CW01630798

One Year at the Dog and Duck

by

Karen Stanley

Mabel & Stanley Publishing

MABEL & STANLEY

PUBLISHING

Contents

Dog & Duck series:

A Very Public House: New Beginnings...	1
Spring: A Time For Change...	103
Summertime Blues...	225
Autumn Chills...	339
Christmas Gifts...	451

A VERY PUBLIC HOUSE

New Beginnings

at the

Dog & Duck

Chapter One

Kim looked in disbelief as her husband Keith swung into the car park of The Dog and Duck pub – the pub that had taken them four sodding hours to get to, one hour of which had been spent going up and down the same country lanes because Keith had refused to listen to the SatNav. With his usual questionable wisdom and unshakeable arrogance, Keith had of course, felt certain he had a better notion of where he might find a pub in the arse end of nowhere, in a place he'd never been to, than a machine programmed by really clever technicians using an actual sodding map!

"Lick of paint and it'll be alright," said Keith.

On the outside he was attempting to radiate positivity but on the inside Kim knew for sure he was probably just as horrified as she was at the sight before their eyes. The thing about Keith though was that he would NEVER admit that he might be wrong about anything!

Kim didn't trust herself to speak. One thing she did know, was that there wasn't a tongue in the world big enough to rectify the ramshackle building before them with simply a 'lick' of paint!

On the other hand, she was desperate to get out of the tiny sports car that Keith had bought during his latest midlife crisis (it seemed he was up to about two such crises per year currently) and that was ridiculously uncomfortable and not nearly as cool as Keith thought it was. She was busting for a wee – her menopausal bladder being what it was – and gagging for a cup of tea...although she thought perhaps a large brandy might be more appropriate given the disastrous circumstances in which she found herself.

Keith prised himself from the driver's seat, his large frame seized up after the long drive, puffing and blowing like an old train – James Bond, he was not!

They made their way up to the front door of the pub. Kim looked up at the window frames, their sad and neglected black paintwork peeling away to such an extent that there were more cracks than colour. A varying selection of grey net curtains hung at the upstairs windows, and a couple of sad old hanging baskets, housing nothing more than a collection of weeds and a few dead petunias, swung from rusty iron brackets either side of the doorway.

A faded chalkboard rather optimistically promised a 'Warm Welcome' and announced 'Curry-oke' happening on Saturday night for just £5 a head from 7pm – dogs and children welcome.

The only thing preventing Kim from running back down the drive and taking off in Keith's pathetic excuse for a sports car was the fact that she was literally about to wet herself. This 'new start' was pretty horrific already and she didn't think it would be made any better by the new landlady peeing her pants on the doorstep.

Kim's Uncle Frank had passed away peacefully in his sleep at the grand old age of 92 and, without any children or close family, he had left everything he owned to her. At first, Kim had been touched by his generosity (they had always been close) but that was when she thought she might end up with a few quid in her bank and maybe the collection of mugs depicting various royal weddings of which her Uncle had been so fond. But no, apparently not! Her Uncle Frank was one dark old horse it seemed, having owned this pub on the East coast of England with a mate of his from his time in the Army. The mate had died a few years back and Frank had simply left the pub in the hands of the 'manager' without much thought as to what might happen when he himself passed on.

Kim had been dead against moving here. She had thought that they might sell the pub and pay off their mortgage, with perhaps a little left over for a nice holiday and a few rainy days but Keith had had other ideas. He'd always fancied himself as a man with a bit of social standing and the idea of holding court as the landlord of a pub appealed greatly to his over-inflated sense of self-worth. As usual, Keith had got what he wanted and here they were, standing in the doorway of their new 'home.' Kim wasn't sure when she had felt so despondent and that was quite a realisation when she considered the shitshow that was her marriage, which mainly contained three people – Kim, Keith, and Keith's ego! Of course, there was her beloved son Daniel, but she didn't include him in her disappointing union, he was the only thing that kept her sane and she didn't want to tarnish him with her baggage... namely his father! What Kim knew for absolute certain was that any real work that needed to be done would be down to her. It would be her job to organise, refurbish and re-vamp whilst Keith looked busy telling others how to do things and what he would do differently (if he could get off his arse long enough that was!).

"Well come on then," said Keith, "Don't stand there gawping, let's get in there and show them who's boss."

Kim sighed, her stomach sinking at the thought of the first impression that Keith was fairly certain to make; that first impression would differ considerably from how he *thought* he appeared!

After a fair bit of jiggling with the less than efficient door handle, Keith and Kim entered the pub. A juke box was playing 'Everybody hurts' in the corner of the room and Kim almost laughed at the irony – although she didn't dare laugh too hard for fear of peeing herself! The entire occupants of the public bar turned to look at the new arrivals; these occupants consisted of a barmaid whose fake eyelashes were so long that they almost poked Kim in the eye before she so much as stepped forward, two blokes in high-vis jackets and work-worn trousers and a couple in the corner of the pub who were as pissed as newts and obscured by huge clouds of vanilla-scented vape fumes.

"Greetings!" proclaimed Keith, addressing his 'public' like some form of conquering hero.

Kim cringed inwardly. "Hi, we are Kim and Keith. I'm so sorry but could you point me in the direction of the loo please, we've had such a long journey to get here."

Eyelash girl looked Kim up and down with barely disguised disdain and pointed a long scarlet fingernail in the direction of the pub toilets. Kim gave the briefest nod of acknowledgement before breaking into an undignified run. It was always baffling to Kim that you could be busting for a wee literally for hours, and hold it all that time, and yet the closer you got to the toilet the more in danger you were of wetting your pants. She almost fell into the first cubicle and struggled with the button on her jeans, she was so desperate by the time she sat down she had almost forgotten to pull her knickers down! The release was bliss despite the freezing cold toilet seat. Kim closed her eyes as she enjoyed the relief of making the loo in the nick of time. When she finally opened her eyes, she saw everything that she had missed in her earlier moments of desperation. She saw the cracked wall tiles. She saw the line of grime that had entrenched itself in the gap between the floor and the cracked wall tiles. She saw the graffiti on the toilet door – 'Paul is a wanker,' scrawled in surprisingly neat handwriting above the punch-hole in the middle of door – presumably this hole had been created by Paul himself and was perhaps the source of his angry companion's need to share her character description of him. Kim sighed and swallowed down the lump of disappointment and despair rising in her throat; if she gave in to tears now, she may never stop.

She exited the cubicle and tried to wash her hands in the sink with the broken taps, below a tarnished mirror. A sad little bottle of silk flowers sat on the windowsill next to a tin ashtray that appeared to have been nailed down. The sink didn't work – barely a trickle of water came from the tap at a temperature hot enough to remove several layers of skin – the soap dispenser was empty and the 'roll a towel' on the wall was so dirty that Kim could almost see the individual germs marching up and down it. She took the small tube of anti-bac from her bag and cleaned her hands. She attempted to check her reflection in the mirror but gave up, took a very deep breath and steeled herself for the impending meeting of her 'staff,' which she feared was going to about as comfortable as a rugby player's jock strap!

Keith was sat at the bar, pint already in hand, holding court when Kim entered the room.

"...lots of experience in business... very much a people person... self-made man..."

"Self-made man my arse," thought Kim. "I wouldn't trust him to make a bloody bed!"

Eyelash girl looked at Kim. She made a face as if to speak but then decided better of it and went back to hanging on to Keith's every word; it seemed she was keen to make an impression on this 'wealthy self-made man.'

Kim was undeterred. "I take it Keith has introduced us both?" she said. Eyelash girl didn't answer.

"I'll make my own way upstairs if that's okay then?" said Kim. "I understand that the pub is currently managed by off-site managers – I don't want to upset anyone up there singing in the shower!"

Eyelash girl rolled her eyes at Kim's unappreciated attempt at humour. "It's empty if that's what you mean," she replied. "And just for the record, I am the 'off-site' manager."

Great, thought Kim, just great! "I'll go on up then; are you coming Keith?" said Kim looking un-optimistically in Keith's direction.

"Bloody hell woman, I've been driving for hours, let me have a pint and a rest will you?"

Kim ignored the smug grin on eyelash girl's face and made her way behind the bar. She'd already made a note of the door at the back which presumably led to the upstairs flat where they would be staying. She wasn't surprised by Keith's reluctance to get involved and secretly she was always a little bit relieved when he didn't get involved – it meant she could do things her way without too much drama or interference.

As she opened the door, she caught sight of another doorway leading through to the pub kitchen. On first inspection it didn't look too bad. It certainly wasn't grand, and the décor looked just about as tired as she felt, but it looked clean enough and there no obvious signs of vermin... baby steps!

Kim climbed the creaky old stairs. The Dog and Duck had been built in the Mid-19th Century and had several exposed timber beams and period features – mainly because it probably hadn't been decorated since the 1800s but that was beside the point. She noticed that the stair carpet had seen better days and resolved herself to the accommodation being more 2* motel than 5* hotel, although nothing could have prepared her for the carnage that awaited her.

At the top of the stairway was a hallway with doors leading off it; each one open wide so that Kim was privy to a panoramic snapshot view of each room in the whole apartment, and it was fair to say that each room was as visually unappealing as its neighbour. Kim moved from room to room, fighting the urge to cry. Old newspapers, pizza boxes, wine boxes and discarded mail littered the floor in every room. She supposed the carpet was as dirty here as it had been on the stairs, but it was hard to tell with the rubbish that obscured it. There was not one scrap of furniture in the flat apart from an old sofa in the 'lounge area' that looked like it belonged in a skip and an even older iron bed in the main bedroom. There were three bedrooms in total, a lounge, a large kitchen/dining room, a bathroom and some kind of walk-in cupboard that housed an assortment of cleaning items such as brushes, mops and brooms; 'pretty bloody superfluous to requirements,' thought Kim bitterly. To be fair, there was a fitted kitchen of sorts, it's just that the cupboard doors were missing!

The removal van with the contents of their old house was not arriving until the morning and they certainly hadn't been able to pack anything more than two sleeping bags in Keith's pathetic excuse for a sports car. When Keith had decided on their monumental move to a village somewhere near nowhere, he had not given any thought to the actual logistics; beyond selling their house and driving to the new one. Kim imagined that he had expected to swing into the carpark of a far grander establishment than the one they had currently which was more motorway services than Michelin star!

'Happy bloody New Year,' muttered Kim under her breath.

Chapter Two

Kim wandered from room to room making mental notes of the jobs that needed to be done which had already gone way beyond 50! She wasn't sure how this was going to pan out but, once again, she realised that she would be the only active member of this task force. Judging by the raucous laughter coming from downstairs, Keith was already making quite a start on their bar stock. Throughout their 25-year marriage, Keith had drifted from one job to another. Kim had always been the main breadwinner, working hard at the bank where she first joined as a graduate straight out of university. They had never been wealthy – Keith had made sure of that with his frivolous purchases and his desire to impress others with his Dolce and Banana rip offs – but Kim had made sure that the bills were paid, which she did by only allowing Keith access to certain areas of their financial profile. Now that Uncle Frank had died, they had quite a little nest egg which was supposed to be for pub renovations (and judging by the state of the place they'd need every penny) and as a buffer whilst they got on their feet. Kim didn't trust her feckless husband one little bit not to blow the bloody lot, which is why she had taken certain precautions; and as for the cash that Uncle Frank had left her along with the pub... well that was going to be harder to find than a billionaire's tax return!

"Kim! Kim!" Keith's booming voice rang out from downstairs.

Kim had mostly been able to ignore Keith in the same way that someone might ignore a mild case of thrush but since the peri-menopause, her patience was thinner than an after-dinner mint and she wasn't entirely certain she wouldn't end her days wearing an orange jumpsuit, some sliders with socks and sporting a teardrop tattoo on her left cheek! She had asked herself many times why she stayed but the years had ticked by and things had just sort of... gone on.

Kim took a deep breath in, held it, and exhaled in just the way that she had been taught at her Pilates group. She wasn't sure it was quite as calming as her instructor proclaimed but it usually gave her a little time to think before throwing or breaking something – mainly Keith's neck! She picked her way across the piles of paper, making a mental note to find the whereabouts of the recycling bin, and made her way downstairs into the bar. She had no idea where to start but she knew that she would be wise to spend a couple of days in quiet observation before gathering her 'staff' together and finding a way forward; hopefully if it was a total disaster, they could be out of here in 6 months, sell the building and put the whole sorry escapade behind them!

"Where the bloody hell have you been?" said Keith giving a knowing glance to his 'audience.'

"Just taking in our luxurious living arrangements," replied Kim dryly.

"Olivia said it's normally packed in here on a weekend," said Keith nodding in the direction of eyelash girl. "Probably just the new year lull," said Keith speaking with an air of knowledge and wisdom that he certainly did not possess.

"Right," said Kim. "Well hopefully we will have a couple of weeks to prepare ourselves for the rush then, won't we?"

"Olivia's got it all under control," said Keith. "She's our bar manager, she's doing a great job," he continued winking in Olivia's direction.

Kim failed to see how difficult it was to 'control' the clientele when there were precisely four of them; she also wondered about Olivia's definition of 'packed' but she said nothing.

"It's nice to meet you Olivia, we'll leave things the way they are for now and then perhaps we can have a meeting in a week or two to discuss logistics?" said Kim, trying her hardest to wear a warm smile – she couldn't be absolutely certain but she imagined Olivia was going to be a bit of bitch, if the sullen and somewhat defiant expression on her face was anything to go by each time Kim addressed her.

"I've been here two years now," said Olivia with a smug smile. "I've pretty much been left to run the place; I do what I like really."

"Two whole years," said Kim, "that IS a long time, I'm sure there is lots you can show me." The sarcasm appeared to be completely lost on the 'expert' Olivia who had now grown tired of the conversation and had turned her attention back to the motley assortment of 'men' at the bar – namely Keith and the two high-vis boys.

"No need to rock the boat Kim," said Keith draining his pint glass and motioning for another from Olivia.

"Like I said, things are fine as they are... for now," replied Kim. "I'm going to head upstairs and try to create a little bit of order so that we can at least sleep somewhere tonight. Perhaps you could bring our bags in from the car; only if you're not busy of course."

Keith did not reply – mainly because he wasn't listening – and Kim certainly wasn't going to have a showdown in front of an audience, no matter how meagre.

Kim took a better look around the kitchen and managed to find a box of cleaning materials - cloths, anti-bacterial sprays, some bleach and a roll of bin bags. The kitchen was sparse but clean and Kim was encouraged to notice a cleaning rota on the wall along with a hygiene certificate and some safety notices. The fridges however, were barer than old Mother Hubbard's cupboards, so she figured keeping a kitchen clean when there were no visible signs of any cooking going on couldn't be that hard. She took a photo of the staff rota on the wall that showed employee names and phone numbers and resolved that she would contact individuals directly; relying on Olivia was not going to be her plan A… or her plan B for that matter. She would have a ring round throughout the week and try to get a handle on who was who and who wasn't!

The only good thing about having a flat littered with old takeaway menus meant that they would be able to order something for tea. They had no shopping in, there was no food in the kitchen downstairs and Kim certainly wasn't about to risk a dose of Botulism by preparing food in the upstairs kitchen anyway.

She set about cleaning the flat. Her first job was to scoop up all the menus, boxes and general crap that littered the floor – she had hoped to recycle as much of the paper and cardboard rubbish as she could, but David Attenborough was going to have to turn a blind eye for today; she'd sort the recycling 'system' out once she had got her bearings.

She found an old hoover in the cupboard which sucked about as efficiently as a straw full of holes – she could probably lick the dust off the carpet more effectively – but it was better than nothing… just! She decided that she would just tackle the main rooms for now and see how she got on. The process was akin to polishing a giant turd but at least she might be able to kill at least some of the germs that had been living rent-free in the flat for the past few years. She scrubbed the old white bathroom; dousing the corners of the bath surround, toilet rim and taps in copious amounts of bleach – she almost choked on the fumes and closed the door to let the bleach work its magic whilst she performed a similar operation in the kitchen. She wiped down every inch of paintwork, every light switch and door handle and by the time she had finished, she had needed to turn the lights on as the gloom of the January evening descended. Keith had indeed been too 'busy' to get the bags from the car and was probably now on the whisky chasers. At least he'd fall asleep quickly thought Kim with relief – small mercies.

She made a quick phone call to the local Indian takeaway and ordered a couple of bhunas, some rice and poppadoms. She was dying for a shower but decided to wait until the place was empty – it felt weird being in your 'home' knowing that people were still downstairs; something she would have to get used to she feared.

Kim took another of the deep, healing breaths that were meant to steady her temper and steeled herself for the ensuing carnage happening in the public bar.

"You still busy Keith?" she asked sarcastically as she entered through the back of the bar.

Keith's face was an unattractive shade of purple. His eyes were hooded and his lips were shiny – a sure sign that he was well oiled in every sense.

"I'm fucking starving!" slurred Keith.

Apparently, this was absolutely hilarious to Olivia and the high-vis boys who started laughing raucously at Keith's 'joke.'

"Brilliant!" thought Kim. They were all as pissed as newts, including Olivia whose eyelashes seemed to have taken on a life of their own and were crawling their way to freedom across her face.

The couple in the corner of the bar from earlier were now asleep on the bench seats and the jukebox was belting out 'Don't Stop Me Now,' its garish lights illuminating an otherwise darkened room. Kim crossed the room and lowered the volume on the jukebox.

"We were listening to that!" yelled Keith, sparking another round of raucous laughter from the room's idiot convention.

Kim ignored him and walked around the bar collecting discarded glasses and empty crisp packets. She gave the sleeping vapers a none-too-gentle shove and guided them toward the door in their disorientated awakening. She looked at the clock – 10.20pm. She walked back towards the bar and rang the bell.

"Time ladies and gents," she called, ignoring the shouts of objection hurled her way.

"We don't always have a closing time," sniggered Olivia.

"Well, I'm afraid we do tonight," replied Kim, through gritted teeth. "I'm tired, I haven't eaten and I'm afraid I might stab you all to death if I don't get some peace!"

They all laughed... but Kim didn't!

After much cajoling and some careful negotiating, it was another twenty minutes before the revellers finally left the pub. Olivia staggered out of the door with her jacket on inside out, bumping into the takeaway delivery man as he arrived at the threshold.

Kim looked over at Keith who had fallen asleep in one of the armchairs next to the pool table and took her dinner gratefully from the takeaway guy. He looked across at Keith and said, "Busy night?"

"For some of us," replied Kim wryly.

In all honesty, Kim was pleased that Keith was snoring in the corner, whilst it wasn't exactly peaceful, it meant that she could enjoy her dinner without interruption or any more of his crap, slurred jokes.

The curry was delicious, and she realised just how hungry she really was. She ate every last morsel and left Keith's in the bag on the table in front of him. She didn't give a rat's arse if he ate it or not and she certainly wasn't about to try and wake him up! She then went out to the car to retrieve her sleeping bag and pillow and the bag containing her pyjamas, dressing gown and toothbrush. She then poured herself a very generous brandy and sat in the corner of the darkened room taking in her surroundings in all their grim glory and wondering how the actual fuck she had ended up here; not just immediately, but in her life in general.

She felt the soothing warmth of the brandy and resolved to tell her Pilates teacher that it was a lot more effective at calming her nerves than a round of 'circular breathing!' She drained her glass, collected up her belongings, turned off the lights and left Keith snorting like a warthog in the darkness.

The smell of bleach was almost acrid yet strangely comforting, and Kim felt pleased that she had at least made small headway in the fight against grime that had threatened to engulf her when she'd first arrived. In all honesty, she was so knackered that she thought she could probably have slept in a sewer if that had been her only option.

She cleaned her teeth, put on her pyjamas and dressing gown (as clean as the flat might smell she wanted a little protection against the dubious-looking mattress) and took her sleeping bag through to the bedroom. Fortunately, her sleeping bag was designed for arctic expeditions – which had obviously been super useful in the South East of England – but now came into its own as it had a little hood which would further prevent her from coming into close contact with the dreaded mattress.

She snuggled into the bag and was asleep before her head hit the pillow – if she'd had a pillow that was!

Chapter Three

Kim awoke to a God-awful racket downstairs. She tried to extricate herself from her sleeping bag which had somehow twisted itself around her so tightly that Houdini would have found it tricky to escape. She writhed around getting more frustrated and feeling an ill-timed hot flush begin to rise up through her body like a volcanic eruption as she tried to twist herself free. One suspicious ripping sound later, which she feared might be the 'storm zip' giving way, and one rather ungracious fall to the floor, she was free! Having been so tired last night, she had neglected to remove her dressing gown, and this had clearly caused the sweat ridden tangle of hair that was sticking up on one side and stuck to her cheek on the other. Thankfully, the flat was so frugally furnished that there were no mirrors to reflect what Kim feared would be a pretty horrific image currently.

The banging downstairs grew louder and more frenzied.

"I'm coming!" yelled Kim, hurtling down the steep staircase as fast she dared without causing mortal injury.

A little disorientated, it took Kim quite some time to open the door at the bottom of the stairs that led out into the bar. She jiggled the handle, swearing under her breath. One of the many beautiful things that happened to a woman in the throes of menopausal hormonal chaos was the shortening of her fuse. Situations that Kim may once have been able to tackle calmly and with something resembling patience, were now the cause of an incandescent rage that bubbled up inside her and was frankly pretty life-threatening to anything within a 10-mile radius! Just as she was about to lose her shit altogether, the door handle gave way and she tumbled into the bar.

The banging was coming from the front door. Keith was still snoring in the chair, the bag of Indian takeaway untouched on the table in front of him.

“Hang on,” said Kim to the, as yet unidentified, door banger.

She opened the door – it seemed she had forgotten to lock it before bed and a rather uncharitable thought about Keith’s safety in the dead of night from rampant intruders passed through her mind; he certainly wouldn’t get kidnapped, they wouldn’t bloody keep him for long if he did!

On the doorstep stood two men in brown uniforms with the words ‘Riley’s Removals’ embroidered on their breast pockets.

“Oh shit! Sorry!” exclaimed Kim. “I had completely forgotten that our stuff was coming today.”

The two men observed her with an expression of ‘dozy cow’ on their faces.

"Anyway, come in," said Kim. "It might be easier if I open a door out the back, you can bring the stuff through the kitchen – might be easier? Keith! KEITH! Wake up! Our stuff is here!"

Keith stirred and rubbed his face, "What time is it?"

"Time you got off your backside and got our stuff in," said Kim.

She shuddered to think of the impression the removal men were getting. A pub in the backend of nowhere that looked like it was falling down, a 'landlord' who stunk of stale beer and last night's takeaway and a 'landlady' who looked like she had been pulled through a hedge backwards. 'I bet they are counting their lucky stars we've already paid them,' thought Kim, 'we must look like a right couple of vagrants!'

The removal men puffed and panted their way up and down the narrow staircase with the contents of Keith and Kim's old house. There were a few tense moments when it looked like they would be leaving their sofa and one of their wardrobes downstairs but credit to them, they did get the job done. Keith was neither use nor ornament – unless you counted the fact that he gave them plenty of 'advice' without actually once putting his money where his over-active gob was!

Kim ran backwards and forwards unloading the smaller boxes and making cups of tea; she apologised that she couldn't offer them anything to eat but in truthfulness, looking at the state of the place, she wouldn't have blamed them for refusing if she had!

The whole process took around three hours, just in time for 'eyelash Olivia' to arrive for the start of her 12 o'clock shift. Kim had hoped that she would have looked more in control when Olivia arrived this morning but instead, she looked like a slightly psychotic bag lady.

"Morning Olivia," said Keith, appearing suddenly chirpy. "You've arrived at the right time, it's been chaos here, we've only just stopped."

Kim shared a glance with one of the removal men who rolled his eyes and made a less than friendly gesture behind Keith's back. Kim stifled a giggle.

"Thanks so much guys!" said Kim gratefully. "You've been amazing," and she put an extra 50 quid into the hand of one of the removers.

"Spending all my money," said Keith, lording it up, especially now that Olivia had arrived.

"Our money Keith, our money," said Kim. She really wanted to say, 'It's actually MY money,' but she didn't have the energy for a full-on row; and definitely not with an audience!

The removal man gave Kim a sympathetic glance and thanked her for their tip. They barely glanced in Keith's direction and left the pub.

"Not very professional?" said Keith. "Customer service eh? Olivia can give them a few lessons!"

Kim didn't trust herself to speak. "I'm going for a shower and then I'll be back down," she said. "It's Monday, so I'm not expecting you'll be that busy today? Are there any other staff due in?" she asked, looking in Olivia's direction.

"Kitchen staff are off this week," replied Olivia with the apathy of a bored, hormonal teenager. "Just me today. We shut early on Mondays. Darts are in tomorrow."

"Great," said Kim. "If it's going to be quiet then that'll be the perfect opportunity for you and me to sit and have a chat." Olivia looked as though a 'chat' might be about as welcome as a fart in a spacesuit but Kim chose to ignore her attitude... for now!

Keith followed Kim up the stairs, mumbling something about Kim being more friendly and not needing to, 'go charging in and changing everything.'

"You wanted us to move here Keith," said Kim. "So, if we are here, we may as well try and make a success of it. We can't live on fresh air and lager forever!"

Keith began to try and tell her that he knew exactly what he was doing, he had plenty of years in business and he had been to enough pubs to know how it worked! Kim did not bother to point out that his 'years in business' had mainly been a succession of driving jobs and a few years as a painter and decorator which wasn't entirely relevant in this current situation. She also didn't mention that drinking in a pub and actually running a pub were about as similar as sitting on a plane and flying the sodding thing!

The 'shower' in the bathroom didn't work. That wasn't strictly true... it did work but only in short bursts and with two extremes of temperature that alternated without warning. Ice cold, scalding, ice cold, scalding... Kim felt like she'd been to one of those Scandinavian sauna/plunge pool experiences designed to invigorate and rejuvenate, but she didn't feel invigorated, just cold and burnt... if that was even possible?

Fortunately, Kim had packed methodically for their move, and she was able to find her clean clothes in the chests of drawers where they belonged. Her hairdryer was easily accessible, and it wasn't long before she felt a little more human. Keith had plonked himself on the sofa, complaining that he was 'knackered' and that he hadn't eaten. Kim thought that he was confusing her with someone who gave a toss!

A wave of sadness came over her. She had loved Keith when they had married all those years ago and she had always thought it tragic to be shackled to someone for whom you only felt disdain. She had tried so hard over the years, but Keith made it unbelievably difficult at times. She wondered if perhaps a new start might be good for them both and she resolved to be a little kinder. If she made an effort, who knew... what went around, might come around? Kim breathed in for four looooong counts, she held her breath, she counted, she breathed out, she counted...!

Kim poked her head around the lounge doorway to observe Keith snoring on the sofa – bless him, the morning's exertions had clearly taken their toll. She was actually quite relieved, it meant that she could have an uninterrupted conversation with Olivia – she could do without Keith's very useful words of wisdom.

"Hi Olivia," said Kim as she entered the bar area.

Olivia had just been helping herself to a large brandy and coke without a hint of shame and barely acknowledged Kim's greeting. It didn't take very long for Kim to ascertain that the pub was emptier than a politician's promise and she marvelled at how it had remained open for so long. She had requested the books from the accountant upon her inheritance and you didn't need to be a financial genius to realise that things were sailing the wrong way up shit creek without the proverbial paddle. This had been one of the many reasons why Kim would just have been glad to sell up and get rid but... here they were.

"Shall we take a seat?" Kim motioned Olivia to join her at one of the scratched tables with the mismatching chairs.

Olivia joined her, glass in hand, but without a word.

"Ok, so I don't know how much you have been told," began Kim, "but Keith and I are now the owners and consequently the landlords of the Dog and Duck. I'm really keen to get a handle on things and I'd really like to help all of the staff in as smooth a transition as possible.

Olivia took a long swig of her brandy. "We've been doing fine up until now," she said. I'm Doug's ex-wife's husband's niece you know, I didn't expect to be replaced when he died.

'*Well that explains the hostility*,' thought Kim. Doug had been Uncle Frank's friend and co-owner of the Dog and Duck - Olivia had clearly expected to inherit the pub herself – although her family connection was tenuous to say the least.

"Yes, I am sure you've all done a great job of keeping things going, but the pub couldn't remain in limbo forever. As I see it, this could be a great new start for everyone," Kim smiled with an enthusiasm she didn't entirely feel.

"I think the best thing to do is to have a meeting with all staff present and see if we can think of ways to make the pub busier and more successful – the first thing will be to give it a good clean, perhaps a fresh coat of paint on the walls, before we make any big plans," Kim continued.

"I hope you aren't suggesting that I do any painting," questioned a horrified Olivia. "I only work behind the bar."

Kim thought it interesting that Olivia had rather quickly demoted herself from bar manager to barmaid at the suggestion of any hard work, and she also wasn't sure that helping yourself to a large brandy and coke whilst sitting on a barstool and drumming your fingertips counted as 'work,' but she kept her thoughts to herself.

"Do you usually pay for your drinks Olivia?" asked Kim. She had decided that appealing to Olivia's more reasonable side was going to be about as successful as negotiating with a fascist militant and so she resolved to simply pull rank and say it how it was. She was a pretty good judge of character and, judging by what she seen of Olivia so far, she didn't imagine it would be too much of a loss if Olivia got the hump and took her impossibly long eyelashes in search of alternative employment!

"What do you mean by that?" asked Olivia defensively.

"Just a simple question," answered Kim calmly. "I'm not very keen on people drinking on the job if I am honest, you wouldn't do it if you worked in an office would you?"

"But I don't work in an office," said Olivia defiantly.

"I understand that and very well observed Olivia," replied Kim, "but from now on the rule is that we don't drink during a shift. I will honour ONE complimentary drink for all members of staff at the end of their shift but whilst at work it's tea, coffee or water I'm afraid."

"Is there anything else?" asked Olivia with a look that would have turned milk sour.

"Plenty actually," said Kim and she began to ask questions about who worked what shifts, what 'entertainment' was on offer and when the pub served food. She ignored Olivia's reluctance to answer with anything approaching enthusiasm and ploughed on ahead, smiling in a way that meant Olivia could not accuse her of aggression but that would definitely infuriate her. Her original plan had been to wait a while before delving into the way things worked but she now realised that things needed to be taken in hand sooner rather than later.

At one o'clock the door opened and the two high-vis guys from yesterday entered the pub.

"Excuse me, I have a job to do!" said Olivia, getting up from her chair and probably never keener to actually *do* her job!

Kim smiled and thanked her for her 'help.' What she had learned from their conversation was this...

There was a darts team meet-up every Tuesday at 7pm and tournaments and matches were played from March through to August. Food was served at lunchtimes from Tuesday to Friday, but this consisted only of baguettes and there was Sunday lunch, obviously on Sundays. There was no food at all on Saturdays or in the evenings. The pub used to have a pool team but there was a disagreement and all but two members of the team were barred; subsequently, the team had collapsed. Occasionally they had a karaoke night or the odd charity night, but these were few and far between and hadn't happened for ages. A local ladies group met in the pub every Thursday lunchtime, but Olivia said they were stuck up and she didn't know why they met there. The pub was open from 12pm – 3pm and 6pm until 11pm although it was often shut on Sunday and Monday nights if they didn't have staff. There were three barmaids including Olivia who worked shifts and one chef in the kitchen. There was no cleaning lady – this did not come as a massive surprise to Kim – and the chef was also in charge of the cellar.

The most positive thing about this whole depressing conversation Kim thought, was that the only possible way was up; unless they collapsed entirely and faced financial ruin that was!

Kim left Olivia chatting to the high-vis boys and glancing none-too subtly in Kim's direction at regular intervals. It was quite clear that she was bemoaning her situation and telling them all about her highly unreasonable new boss. Kim couldn't have given a single toss; if she didn't like it, she could bugger off... literally!

Kim went into the kitchen and collected the rota from the kitchen wall before going upstairs. Keith had just woken from his slumber and announced that he was going to have a quick pint before getting on with things. Kim just sighed; this was obviously her lot now, Keith propping up the bar while she got stuff done.

She spent the afternoon ringing around the staff and co-ordinating a meeting for the following Tuesday afternoon between 3pm and 6pm when the pub was closed. Dean, the chef seemed really quite pleasant and was very happy to come and meet. Kim made it clear that she would pay the staff for their time – if

Olivia objected then she would just have to accept any changes without consultation… her loss! The other two barmaids – Megan, a single mum from the neighbouring village working shifts around her young daughter, and Rosa, who sounded older and spoke with a strong Mediterranean accent - were similarly pleasant and Kim got the feeling that there was little love lost between any of the staff and the stroppy Olivia.

Kim had stayed out of the way until 3pm when the pub closed, she didn't think there was any benefit to another confrontation with Olivia and she resolved to be an observant bystander for the following week until their staff meeting, when she could be clearer about their current situation as opposed to their preferred situation. She had spent the rest of her time that afternoon, tidying and trying to achieve a sense of order. Anything that hadn't been sorted was stacked in one of the spare bedrooms for another time. She resolved to give Keith some jobs to do. The one way in which he could be useful was to decorate the flat – a liberal coat of white paint on all the walls and ceilings would be fine for now and freshen the place up no end. The biggest expenditure would be a new carpet throughout and a new set of kitchen units. The bathroom was old, but fortunately housed a white suite as opposed to some awful avocado green or peach monstrosity; another good clean, a new blind and a bit of vinyl and it would be perfectly okay for the time being. If Keith wasn't kept busy, he'd end up as a permanent fixture in the corner of the bar!

Once she heard the front door slam and the chatter of voices fade away, Kim went downstairs.

"I thought I'd go into town," said Kim. "We desperately need some shopping and I'd like to get my bearings – we haven't stepped outside the pub since we arrived yesterday."

"You don't need me do you?" asked Keith. "I thought I might take a break this afternoon."

Kim wasn't sure what he was going to be taking a break from exactly, but she was quite happy to go alone.

"No, that's fine but I'll need the car."

"Just don't scratch it," said Keith.

"I'll do my best," replied Kim, thinking that he showed more affection towards his less-than-cool sports car than he did her.

Chapter Four

Even though she was quite small, Kim still struggled to get in and out of the impossibly impractical car. It was so low to the ground that a limbo dancer would have had difficulty and the two rear seats were designed for Oompa Loompas only. She resolved to buy herself a nice, practical little runaround with some of the money – nothing fancy, just something with a roomy boot and four doors and maybe in a nice shade of pink or purple; that way Keith would never want to borrow it.

Kim drove the short distance to the local village; it was actually almost close enough to walk. It had seemed miles away when they'd arrived but then they *had* gone round and round in circles for at least 10 miles whilst Keith refused to admit that he didn't know where they were going! Kim was quite relieved to discover that they weren't as far off the beaten track as she had feared.

The village of Foxley was big enough to be considered a small town. There was a shopping complex on the outskirts of the village which housed a large supermarket, DIY superstore and one of those budget shops that sold everything from housewares to coal and from toys to pet food. Kim deliberately drove past the supermarket and into the town car park, she figured that the supermarket would stay open later than the local shops and she quite fancied a look around. She paid her car park ticket with the few coins she found in her pocket and once again promised herself that she would get one of those apps that allowed you to park with your phone – next time Daniel came to visit she would get him to set it up for her. Kim was not a lover of technology, and it definitely wasn't her strong point, but she knew she needed to join the 21st century sooner or later. She'd just about mastered posting a few pictures on social media and she could email and FaceTime, but she realised this was hardly cutting-edge stuff!

She left her car and followed the sign for 'town centre'. The sign itself seemed fairly pointless as there was only one exit from the car park and only one viable direction to walk in! Within the town itself was a pub, a butcher, bakery, hairdresser, post office and a quaint little café. The shops encircled a village green which was so quintessentially 'quaint English', that Miss Marple herself would not have looked out of place on the little bench that sat on the border of the green. Just beyond the shops Kim could see the river that bordered Foxley and that led to the larger harbour town about 10 miles east.

She decided to support the local economy by making a few of her purchases in the local shops – well that, and the fact it gave her a chance to be nosey. In the butcher's shop she met Jim, at least she assumed he was Jim because he said he owned the place and there was a large sign above the door that read 'Jim's Butchers'.

"You not from around here?" asked Jim as he wrapped up six rather plump 'Grandfather's recipe' sausages, a couple of pork chops and a kilo of chicken breast.

"No, I've just moved into the Dog and Duck. Do you know it, it's about two miles from here?" asked Kim.

"The Dog and Duck you say," said Jim. "I know it although I didn't know they took lodgers."

"I'm not lodging," said Kim. "I'm the new landlady."

"Well, you've got your work cut out there," laughed Jim, causing all of Kim's misgivings to rise directly to the surface!

After a little more small-talk during which Jim promised to pop in for a pint some time and had given her a card for the local gardener, the chimney sweep and the taxi company, Kim left in the direction of the bakery. She wondered if Jim was on some kind of commission from the local businesses but maybe that was how it worked in smaller towns; less anonymous than more populated areas where you hardly knew your neighbours, let alone your local shopkeepers!

She had a similar conversation in the bakery, another in the post office and by the time she popped into the little café for a cup of tea, she was practically a local celebrity!

"You must be the new landlady at the Dog and Duck," said the waitress who, as it turned out, was also the café owner and cousin of Jim the butcher!

'Christ, I better not murder anyone,' thought Kim, *'I'll be tried and committed before the blood is dry on my knife!'*

She hoped this wasn't the kind of place where everyone knew your business but on reflection, she decided that there wasn't really much worth knowing about her business anyway. Kim finished her cup of tea and made her way back to the car; the drive to the supermarket took less time than it did to get out of the car park. After fumbling around in her coat pockets and shoving her hand down the back of the seats, she swore softly to herself as she realised that she didn't have a pound coin for the trolley.

"Need a pound?" said the voice beside her – clearly, she had sworn a little louder than she realised!

"Oh bloody hell, sorry," said Kim. "I need to get one of those token things but I'm not nearly that organised."

"I've only got a coin, cos I found it on the floor," said the voice. "I'm not that organised either."

Kim looked up and saw that the voice belonged to a man who she guessed was roughly her age. He had a nice face and eyes that twinkled with just the right amount of humour. He wore a mustard-coloured beanie hat and black puffa jacket.

"I couldn't really," said Kim. "I'm sure they'll give me a token in the store."

“Seriously,” said the man. “I honestly did find it on the floor, put it in the charity box when you’re done.”

“Well, thank you,” said Kim, smiling.

The man turned on his heel and gave her a backward wave as he got into his car.

Kim waved the hand that clenched the coin in his direction before heading into the supermarket. She filled her trolley with everything she thought they might need considering they had absolutely nothing in the place; toiletries, cleaning products, groceries, tin foil and washing up liquid, toilet roll and washing powder. When finally she got to the till her trolley was groaning. It wasn’t until she got back to the car that she realised she may have more than a little difficulty to get the shopping into the diminutive vehicle… she pushed and shoved, grunted and groaned, swore and cursed. By the time she had finished there were bags of shopping in every conceivable space; some crammed into the tiny boot, behind the seats, in the footwell and piled high on the passenger seat. Back home she had always shopped online, especially as Keith was always ‘too busy’ to do the shopping and working long hours in her job meant it had been easier to get it delivered. She had no car of her own and travelled to work with a colleague. The knackered old van that Keith had for work had been laid to rest at the big scrap heap in the sky just before they moved, and he’d traded their perfectly sensible car in for his midlife crisis testosterone vehicle the year before. Kim sighed at the memory; one of many memories about Keith that made her sigh for all the wrong reasons!

Kim drove the mercifully short distance back to the Dog and Duck, barely able to see out of the front windscreen and with the seatbelt alarm beeping its disapproval at the untethered 'passenger' in the front seat! She drove to the rear car park and heaved the shopping in through the pub kitchen. She called out several times to Keith as she lumped bag after bag of shopping up the stairs, but he only appeared to help when just two bags remained.

"You should have called," he said. Kim held her breath.

By the time Kim had unpacked it was getting dark and she chucked the ready-made lasagne into the oven in the cleaned but tired kitchen. They ate on their laps sharing a bottle of red and watching TV. They had just finished eating when Kim's phone rang...

"Hi Mum, how's country life?"

"Daniel!" cried Kim. She was so pleased to hear from her only son. He was her pride and joy and the absolute light of her life. "It's okay babe. Not too bad. The pub's a bit of a dive but it might be ok." She hoped her voice portrayed more enthusiasm than she felt, she didn't want to worry him.

"And Dad? Is he alright?" asked Daniel.

"Yep, all good," said Kim. She knew that although Daniel loved his dad, he also didn't have a huge amount of respect for him. He was often frustrated at the way Keith treated his mum and had called his father out on more than one occasion. Keith always said that Kim 'mollycoddled the boy' but Kim knew that was because Daniel had the measure of his father and wouldn't tolerate any of his crap.

"Anyway Mum, I've got some news! I've got a week off work so I thought I'd come up to visit; I could bring Nan if you like?"

"Oh Daniel that would be so lovely. When are you coming?" Kim noticed Keith's reluctant smile as she beamed in his direction. '*Oh sod him*!' she thought, just delighted at the thought of her son and mum coming stay.

"Is there enbough room for us? Can we stay?" asked Daniel. "We'll be up Friday week, is that too soon – it's only ten days away?"

"Of course you can stay," laughed Kim. "Your dad can get your rooms sorted out before you come, it'll do him good to be busy." She ignored the glare that Keith shot her way.

One of the things that had pained Kim the most when they moved was leaving behind her beloved mother. Her father had died when she was a teenager and she and her mum had grown increasingly close over the years. Of course, she'd offered for her mum to come with them, but her mum had assured her that she was fine in her little bungalow in the sheltered complex where she lived. In all honesty Kim imagined that her mum would rather live anywhere than with Keith and she couldn't say she blamed her. Kim's mum had always tolerated Keith for Kim's sake, but Kim knew there was no real love lost on either part. Daniel adored his nan and Kim knew that her mum would go anywhere with her blue-eyed boy.

She got off the phone feeling quite tearful. The enormity of this new life, of leaving behind her work, friends and family, to live with a man who she wasn't sure she loved anymore seemed to rush over her in a wave; she wasn't sure she could do it. Kim took a deep breath and returned to the sofa, taking a long glug of her wine.

"Well thanks for organising my time," said Keith sulkily.

Kim swallowed down the lump in her throat. "It would just be nice to see them," said Kim quietly.

"Them?" said Keith. "Bloody hell Kim, haven't we got enough to do?"

Kim didn't reply. They spent the rest of the night in silence, drinking wine, watching TV and each of them seething inside.

Chapter Five

In the morning, Kim decided to try and keep the peace, perhaps if she made a little effort then Keith might behave less like a pre-pubescent teen. She made him a cup of tea and a bacon sandwich; most of Keith's good nature seemed to be located in the area of his stomach and below, and Kim knew that if she wanted a quiet life she would have to feed him or... well anyway, she decided this morning that she would feed him!

"I'll go and get some paint if you like," said Keith, the bacon sandwich seemingly working its magic on his demeanour.

"Thanks love," said Kim. "That would be very helpful – just white will do for now, freshen things up a bit. I'll get on with clearing some of the boxes so you've got room to work."

Not for the first time, Kim wondered why it was that men seemed to need so much praise and adoration every time they did a job; no one played a fanfare when she brought the washing in or cleaned the bathroom!

Kim left Olivia to it for the day, just popping her head in now and then to see the state of play. There were never more than five people in the bar at any time when she looked in. The high-vis boys were back – she wondered when they actually got any work done – an elderly man in a jacket with what looked like war medals pinned to his chest, a respectable-looking couple who only stayed for one drink and looked like they had only stayed to be polite, and a flustered-looking woman who came in asking for directions. If there were other patrons in between, Kim didn't see them.

In fairness to Keith, he worked pretty hard. Kim emptied one of the spare rooms completely, except for the bed that they had brought with them, and spent the rest of the time organising through the stuff in the other bedroom, making sure that it was in some kind of system ready to be distributed throughout the flat and find its proper place. By the time evening came, Keith had painted the ceiling and put the first coat on the walls and woodwork.

"I think I've earned a beer," said Keith and Kim really didn't think she could argue.

She left Keith to go downstairs while she got bathed and changed. Apparently, the darts team were coming for a warmup match tonight and she wanted to be there to meet them and find out who was who. She didn't imagine they would be posh, but she didn't want to meet them looking like Cruella de Vil either!

Kim washed, dried and curled her collar-length blonde bob, the grey hairs hidden by some cleverly placed highlights. She chose a black roll-neck and fitted trousers with a wide belt. She still had a good figure and had been blessed with her mother's metabolism meaning that she had never needed to diet. Having watched some of her friends as they tried one faddish diet after another, drinking shakes with the consistency of plaster of Paris, and probably tasting fairly similar, only eating meat and eggs, going gluten free, dairy free, taste free while they battled the dreaded middle age spread, Kim felt never more grateful for her fortunate genetic inheritance.

She felt strangely nervous as she descended the stairs, a reluctant leading lady about to make a grand entrance.

The bar was the busiest it had been since they arrived. The darts team had arrived and there was a friendly game of mixed doubles taking place. The juke box was on and several people stood at the bar. A group of lads were playing pool in the part of the pub that led out into the overgrown back garden. Several people were vaping, blowing great plumes of perfumed smoke into the atmosphere; Kim was sure she would have a battle on her hands putting a stop to that! Megan, the other barmaid had come in to work her shift with Olivia and the two of them were running up and down the bar serving the thirsty customers. The pub itself looked like a bomb had hit it and Kim set about clearing the backlog of glasses from the tables and loading the dishwasher. Keith was propping up the bar revelling in his role as 'lord and master'.

At least an hour passed before the initial rush died down and the customers had been watered... for now at least. Keith had motioned to Kim to pour him a drink but the look she shot him made him think better of it and pour his own bloody drink! That eventually turned out to be his sole input to the evening's demands.

When they had five minutes to spare, Kim took the opportunity to introduce herself properly to Megan.

"Well, I'm Kim in case you wondered," she laughed. "Bit tricky to chat with this lot arriving, but it is nice to finally meet you properly."

"And you," replied Megan. "It is always like this on a Tuesday when they first arrive, but it gets steadier once they've had the first one. You've got your work cut out here, the old place definitely needs a bit of TLC. It'll be nice to have fresh eyes on it; we've got some really nice customers - and some you might not rate so highly - but it would be a shame for the pub to close. I've always thought it could be great with some careful management."

Having overheard their conversation, mainly because she was eavesdropping none-too-subtly, Olivia gave Megan the kind of look that would have rendered a less healthy person dead on the spot at this last comment.

"The pub has a manager!"

Kim and Megan shared a silent exchange that confirmed that they were both fully aware of the issues regarding the pub's current 'management'! Twice that night already, Kim had caught Olivia trying to pour herself a sneaky brandy and coke despite their conversation about drinking on the job the day before.

"I think you have done your best Olivia, but I'm sure that if we work together and support each other, things can be even better," said Kim attempting to soothe the tension in the room.

Olivia not only ignored the olive branch offered by Kim, she may just have well whacked her over the head with it; she turned on her heel and went to collect glasses with the air of a teenager who's had their wifi confiscated.

"Seems she does her best work when I piss her off," laughed Kim quietly. Megan stifled a giggle and went back to serving the customers who were making their way back to the bar for round two.

The evening progressed without further confrontation and the steady stream of thirsty drinkers kept the girls busy; it seemed nothing was able to keep Keith busy apart from his re-fillable pint glass. Once Olivia and Megan had got themselves into a steady rhythm Kim took the opportunity to spend a little time in amongst her customers.

She met Doris and Brian, an absolutely lovely couple with a chocolate brown Labrador who lapped up every morsel of attention from anyone who was willing to give him a tummy rub. Then there was Kate and Jackie (affectionately known as Jax), two members of the 'Women Who Wine,' a local female entrepreneur group who met weekly on Thursday lunchtimes at the pub and who Olivia had previously labelled as 'stuck up'. They were not in the least stuck up, in fact they were great company and Kim suspected that Olivia's character assassination of them had been down to the fact that they had probably taken very little of her nonsense – she imagined they suffered fools very un-gladly! Kim had a feeling she would get on very well with the Women Who Wine and was cautiously optimistic to have found some potential allies; she looked forward to meeting them all properly on Thursday.

Some of the patrons were definitely *not* potential allies and some were positively intriguing. There was Steve, a loud-mouthed bloke who seemed to have an opinion on everything, along with an optimistically high opinion of himself...it did not come as a great surprise to Kim that Steve and Keith appeared to be getting on like a house on fire!

And there were Bobby and Fran. Bobby was a giant of a man with a face the colour of beetroot. He was tall, broad-shouldered and sported an enormous stomach that protruded in front of him like an over-inflated beachball, his bright-coloured football shirt straining at the seams. Kim was not a nurse, but she suspected that Bobby's blood pressure was on the high side of normal (if his complexion was anything to go by) and also, judging by the way he was downing pints of beer and whisky chasers, she thought he might also be a bit of a slave to the demon drink. By contrast, Bobby's girlfriend Fran was tiny. She was a little mouse of a woman, sitting hunched in her chair looking as if she wished it may actually swallow her up and allow her to disappear from the room altogether. Where Bobby was loud and gregarious, Fran barely spoke. She was as pale as he was puce-coloured. He looked out and faced the room, whilst she looked down, her head and eyes lowered to the floor. In front of her on the table was an ice bucket and a tall-stemmed glass; a 'champagne' flute. At first glance Kim wondered if perhaps they were celebrating, although Fran didn't look exactly exuberant, but on closer inspection she realised that the bottle held in the ice bucket actually contained an alcohol-free sparkling 'wine'. No wonder Fran looked so bloody miserable – sitting in a pub with the brash Bobby who was slinging lager down his throat like it was going out of fashion and getting redder and drunker by the minute whilst she sipped her fun-free fizz; the drunker he got, the sadder she looked.

The dart match was in full swing and there was lots of good-natured banter coming from the players. Kim thought that, if only for appearances, she and Keith ought to attempt to portray a united front for at least a small part of the evening and so she went and sat beside him at the bar.

"What do you think?" she asked. "The pub at least seems to have some regulars, so I suppose that is something."

"I reckon we have taken a fortune," said Keith, a little prematurely in Kim's eyes but she had to agree that the takings would certainly be up from the handful of guests they had on Monday.

At that moment Steve came over to join them and Kim was only able to manage about 15 minutes of his company before work seemed a more attractive option – in fact five years' hard labour in a coal mine would have passed quicker than a conversation with Steve!

"...been coming here since it opened," said Steve, "... not much I don't know about the people round here..." Kim assumed that Steve meant since the pub opened when her Uncle Frank and his friend Doug took it on after a period of closure, not since it was built in 1857!

Kim left Steve and Keith to bore each other shitless with their tales of whose cat was blacker and who'd bought and worn the most T-shirts!

"I see you've met Steve," chuckled Megan. "Me and Rosa call him 'Brag Pitt', thinks he's God's gift to women and is an expert on absolutely everything!"

Kim laughed, she already liked Megan. "Love it! Not to his face I guess?"

"No, but he's so thick-skinned, he'd probably take it as a compliment!"

"Did you say you have a little girl?" asked Kim. "Where is she tonight?"

"She's at her Nan's tonight. My mum is great, but I can't always do the day shifts because she works in the daytime. It's okay during term time, it's just the holidays that are a problem."

"How old is she?" asked Kim. "I know it isn't ideal, but you could always bring her with you if you get stuck."

"She's nine," said Megan," and I know she's mine, but she's a great little girl. She'd happily sit in the corner and do some colouring and if you gave her a job to do, she'd love it!"

"Well, she's welcome any time," said Kim. "I'm really hoping that we can turn the Dog and Duck into more of a family venue, at least during the day, so she can be our guinea pig so to speak!"

"It's not a bloody creche," sniped Olivia as she walked past.

"Well you'd better grow up and change your sulky attitude then," said Kim. She was trying very hard to be nice but quite frankly her thin patience was growing positively threadbare, and she was at a time in her life when she gave less and less of a rat's arse what people thought of her – especially when they were behaving badly.

Olivia looked indignant and slunk off in Keith's direction, presumably to try and ingratiate herself to at least one of her new bosses. Kim and Megan simply smiled at each other.

Before Kim knew it, the clock had ticked its way round to 11 o'clock. Last orders at the bar had been rung and a flurry of punters desperate for one last drink had been served and told to drink up quickly. Several taxis had been rung to take home those that were unsteady on their feet, but Kim also noticed that a few had left the pub on less than steady legs and with their car keys in their hand. She wondered where she should draw the line when it came to letting adults decide their own fate and taking action to avoid dangerous drivers leaving her pub. She definitely felt a sense of responsibility and she had her own strong views about drink driving; that would be another challenge she would have to face she guessed.

By the time the Dog and Duck was empty, and the last load of glasses had been cleaned, Kim was shattered. She bolted the front door noticing Keith watching her from the bar stool that he had barely left all night.

"I don't know why you've got such a problem with Olivia," he said, slurring his words slightly.

"I haven't got a problem with her Keith, I'm just not putting up with any of her crap. If she wants to be polite then so shall I, if not then she'll just have to take what comes her way."

"Running a pub is about getting along with people," said Keith helpfully.

"Well thank you Keith, that is good to know. Running a pub is also about not drinking all the stock, serving the customers and clearing the glasses, so perhaps we can each make an effort to do our bit," said Kim heading off to the toilets to turn the lights out and to make sure that no-one had left a tap running. She observed that Paul was still a 'wanker' on the toilet door, and she made a mental note to paint over that as a matter of urgency; although the way she felt right now she was tempted to cross out Paul and add Keith's name!

Chapter Six

As the week passed, the pub was more quiet than busy. It seemed that Tuesday night was not a regular occurrence in terms of bums on seats. Wednesday had been quieter than the grave and Thursday was similar, apart from the Women Who Wine group, who met between 12 and 2pm.

Kim made a point of being in the bar when they arrived so that she could pick their brains about what they liked about the pub and what they didn't; although she reckoned the first list might be considerably shorter than the second!

There were six women in the meeting on this particular Thursday, but apparently the entire group consisted of about twenty-five members in total; the other members came along when they could, when work commitments allowed or when they had their quarterly progress meetings. Kim learned that when the whole group met, they often used another venue mainly because they would have liked food whilst they talked and Olivia had told them that twenty-five people was too large a group to cater for!

"I'd love you to use the Dog and Duck for all of your meetings," said Kim, "but obviously I appreciate that things are going to need to change a bit in order for you to consider us – what could I do to persuade you to meet here?"

Jax was the first to speak. “We’d like some food other than baguettes, maybe afternoon tea or perhaps some tapas-style dishes; you know olives, bruschetta, maybe some meats and cheeses?”

“That seems easy enough,” said Kim. “We’ve got a big meeting on Tuesday – well when I say big it’s me, the chef and the two barmaids; and Olivia of course. I’m sure she’ll be very amenable!”

Kate laughed, “Yes Olivia is well known for her friendly and flexible attitude so I can’t imagine you’ll meet any problems there!”

Kim rolled her eyes... “Anything else?”

“I mean it would be great if the place had a little tidy up, but I understand that will take time... and cash,” said Jax.

“Yep, already got some plans,” said Kim. “I’m thinking a good freshen up, remove the toilet graffiti for a start and revive the menu. I’m happy to section off the area at the back of the pub so you can have a bit of privacy and if you phone ahead with your orders, we can make sure we book your lunch for a convenient time – it also means we can be prepared if we are busy,” she looked around the empty bar and raised her eyebrows.

“This place used to be quite a desirable venue a few years back,” said Helen, a local businesswoman from Foxley who owned her own hair and beauty salon. “They used to do a great Sunday Lunch and often had special nights on but since Doug died, Olivia has pretty much run the place into the ground. It's not entirely her fault, I think she is out of her depth to be honest."

"Oh come off it Helen, Olivia's a lazy cow. She's more interested in flirting with the work men and drinking the brandy than she is actually doing any hard work," remarked Fleur, "it takes all her energy to lift those bloody eyelashes of hers. She's a back-stabbing bitch as well!"

"Say what you mean Fleur!" laughed Hanna.

Kim giggled, no wonder Olivia thought they were stuck up, it seemed they had more than the measure of her. She chatted with the women for over an hour, enjoying their company and laughing about everything from menopause to men and family. She learned about each of them in turn; Fleur was a very successful social media and marketing consultant and had an impressive client list, Hanna was a teacher of Pilates and specialised in wellbeing, Kate ran her own catering business baking an assortment of special occasion cakes and cookies, Jax was a florist and Bridget was a potter who ran several workshops and community interest groups.

Olivia huffed and puffed her way past the group of women, clearly put out by the fact that she hadn't been so readily welcomed by the group as Kim appeared to be.

"Anyway, I'd better leave you lovely ladies to it," said Kim, rising from her chair. "I can't promise that everything will be done tomorrow but if you give me a bit of time then I'm sure I can make you feel much more welcome than you have been."

"I'm so glad you're here," said Fleur, squeezing Kim's arm. The two women seemed to have formed an instant connection and Kim felt sure they would become friends.

"I wasn't too glad to be here to begin with if I am totally honest," said Kim, "but hopefully things will get better from now on. When is your quarterly meeting?"

"Last Thursday in January," said Kate.

"Right, give me a couple of weeks and if you're happy to come here then I will promise you a nicer workspace, some great food and a free bottle of bubbles, how does that sound?" said Kim, she knew that a regular party of twenty-five was an opportunity not be missed.

"Sounds perfect," smiled Hanna, the rest of the women nodded their agreement.

Chapter Seven

Considering Friday should have marked the beginning of a weekend and a chance for small celebration, the Dog and Duck was positively depressing. Bobby and Fran came back in, she looking no more joyful than she had the last time Kim had seen her, sipping on her alcohol free wine dressed up to look like something altogether different, and he slinging lager down his throat like his life depended upon it. Kim lost count at pint number sixteen and suspected that Bobby's life may be in question sooner than he hoped.

The old man with the medals was back, as were the vaping couple. Olivia went home early with a 'headache' and Kim had been left to run the bar with Rosa. This hadn't been much of a problem when the staff outnumbered the guests at points in the evening and Kim had been pleased to meet another member of her team.

Rosa was originally from a small town in Italy and had moved to England with her husband 25 years ago. Her husband had passed away two years previously and she admitted that she had taken the job at the Dog and Duck as a way to fill her empty evenings more than a source of income. She had two sons and multiple grandchildren who she clearly adored and saw as often as she could, but it was no substitute for the companionship she had shared with Paulie. Rosa was barely five feet tall and possessed a curvy figure. She wore her long dark hair in a bun at the nape of her neck and her eyes were the colour of chocolate. She had a warm smile and a similarly warm disposition. She laughed often and with unashamed volume. Kim loved her instantly. Kim thanked her lucky stars that so far, with regards to her staff, and in the words of Meatloaf, 'two out of three weren't at all bad!"

In contrast to Olivia, Rosa was a hard worker and loved to be busy. Whilst they chatted, she cleaned and polished every inch of the bar, shining the counter tops and polishing the glasses. She was enthusiastic about making the pub a success and Kim knew that she would be an asset in the future.

"I almost left," said Rosa. "It is so quiet in here, like a dying swan, but I 'ave nothing else to do."

"Well don't leave just yet," said Kim, "I promise you this much, if the pub still looks like this in six months, we'll be leaving together!"

Kim noticed that Keith had left his favourite spot at the bar whilst they had been chatting and wondered if the excitement had been too much even for him!

When closing time came, Rosa hugged Kim like a long-lost friend and Kim felt a warmth that was not often present in her daily life.

"See you tomorrow Rosa."

"Tomorrow mia cara."

Kim locked the door behind Rosa and turned off the lights expecting to find Keith in their flat when she went upstairs. She heard the kitchen door slam as she reached the top of the stairs.

"Who's that? Rosa?"

"No it's me," replied Keith. "I went out to the car."

"The car?" asked Kim. "What is in the car? At this time of night?"

Keith mumbled a reply that Kim didn't quite catch but when she heard the clinking of glasses, she assumed that it was time for yet another night cap!

Keith was unusually helpful on Saturday, finishing the painting in both of the spare bedrooms and helping to move the furniture without his usual griping. Kim had been quite heartened that they had managed to work together in such a harmonious manner and dared to allow herself the notion that maybe the move to the Dog and Duck could perhaps be a step in the right direction for the future of their marriage and their life together.

Kim's earlier optimism was soon dampened when Keith announced that he was meeting Steve in town to, 'check out the competition.'

She inwardly chided herself for her wishful thinking realising, not for the first time, that Keith was only ever accommodating when he had an ulterior motive – in this case, a pub crawl around the watering holes.

"You don't mind do you love?" asked Keith planting a kiss on the top of her head.

"No it's fine," said Kim. She hadn't the energy to argue. She didn't even mind him going out, it was more the fact that she felt she had been played and also that she felt a bit foolish for believing things were better than they were.

"It's just a few drinks and a chance to get to know people," said Keith. "I've worked hard today."

"Yes, you're right. You have worked very hard. Just me being daft, bit tired I guess. I thought we got on pretty well today."

"We always get on okay babe," said Keith, leaving the room to run himself a bath.

Kim wasn't as convinced as Keith that they 'always got on ok,' but perhaps she had unrealistic expectations about how a marriage worked. The flat was a lot cleaner and tidier than it was before and at least her Mum and Daniel now had a clean and comfortable room to sleep in. She didn't really have much room to complain.

Keith left the pub by car at about 7pm just a few minutes before Rosa arrived for her evening shift. Megan arrived at 8pm and it was Olivia's night off. Apparently, Olivia often took the night off and there wasn't always a clear timetable for her shifts unlike the rest of the staff. Kim was making a mental note for 'things to discuss' for their Tuesday afternoon meeting and she had a sneaking suspicion that Olivia was going to be the unwilling focus for most of these discussions.

The evening went by without event, or customers, and the three women easily managed the bar between them. Rosa had them in stitches recounting the time when her dear husband Paulie had asked for a pound of beef curtains in the butcher's instead of a pound of beef skirt. New to England and still learning the language he had struggled to find the words for his order! The butcher who was Jim Senior at the time almost spat out his false teeth at the request and had a pretty hard time trying to explain Paulie's mistake to him – they became firm friends from that day forward.

Keith did not return until almost midnight and Kim thought it strange that he came home by car. She had been sitting in the bar enjoying a small night cap when he came in through the back kitchen.

"How come you drove, you're not over the limit are you?" asked Kim.

"No, I only had a pint in the end."

"I thought you were going on a pub crawl, how come you didn't drink? How did Steve get home?

"Bloody hell woman what's with all the questions? There are no taxis around here, so I decided to take it easy," said Keith irritably and pouring himself a large scotch.

"What are the pubs like?" asked Kim deciding not to pursue the issue of the invisible taxis.

"Yeah alright," said Keith vaguely.

He offered no further information about the evening and switched on the wall-mounted TV to catch up on the day's football scores. Kim sighed and gave up – any hope that she had earlier held for their future disappearing quicker than Keith's whisky.

Chapter Eight

The weekend came and went, and Kim was glad that the pub was so quiet as it gave her plenty of time to give the place a thorough clean. Their upstairs living accommodation was now tidy and painted except for the bathroom and kitchen which needed more of an overhaul and would have to wait a little longer - at least they were clean and as organised as could be expected given the circumstances. They needed a new carpet throughout, but Kim still wasn't altogether sure that she was going to stay in her heart of hearts, so she held off... just in case.

She was however looking forward to their Tuesday staff meeting. She still hadn't met Dean the chef and she figured that even if she built the business up a bit, at least it would look more attractive to a prospective buyer in the future.

When she awoke on Tuesday morning, Keith was in a foul mood. She did her best to ignore him but he seemed hell bent on picking a fight – everything she did annoyed him; using the bathroom when he needed to clean his teeth, forgetting the sweetener in his tea... all the usual first world problems of a middle aged diva!

"Will you stop bloody moaning," she snapped after Keith had made his 110th demand of the morning.

"That's rich coming from you," replied Keith.

Kim rolled her eyes and chose not to respond. She was mighty relieved when Keith finally left the building to go and 'take a breather,' whatever that meant. She suspected he had a thick head (in more ways than one!) after propping up the bar for an entire weekend, his over-indulgence affecting his mood and his health. Keith had always liked a drink but even he wasn't used to drinking like he was 'out, out' seven nights a week!

Kim made an extra effort with her appearance, she wanted to make a good impression and to appear calm and in control. She chose a pair of black jeans and a pale pink roll neck with sleeves that had been described rather unflatteringly as 'mutton' sleeves by her mum; she hoped she didn't look like mutton dressed as lamb, as her grandmother used to say! She applied some light makeup and added a few wavy curls to her shoulder-length hair. One of her best friends before she moved away often joked that the older a woman got, applying more makeup just made you look worse instead of better; like an ageing drag queen. With that in mind, Kim went for the 'less is more' approach and hoped it would do.

She went downstairs to set things up for the day, turning on lights and chucking one last slosh of bleach down the toilets; no matter what she tried they still smelled a bit like a cross between a nightclub urinal and a Portaloo. Unfortunately, she feared that they were probably the one bit of the pub that could not be rolled in glitter but would need a total refurb; whether she stayed or not, they needed sorting out.

At 10.30am, she heard the kitchen door creak open and the sound of whistling cheerfully breaking the silence. She hoped it was Dean the chef, otherwise they had a very jolly intruder! Olivia would not be in until five minutes before her shift began at midday – one thing that was definitely going to change was Olivia's highly 'flexible' rota.

"Hi, you must be Dean," said Kim, entering into the kitchen.

Dean turned around, yellow beanie hat still in place as he put on his chef's apron.

"Yellow beanie hat! Aren't you the one pound man?" exclaimed Kim, instantly recognising her helpful stranger from the supermarket carpark.

"Not quite as flattering as the million dollar man, but I'll take it," laughed Dean. "How weird is that? Meeting before meeting if you know what I mean."

"It's a small world," smiled Kim. "I'm Kim, your new landlady, lovely to meet you... again."

"Likewise. Anything you want me to do other than what I normally do?" asked Dean. "Although to be honest, these days I don't do much at all... not that I'm lazy, just a lack of clientele," he added, hastily.

"It's ok, I get it, I've not exactly been rushed off my feet either, well I have but more with moving in than serving drinks. I'm hoping things can change. Let's face it, if they don't change then this place will close down."

"If I'm brutally honest with you, I probably wouldn't stay much longer with things as they are. I like to be busy and I do have some professional pride – making a few cheese baguettes of a lunchtime hardly gets my creative juices flowing," sighed Dean.

"Oh no, not you as well," said Kim. "I know Rosa had one eye on the door, but I'm hoping I've convinced her to hang for a little while longer."

"Listen I'm happy to give things a try, especially if there is somebody at the helm who actually wants things to change if you know what I mean. I don't suppose Olivia is in yet?" asked Dean.

"Erm... Olivia never seems to be *in,*" sighed Kim. "I don't wish to speak ill of absent people but even when she is here, she does the bare minimum and I've got to be honest, I've found her pretty heavy-going. She doesn't exactly radiate enthusiasm and positivity does she?"

Dean laughed. "Olivia is only positive about a few large brandies and getting away with as little as possible. She fully expected to inherit this place when Doug died but he only employed her as a favour to his ex-wife. He couldn't bloody stand her, but by that time he was too old to manage by himself. Olivia wants the title of bar manager but with none of the effort; she wants to swan around, fluttering those huge eyelashes and doing very little else. She has not got a bloody clue. I guess I'm not afraid to speak ill of absent people... but it's not something I haven't said to her face on more than one occasion!"

Kim smiled. "Phew! At least I'm not the only one who thinks that way – I don't think Megan or Rosa are super fond either. Anyway, why don't you give me a quick rundown of your usual morning and I can add it to the list of things to mull over for our meeting this afternoon?"

"Sounds like a plan," smiled Dean. He really did have the loveliest eyes.

For the next hour or so, Dean gave Kim a tour of the cellar and showed her how he maintained what little stock they had. Since leaving the army eight years ago, where he had trained as a chef, Dean had managed his own pub for a few years but when his marriage broke up, he was forced to leave and find a job. The Dog and Duck had been an easy quick fix for the past year, but he knew that he needed a job that would challenge and fulfil him more than his current position. His army training meant that he was methodical and well-organised, and Kim hoped he would stay – at least while she stayed that was.

Just after 11.30, Kim returned to the bar and left Dean whistling in the kitchen whilst he prepared the meagre quantity of baguettes likely to be needed for today's 'rush.' She had tasked him with the job of preparing a nice lunch for the staff during their meeting; something that could be eaten with fingers whilst they talked; she had felt like one of those shouty chefs off the telly, "...today your challenge is to prepare a lunch for five, using half a pepper, some cheese with the mouldy bits cut off and a couple of part-baked baguettes. You have three hours and your time starts... NOW!"

Kim opened the front doors just before 12pm and waited for someone, anyone, to arrive. By 12.45pm no-one had arrived, not even Olivia who was now unfashionably late, even by her standards.

Just before 1, a flustered Olivia entered the bar via the back kitchen, "Sorry I'm late, car trouble," she said, appearing neither convincing nor sorry.

Kim gave her a look that she hoped was suitably menacing. As a child Kim's mother had been able to silence even the thought of a tantrum with a look that could stop the most wilful of protestors. Kim wasn't entirely sure she had quite inherited her mother's death stare, but age and a lack of patience were certainly helping her to perfect the art.

"Do you have a phone, Olivia?" asked Kim.

"Yeah, battery's dead," replied Olivia, just as her phone started ringing in her bag.

"Your phone's ringing," said Kim, dryly. "I'll take an hour off today's pay," and she walked away leaving Olivia scrabbling to turn off the offending phone and muttering something under her breath which sounded a lot like a witch's curse!

"Yes, she's fuming," whispered Olivia into the phone that had refused to stop ringing. "Ok, but it's not ideal."

Kim heard the whispered conversation and had no doubt that she was the 'she' that had been mentioned. At that moment Keith entered the pub through the front door.

"Nice time?" asked Kim. "Any plans to help out in the business you wanted us to run today?"

"Still in a bad mood then?" asked Keith.

Kim didn't trust herself to reply. "Are you joining us for the staff meeting today? Might be good to appear as a team?"

"Er, I might pop in. Probably best if you deal with all that, I've got to pop out later anyway."

"Pop out where exactly?" asked Kim.

"These jobs won't do themselves," said Keith vaguely.

Kim didn't think for one minute that he was going out on 'official business', she more suspected that he didn't want to be involved in any situation where he might be required to negotiate or have any potentially difficult conversations. As much as she had expressed an interest in him taking part in the meeting, she didn't realise that she had in fact been clenching her jaw tightly when he replied – deep down she had hoped that he would refuse and keep out of the bloody way!

Olivia did not speak another word to Kim for the rest of her shift and Kim was absolutely fine with that. At three o'clock they ejected the three customers in the bar who had been prepared to take up residence had they been allowed and Kim pulled a couple of tables together to given them plenty of room. Megan and Rosa arrived on the dot of 3 and Dean called through from the kitchen to check if they were ready for lunch to be served.

He had obviously relished the challenge of preparing a nice lunch and had pulled out all the stops considering his less than bountiful supplies. A platter full of delicious finger-food goodies was placed proudly on the table in front of them...

"We have olive and parmesan bruschetta, roasted peppers with goat's cheese, paprika wedges with a sour cream dip and savoury rice with prawns, courgette ribbons and a chilli and lemon dressing – basically posh pizza and chips," laughed Dean.

"It looks amazing Dean, thank you," said Kim. "This is definitely the kind of food we should be serving at the Dog and Duck."

"Our customers won't like this," said Olivia sulkily.

"Olivia, we don't have any customers," laughed Kim.

The rest of the group laughed with her whilst Olivia sulked and folded her arms across her chest.

"Right let's tuck in and I say we can talk whilst we eat; that okay with everyone?" asked Kim. "We've got a lot to talk about so we could be here a while."

"Fine with us," replied Dean. "You ladies tuck in and I'll go and get the pot of coffee and some mineral water."

"Lottie is going to after-school club today," said Megan, "and then my mum is collecting her so I am good for a while yet."

"Perfect," said Kim. "Let's make a start – I've made a list..."

Kim began to share her ideas for the pub.

"I don't think we can run a pub that doesn't serve food and we certainly can't be closed on certain days. I think we should run the pub as if it were busy and start as we mean to go on. I suggest we open every day from 11am until 3pm and then again from 6pm until 11pm.

If we get super busy then we can consider opening all day but that can wait for now. I propose that we serve food between 12pm and 2pm and again from 6pm until 9pm and Dean how do you feel about devising a menu; I'm thinking good no-nonsense pub grub and perhaps some sharing platters for lunchtimes, a bit like you've done today?"

"That would be my pleasure," said Dean with real enthusiasm. "I don't know if you realised it but Rosa is an awesome cook, she makes a mean lasagne."

Rosa blushed, "Oh Dean, mia cara, you so sweet."

"Well I'm up for it if you are?" said Kim. "Of course, we will buy the ingredients and you can have extra time to prepare it in-house ready for service – anything we don't use can be frozen and re-heated on another day. Might be good to make it in nice big batches!"

"I would be 'appy to show you a proper Italian lasagne," smiled Rosa.

"Great," said Kim, "that's dish number one sorted then! The next thing we need to sort is a cleaning lady. I'm happy to help clearing up but I think we need a good daily clean, especially for those grotty toilets, which are another thing on my list!"

Megan raised her hand nervously. "I don't if this would be okay with you but I could really do with the extra hours, I'd be happy to come in an hour or so each day. I could come straight from dropping Lottie off at school if that would work? Any days that I'm working the bar too I could just stay on."

"That would be perfect," replied Kim, "and if you need to freshen up and change you'd be welcome to use a spare room upstairs."

The enthusiasm in the room was infectious and Kim was starting to feel more motivated about the pub than she had so far. They talked about changing the layout a bit, moving the pool table nearer to the dart board area to create a games area. The room that housed the pool table currently had doors onto the garden and they all felt this would be a great space for a dedicated restaurant and hospitality area for functions and parties or meetings.

"I'd also like to decorate and maybe get some nicer seating, some sofas and comfier chairs. I'd also like to get the chimneys swept so that we can have a fire at both ends of the pub, especially in the winter months, it seems a shame not to use them and it would make the place feel much cosier."

Kim took a deep breath; she had deliberately left this part of the meeting until some positive things had been decided. During her career in the bank, she had been taught to start meetings with positivity before addressing sensitive issues. She knew that what she was about to discuss was likely to be met with some resistance; although in fairness she suspected that the person that was likely to resist most strongly was the one who had barely said a word and who sat with arms still folded and an expression of boredom and defiance on her heavily-lashed face!

"This next part could be a little sensitive," said Kim, "but I really feel it's important to make sure we have good systems in place – makes things fairer and clearer I think." Olivia sat up in her chair and uncrossed her arms.

"With regards to working hours," continued Kim, "I would like everyone to arrive 30 minutes before their shift starts so that they are ready and prepared. It goes without saying that you will be paid for that time. Dean, I imagine you might need to arrive an hour before your shift, that gives you two hours of prep before service. Is that enough?"

"That's fine by me," said Dean. "If... I mean *when,* we start getting busy we may need to re-think or get some extra help but it's certainly fine for now. I'll make sure the menu is easy to prepare with minimum wastage."

"Wonderful," said Kim. "Now, with regards to drinking on the job, I'm afraid I am going to be a spoilsport and say no more. I'm happy to buy you all one free drink at the end of your shift and of course, you can have as much tea, coffee and water as you like but no more alcohol during work time, is that ok?"

Olivia re-folded her arms. "I suppose you're talking to me now?" she asked sarcastically.

"I'm talking to everyone Olivia," replied Kim calmly. "I won't treat anyone any differently."

Olivia huffed. "I don't think any of you smoke," continued Kim, "but just for the record I'm going to be banning vaping from inside the pub too – customers and staff."

"Fine by me," said Megan, "I hate it!"

“It might not be popular but if we make a nice little smoking area out the back it might soften the blow a bit. I’d also like to suggest that we all have a list of agreed jobs to do for when things aren’t busy – nothing too strenuous just cleaning the bottle shelves, tidying the bar area things like that…”

“I thought we had a new cleaning lady,” Olivia snapped.

“Well yes we do, Olivia,” said Kim, as calmly as she could, “I just think it would be a good opportunity to keep on top of the little random extra jobs when we are quiet. Dean, are you still happy to manage the cellar?”

“Fine by me,” said Dean, “I’m sure we can work out some kind of rota for the time it takes me…”

“So am I a bar manager or a fucking cleaning lady,” growled Olivia, interrupting Dean and sitting forward in her chair.

“Sorry?” asked Kim, a little taken aback at the venom with which Olivia had spoken.

“I said, am I a bar MANAGER or a fucking cleaning lady? So far you have done nothing but make digs about how I run the place, don’t drink, don’t vape, arrive early, polish the fucking shelves… is this a pub or a fucking workhouse?”

An awkward silence descended on the group and Kim wouldn’t have been surprised to see a big ball of tumbleweed roll in through the door and across the room in front of them. Astonishingly, it was Rosa who spoke first…

"Oh for fock's sake Olivia stop bloddy moaning. This place is definitely not a *work* house where you are concerned. If you don't like it you can bloddy well peess off!" she said, sucking a large intake of air through her front teeth and gesturing with her hands in quite the most Mediterranean of gestures that Kim had ever seen!

"Yes, well, I have somewhere I need to be, you can add the last hour of my *wasted* time to my wages," shrieked Olivia, her face flushed, her eyes blazing.

Olivia snatched her bag up from the floor, tugging at the strap as it caught under her chair. In her fury she yanked at the trapped bag with such force that the strap broke free, she lost her balance and fell flat on her backside! The rest of the group stared in disbelief, mouths open and closing like a bunch of bewildered goldfish. Olivia scrambled to her feet, wrenched her coat from the back of her chair and stomped out of the pub slamming the door so hard that Kim swore she saw a little more of the peeling paint detach itself from the door frame and float down onto the carpet.

For a few seconds, the room was deathly quiet until Dean began to laugh and pretty soon, they were all rolling around, tears streaming down their faces, barely able to speak.

"Should I send her Oscar in the post," chuckled Dean, "that really was quite entertaining!"

"Oh don't," said Kim. "I knew she probably wouldn't be too happy but I'm not sure even I expected that! You don't think I'm being unreasonable, do you?"

"Listen," said Megan. "All you've asked is that we have a clear and fair system with a few rules that are perfectly reasonable. I'm sure I'm not the only one who is very keen for things to change around here. It's about time Olivia pulled her weight and if she doesn't like it, well then, she can 'bloddy well peess off," she said, imitating Rosa.

With that, everyone started laughing again.

"It will be lovely," said Rosa looking in Megan's direction with mock indignation, "to work somewhere nice and clean, to be busy with nice customers and to serve nice food."

"Hear, hear," said Dean, standing up and starting to clear the plates. "Why don't you work on a rota that you think will work and then we can all take a look and let you know what we can and can't do."

"Wonderful," said Kim, relieved that at least three quarters of her staff were 'normal' humans! "And in the meantime if you just jot down any times that you absolutely can't do then I'll do my best to accommodate; like childcare and family stuff, although don't forget Lottie is welcome here during the day with you, Megan, if you're stuck."

At that moment, Keith barged in through the door, "What the fuck have you done to Olivia?" he yelled.

"We are just cleaning up the toys that Olivia has chucked from her pram Keith, and I didn't *do* anything to her – unless you count me asking her to actually do her job, that is," replied Kim, furious at Keith's very public chastising of her.

"She's in a right state," said Keith. "I've spent ages persuading her not to leave us!"

Kim held her breath. Keith shot a smug glance in her direction, "Good job I'm here to sort out your mess, isn't it?" he said, leaving the bar and heading upstairs.

Once again, a silence descended on the room and Kim fought back the tears of humiliation burning the back of her throat. Dean retreated to the kitchen with the dirty dishes and Megan busied herself wiping down their table. Rosa came across to Kim, put her arm around her shoulder, squeezing her tightly and placing a kiss on the top of her arm.

"Mia cara," she whispered, "mia cara."

Kim gave a feeble smile and exchanged a look with Rosa that spoke volumes. Rosa knew. Rosa *saw* everything.

Chapter Nine

The only thing that had kept Kim from running away or taking a blunt instrument to Keith's precious sports car was the fact that her mum and Daniel were arriving on Friday. Olivia did not say one word to her for the rest of the week except when absolutely necessary. Kim knew that she was still defiantly stealing the brandy and although she did now arrive early for her shift, it was never the full 30 minutes as agreed. Sometimes Olivia would make a theatrical show of polishing a teaspoon or some other inconsequential object when Kim looked her way, but Kim refused to bite; she was pretty sure the bubble would burst eventually. Let her have her little victories... for now.

Keith was still strutting around like William the sodding Conqueror, Kim was sure he felt satisfied that he had waved his willy around sufficiently to show his dominance, to stake his claim as the man in charge. Kim kept the peace and let him think he was in charge for the time being; she didn't want to rock the boat before Friday.

On Friday morning, Kim felt the kind of excitement usually felt by small children on Christmas Eve, like she was about to get the best present on her list. Even Olivia couldn't dampen her mood. She spent the morning polishing the flat and the bar until it shone, if not like a new penny, but certainly a slightly buffed one! She checked the time at least every half an hour throughout the day, watching the door every time it opened, even though she knew they wouldn't be arriving until around 7pm.

A few minutes before 7 and the one time when ironically Kim hadn't been watching the door, Daniel and her mum burst in, stamping the rain off of their boots and looking for all the world like a pair of Dickensian travellers who'd battled the elements to arrive, windswept and weary!

Daniel and his nan stood in the doorway, their eyes scanning the pub. Daniel noticed the familiar bulky frame of his father who sat on his usual bar stool, with his back towards the door. He didn't bother to call out, he wanted to see his mum first – he knew she would be much more pleased to see them than Keith would pretend to be.

At that moment Kim bobbed up from behind the bar where she had been crouched down sorting the empty bottle crates. She banged her head on one of the beer pumps as she stood up,

"Shit! Ouch!" she exclaimed rubbing the offending area.

Her eyes drifted towards the door and then, "Daniel! Mum!"

She hurtled across the room, her sore head forgotten, as she flung herself upon her two eagerly awaited guests.

"Oh my God, I thought you'd never get here," she exclaimed, showering them both with hugs and kisses.

"Steady on, Mum," laughed Daniel, "you'll have us over!"

"It's so good to see you darling," said Kim's mum Judy.

"You have no idea how excited I've been... welcome to paradise!"

Judy raised her eyebrows, "Not exactly the Ritz is it, but then I know you'll have it lovely in no time. How are you, sweetheart?"

At the sound of the commotion, Keith turned round on his bar stool, barely a quarter turn, and nodded in the direction of his son and mother-in-law, "Son... Judy."

Daniel and Judy smiled and greeted Keith in return, but it would have been obvious to even a complete stranger, that the welcome did not possess a fraction of the warmth flowing between themselves and Kim.

Keith had never exactly been 'father of the year.' He'd never been unkind, and Kim knew that he loved Daniel in his own way, but theirs was very much one-dimensional kind of relationship. It had always been Kim who had taken Daniel to birthday parties, to swimming lessons, invited friends for tea, read bedtime stories; all the nurturing stuff and consequently Daniel and Kim were close whilst Daniel and his father were much more distant. The truth was that Keith always put Keith first and he hadn't changed just because a baby entered their lives. If Kim was brutally honest, she kind of liked having Daniel to herself, if Keith wasn't going to be 'hands-on' then she had preferred being able to dote on her beloved boy, without 'interference.'

"Come on, let's get your bags upstairs and then we'll open a nice bottle of something bubbly to celebrate," smiled Kim taking her mum's bag and leading them upstairs.

It didn't take long to give them a tour of her less-than-palatial accommodation, but she was pleased that it was clean and tidy; it actually looked quite homely if you compared it to the sight that had greeted her when she first arrived!

"Well, it's not too bad at all," said Judy. "Mine and Daniel's rooms are really quite cosy."

"It didn't look like that when arrived," laughed Kim, "but to be fair to Keith he has been quite busy with a paintbrush."

Judy raised her eyebrows but didn't reply.

"Just a new carpet and then it will be much better – if you ignore the kitchen and the bathroom that is!"

"So, are you okay here, Mum? I mean, *really* ok?" Daniel asked.

He knew that his mum hadn't been keen on moving and he cared deeply about her happiness. He also worried that now she was much further away from him, he was less able to pop in and check on her; he was under no illusion about how difficult it could be living with his dad at times.

"I'm okay son," said Kim. "I have had the notion to turn on my heel and run on a few occasions but I'm just taking it a day at a time. If it doesn't work out, then we'll just sell the place. I've actually met a few nice people since I've arrived and three out of the four staff are lovely."

"Do you mean her with the big lashes," asked Judy. "Is she the one out of the four?"

Judy was not your average 72-year-old. She was smartly dressed and even smarter of mind. There wasn't much that got past her and even though she was one of the kindest souls that Kim had ever known, she didn't suffer fools gladly and she had the kind of intuition for a person's character that bordered on witch-like!

"Oh she's the one alright," laughed Kim. "Anyway, enough of her, let's go and get a drink. Rosa has cooked one of her amazing lasagnes and left it in the kitchen for our tea."

"Good, I'm bloody starving," said Daniel.

"I take it Rosa is one of the three," laughed Judy.

"Rosa is just wonderful, you will love her, I know you will."

The three of them went back downstairs and settled themselves around a table. Keith came over briefly, but the conversation was stilted. He stayed long enough to eat some of the amazing meal that Rosa had prepared before resuming his favourite stool at the bar and chatting to Olivia who was simpering and fluttering her lashes at his every word.

"She'll have his bloody eye out if she's not careful," remarked Judy with more than a hint of contempt.

Kim laughed. “I think she’s trying to get at me for telling her off the other day. I told her she couldn’t drink all the brandy and had to actually turn up for work on time.”

“No wonder she’s pissed off,” laughed Daniel, “you can’t half be unreasonable at times, Mum!”

They continued laughing and chatting and Kim felt so content. She didn’t care that Keith and Olivia were busy flirting, she didn’t care that the pub still looked like a tired old social club, she was just so pleased to spend time with the people she loved the most.

Chapter Ten

Daniel and Judy were staying for the whole week and didn't plan to travel back until the following Saturday morning. Judy got quite into her role as temporary bar maid and the customers absolutely loved her. Daniel was wonderful, helping Kim to re-arrange the pub furniture, creating designated areas for pub games, dining and relaxing; just the re-arrangements alone made the whole place look ten times better. The old threadbare carpet that had stuck to their feet a fortnight ago had been ripped up to reveal the most amazing flagstone floor, and a trip to the local charity shop had yielded a couple of comfy old leather sofas in great condition, that looked really cosy around the big old fireplace. Judy was extremely house proud, and she and Megan scrubbed and cleaned the place so that the windows actually gleamed, and the floors shone. A smell of white linen furniture polish had replaced the smell of damp and neglect, and scented tealights adorned every table.

Keith had made less and less of an appearance, always having to dash off to 'pick something up', or being spectacularly conspicuous by his absence; especially when there were jobs to be done. The only real contribution he had made was to replace the broken door in the ladies' loo which at least meant that the tribute to the masturbating Paul had been removed! They had shared a few meals together as a family, but Kim always felt relieved when he left, and the conversation flowed more naturally again. She felt sad that Daniel and his dad seemed to have grown further apart than ever and she knew that it wasn't just because of geography.

Dean and Rosa had worked a miracle in the kitchen and Rosa's Italian influence on the new menu had made for some exciting new dishes. The best thing about all of this, apart from the harmonious working atmosphere, was that Kim and her family had been used as willing guinea pigs for any new ideas, and she couldn't remember a time when she had eaten so well. Pub grub favourites such as shepherd's pie, beer-battered cod, and bangers and mash were joined by Rosa's authentic lasagne and some antipasti sharing platters which looked as good as they tasted.

Dean managed the kitchen and cellar with military precision and everyone, apart from Olivia who walked around with an expression that resembled a smacked arse most of the time, was more than happy with their new structured and productive work routines.

On Wednesday evening Kim had accidentally overheard a muffled conversation between Daniel and Keith and it sounded very much like Daniel was unhappy about something..." make an effort... selfish... where were you...?"

Kim had been on her way downstairs and it sounded very much like the voices were coming from outside the back kitchen door. She had faltered on the stairway to see if she could hear, but then the phone in the kitchen rang and the voices dispersed. She entered the bar just as Daniel came through from the kitchen and they almost bumped into each other.

“You okay babe?” she asked, noticing Daniel’s pained expression.

“Don’t stay because you *have* to Mum, stay because you *want* to, ok?”

Kim went to reply but Daniel had already started walking away. She was a little puzzled by his somewhat cryptic message but knew that without doubt his father was the source of his exasperation; and definitely not for the first time.

Chapter Eleven

Thursday lunchtime was the date for the Women Who Wine's quarterly meeting and Kim felt strangely nervous. She had grown quite fond of the few members she had met, especially Fleur, and she was really keen to make them feel welcome. She also wanted them to be impressed by the efforts that her little team had made (although Olivia's contribution had been minimal at best), and to enjoy both the food and the newly arranged meeting area.

On Thursday morning, Dean had come in extra early and set about preparing the platters for the ladies' lunch. Judy and Megan had put little vases of flowers on each of the tables and had laid a top table with a bright white cloth. On it, they arranged a larger vase of flowers, some water jugs, glasses (shined especially for the occasion), and some pens and post-it notes, along with a bowl of vibrant fruit.

The rest of the tables were arranged neatly around the room with places and chairs for 25 members. Plates, cutlery and serviettes had been laid and carefully arranged. Kim had to admit that the result was pretty amazing.

"Thank you so much, it really does look beautiful, you've both worked so hard."

Megan and Judy smiled. "Team effort," said Judy placing an arm around Megan's shoulders. "She's a little treasure, this one."

Megan blushed.

“Oh don’t worry, I know that,” smiled Kim.

At that moment Olivia walked into the room. “Foster’s is off!” she said, barely acknowledging her colleagues.

“Thanks for letting me know,” said Kim through gritted teeth.

“Little madam,” exclaimed Judy.

“I heard that!” shouted Olivia as she left the room.

“Good!” said Judy under her breath. “Seriously Kim, she needs to go,” she mouthed, making a ‘get lost’ gesture with her thumb over one shoulder.

Megan and Kim smiled. “Her time will come Mum, don’t you worry. For today I just want us to be proud of what we have achieved here. Now let’s go and grab a quick cuppa before the rush starts. I want to make sure Dean and Rosa get a break too, they’ve been in that kitchen all morning.”

Kim knew it was probably a little excessive having *all* the staff in for the day but, not only did she want things to run like clockwork, she also wanted to share her success with the people who had helped to make it happen; even though Olivia had only been an accidental bystander in proceedings!

They went through to the bar and sat on the barstools. Dean and Rosa came through to join them and Kim poured coffee from the percolator that was now a permanent fixture behind the bar. Pretty soon, Daniel came to join them and they chatted excitedly about the day ahead, making sure they hadn’t forgotten anything. After a few minutes, Dean said,

"Where's old sweetness and light got to?"

Rosa and Megan giggled at Dean's description of Olivia.

"Oh Christ," exclaimed Kim. "She came and barked something about the Foster's being off. I bet she's had to go and change it; I completely forgot!"

"Stay there, I'll go and give her a hand. That lager will be pouring like a Mr Whippy by the time she's finished with it!" said Dean, getting up from his stool.

"Do you need a hand?" asked Daniel.

"No, I'm good mate, but you're welcome to come and have a nose."

Daniel got up and followed Dean in the direction of the cellar, "Won't hurt for me to see how it's done I guess."

The girls continued their conversation where they had left off.

All of a sudden there was an almighty crash.

"What the bloody hell was that?" shrieked Megan almost jumping off her stool.

The noise seemed to be coming from their cellar. There was more crashing and the sound of shouting followed by a high-pitched wail. The girls looked at each other in confusion and stood up almost in unison. At that moment, Dean appeared at the cellar door, his face as white as a sheet.

"Kim, I think you need to come through the back, this can't happen in the pub," he said.

“What can’t happen in the pub?” asked Kim. “We open in five minutes, what do you mean? And why do you look like you’ve been in a fight? Hang on... what’s gone on....?” Kim’s voice was now raised and becoming increasingly frantic.

“Kim trust me, just come through to the kitchen. Rosa, Megan, you need to open the pub. Judy, I’d stay where you are if I were you.”

“Dean, you’re scaring me, what’s happened? Where’s Daniel?” said Kim, now almost panic stricken.

“Daniel’s fine, just come through to the kitchen.”

The door to the cellar was located between the kitchen door and the door to the upstairs flat. Going out through the back of the bar, it was necessary to pass first the apartment door, then the cellar door before reaching the kitchen door, although this whole passage was little more than a few steps.

As Dean and Kim passed the cellar door, it flung open and Daniel emerged, his hair decidedly ruffled. He had the beginnings of a black eye, and he was rubbing the knuckles on his right hand with the palm of his left.

“Daniel are you okay, what happe.........” Kim began, but faltered as first she saw Olivia and then Keith following behind Daniel.

Olivia’s long eyelashes had begun to clump together, soaked by the tears that were making long black tracks down her cheeks. Keith’s lip was swollen and bloody, his T-shirt ripped at the collar.

"Oh my fucking Christ!" shrieked Kim, as reality dawned. "You were with *her*, weren't you?"

Dean guided Kim through into the kitchen, eager to avoid a spectacle for any early customers. The five of them stood in the kitchen, Olivia making frequent sniffing noises, Keith looking indignant.

"So Dad, do you want to tell Mum or shall I?"

Keith opened his mouth to speak but Kim held her hand up to silence him; the last thing she needed now was a stream of false protestations from Keith. "It's okay Daniel, I know exactly what has happened. It's not exactly rocket science, is it?"

Suddenly all Keith's mysterious disappearances, the pub crawls without any drinking, the phones with 'dead batteries' that rang unexpectedly, the furtive glances and vague explanations, it was all making sense; two and two were definitely starting to make four!

Keith opened his mouth as if to speak again. "Shut the fuck up, Keith!" said Kim with more control then she felt.

At that moment, Judy came through from the bar, "Everything alright?"

She looked at the scene before her. She observed Keith's swollen lip and Daniel's bruised knuckles. She directed her steely gaze at Olivia, "Finally shown your true colours, have you?"

"Now hang on a minute," Keith protested.

"Don't you 'hang on' me, you arrogant, jumped-up little snot!" spat Judy. "I've known from the moment I set eyes on that girl she was trouble and I've known *you* were trouble for the last thirty years. I've tolerated you for the sake of my daughter and my grandson but you're nothing but a waste of space!"

Kim almost smiled at her mum's outburst. She might be small in stature, but she was a force to be reckoned with if you upset her family!

"It's okay Mum," said Kim. "It's funny though Keith isn't it, that none of us are altogether surprised at what a terrible human being you are? I think you both need to leave. I've got twenty five people coming for lunch and I'll be damned if I let either of you spoil it; especially when you have both contributed bugger all to the efforts."

"What do you mean, leave?" snarled Keith. "This is half my pub, where will I go?"

"I suggest you go and stay with Olivia, it's not like she's got work in the morning!"

"You can't do that," shrieked Olivia, "I've got rights!"

Kim suspected that Olivia was less than delighted at the prospect of welcoming the feckless Keith as her new lodger so soon in their 'relationship.'

"I think you'll find, *OLIVIA*," said Kim, placing sinister emphasis on the girl's name, "that your rights just disappeared when you decided to cop off with my husband. But honestly, you are very much welcome to him. And Keith... my dear Keith, once she realises you are neither as successful nor as wealthy as you profess to be, you may be disappointed to find that you are not as irresistible as you once were. And, once it becomes clear that she is more interested in staking her claim on a pub, which is not even in your name, than she is in your questionable charm and wisdom, your relationship will have less shelf life than a week-old kipper!"

"Now listen to me," said Keith. "This is still half my pub!"

"I'm done listening to you Keith, and I would sincerely recommend that you take a look at the deeds; when you have a spare moment that is!" said Kim, feeling her brave face beginning to slip.

Daniel stepped forward, "You need to leave, Dad, otherwise I will push you out myself!"

Keith looked as if he might try to protest but declined when Dean took a step forward to stand beside Daniel. Kim knew him well enough to know that his mind would be reeling about her last revelation, and she didn't dare to imagine what would happen when he found out the truth; she'd rather he found that out when he was on his own!

"I'm going back through," said Judy, placing a kiss on her daughter's cheek. "I'm going to tell the girls quietly just so they know to look after you."

Kim nodded gratefully. She didn't think she had the strength to talk about events publicly just yet.

"Right, OUT!" said Daniel, guiding his dad roughly to the back door.

“What about my bag?” whimpered Olivia.

“I’ll throw your bag through on my way back,” said Judy.

...And true to her word, moments later, Olivia’s bag was slung through the kitchen door with neither a word nor a glance from Judy!

Keith and Olivia left before they were forcibly removed, and Daniel closed the door behind them. They could be heard arguing on their way to the car.

Kim had been standing with her back to the fridge and, at the sight of their departure, all her resolve faded. She slumped backwards and slid down the fridge door settling in a seated position on the kitchen floor. She hugged her knees to her chest, dropping her head and allowing the tears to fall.

Daniel crouched down on the floor beside his mum, pulling her in towards him and hugging her tightly.

“I’m so sorry Mum, please don’t cry. He was never good enough for you.”

“What about the lunch?” sobbed Kim. “All our hard work?”

“Now listen to me,” said Dean, having remained silent throughout the whole sorry saga. “I don’t want to speak out of turn, but we are *not* going to let that selfish bastard ruin our hard work! It’s eleven o’clock, which means we have a whole hour before they arrive. The girls can manage the bar while you go and get yourself together. Take a shower, wipe your tears and pour yourself a stiff brandy. Then come down here, put on your game face, and take the credit you deserve. You've got this far without any help from either of those two feckless idiots, so you definitely don't need them now!"

"He's right, Mum," said Daniel kindly. "You can't let them spoil this for you. I'm here and I can fetch and carry with the best of them; you might even get me doing the washing up!"

Kim smiled. "Thank you darling, thank you. I love you so much. I'm so sorry you had to be involved in that."

"Listen, I'm a big boy now and I love you too. So, what do you say?" asked Daniel.

Kim turned to look at Dean, "And thank you too. I feel so embarrassed."

"You aren't the one who should be embarrassed," said Dean.

Kim stood up, brushed herself down and scooped her fingers under her eyes to remove the mascara that would undoubtedly have found its way there. She took a deep breath, "Let's do this!"

"Good girl, now go and smarten yourself up before you frighten the customers," laughed Dean.

Kim left the kitchen and went upstairs to shower and freshen up, taking Dean's wise advice. Daniel stepped forward and shook Dean's hand.

"Thanks mate, I really appreciate your support."

"Don't be daft, I feel bad for your poor mum, that's all. I know he's your dad but he's a bit of a knob isn't he?" Dean laughed.

"And some," said Daniel. "To be honest, I know I should probably feel sad that he's gone, I'm pretty sure we won't really speak again, but he's never really been a dad in the proper sense of the word, and he's made my mum's life miserable at times. I'm kind of glad he's gone. Is that awful?"

"Just because you're related to someone doesn't automatically make them a good person. Now, you better wash your knuckles and clean your face up," said Dean. "And I'd stay in the kitchen if possible, looking like you've gone a few rounds in a boxing ring isn't the best look for a publican!"

"No, you're probably right," laughed Daniel. "I'll chuck a bit of ice on it. Feel free to boss me about today, consider me your manservant. I'm not a natural kitchen hand but I can take an instruction!"

"You might live to regret that," chuckled Dean.

Chapter Twelve

In the bar, Rosa and Megan had opened up for custom and Judy had given them a brief chat about what had transpired in the cellar. Once again, they too, had not been surprised to learn about Keith or Olivia's poor behaviour. They had experience of Olivia and knew she could a manipulative devil but, even though they had only known Keith a couple of weeks, neither of them had warmed to him. It would have taken a pretty oblivious soul not to notice the disrespect that Keith often showed his wife, nor the fact that he mainly sat at the bar whilst Kim did all of the running. By contrast, they had all warmed to Kim instantly, finding her warm, funny and smart; the polar opposite of Keith!

"Just act as if everything is perfectly normal," said Judy. "Try not to be too nice to her otherwise I worry she'll just get upset. Of course, we can give her a shoulder to cry on when today is over, but for the meantime we need to be strong and get on with the job in hand, I'm not letting that selfish idiot spoil things for her."

"Agreed!" said Megan and Rosa together. They both knew there was no time for Kim to be licking her wounds today – that would have to come later.

At a quarter to twelve, the first of the Women Who Wine began to arrive. Fleur was first, closely followed by Jax and Hanna.

"Oh wow!" they exclaimed upon entering the back room. "This looks totally amazing, thank you so much!"

"You wait until you taste the food," said Megan, "I'm sure you are going to love it."

At that moment, Kim arrived, makeup freshly applied, hair brushed and sporting a bright red jumper – nothing like a bit of colour to boost the mood. She smiled at Fleur, "Happy?" she asked.

"Amazed," said Fleur. "You've all done such a brilliant job. I can't quite believe the change to be honest."

Kim felt really chuffed. Despite the morning's events she was so proud of what they had managed to pull off in such a short time; sure, there was a long way to go, but this was certainly a good start.

Chapter Thirteen

The meeting was a great success. There were oooos and ahhhhs of delight as the platters came out from the kitchen. Rows of cured ham and salami, succulent marinated olives, feta and sun-dried tomato antipasti along with Dean's fantastic bruschetta. There were bowls of spicy potatoes, roasted peppers and homemade ravioli parcels courtesy of Rosa. For dessert, a selection of mini fruit tarts, chocolate brownies, peanut brittle and crème brulee. All the food had been carefully prepared to be eaten with forks or fingers, allowing plenty of time for chatting and planning.

Kim, Rosa and Megan ran back and forward between the meeting, the main bar and the kitchen. Several customers appeared who Kim had not seen before, and they were busier than they had ever been. In the kitchen, Daniel was true to his word and took orders like a pro; washing dishes, collecting crockery and emptying bins. Dean didn't stop to breathe as several orders for bar food came in on top of the large party – thank goodness he'd been well prepared. Judy was on dishwasher duty and the tables were kept clean and glasses washed with speedy efficiency.

There had been a slightly awkward moment when Fleur had asked where Olivia was. Kim had felt her throat tighten but bless Rosa, she had jumped in and told Fleur that Olivia didn't work here anymore, giving Kim a chance to move away and find a task to distract her.

By the time the shift was over, they were all exhausted – exhausted but satisfied.

The Women Who Wine had already made reservations for their next meeting and had also asked for the opportunity to phone ahead their lunch orders for their smaller weekly meetings. Messages of congratulations for the chef filtered their way through and there was actually money in the tip jar.

"Well done ladies!" said Dean, as he and Daniel came and plonked themselves at the table where the girls were sitting.

"Well done everyone," said Kim. "I am so proud and so grateful...." Her voice began to waver as tiredness and emotion swept over her.

Rosa took her hand and squeezed it tightly, "Strong mia cara. Stay strong."

Daniel broke the tension in the room by collecting a bottle of chilled cava from the wine fridge and popping the cork at the table. A little shout of delight went out from the group and glasses were held out, eagerly awaiting a well-earned refreshment.

Epilogue

It had been a month since Keith and Olivia's dramatic departure. Daniel had left for work a couple of days after the drama, but Judy had stayed on to give her daughter a little moral support. Kim knew it wouldn't be forever and was actually dreading the time when she went back, but Judy was fiercely independent and had a better social life than most twenty-year-olds!

The pub was going from strength to strength and little improvements were being made all the time. Their food orders had increased ten-fold and Kim was finally starting to enjoy her fresh start; although it definitely hadn't been what she had expected in more ways than one.

When Keith had left, he'd taken his stupid little sports car with him and Kim had taken delivery of a new, more practical vehicle, with four doors, a boot bigger than a teacup and in the most glorious shade of pink – Keith would have hated it!

Kim knew that difficult times were on the horizon. Keith had deliberately stayed quiet whilst Daniel and Judy were around, but she knew that it wouldn't be long before he would be staking a claim on his territory and when he found out what she had done to protect herself, the battle wasn't going to be pretty!

But for the time being, she would enjoy her new start, her new friends and her new-found freedom. She was finally her own woman and she felt invincible!

SPRING
A time for change

at the

Dog & Duck

Chapter One

Dean sat up with a jolt, his back drenched in sweat, his heart racing, his hands trembling. It had been quite some time – maybe one month, maybe two - since the nightmare that had once plagued his sleep one relentless night after another had occurred, but it was still there, still waiting in the wings to rear its ugly head when he least expected it.

He rolled over and switched on the bedside lamp; the clock on his phone showed 2.45am. He'd barely been in bed more than a couple of hours, having finished his shift at the Dog and Duck public house where he worked as a chef, just before midnight. He had helped Kim, the new landlady, to close the pub, making sure that every door and window was firmly locked, helping her to lock out any unwelcome visitors - if only it were that simple for the demons in his head.

He climbed out of bed and made the few short steps from his bed to the kitchen area in the small studio apartment where he had lived for the past two years. The flat was in a modern complex close to the up-and-coming riverside development, with stunning views that overlooked the harbour; it was the small balcony and the view that had softened the blow of his fall from grace. Dean flicked the switch on the kettle and took a mug from the immaculately-ordered cupboards; army life had taught him nothing if not to keep a tidy and well-kept home. He approached both his life and work with order and logic, and he had lost count of the number of times that he wished he had applied his usual logic on that fateful night; he'd lost his cool and he'd paid a high price.

He added a camomile teabag to his mug and poured the boiling water onto it – he would have much rather had a large whisky and a sleeping tablet, but that was a slippery slope that he refused to slide down. He ran a hand through his hair and rubbed his tired eyes. He knew that his constant self-recrimination served little purpose and mostly he had managed to place his past into a box with the lid kept tightly closed, but just now and again the worry that his secret may burst free and ruin everything threatened to consume him; he had resolved to be a better man and he was determined to do just that.

Dean took his tea over to the couch and turned on the TV – a late night 1970s cop show was showing, the two hero partners jumping in and out of sleek, souped-up cars that looked little like standard police issue. He sipped his tea and pulled a blanket over his legs, he was resigned to the fact that this would probably be his resting place for the night; once the dreams took hold, he rarely went back to bed – as if that was the place where they resided.

Chapter Two

Dean awoke with a stiff neck and a cold back, the blanket having slid off him during his fitful sleep. Despite feeling less than well-rested, he was just grateful that the night was over; it was much easier to maintain a positive and hopeful demeanour once morning came. He ran himself a nice hot bath, made his bed with military precision and popped a couple of slices of bread into the toaster.

His shift at the pub began at 10am; they were getting steadily busier with food orders since the new menu and also since Olivia's departure. Dean had really felt for Kim when she had caught her feckless husband Keith getting up close and personal with their work-shy bar manager in the cellar, but he couldn't honestly say that he hadn't been glad to see the back of either of them. Olivia had been a nightmare to work with and had been steadily running the pub into the ground, seeing it purely as her own personal brandy store. Keith had been a bully and a know-it-all knob in Dean's eyes - he was pretty sure he wasn't alone in his opinion - and he also knew that Kim was way too good for Keith and probably always had been. Now that Kim was running the pub on her own, Dean had begun to feel increasingly protective of her and was also enjoying her company more than he probably dared to admit to himself, let alone anyone else.

After a hot soak in the bath to ease his aching muscles, Dean felt much more like himself – the 'self' that he had worked so hard to achieve and the 'self' that hid his past.

He walked the twenty minutes to work at a fast pace, enjoying the exercise. The March morning was crisp yet clear and signs of Spring were definitely in the air. It was not yet quite warm enough to ditch his favourite yellow beanie hat, but Dean hoped it wouldn't be too long – life felt more hopeful in the sunshine.

He let himself in through the kitchen door at the back of the Dog and Duck using the key that Kim had given him and filled the kettle ready for his morning drinks round. He could hear Megan in the bar, her voice ringing out above the sound of the Hoover as she completed her morning clean up.

"....why do you build me up, Buttercup baby, just to let me down..."

"Morning!" he called...no answer. "MORNING!"

"Oh bloody hell, you scared the life out of me," laughed Megan, turning off the Hoover. "Sorry about the terrible singing!"

Dean laughed, "You go for it girl! It's nice to hear someone enjoying themselves."

"Oh Dean, it's so much nicer working here without Olivia, isn't it?"

"Different place altogether," smiled Dean, looking around the pub that already looked so different to the tired old place that had greeted Kim and Keith when they had first taken over as landlords. "Is Kim here?"

"She's upstairs," replied Megan. "She'll be down in a bit; I'm just about finished here."

"Breakfast?" asked Dean. He loved looking after his 'girls' as he called them – although he knew it probably did him every bit as much of a favour as it did them.

"I thought you'd never ask," smiled Megan. "You spoil us you know!"

"Did I hear someone say breakfast?" asked Kim, entering the bar from the flat upstairs.

"You're like vultures you lot," laughed Dean. "Breakfast on its way!"

Twenty minutes later, Dean, Kim and Megan were sat at one of the tables enjoying a pot of fresh coffee and some delicious Eggs Benedict.

"These are delicious Dean; you really do spoil us!" said Kim, taking a slurp of her coffee. "I was thinking that if we have the demand, we could maybe even start doing a breakfast trade if you're up for it?"

"Fine by me," said Dean. "The busier the better for me."

"As long it doesn't mean we don't get breakfast too," said Megan, "I wouldn't half miss this!"

"Don't worry we will keep you well fed," replied Kim. "Are you all set for today Dean? We've got the Women Who Wine group meeting at 12 but I think they've pre-ordered, and we've got three tables of two and a group of five, plus any walk-ins."

"Yep, all good boss," said Dean. "Rosa batch-cooked one of her lasagnes yesterday and I've got today's special already prepared. Just need to prep the salad garnish and get some baguettes in the oven. I'll give the cellar a quick once-over and we are good to go."

Kim smiled. She was so happy with her little team. When she had arrived at the pub just a few months ago, she would never have believed that she might actually stay. The place had been a dump and she had been less than impressed with the 'charming' Olivia, but a lot had happened in such a short space of time. Keith had gone, and she was surprised how little she missed the man to whom she had been married for practically her whole adult life – she felt a bit sad that she had wasted so much time on him and also cross with herself for putting up with his crap for so long, but she was now determined to enjoy her new-found freedom.

"I'll check with the neighbours and see if we can have a bonfire this afternoon, try to get rid of the rest of that tree," Dean called, sticking his head round the kitchen door.

There had been a mighty storm during the month of February: "Storm Agnes", Kim seemed to remember –

why they named hurricanes after little old ladies Kim didn't know... something to do with irony perhaps! The winds had reached ridiculous speeds and many of the surrounding trees and hedges had taken a battering. The storm had been bad enough in itself but was made much worse by the pub's closest neighbour at the back of the garden. Fearing that one of his trees had become unstable, the neighbour had climbed up it and tried to remove a particularly low-hanging branch. Instead of solving the problem, the branch had fallen straight through the old shed roof with the neighbour still attached. Fortunately, the neighbour had wounded little else other than his pride and had left the garden.... *without* the sodding great branch that had decimated the shed! In truth, Kim had to admit that the shed had probably not been long for this world, but she was a little peeved that she was being left to clear up her dozy neighbour's mess – he hadn't even offered to help! But, in the spirit of harmony and not wishing to alienate any of the pub's potential future allies she had agreed to dispose of the offending branch. Dean had spent the last few weeks dismantling the tree-shed combination and chopping it up ready for a bonfire; if it had been closer to November 5th, they would have been set!

"Great, thanks Dean," called Kim. She didn't know what she would have done without his help these past few weeks.

"Right, I'd better get this Hoover away before the doors open," said Megan rising from her seat.

“Bloody hell, is that the time?” exclaimed Kim, looking at the clock. It was only ten minutes to opening time. “How was your blind date?”

“Oh my God, you don’t want to know,” laughed Megan. “He arrived at the restaurant 25 minutes late, I’d almost given up on him. He spent the whole night talking about his ex-girlfriend who was apparently ‘a right bitch,’ and must have told me that he had a BMW at least 25 times! I think I’m going to give dating a miss for a while, it’s too much like hard work.”

Kim laughed, “But did he have a BMW though?”

“Yes, it was at least 20 years old and had those funny little skirts around the bottom and tinted windows!” giggled Megan. “Very cool!”

“I shan’t buy a hat just yet then?” joked Kim.

“By the time I find a decent bloke you’ll be wearing one of those crocheted berets that only really old ladies wear!”

“I’ll take that to mean it’s going to take ages... not that I am already quite old!” laughed Kim.

Chapter Three

Kim and Megan cleared away the plates, put the Hoover in the cupboard and opened the doors bang on 11am. There wasn't exactly a huge surge of customers but then it was still early, and Kim was thankful that the majority of their clientele weren't the type who started drinking at breakfast time. The good thing about having hardly any customers had meant that there was hardly any trouble – unless you counted Steve (aka Brag Pitt – the resident pub know-it-all and self-proclaimed God's gift to women!) puffing his chest out like an over-inflated pigeon because Brian had told him to wind his neck in after a recent opinionated rant on Steve's part! Brian and Doris were two of Kim's favourite regulars. They were both in their late sixties – sweet but straight-talking – and didn't suffer fools gladly. Watching Steve squirm his way out of his latest stream of bullshit had been enormously entertaining and Kim and Rosa had been in fits of laughter.

Megan had just popped upstairs to change her cleaning clothes and Kim busied herself setting the tables that had been reserved for lunch. The Women Who Wine group were popping in for their usual Thursday lunchtime meet but there would only be four of them today – their big quarterly meeting wasn't until next week on the last Thursday of the month. She laid up the rest of the reserved tables with a sign and a small vase of daffodils; Kim knew that the place hadn't looked this welcoming in years.

At a little before 12, the table groups began to arrive and Kim and Megan dealt with the sudden influx of drink orders. Dean began serving and taking orders with calm efficiency and within just over thirty minutes people were seated, watered and either eating or about to eat.

Kim had taken the opportunity to go over and chat to the Women Who Wine group, especially Fleur with whom she had become firm friends. Fleur was a very successful businesswoman whose expertise was in social media marketing, and she was trying her very best to drag Kim into the 21st Century. Her first mission had been to get Kim a smart phone that was able to send photos and access the 'must-have' apps to replace the pay-as-you-go mobile that Kim had previously had, and which was similar to the disposable 'burner'-type phones generally purchased in late night garages by drug dealers and men cheating on their wives!

Kim's son Daniel had almost fainted when he got a friend request from his mum on social media and there had been much hilarity as Kim struggled to deal with the pitfalls of tagging and FaceTiming. Before Kim had moved to the pub, she had seen Daniel face-to-face regularly and had called him almost every day so there had been little need for screen calls, but now she loved to call and see his face as they spoke, and she had become pretty good at positioning the phone so that Daniel saw more than the top of her head or the inside of her left ear! Even Kim's mum Judy had got in on the act, tagging Kim into countless humorous videos of people falling over and orphan dogs being rescued and re-homed. Kim was hoping that Judy would come back to visit over the Easter break when Daniel had a few days off work – she missed them both very much.

"Afternoon ladies," said Kim to the Women Who Wine group. "How are you all doing?"

"All good," came the unanimous reply.

"I must say the pub is looking amazing Kim," said Jax, a local independent florist. "It is practically unrecognisable from when you first took over."

"Oh God, don't remind me," laughed Kim. "It looked like a bloody squat. I don't know how I didn't turn and run in the opposite direction. I must admit it is starting to feel like home now. I can't really remember not being here and I never thought I would say that."

"You've worked wonders," said Kate. "I wanted to have a chat with you actually, I've just started a new range of breakfast muffins and pastries, I didn't know if it would be something you would be interested in?"

"Do you know, I was just chatting to Dean earlier about doing a breakfast trade; that could definitely be something you could help us with, and I'd love us to be able to support each other," said Kim, loving the prospect of working together with her locals.

"It'll make some great content for social media photos too," said Fleur. "Nice arty shots of croissants and a cup of fresh coffee next to a vase of daffodils… now you're an expert!"

Kim laughed. "Well, I've moved on from Polaroids if that's what you mean – I guess that can be called progress!"

"I've booked our spa treat for Sunday if that works for you?" asked Fleur.

Kim and Fleur had decided to take a well-earned mini-break – if only for a few hours – at a local hotel that offered Sunday afternoon spa packages. They had been meaning to get together to unwind and chat about their plans to promote the pub moving forward but they never seemed to get the time without being interrupted. Kim reckoned that a little spot of relaxation by the pool and a hot stone massage would provide the perfect conditions for some inspiration and planning – as business meetings went, she felt sure this would be right up there!

"That's great," said Kim. "Rosa and Megan are both going to cover the lunchtime shift and Dean is quite capable doing Sunday lunches – you know what he's like, Mr Organised! Anyway, better dash, it looks like Megan has a bit of a rush on behind the bar, enjoy your lunch!"

Kim hurried away to help Megan with the flurry of customers wanting Round Two.

The rest of the shift passed fairly uneventfully apart from one small tantrum from Bobby when Brian and

Doris's dog Chester had helped himself to the contents of Bobby's sausage baguette. Bobby had been about twelve pints up as usual – he was not averse to drinking around twenty pints in a solid session. Kim genuinely didn't know how he didn't drown on the inside with all the fluid floating around inside of him. His giant belly stuck out like an over inflated beach ball, and he looked like he might go pop at any time. Bobby would occasionally order a baguette during a drinking session but rarely ate more than about half of it – probably because there wasn't much room – and trying to use a baguette to soak up the amount of beer he drank was about as effective as using a flannel on a sodding tsunami!

Typically, Bobby had left his half-eaten baguette precariously balanced on the edge of the table and Chester, not wanting to miss such a golden opportunity, had very carefully – and pretty impressively Kim thought – removed the sausage from the inside of the baguette. Chester may even have escaped detection – it was unlikely Bobby would have noticed that his sausage baguette was now missing one fairly crucial ingredient – if it hadn't been for the fact that at the exact moment he was making his getaway, Bobby stood up to go for his twenty-fifth piddle of the session and accidentally stood on Chester's tail. Chester yelped, knocked the table, and the remainder of Bobby's lunch had landed on the floor.

"Fucking dog," moaned Bobby indignantly, "he's got my sausage!"

Kim had stifled a laugh at this point especially when she had spied a very guilty-looking Chester who was sat, trying to look innocent with half a Cumberland hanging out of his chops!

"Oh dear, bang-to-rights I think, Chester," laughed Dean, who had come through to the bar after hearing the commotion.

Brian and Doris had begun to apologise profusely as they tried to usher the opportunistic Chester back to their table and out of harm's way.

"No harm done!" said Kim.

"What about my sausage?" exclaimed Bobby.

Once again, Kim tried not to giggle and resisted the temptation to suggest that, judging by the size of his belly, this was probably the first time Bobby had seen his 'sausage' in quite a while! Instead, she had suggested that Bobby go and empty his bladder and she would get Dean to replace his missing lunch. As it turned out, Bobby was not all that fussed about the sausage baguette after all and was much happier with the free pint that Kim offered by way of consolation – pint number 13, lucky for some it seemed!

All the while, Bobby's long-suffering girlfriend Fran sat motionless, silently sipping her glass of 'Nosecco' and looking like she wished the world would open up and swallow her whole. Rumour had it that Fran had herself once been partial to a drop of the hard stuff; so much so, that she had taken to hiding vodka in a water bottle that she had carried around with her permanently. To the untrained eye, it had looked like Fran was simply keeping herself hydrated when in fact she had been doing the exact opposite. It wasn't until she had collapsed and turned a rather fetching shade of mustard that she had been rushed to A&E and the full extent of her problem was revealed. Fran spent several weeks in hospital clinging to life before emerging to live a very different kind of life. This different kind of life involved still visiting the pub every day to watch Bobby consume a daily amount of beer equivalent to that of an entire football team on a stag night, whilst sipping non-alcoholic drinks and looking for all the world like she had landed in purgatory! Bobby was hardly culture personified, and his conversation was pretty much limited to 'tits and tyres', which left Kim wondering whether Fran had actually been 'saved' at all.

"I'm so sorry about that," said Doris as she came to the bar to order another drink. "I'm so embarrassed!"

"Don't be daft," said Kim quietly. "Let's face it, he always leaves half the bloody baguette anyway and I think he's secretly much happier with a free pint. If he didn't leave his lunch hanging off the edge of the table, it would never have happened. You've got to take your hat off to Chester; he almost got away with it!"

Doris laughed. "It was quite funny. And Bobby's not exactly our favourite person anyway; poor Fran, I wouldn't want her life for all the sausages in the world!"

"It is pretty grim, isn't it?" agreed Kim. "Did you know her before she got ill?"

"I don't think any of us have ever really *known* her," replied Doris. "She's never been a talker; she's always looked a bit downtrodden. I guess the only good thing for her was that she was just a bit numb to him before. Although she did used to like a bit of karaoke – she can actually sing you know?"

"Bloody hell. She doesn't look like she has any kind of voice, we'll have to get her up there one night... put Bobby in the shade for a change!"

Chapter Four

Kim closed the doors at 3 o'clock. The pub was empty, and Megan had worked hard to keep things tidy as they went. Just a few glasses to go into the dishwasher and they could have a few hours off.

"I've checked with the neighbours, nobody minds if we have a bonfire this afternoon," said Dean, popping his head around the kitchen door. "If you like we can have a bit of a burn-up and a coffee in the garden whilst we get rid of our 'tree-meets-shed' sculpture!"

"That would be great," said Kim. "I'd like to tidy the garden up for the summer if we can, we could have some barbecues out there instead of indoor lunches at weekends maybe."

"That would be lovely," said Megan. "We could have some really nice family days out there."

"Exactly what I thought," smiled Kim. "You staying for a bonfire?"

"No, I'd better go," said Megan. "Lottie hasn't got any after-school clubs today, so she'll be out normal time. I'd better shoot off if that's ok?"

"No worries," said Kim. "See you in the morning and thanks for today, love."

Megan smiled and waved goodbye as she left through the back kitchen door to collect her tired old Ford

Fiesta from the carpark. The bumper was held on by some black tape and the bodywork was decorated with several marks and dents but at least it got her from A to B… just about!

"Bless her, she works so hard. I'd like to see her have some nice things of her own someday," said Kim.

"Yes, she's a good kid," said Dean.

Dean put the coffee machine on and began to prepare a decaff cappuccino for Kim and a skinny latte for himself. He knew exactly what she liked, and they had settled into quite a nice routine at the end of each shift, chatting and laughing comfortably with each other. Dean helped enormously and was keen to do some of the more physically-demanding chores that they jokily referred to as 'man jobs'. In truth, there were many of these so-called 'man jobs' that Kim was quite capable of doing of herself – she definitely wasn't the helpless little woman type – but she enjoyed Dean's company and of having the support of a man who gave it willingly rather than the Keith-style of support that she was used to, which had involved a whole load of whingeing and playing the martyr. There had been several times in their marriage when she had considered erecting a bloody stake in the front garden so she could tie him to it and set light to him!

As much as she enjoyed Dean's company - they had talked about everything from their ambitions to their taste in music, to cringy childhood memories – she still knew very little about his immediate past. He played his cards pretty close to his chest whenever she asked him anything about his time in the army or his personal life. She knew that he had been married before, but he was reluctant to talk about it and would change the subject or divert to the kitchen to make a drink or something to eat when the conversation veered in that direction. Whilst Kim respected his privacy, she also felt just a little bit put out that he didn't feel that he could share those experiences with her. Let's face it, he knew everything about her disastrous marriage; he'd been witness to most of Keith's indiscretions in all their sordid glory!

Kim also knew that when it came to emotional stuff, she was very much an open book. She had never been very good at being mysterious and, even when she did try to internalise what she was thinking, her face would display her inner thoughts with such blatant accuracy that she didn't need to open her mouth at all! She decided to accept that it was Dean's prerogative to keep his private life just that and maybe there wasn't much to tell – not everyone's marriage ended with the same technicoloured drama that Kim's had after all!

Kim and Dean spent the afternoon adding bits of shed to the blazing bonfire. At one point, the flames reached a rather alarming height and Kim was afraid they might actually set light to next door's shed as well, but they just about managed to keep it under control. By 5 o'clock most of the wood had been burnt and the flames reduced to a less hazardous intensity.

"Right, I don't know about you, but I need a shower," laughed Kim. "I smell like an old ash tray!"

Dean laughed. "Yes, I think we are both a bit smelly. I'll shoot home and see you back in about an hour. We haven't got any reservations and I'm all prepped – see you in a bit."

Kim went back into the pub to shower and change for the evening shift. Rosa was in tonight, and she would be quite capable of opening up if Kim was a few minutes late.

As she entered the kitchen, she saw that her mobile phone was ringing. She sighed as she recognised the number flashing on the screen and prepared herself for the conversation that she was not looking forward to.

Chapter Five

Kim put the phone down to her solicitor. As she feared, Keith had been in touch, and he was not happy… AT ALL!

When Kim had inherited the pub from her Uncle Frank it had been left solely to her – a fact that she had not mentioned to Keith. Uncle Frank had not been alone in his contempt for the feckless Keith. In fact, when she thought about it, Kim didn't actually know anyone amongst her friends or her family who had liked Keith at all. They had all tolerated him in the same way you might tolerate a best friend's odious offspring!

Fortunately for Kim, Keith had always been far too lazy to take an interest in their financial affairs – in truth, Keith was too lazy to take an interest in anything that didn't immediately benefit him – and so Kim had been able to keep secret the fact that the pub was actually nothing to do with Keith at all. Looking back, she found it quite ironic that only *she* had a claim to the place that only Keith had wanted initially! It must have been some kind of sixth sense that had driven Kim to pigeonhole their assets so effectively before their move as at that time they had not been at the stage of imminent divorce as they were now.

The long and short of it was that the Dog and Duck was Kim's and Kim's alone. Whether they divorced or not Keith would have no entitlement to any part of it. Over the years, Kim had been quite careful about where she had spent her money – working for the bank it was mainly her who had supported the family and she had more than a little financial savvy – and so she had various policies and investments in her name alone. The proceeds from their house sale would have to be split 50/50 after the mortgage had been paid off and, whilst Keith would leave with a fairly tidy sum, Kim knew it wasn't anything close to what he thought he would get. Finally, Keith's delusions of grandeur had come to bite him in the arse – karma was working her magic!

Since Keith had left the pub, they'd kept in contact via their solicitor only. Keith had demanded a couple of in-person meetings, but Kim had always declined; she was not about to put up with him stomping into her pub, waving his willy about and shouting the odds about his 'rights' anytime soon!

Keith had been busy enough with the gold-digging Olivia who was carefully massaging his ego – along with God knows what else – and had reluctantly agreed to communicating via the third party. Up until know, Kim supposed he had smugly been telling Olivia it was all just a formality and before long they would be Lord and Lady of the manor, basking in his considerable 'wealth' and questionable status. Now, it seemed, that realisation had dawned; Keith was in full possession of the facts – as opposed to his fantasy – and to say he was pissed off was an understatement!

The solicitor had advised Kim to be on her guard as Keith had made some rather alarming threats as to the safety of the windows at the Dog and Duck - mainly that he was going to put a bloody brick through them - and that Kim would live to regret taking him for a fool.

Kim had said that with regards to Keith being a fool, then... if it looked like a duck, walked like a duck and quacked like a duck, then it actually probably was a sodding duck! She had left the phone call a little shaken but unsurprised. She had known all along that Keith would not take this lying down and she also knew that the more he began to realise that there was fuck all he could do about it, no matter how much he stamped his feet, the more furious and indignant he would become. She wasn't afraid of him - she was pretty sure he was mainly hot air - but she didn't relish a confrontation.

As it was, she would leave it to the solicitors to converse with her wounded, soon-to-be ex-husband and hoped that the matter wouldn't be dragged out over too many months. Although she didn't want to be a bitch, she couldn't help but feel a tiny bit satisfied that Keith had finally met his match, even if it had taken thirty years!

Chapter Six

Dean made his way back to his flat quickly and jumped into the shower. It had not escaped his notice that he was finding more and more ways to spend time at the pub with Kim. He could easily have got the local handyman to help clear the tree and it certainly wasn't in his job description, but being with Kim was a welcome distraction to the turmoil he sometimes felt inside.

They got on like a house on fire – literally! He was relaxed in her company, and it felt good to be useful, to know that you were able to help someone you cared about. He knew that deep down he was essentially a good bloke who had cocked up… royally! Perhaps now he could put his past behind him. Perhaps it was time to enjoy the present and look forward to the future. He'd paid his debt and maybe this was finally the real start of his new beginning. He knew that he was still a bit cagey around Kim; he didn't share his secrets easily and he knew this peeved her a little bit at times – the woman was an open bloody book for Christ's sake, she bared her soul as easily as some people bared their teeth! But that was one of things Dean loved about her the most – with Kim, what you saw was exactly what you got. She was open, uninhibited and honest to a fault, something which could have saved him a lot of trouble in the past had it been practiced by the very people he should have been able to trust.

Perhaps he would tell her. One day he might. But for now, he didn't want to risk scaring her off. For now, he was going to concentrate on being a good friend and feeling more settled in his life than he had done in years.

Chapter Seven

The rest of the week flew by with very little drama but with a lot of customers. Many times, as they were rushing up and down, Kim took a moment to reflect on how different the pub had become in such a short space of time. The tired old building that she had encountered on her first day, inhabited by little other than a few mice perhaps, seemed a distant memory. Now the place was much more alive, and it felt warm and welcoming. The regulars who had drifted away, disenchanted with the grubby surroundings, meagre menu and the hostile Olivia, were now eager to return.

Kim had taken the time to find out just what her regulars favoured; like serving a new draft bitter for the retired Navy man whom they fondly referred to as Uncle Albert and who had taken up permanent residence in the old club chair by the fire. A selection of posh new gins – everything from blood orange to rhubarb and ginger – made for an impressive display along the top shelf of the now gleaming bar shelves. The 'social club' glasses had been ditched in favour of some long-stemmed wine glasses, some bespoke gin balloons, and some high ball tumblers that meant you didn't have to drink your spirit and your mixer separately because the glasses were too small to fit a whole drink!

A little unpopular had been Kim's decision to ditch the 'free' bar snacks which had consisted of a few bags of mini cheddar biscuits, roughly presented in white plastic bowls that were supposed to look like mock woven baskets. Kim had pointed out that these snacks were mainly urine and grime by the time you got to the bottom of the bowl and were basically only eaten by those punters who were too tight to buy a sandwich! Once the kitchen started serving a proper menu, it was surprising how many more of their former 'beer drinkers only' customers started to buy themselves a lunchtime snack as they watched plate after plate of delicious looking food pass before their eyes on the way from the kitchen to the bar! Not only did this do wonders for the lunchtime takings, but Kim also felt she was doing a public service, making sure her customers took a short break from destroying their livers and actually putting some decent grub inside their bellies!

Friday night had been Quiz Night – the first of a proposed, regular monthly occurrence. The questions had been created by Jim the butcher's daughter-in-law Laura, who worked at the local library and fancied herself as a bit of a general knowledge guru. Laura had been a stickler for the rules and there had been several calls of indignation when marks were not given because Brian and Doris's team had said that Prince Charming had been a hit for Adam Ant in the 80's and not Adam *and the* Ants. This decision had caused Brian's team – named Brian's Brains – to miss out on the winning title (and the prize kitty which equated to about £4.50 a head once it was shared out) by just one point. Not wanting to oversee a full-scale riot, instigated by an old pop singer wearing guy-liner and a frilly shirt that he had likely borrowed from his Nan, Kim had calmed the situation with a compensatory drink for each member of Brian's Brains, which had cost her about the same as the prize kitty!

Uncle Albert had watched the proceedings from his favourite chair, spectacularly bemused by most of the questions and even more bemused by the answers. At one point someone had to Google a picture of Adam Ant on their phone to show him the focus of their dispute, to which he commented, "She looks a bonnie lass. Not sure about the shirt, though!"

"Anne Robinson eat your heart out!" laughed Megan to Kim, nodding in Laura's direction.

"I know, bless her. She's taken it all very seriously!"

Once the prizes had been distributed and peace restored, good-natured banter and laughter filled the room once more. Rosa walked past Kim and kissed her on the cheek.

"What was that for?" asked Kim.

"You have done so well, mia cara," smiled Rosa. "My Paulie would have been here every night – he loved to laugh. We never came before. He hated that bloddy Olivia!"

Kim laughed. "It's great isn't it? I couldn't have done it without you and Megan though... or you!" She giggled seeing Dean's expression of mock hurt as he overheard their conversation. "I'm glad we stuck at it."

There were no events on Saturday, just the usual diners and drinkers. On Sunday both Megan and Rosa were coming into work so that Kim could enjoy her spa treat with Fleur. She couldn't wait.

Fleur came to collect Kim at midday and Dean and Rosa shooed her out of the pub like doting parents.

"Off you go, have fun, you deserve a break," said Rosa. "We will be fine here."

"Are you sure you don't mind – this is actually a business meeting you know!"

"Yeah, course it is," laughed Dean. "It's tough at the top!"

Kim smiled, "Well I guess there are worse ways to spend an afternoon. I'll be back around teatime."

"Please don't worry," said Rosa. "I will be here early just in case and there is no food on Sunday nights so you don't need to worry."

"I was going to take this evening off, but I can come in if you like?" said Dean.

"You need a break too," said Rosa. "You are always here! If I need anything I can call but I will be fine. Sunday night is not busy for us. Now Kim... shoo!"

Kim laughed. “I get the hint – no drinking the brandy while I am out! See you later… and thanks guys, you really are the best.”

Chapter Eight

Kim climbed into Fleur's posh Mercedes. As much as she loved her new pink, midlife-crisis car – bought especially because she knew that Keith would have hated it! – it was really nice to travel in luxury. The dashboard of the car looked like something you might find in the cockpit of an aeroplane and there were beeps for every eventuality: beeps to tell you to wear your seatbelt, beeps to tell you that the car in front was too close, beeps to tell you the speed limit...!

"Bloody hell, this car interferes more than my old man," laughed Kim.

"I know," said Fleur. "It drove me mad when I first got it, but now I treat it like you'd treat any other husband - I just don't take any bloody notice!"

Fleur was not married. She had a long-term boyfriend, but they didn't live together, and Kim had learnt that Fleur quite liked it that way. She was fiercely independent and very ambitious. She earned her own money – and plenty of it – and was not the sort of person to be controlled by anyone. She'd never had children and Kim suspected that this upset her more than she let on and was probably part of the reason for the protective shell that she had constructed for herself over the years. Fleur had replaced children with her beloved fur babies; two enormous huskies named Bonnie and Clyde whom she doted on and whom she treated better than most people treated their actual children! They had babysitters, dog walkers, groomers and trainers...in fact, Kim wouldn't have been surprised to find them at the spa rooms, eating fillet steak and enjoying a hot stone massage!

"How're the kids?" joked Kim.

"Yep, all good, they've got Aunty Tanya round to babysit this afternoon, so they'll be stretched out, getting cuddles and watching Lady and the Tramp," laughed Fleur.

"The sad thing is I know you're only half-joking," sighed Kim.

They arrived at the 'Fit 4 Life' leisure centre. The spa rooms were in an annexe to the left of the main building. There were three private treatment rooms, and a communal relaxation area that had a small plunge pool with heated, tiled beds around the edge, a help-yourself bar area that served hot and cold drinks, a sauna and a jacuzzi. Sunday afternoons were their quietest times and so Kim and Fleur had the place to themselves. They collected their fluffy robes and slippers from reception and followed one of the beauty therapists through to the locker rooms where there were showers, toilets and a bank of hairdryers.

They placed their clothes and shoes into one of the lockers and donned their robes. Inside the relaxation area some calming music featuring pan pipes and sounds of the ocean played on a loop, and the fragrant aromas from a scent burner filled the air – it was all very zen. Kim made sure she had a quick wee before leaving the locker room – the ocean sounds were all very nice but at her age the sound of running water kicked her menopausal bladder into overdrive!

They settled themselves onto the heated beds that were constructed in a kind of gentle 'S' shape that meant your feet and head were raised and your bottom could sink into the curve of the beds. Kim laid back and revelled in the comforting warmth as the music transported her to the misty mountains of a distant rainforest.

"I could get used to this," said Kim.

"We should make it a regular thing," said Fleur.

A therapist called Jasmine came into the room and asked if they had everything they needed. Kim wondered if therapists were ever named something that wasn't entirely appropriate. Perhaps when you became a therapist you chose a kind of 'stage name' if yours was less than beautiful? She had never once been introduced to a therapist called Ethel or Madge, for example. Granted, her experience of spa days was not exactly prolific, but she had been to enough to know that ugly therapist names seemed to be a no-no!

Kim and Fleur assured Jasmine that they were more than happy and accepted her offer of a pot of ginger and lemon tea for two. The tea was presented in a white china teapot with fancy little teacups and one of those wrapped biscuits of a familiar, yet indistinguishable flavour. Jasmine – wearing a black, tailored tabard with pink edging around her size 6 figure, blonde hair neatly curled into a perfect bun, perfectly-applied make-up and perfectly-manicured nails designed to look professional but also slightly intimidating - placed the tea down on a small table and informed them that their first treatment would be in thirty minutes when herself and Lily (another appropriately-named therapist!) would come to collect them. With that she left in a waft of shower gel, body lotion and perfume, the mark of a well-groomed and fastidious young girl who had few commitments beside her job and her appearance and who likely still lived at home with her parents.

Kim and Fleur began relaxing and sipping their tea.

"How much time do you think she spends to get herself looking like that every day?" asked Kim.

"Not as long as we'd have to spend at our age, that's for sure," laughed Fleur.

"True, although I'm not sure I ever looked that slick even when I was young. I always seemed to be one haircut behind what was cool. I'd just caught onto the perm and suddenly everyone was going short and choppy. I tried to catch up and ended up with a 'half perm, half choppy' combination which made me look like Worzel Gummidge. I never looked cool in those pinafore dresses, and I never once mastered how to dance to the 'slow-to-weirdly-fast' bit in 'Come on Eileen' either!"

"I know what you mean," laughed Fleur. "I have horrible memories of the school disco, sitting round the edge for someone to ask me to dance and then the only one left to ask you would be the boy who was even less cool than we were!"

"Some of my memories are so cringy, they actually make me shudder," laughed Kim. "Although not as bad as poor old Tina Briggs. She was desperate for some boobs so she put cotton wool in her bikini top during our outdoor swimming lesson in a pool that was so frigging cold it literally would freeze your tits off! Unfortunately for her, David White had just done a massive turd in the pool which floated past her nose and made her jump up and scream. The cotton wool, which had now shrunk to little more than a wispy, wet thread, escaped from her bikini top and floated to the surface of the pool along with David White's turd! Poor girl – I think she was known as the 'ironing board' for the rest of her school days!"

Fleur giggled. "If you want a turd story, I've got one much better than that! A friend of mine, Sarah her name was, who I used to hang about with in my younger days, was known for being a bit ditzy. Anyway, we were at a house party and the drink was flowing well. Partway through the evening Sarah unfortunately needed to go for a poo... and you know what it was like when we were younger... needing a poo when you were out was literally the worst thing that could happen to you!"

Kim laughed, "Mad isn't it?!"

"Anyway, Sarah bided her time until she thought the coast was clear and snuck up to the bathroom to relieve herself. Poo done, and then, what's the next worst thing that could happen…?"

"…the flush won't work," said Kim and Fleur both together.

"Exactly," said Fleur. "She tried and tried but could not get the poo to go away. She started to panic and worried that someone was at the door waiting to come in, so she did the only thing that she could think of and fished the poo out of the toilet and threw it out of the bathroom window!"

Kim shrieked, "Oh my God, NO!"

"Yep!" laughed Fleur. "There was only one problem that she hadn't accounted for – the bathroom window didn't open into the garden but was directly over the conservatory roof where the majority of the party goers were gathered! I remember hearing this thud on the roof but fortunately for Sarah the music was reasonably loud. I do remember a couple of people commenting on the size of the bloody seagulls!"

Kim clutched her side as she laughed. "That is so funny! What did she do?"

"She came down the stairs with a face as white as a sheet. She grabbed my arm and dragged me out of that party at break-neck speed. I wondered what the bloody hell was going on," laughed Fleur. "When she told me what had happened, I thought I was going to wet myself! God knows what the owners thought in the morning. We never knew if they found it – Sarah never went near their house again. If she saw any of them out in the town after that, she'd make a wide berth..."

At that moment the immaculate Jasmine re-entered the room, joined by the equally immaculate Lily, "Are you ladies ready?"

Kim wiped the tears of laughter from her face and followed Jasmine into the treatment for her first treatment of the afternoon – a deluxe facial designed to regenerate and rejuvenate mature skin. She was looking forward to nothing short of a miracle!

Chapter Nine

Kim and Fleur returned to the Dog and Duck still laughing about the 'unfortunate poo' story. Kim realised that it had been a long time since she had laughed that much with a friend, and it felt really good. Her life hadn't been all doom and gloom, but she realised that she had wasted a lot of time just going through the motions. This was her time now. Her time for change. The only thing that she supposed she had to thank Keith for was his insistence on them moving into the Dog and Duck. If it had been down to Kim, they'd have sold it without stepping one foot inside its grubby old doors. Then he would also never have copped off with Olivia and her ridiculously long eyelashes, and their marriage may still have been limping along with Keith going through her inheritance like an over-entitled rich kid!

The more she thought about it, the less sad she was that she was on the brink of divorce – in fact she wished it had happened years ago. It also occurred to her that had they not moved here, she would not have met Fleur, or Megan, or Rosa, or Dean and each one of them had enriched her life more than they realised. Was it too soon for her to have the fluttering of a crush each time she thought of Dean? (Not that she was sure she remembered what having a crush felt like; it could quite possibly be just another of her hot flushes!) The last thing she wanted was to make a twat of herself especially if Dean just considered her to be a slightly high-maintenance boss who needed looking after; although she was sure he did actually like her, if only as a friend.

The pub was as quiet as expected when they entered the bar area. Sunday evenings were usually fairly relaxed – the busiest time was obviously during Sunday lunch when the place was a veritable hive of activity. Tables of families enjoying a shared meal, the smell of roast beef and Yorkshire puddings working its way out of the kitchen like the trail of steam on the old Bisto advert. The hum of conversation, the old favourites on the jukebox, the clink of glasses as they were loaded into the dishwasher ready to remove lipstick stains and beer foam – all of these sounds had become familiar and well-loved by Kim, and made the Dog and Duck actually feel like home.

"Shall we open a bottle?" asked Kim, collecting a bottle of Prosecco from the wine fridge.

"Remember the rules," laughed Fleur, "no drinking on duty. What would Olivia say?!"

"Bollocks to Olivia," said Kim. "Technically I'm not on duty today. Rosa is on tonight; I wonder where she is?"

At that moment the pub door flew open, having been pushed so forcefully that it banged against the table and chairs that sat next to the entrance. The glasses on the table rattled and fell to the floor.

"Jesus Christ!" exclaimed Kim. "What the fu....?"

She stopped dead in her tracks as she looked up to see the cause of the disturbance, her eyes wide with shock. Before she had the chance to react or properly take in the scene before her, Keith strode towards her in three large steps, his eyes black with fury, his index finger aggressively pointing in her direction.

"Now hang on a minute..." said Fleur stepping between Kim and the ever-advancing Keith.

"Fuck off FIONA!" yelled Keith, pushing Fleur to one side. "This is none of your business, this is between me and my WIFE!"

"Now hang on a minute," echoed Kim, moving behind the bar and slamming down the hatch in an attempt to put an obstacle between her and Keith.

"I don't think anyone is doing any more hanging on," came a shrill voice from behind Keith. "We know what you have been up to!"

"Oh fuck me, it's the organ grinder's monkey," said Fleur as she caught sight of Olivia bringing up the rear.

Kim almost laughed at the ridiculousness of the situation. "First of all Keith, I am your *estranged* wife, soon-to-be ex, thankfully! Secondly, I am not going to do this without a solicitor. If you want to talk to me, you can go through the proper channels. I presume this is about you realising you are not going to be a pub landlord anytime soon – although granted you have found yourself a cracking Bet Lynch substitute,"

Kim raised her eyebrows in Olivia's direction as she spoke.

"You smart-arse little bitch," sneered Keith through gritted teeth, flecks of spit collecting in the corners of his mouth.

"Get out of MY pub," shrieked Kim, feeling for all the world like she belonged in an East End soap.

"Now you listen to me," snarled Keith, stepping forward and grabbing Kim roughly by the collar.

"Whoa, whoa, whoa," yelled Fleur, "you get your bloody hands off her!"

Fleur stepped forward to try and move Keith away from Kim, but Olivia stepped in and blocked her path, "I don't think so, you stuck-up bitch, this has nothing to do with you!"

Fleur and Olivia began to wrestle each other, each trying to jostle the other out of the way and with neither making any ground; until that was, that Fleur took an almighty swing and managed to crack Olivia in the shins with the toe of one of her rather pointy and equally strong Italian leather boots.

"Aargh!" screamed Olivia, clutching at her bruised shin and losing her advantage in the fight for her feckless boyfriend's 'rights.'

Fleur reached into her coat pocket and pulled out her mobile phone. "Enough's enough, Keith. I'm calling the police. I don't know who the bloody hell you think you are!"

"He is the landlord of this pub," shrieked Olivia desperately.

"WAS darling, WAS!" said Fleur with an icy glare that even scared Kim a little bit, and Fleur was on her side!

By this time, Kim was actually feeling quite frightened. Keith had tightened his grip on her collar and had managed to trap a piece of the skin on her neck between his fingers. She was buggered if she was going to cry out and show weakness, but it was really starting to hurt, and she could feel herself struggling to breathe.

At that moment the door behind the bar opened with a bang – there was more door-banging and opening than in a Texan whisky saloon. Any minute now, Kim expected the Sundance Kid to turn up and declare a bloody gunfight at the O.K. Corral!

Unable to look round, Kim only saw the look of surprise on Keith's face as a fist whistled past her ear and placed itself firmly on Keith's nose. There was a rather alarming crack and Keith's nose sort of imploded, blood began to ooze its way down his face and his head flicked back with the force of the blow. Almost immediately, he loosened his grip on Kim – well, to be more exact, he let go completely – and Kim staggered back. She would have fallen to the ground had it not been for two strong arms that caught her just before she fell.

"You ok, love?" asked the voice which she now knew to be Dean's.

With all the dramatic expression of a helpless damsel in distress, Kim collapsed into Dean's arms and began to shake uncontrollably.

"If I see you in this pub again Keith, I swear I will remove your balls and make you wear them as earrings.... *IF* I can find them that is! Do I make myself clear?" snarled Dean.

"Come on Keith, let's go," snapped Olivia. "This isn't the last they have heard of this!"

At this point, Kim quite literally lost her cool. All the anger that she felt – both from this latest episode and from years of being married to a man who was quite frankly showing himself to be more than just a bit of an arse – bubbled over like a can of over-shaken cola.

"Olivia, as much as I am overjoyed that you and Keith have found each other, if you think you are getting even the tip of one of your over-manicured talons on MY inheritance then you can think again. I am pretty sure you have had the 'Keith' version of events in which he has puffed himself up like a strutting peacock and told you how important and wealthy he is but, unfortunately, I am here to tell you that, as with everything else about Keith, whatever he has told you is likely to be deluded nonsense. Unfortunately for both of you, I have gone through the proper channels and made sure I have done things legally and with better information than just the vague notions of my imagination. So you can fight all you want, but legally, I am afraid to say that you are both fucked!"

At this point Kim turned to address Keith personally. "And as for you, Keith, if you ever lay another finger on me, I will remove your balls myself as, unlike Dean, I still know where they are... just about. I shall be logging a complaint with the police, and I will be serving an injunction on both of you. You will not be welcome anywhere near this pub. Now please leave before I have you arrested immediately."

"Too late," said Fleur, opening the door to two uniformed coppers who had arrived during the commotion.

"Did you call them?" asked Dean.

"No, I did," said Rosa, emerging from the direction of the pub toilets. "I saw them sneaking around outside just before you and Fleur got back. I knew something was going to go on. I hid in the toilets so I could phone them quietly."

Once the situation had been explained to the visiting officers, Keith and Olivia were marched unceremoniously from the premises. A complaint was logged against both of them, and the police lady assured Kim that she would have no trouble securing an injunction. They were released without arrest on the condition that they did not return at any point in the near or distant future. Keith shot Kim a withering look as he left, his nose now seemingly spreading itself across his face looking for all the world like it was made from a lump of old dough.

"He hit me," he whined, pointing at Dean.

"I think you are quite lucky that you have escaped with just a broken nose. Assaulting a woman doesn't tend to make you very popular," said the female police officer.

Keith opened his mouth as if to speak, but for once in his miserable life, chose wisely to keep his thoughts to himself!

"Well *that* was dramatic," exclaimed Fleur. "Are you ok, Rosa?"

"Mia cara," exclaimed Rosa, throwing her arms around Kim. "He is such a bloddy bastard!"

Dean and Fleur laughed at Rosa's comment. "He's that alright," said Dean. "I swear I could have knocked his bloddy block off!"

"Well you did a pretty good job on his nose," said Kim shakily. "Thank you. How did you know he was here?"

"Rosa phoned me before she phoned the police," replied Dean.

"I just knew he was going to be trouble," said Rosa. "I was worried in case the police took too long."

"Thank you both," said Kim. "I'm very lucky to have you."

"Any time," said Dean, "I dread to think what he would have done if there was no one here."

"I think he knew that the pub would be empty about now, sneaky bugger!" said Fleur. "Now, let's all have a nice medicinal brandy, I think we need to calm our nerves. I'm going to stay here with you tonight Kim... just in case."

"You don't have to," said Kim weakly and with less conviction than she felt.

"Nonsense," said Fleur. "It's decided. Now Dean, get the brandy out!"

The four of them sat, each with a generous measure of brandy, and Kim was not alone in feeling the calming sensation of its warmth as she struggled to take in all that had happened. She knew Keith had a temper but that was the first time in thirty years that he had actually grabbed her like that – it seemed that for Keith, money was quite a trigger! She thanked the Lord that the pub had been empty, she would not have wanted her dirty laundry aired in public, but then she guessed Keith had bided his time to make sure that she was alone and defenceless – he wouldn't have wanted a showdown with all of her customers there. She hoped that this was a one-off event, no matter how much he kicked and screamed; the legalities were well and truly sewn up whether he liked it or not!

"I think we should have a sweepstake," said Fleur, "on how long it takes Olivia to ditch Keith once she realises he really isn't getting his hands on the Dog and Duck."

“Fleur you’re such a cynic,” laughed Kim. “It’s true love!”

They all laughed, releasing the earlier pent-up emotions.

Chapter Ten

It was gone 10 in the evening by the time Dean left the pub. He hadn't meant to stay quite so long, and he wasn't scheduled to work on Sunday evenings as they didn't serve food, but he'd felt compelled to make sure that Kim was ok after her confrontation with Keith. If he had thought Keith was a twat before he'd attacked his estranged wife, especially after waiting until he knew she would be alone, he was certain he was a twat now. What a coward!

The only good thing to come out of the whole sorry episode was that Dean did at least feel a bit less ashamed of his past. Sure, he'd made some catastrophic mistakes, but he'd never stooped so low as to attack a woman. He wondered if perhaps he could tell Kim about the events that had led him to a rented bedsit without the proverbial pot to pee in but then again, he still wasn't sure that she would ever respect him again once she knew. He wasn't even sure why he felt the urge to tell her – after all she didn't need to know and perhaps in circumstances such as this, ignorance was bliss? When he thought about it, and if he was really honest with himself, there was a part of him that would have liked their friendship to develop into something more and he didn't know if you could do that with a sodding great skeleton in your cupboard – mind you, it seemed to work for politicians and celebrities, but then again he was neither, and knowing his luck the truth would bite him in the arse the moment his back was turned.

He arrived at the little bedsit he called home and resolved to quit the over-analysing – he felt sure he would be awake in the early hours doing some more over-analysing - but he would give it his best shot. He hadn't been happy about leaving Kim to lock up the pub, but Fleur was staying the night with her, and a couple of the regular lads had promised to stay until she locked the doors in return for a free pint. Kim had assured him that she would be just fine and once she and Fleur had started chatting and knocking back the brandy, Dean had felt a bit awkward and in their way – he felt like a gawky 15-year old with a crush whenever he was around her! He'd reluctantly left them to it knowing that she had enough back-up from her regulars should she need it… besides, Keith wasn't enough of a moron to come back in the short-term, at least.

Dean ran himself a hot bath, something he always did when he needed to unwind, hoping that it would help him to sleep. He still had the remains of Keith's blood on his knuckles from when his fist had made contact with his nose; he did have a little chuckle to himself when he remembered the look of absolute shock on Keith's face!

Chapter Eleven

The following week progressed with much less excitement than the TV soap-style shenanigans of Sunday night and Kim was mighty relieved for a little slice of normality – for the time being at least.

Fleur had stayed for the night after the events they now labelled 'twat-gate,' and bless her, she had phoned Kim daily just to check in. Dean had arrived early and left late for every shift and Kim knew that he was doing his best to keep a watchful eye on her. Rosa had done what Rosa always did in a crisis and tried to 'feed' everyone better! Each day she had brought in homemade treats like some kind of real stereotypical Italian Mumma, and Kim felt sure she had gone up a dress size in just a week! Even Megan had taken to popping in on her way home from the school run, even when it wasn't her turn to work.

"Honestly guys, I'm fine!" Kim had exclaimed on more than one occasion, but they had all shrugged their shoulders as if it was perfectly normal for them to spend more time at the Dog and Duck than it was for them to be in their own homes!

In truthfulness, Kim was really touched by their concern and was genuinely grateful to have made what she considered to be friends for life, regardless of whether they worked together or not.

When Daniel and her mum had phoned for a catch-up, Kim had not given graphic details about Keith's little testosterone tantrum and had played it down somewhat. She knew that her mum Judy would really fret if she thought Kim wasn't safe and she was worried that Daniel would lose his cool completely and give his dad a taste of his own medicine. She had no sympathy for anything that came Keith's way, and sincerely hoped that Karma was one hell of a bitch, but she still didn't want Daniel caught up in her crap, nor did she want him to get into fisticuffs with his father – that was all a bit too 'big fat gypsy showdown' for Kim and not likely to end well for Daniel who would always be her first priority.

Dean and Kim had worked hard in the garden in between shifts, and it was starting to look clean and inviting with the signs of new life and the air of hope that Spring always seemed to bring. The neighbour's tree had now been completely removed and the last branches burnt on the fire, tubs of colourful bulbs and winter pansies adorned the patio and the tired old garden furniture had followed the same fate as the neighbour's tree; having been replaced with some swanky weather-proof rattan-effect tables and chairs. A few colourful umbrellas completed the look and Kim was really looking forward to the summer barbecues that they had planned for the warmer weather.

The pub was busier than ever, and they were starting to get a reputation for their great pub grub and welcoming atmosphere. Several new groups had taken to holding their meetings at the Dog and Duck and this week had been no exception. Tuesday night was darts night, Wednesday lunchtime saw the meeting of what Kim called her 'Saga Louts' – a group of octogenarian old boys who arrived on mobility scooters and cars that were practically relics, which they parked with no regard for the bay markings or for whom they may potentially block in. Every Wednesday there would be a whole load of loudly-voiced messages from the bar for 'the owner of car x' to remove it from the front of the car park where it was blocking the exit of several customers, whilst simultaneously straddling the grass verge and pavement. The messages always had to be repeated several times at full volume on account of the hearing deficiencies of the clientele, before the very slow search for the car keys, followed by the even slower exit of the offending car owner on creaky old limbs supported by a myriad of walking aids. By the time the car in question had been moved, there was usually a second parking drama to resolve on account of the fact that a new precariously parked car had joined the party! Kim couldn't help but notice the amount of time it took her aged patrons to move their cars with not the merest sense of urgency and yet, they could skip up to the bar like veritable spring chickens at the mere whiff of a pint of bitter! She also noticed that when it came to Megan, her pretty young barmaid, the spring in their steps was noticeably springier – randy old buggers!

Thursday had been the quarterly meeting for the Women Who Wine and Kim had been pleased to see them all. As usual, she had made a real effort with the function room where they met, decorating the tables with flowers and making sure they had everything they needed. She knew that their custom had been a real coup for the pub, and she also knew that they had spread the word, bringing other customers into the pub.

Friday night was going to be 'Curry-oke.' This had been the dubious brainchild of Fran's boyfriend Bobby. He had voiced his suggestion – loudly – in the pub one evening and before Kim knew it, she had been railroaded into submission. Apparently, Bobby's brother's daughter's friend, had set himself up as a DJ and was also running karaoke nights to make ends meet.

"It'll be great," Bobby had said. "Really put this pub on the map."

Kim had been dubious at the scale of impact that a karaoke night run by a spotty faced teenager with a new set of speakers and laptop would have on the overall success of the pub and had just been about to make some polite refusal when Steve, aka Bragg Pitt, aka "if you've been to Tenerife, then he'd been to Eleven-er-rife" pub know-it-all, had piped up to declare his as-yet undiscovered singing talents.

"Blinding idea, Bobby. 'Bout time we had some entertainment in here."

Kim couldn't deny that watching the uber-confident Steve fall flat on his arse when he inevitably tried to deliver a song that was way beyond his musical capabilities and deluded sense of talent, would surely be more than a little entertaining, but nevertheless she remained unconvinced.

“Maybe, it’s something we could look into for the future,” she had suggested diplomatically.

Unfortunately, the over-zealous Bobby was already on the phone to his brother and had booked Zane for that Friday – it seemed that fortunately Zane had a ‘window’ in his calendar.

“You should do a themed food night,” suggested the ever-helpful Steve, who Kim was now beginning to wish would just piss off and stop making ‘helpful’ suggestions.

“What about a curry?” said Bobby, taking a sip from pint number fifteen of the evening while his long-suffering girlfriend Fran sat without a word, sipping her ‘Gin without sin,’ and looking like she wished she was anywhere but there.

“Curry-oke!” yelled Steve, mighty pleased with his dubious wit and wisdom.

“I could definitely do a curry evening,” said Dean as he walked past Kim, ignoring the glares from her direction.

“That’s settled then,” exclaimed Bobby. “I’ve booked him for 8 o’clock and he said he won’t charge you as long as he gets a free VRB.”

"Absolute bargain" replied Kim dryly. "Tell him we are eternally grateful."

Bobby was impervious to sarcasm it seemed and returned to discussing favourite karaoke tunes with Steve and who could eat the hottest curry.

Kim had returned to the kitchen and given Dean a playful punch on the arm, "Thanks, *FRIEND!* I was about to wriggle my way out of that one."

"I reckon it could be quite a laugh," said Megan, entering the kitchen to place an order for bar food on the service board."

"Don't you bloody start," laughed Kim. "You do realise that we will have a whole evening of Bragg Pitt to listen to now don't you!"

"Just think of the money," laughed Dean. "And besides, I'm going to do a special curry just for Bobby and Brag. It's going to be hot enough to blow their bloody heads off and neither of them will want to back down or lose face. By the time they've eaten my curry, you'll have sold them about twenty five pints of lager!"

Kim chuckled. "I must admit, that could be quite funny – but for God's sake don't muddle it up with any of the meals for our older customers. We'll be carrying them out on stretchers!"

And so, it had transpired that 'Curry-oke' was a goer and Kim had been surprised by the amount of interested participants. She'd booked forty places for food in under a week and she was bound to get walk-ins and other Friday night-ers coming along. As much as she hadn’t been too keen on the idea, it did look like the takings could be pretty good.

Chapter Twelve

Friday night had come around alarmingly quickly. Zane had arrived at 6pm to set up his gear – literally banging on the door before the pub was even open. Kim suspected that this was his first booking and that was why he was so keen – she tried not to think about the car crash that this event could be when in the hands of a 'DJ' who looked about fourteen and who probably weighed little more than a stick of rock. He was dressed entirely in black, with a floppy fringe that covered most of his face and a couple of those earrings that created huge holes in your ear lobes and made your ears hang down somewhere by the bottom of your chin. Kim wondered what the bloody hell all these young, ear-stretched fashionistas were going to do when they reached middle age and their ears looked like they'd been put through a pasta machine!

"I'll set up over here, the acoustics will be sick," Zane said. "I just need a couple of tables, a chair, an extension lead and some tape for the leads on the carpet... just in case."

"Are you sure that's all?" asked Kim, wondering if he wanted her to do the bloody gig for him as well!

"Yeah, that should do it for now," replied an oblivious Zane. "A drink would be nice too."

Kim had walked away at that point, not trusting herself to be polite!

Once Zane had set up his gear and pretty much rearranged the entire pub in the process, the place was really beginning to fill up. He'd also used the pub TV to hook up to his karaoke machine and Kim wondered at the prospects for his venture with so little actual equipment of his own!

"Blimey they are keen," exclaimed Rosa.

"I know," said Megan. "You going to sing Rosa?"

"Not bloody likely," exclaimed Rosa. "I have a voice like a screeching cat. My Paulie said it made his ears hurt!"

It had been decided that Dean would serve dinner before the Karaoke got underway properly; nobody relished the idea of trying to serve food whilst intrepid wannabe singing divas were up and down to the 'stage' like the proverbial fiddler's elbow!

Fortunately, they were fully-staffed and Dean, like the trooper he was, had made sure that everything was well prepared, and they could be sure of a slick service. They had kept the menu simple. A plate of poppadoms for every table to start, followed by a choice of three curries – a chicken korma for the curry wimps, a 'not-too-hot' korai for the more adventurous curry lovers and a tangy chickpea, spinach and red pepper dish for the veggie diners; all served with a slice of naan and a generous portion of basmati rice. The menu did NOT include the 'burn your bum' special that Dean had created just for Bobby and Steve; their curries had been 'spiced up' in due response to their bragging and bravado about how many curries they had eaten in their lives, how many 'spice-offs' they had won and how nobody would be able to eat a hotter curry than them. Dean had taken up the gauntlet with enthusiasm and duly purchased some bullet chillies from the specialist Indian supermarket on the outskirts of town. His idea was to pass their curries off as just something from the menu. He knew they would never be able to back down from eating it, especially if the rest of the clientele were happily munching away without a pause – if nothing else it would shut the pair of them up for a few minutes at least! Kim had let Brian and Doris in on their little secret, they were two of her favourite regulars and both thought that Bobby and Steve were a pair of opinionated plonkers. Kim knew they would not breathe a word to anyone and also knew that they would really appreciate the joke; it could be payback for the hours of waffle they had endured each time Steve and Bobby got together to hold court! Of course, Rosa and Megan were also in on the joke – they couldn't risk serving Dean's special to anyone else!

Zane had been asked to put on a little background music whilst people were eating which he did, although Kim had to suggest that Motown and perhaps a bit of Ed Sheeran might provide a more suitable ambience than the angst-ridden screaming rock music that he had originally chosen!

Kim and Megan took control of the bar, whilst Rosa and Dean made sure that everyone was fed. Kim was so proud of the way they all worked together as a team – everyone pulled their weight and the whole machine ran smoothly and harmoniously. Tray after tray of steaming hot curries emerged from the kitchen and the smell was mouth-watering. With a little subtle coercion, Kim had managed to make sure that Steve was seated on Bobby and Fran's table and because the pair of them were such bragging bores once they got going, everyone else tended to keep a wide berth. Brian and Doris were seated on a table to their left – ringside seats for the ensuing entertainment! – and to the right of them was the karaoke 'stage' and the expectant Zane who was knocking back the VRB's like a seasoned pro. Kim wondered how he had become so good at drinking when by the looks of him, he still looked like he should be on milk and cookies!

"He needs to slow down on the drinks," said Kim to Rosa, "otherwise this karaoke is going to be an even bigger disaster than I fear."

Rosa tapped her nose secretively, "It is all RB and no V if you get my drift?"

Kim looked puzzled.

"No Vodka!" laughed Rosa. "I'm not clearing up after him when he is sick on the carpet!"

Kim laughed. She loved Rosa so much. Let Zane believe he had an enviable capacity for alcohol when in reality, all he was drinking was high energy pop; although with the amount of sugar and E-numbers coursing through his digestive system currently, he was unlikely to need any other form of stimulant; they'd most likely be peeling him off the bloody ceiling at this rate!

Dean added the final 'garnish' to the two korai curries that Steve and Bobby had ordered. Predictably, they had both ordered the hottest thing available on the menu and just as predictably, they had both bemoaned the fact that Dean had not chosen to cook a Phall.

"Thing is Bobby, your average punter is not going to be able to stand that kind of heat, so I guess they have to make it mild. Not everyone is going to have that kind of tolerance," Steve had said, whilst both of them sat revelling in their own self-importance and cast-iron constitutions.

"I'll take these last two over if you like," said Dean, winking at the girls as he made his way over to their unsuspecting curry connoisseurs.

Brian and Doris sat up in their seats as they watched Dean place the dishes in front of their recipients. Fran continued to pick at her korma, eyes downcast and silent as ever.

"About time," roared Bobby, looking to Steve, his audience of one to join in with his 'joke.' "My stomach thought me throat had been cut!"

Dean smiled, "Sorry mate, last but not least, eh?"

As he walked away, Dean gave Doris a wry smile and suspected that in less than a few minutes both Steve and Bobby might actually be wondering if their throats had indeed been cut!

Dean joined the girls behind the bar as nonchalantly as he could manage. The rush had died down for a few minutes whilst people were eating, and everybody had now got something to drink. Kim had deliberately put jugs of water on each table except Bobby and Steve's as she knew they would never dare go to another table to ask for a cooling drink! They stood behind the bar and waited for the show to begin.

To everyone else, business was proceeding as usual. There was a low stream of jovial chatter, the clinking of glasses and the scrape of cutlery on china plates, as Barry White declared his love, '*just the way you are*,' through Zane's speakers. Kim was beginning to wonder if anything was going to happen all but then she began to observe Steve shifting uncomfortably in his seat. Bobby's face, which at the best of times was the wrong side of rosy, began to glow like a radioactive tomato. He looked like he was being lit up on the inside like a Halloween lantern – if it were possible for steam to have poured from his ears, then now would have been the time.

Steve stood up in his chair banging his knees on the table. "Shit!" he declared.

"You ok mate?" squeaked Bobby, his voice barely a whisper.

"Yeah, just banged my knee," lied Steve, reaching for his pint of lager.

Bobby grabbed a serviette from the table and began dabbing at his now-leaking forehead. The sweat was pouring down his face as though someone was holding a shower above his head. At this point the invisible Fran looked up, a look of surprise crossing her face as she observed her husband's complexion.

"You ok Bobby, is your curry too hot?"

Kim thought this was the longest sentence she had actually ever heard Fran speak.

"Don't be bloody daft woman," shrieked Bobby, downing the remains of his pint in one swallow.

Steve was now shovelling bread and rice into his mouth at break-neck speed as he attempted to reduce the fiery onslaught of his curry, squirming around in his seat like he was having some kind of fit. Unfortunately for both of them, they had mistaken the bullet chillies for cherry tomatoes and had consumed the entire fiery bullets in one bite.

"Do you want another pint?" asked Steve, clutching his throat, his voice hoarse and rasping. "Is your curry alright?"

"Not as hot I am used to," squeaked Bobby, now visibly trembling.

Brian and Doris watched the whole scene unfold, trying desperately to contain their laughter as the two macho idiots tried to downplay their obvious discomfort.

Steve leapt up from his chair, anxious to get to the bar and to not only get himself a drink, but to take a break from the molten lava that he had just consumed.

“Would you like some water?” asked Kim innocently. “I think I forgot to put yours on the table.”

Steve shook his head, his throat now on fire and rendering him unable to speak. If nothing else, this was the first time that Steve had ever been at a loss for words! He raised two fingers in a gesture that demonstrated his order for two lagers.

“Yeah won’t be long, just got to change the barrel,” said Dean disappearing in the direction of the cellar.

Megan and Rosa barely contained a full-on belly laugh, knowing that Dean had only changed the barrel less than an hour ago, but his delay tactics were causing quite a performance from the hapless Steve.

“You sure you’re ok?” asked Megan, “You look a little pink!”

Steve shook his head as he placed his elbows on the bar and put his head in his hands; the poor bloke looked like he might explode. At that moment Brian left his table and went to whisper something into Zane’s ear. A few minutes later, the sound of Jonny Cash’s ‘Ring of Fire’ was being played at full volume and Kim had to leave the bar and collect some glasses before she collapsed in a fit of the giggles.

A painstaking 10 minutes later, Dean emerged having 'changed' the barrel and Steve practically grabbed the glass of beer from Rosa's hand pouring it down his throat like he was dying of thirst. Bobby, who barely ever left his seat for anything, appeared at Steve's side and downed his own pint in a similar fashion. Rosa had not given them their change before they ordered two more pints which didn't last any longer.

"You were thirsty," exclaimed Rosa. "Feeling a bit warm?"

Steve and Bobby gave Rosa a look of disdain before returning to their seats, significantly more subdued than they had been at the beginning of the evening and with lips that looked pretty similar to those of a super model with a Botox addiction!

"Oh my God, that was bloody hilarious," laughed Megan.

"That was reasonably entertaining," smiled Dean. "That's going to burn a lot more on the way out!"

Steve and Bobby remained quiet for a whole 30 minutes before they were back to full volume and the karaoke was well and truly underway. There had been one of the worst renditions of Wuthering Heights that Kim had ever heard from a usually quiet and fairly frumpy customer. She had shrieked and warbled her way through the lyrics in a voice that only dogs could hear, clearly imagining herself with more talent than she possessed! Kim was sure that Kate Bush's eardrums were bleeding wherever she was in the world!

The most surprising performance of the evening came from Fran who stood up in the shapeless cardi-and-leggings combination that she always wore, shifting nervously from one Minnie Mouse trainer to another, before she gave the most incredible version of Memories from the musical Cats. She sang with the voice of an angel, her sweet and perfectly pitched voice rendering a surprised silence throughout the pub. You honestly could have heard a pin drop as people watched in utter amazement as the woman who was barely ever noticed by anyone literally had an entire audience transfixed.

“Bloody hell,” exclaimed Kim, swallowing down a lump in her throat as Fran returned to her seat. “Who knew?”

Rosa wiped a tear from her eye. “Voice of an angel, married to a slob!”

There were no performances that could hold a candle to Fran after that, although the sheer comedy value of Steve’s deluded impression of Tom Jones, complete with hip thrusting and mic swinging left the crowd also thinking, ‘Why, Why, Why, Delilah!’

To be fair to Zane, he had done a pretty good job and Kim was pleasantly surprised. The evening had been a success all round and, as they closed the door on the last of the customers, Kim and her team collapsed with tired satisfaction at a job well done.

"Let's have a little night cap," said Kim, "I think we have earned it!"

The four of them sat and enjoyed their treat as they laughed and remembered the events of the evening and wondered how Bobby and Steve would fare in the morning – as Dean had said, "That curry will burn both ways!"

Chapter Thirteen

Fran looked at the sleeping, snoring form of her boyfriend Bobby. Her favourite times were when he was asleep... or out. But then he never went anywhere without dragging her along with him. She suspected it had much more to do with the fact that he liked to be in control of her – Bobby liked to control everything – than because he couldn't bear to be without her company.

She looked at the half-drunk bottle of whisky on the coffee table, its contents shimmering in the moonlight that was peeping in through the half-closed curtains; the bottle that Bobby had reached for on their return from the Dog and Duck. He'd poured himself a large measure, slurping it down in front of her, taunting her, knowing what she craved but couldn't have.

Surely a sip wouldn't hurt? Just one little sip to fill the emptiness that sat in her stomach like a brick, threatening to drag her down into the abyss. But deep down she knew that it wouldn't stop at one little sip. One little sip would become a mouthful, a mouthful would become a whole glass and before she knew it, she'd be straight back to where she had been before; before that fateful day when all she remembered was the blue lights and the sirens that had carried her to the hospital ward where she had laid for weeks, hooked up to a life support machine whilst her liver battled to recover. Fran knew that one sip could probably kill her, but she also knew that living this way was already killing her in a much more torturous way than a bottle of whisky ever could.

Bobby snorted and let out a loud fart as he rolled over on the sofa. He reminded Fran of a warthog – a big fat snorting pig – minus the tusks and the pleasant demeanour! She scooped up the bottle of whisky, screwing the lid on tight and resisting the urge to sniff its tempting aroma. She placed the bottle back in the cupboard beside the TV in their sparsely decorated home. Despite the generous inheritance that Fran had received from her father when he passed away, they still lived a meagre existence. Bobby refused to spend money on anything that he couldn't sling down his neck and Fran wasn't sure she cared much anyway – nice things and Bobby just didn't belong together.

The only saving grace was that Bobby was unlikely to move from the sofa until the morning which meant that Fran could have the bed to herself. She could sleep uninterrupted and dream of a better life.

Chapter Fourteen

"Oh my God, Fleur it was bloody hilarious," laughed Kim on the phone to her friend the next morning. "The pair of them didn't dare admit that they were on fire, puffing their chests out like a couple of pigeons. I dread to think how they are feeling this morning. Dean said he loaded them up with the chillies!"

Fleur chuckled. "I wish I had been there to see that, I really do! Have you heard anymore from your ex-twat?"

"Nope, not a dicky bird," replied Kim. "I don't think much will happen for a while. I'm sure he'll wait until he gets his money from the divorce and then he'll be getting himself one of those 'no win, no fee' type solicitors for sure. I'm not worried to be honest. My solicitor says there's bugger-all he can do about it and even Keith isn't daft enough to get himself arrested a second time. The injunction means he must keep his distance, so I reckon I'm good for a while at least. I don't know what I would have done without Dean here."

"Is there a bit of crush going on there?" asked Fleur. "You do seem to go a bit gooey when you talk about him."

"No!" declared Kim a little too defensively. "Well, I do like him. But as a friend, I think. If I am honest, I'm not really sure how he feels about me. He's very protective, and he definitely goes above and beyond to help me out, but he's pretty much a closed book when it comes to talking about anything more personal than what he had for breakfast! It's all quite superficial. I'm not sure he's up for anything too deep – and besides I've still got to sort things out with Keith before I get myself involved in anything else."

"Listen babe, you're not getting any younger so if you like Dean then go for it; I'm telling you now, men don't look after a woman the way Dean looks after you if they aren't interested."

"Yeah, I guess you could be right. I'm not sure how the whole dating thing works anymore," sighed Kim. "I can't exactly ask him out for a drink when we work in a bloody pub can I?"

Fleur laughed, "You might have a point there! Oh well, just make sure you look gorgeous when he's around and let nature do the rest!"

Kim wasn't sure she had the time or the inclination to look 'gorgeous' at a moment's notice; at her age looking presentable was enough of a challenge... let alone gorgeous! She said goodbye to Fleur and got ready to go into town. She'd asked Rosa to open the pub up so she could run a few errands; they'd been so busy she'd barely had time to put bins out, let alone leave the actual building. They were going to need another member of staff before too long, but Kim was reluctant to employ anyone who may upset the equilibrium; they did not need Olivia mark two!

She climbed into her little pink car, smiling as she always did at how much Keith would have hated it! She made a stop at the local charity shop to dispose of a few bags of clothes and pointless nick-nacks that she had cleared out of the last few boxes that she had been meaning to sort through since their move to the pub. She could hardly believe that was merely a few months ago, so much had happened in such a short space of time.

She popped her head into Jax's florist shop marvelling at the beauty of the displays: artistically-placed pots of various colourful blooms positioned on old ladders and upturned apple crates, and the most spectacular assortment of cacti she had had ever seen.

"It looks gorgeous in here Jax, you are so clever."

"Aw thanks," said Jax, shyly. "I get my creative streak from my mum, I spent years out in the garden with her when she was younger, she always had a great eye for colour."

"Well you have definitely inherited that," smiled Kim. "I wonder if we could have some nice floral displays at the pub, you know? Nothing too outrageous but something stylish."

"I do a subscription service," said Jax. "You pay a monthly fee and I deliver an arrangement of seasonal flowers. If you were prepared to have whatever I've got left over from my other orders, I could do you a special price; as a friend and host of our WWW meetings?"

"That would be amazing," said Kim. "And I love the idea of using up what is left – nothing going to waste. Much more organic that way."

"If you give me your email, I'll send you a quote and you can set up your subscription – have these as a little new customer treat," smiled Jax, handing Kim the most beautiful bunch of wild springtime flowers in bright blue and snowy white.

"These are gorgeous, thank you – and now I am a technical whiz thanks to Fleur, I can sort out an email no problem," laughed Kim.

"Perfect, it's so lovely that we can all support each other," said Jax, "it's kind of the whole reason behind the Women Who Wine... well, that and the wine of course!"

Kim smiled in agreement. She certainly was very grateful to have found such a lovely little community of amazing women. She put her flowers into her bag, taking care not to squash them, and said goodbye to Jax. Next, she visited Jim's butcher's where she paid her bill for the pub's meat order; Jim was going to drop the meat off on his way home as it was far too much for her to carry in one go.

By the time she'd been around the whole village she'd collected a trial pack of breakfast muffins from Kate – they were going to sample these for the new, prospective breakfast service – caught up on the gossip in the post office, and snagged herself a quick set of gel nails in Helen's salon (another of the Women Who Wine group's members).

On the way out of town she made a stop at the local supermarket where she picked up some basic provisions such as cereal, washing powder and a few personal toiletries. One of the great things about running the pub was that she never really had to do 'proper' supermarket shopping anymore. She practically had her own private chefs in Dean and Rosa and she always had a ready supply of normal items like bread and milk for the pub if she needed them. She certainly didn't miss wondering what to cook every night and with Keith gone, she didn't make much mess at all upstairs although in all honesty, she was working so many hours that she barely did more than lay her head down and take a bath in the upstairs flat. If she sat down and thought about the number of hours she was putting in, she might have felt over-worked, but she was enjoying her life and the people in it so much that it didn't feel like work at all!

She navigated her way around the supermarket aisles, still a little unsure where everything was kept. On a couple of occasions, she noticed a dark-haired, attractive woman standing beside her as she searched for the things that she needed. The woman looked about Kim's age, she thought – although the older she got the less able she was to judge whether someone was 29 or 59! She wouldn't have noticed the woman at all if it hadn't been for the fact that they seemed to be 'meeting' on almost every aisle; by the shampoo, next to the fresh sushi that Kim often bought but never ate, near the tea lights and scented candles.... At one point the woman had looked in Kim's direction and smiled and moved as if to speak but said nothing. Kim had smiled back and hurried off in search of a bargain in the 'miscellaneous crap' aisle where she picked up a candle holder in the shape of the Buddha and a new toilet roll holder for the upstairs bathroom

Kim noticed the woman again whilst she queued at the checkout. She was sure the woman had been looking her way but when she caught her eye, they both did that awkward 'look away quickly' thing that people do when they don't want someone to think you have been staring at them. Kim put it down to coincidence and menopausal paranoia; she'd unwittingly stared at many strangers herself in her time!

When Kim got back to the pub the place was buzzing. Dean and Rosa were running between the kitchen and the bar and Kim had barely got her coat off before she was serving drinks and clearing tables. It was possibly the busiest lunchtime they had ever had, and Kim was becoming resigned to the fact that they would definitely need an extra member of staff.

Just at that moment, a friendly face appeared at the serving hatch, "Would you like an extra pair of hands? We were just on our way back from ballet lessons, if you don't mind an extra little one?"

"Megan!" exclaimed Kim. "Yes please and if little Lottie wants to earn herself a drink and a bag of crisps, she can help us wipe the tables."

Megan's daughter Lottie smiled, "I love helping!"

Kim loved it when Lottie came to visit, she was very grown up for her eight years and absolutely loved helping at the pub. She had been in several times during holidays or weekends with Megan and she was a little ray of sunshine – the older regulars especially loved her.

"What made you call in?" asked Kim. "You must be psychic!"

"We were driving this way home and I saw the car park was packed; I reckoned you might need some help," said Megan.

"Mia cara!" exclaimed Rosa, kissing the top of Lottie's blonde head and pulling her in for a bear hug.

Lottie giggled, she always lapped up the attention she got at the pub.

"Right come on you lot, enough of the gassing, I need a hand here!" said Dean as he burst out of the kitchen carrying a tray of club sandwiches.

"Right you are boss!" replied Kim, passing a cloth to the eager Lottie as Megan began efficiently helping Rosa to serve the customers, pouring a pint of Guinness and preparing a couple of Gin and Tonics with impressive multi-tasking ability.

Chapter Fifteen

For the first time in a long while, Dean slept like a log. The pub had been packed for pretty much the whole of Saturday. They'd served so many lunches that Dean had needed to stock up on supplies for Saturday evening and thank goodness he had, because the evening trade hadn't been any less busy. Sunday lunchtime was looking to be similar, especially as it was Mothering Sunday, and he was glad that he would get a break on Sunday evening.

He was really proud of what he had done with their food trade. With his expertise and Kim's vision, he really felt like they were beginning to crack it. He hadn't thought about 'it' for quite some time now and was allowing himself to believe that perhaps it was time to finally move on. He hadn't quite decided whether he would share his burden with Kim yet; he was torn between wanting to be honest and believing that ignorance may be bliss!

He got to the pub early on Sunday morning; if nothing else, army training had taught him the slightly cliched but very useful mantra that, if you 'fail to prepare you prepare to fail!'

"Blimey, did you wet the bed?" laughed Kim as she bumped into Dean on his way into the kitchen.

"I was so tired yesterday I think I got eight hours sleep in four," Dean smiled. "We are booked right out, and I need to be super-ready – I really want to smash this today, Mother's Day and all that."

"Aw bless you, not sure what I'd do without you," replied Kim touching Dean affectionately on the arm.

There had been a slightly awkward moment when they had both paused at the touch, a small hesitance that suggested each of them wanted the close contact to linger.

"Anyway, best get on," said Dean breaking the moment's intensity.

He had wanted to kiss her then, for the first time since their friendship had begun to blossom, and the strength of his feelings had somewhat surprised him. The last thing he wanted was to misread the signals, to make her feel uncomfortable; after all, he had history where reacting inappropriately was concerned!

Kim ran her fingers through her hair suddenly feeling self-conscious, "Yep, no rest for the wicked!"

She then started waffling on about table flowers and the new hand soap in the ladies' loos in an attempt to appear cool and nonchalant; unfortunately, she feared that all she had done was give the impression that she'd been at the cooking sherry!

As predicted, Sunday lunchtime was carnage. Kim had made sure they were fully staffed but as efficiently as they worked together, they were still run off their feet. At one point, Doris had helped by collecting some glasses and helping to clear tables and Kim resolved to search in earnest for a fourth member to add to their happy team.

"Thanks Doris," she puffed gratefully as she whistled past with two more plates of Roast Beef and Yorkshire Puds. "I owe you a drink."

"Don't be silly," replied Doris. "I'm just so glad to see your hard work paying off; this place has never been so good... but I won't say no to a gin and tonic!"

When the last of the guests had gone and Megan and Rosa had left for a well-earned rest and to enjoy what was left of Mother's Day, Kim entered the kitchen where Dean was loading the last of the plates into the dishwasher. He still had a few pots and pans to wash, and Kim rolled up her sleeves and began helping.

"You don't have to do that," said Dean.

"I'm happy to help," replied Kim. "Dinner was absolutely amazing; I am so grateful – it literally couldn't have gone any better."

"Yeah, my Yorkshires were a bit of a triumph, if I say so myself. Fancy a coffee?"

"I'd love one," said Kim. "Let's have it in the garden."

The day had been unusually warm for March and the last of the Spring sunshine was warming the little corner of the patio that seemed to catch the sun all day long. Dean made them a couple of frothy cappuccinos. He also brought out a small plate of leftover roast potatoes and a jug of his now-famous homemade gravy.

"Now you're talking," laughed Kim as Dean set the treats down on the table.

They sat together in companionable silence, enjoying the sun's warmth, dipping crispy roast potatoes into the gravy and resting their tired feet.

"Well this is nice," said Kim eventually, "makes all the hard work worth it."

"I know what you mean," Dean replied. "The harder you work, the more you appreciate the time off."

"So how long were you in the army?" asked Kim, finally plucking up the courage to ask Dean about his past.

"Since I was sixteen," he said. "It was all I'd ever known. I loved it for so long. My childhood wasn't great and to be honest it was the first time I had ever really felt part of anything; it was my first family if you like."

"That's sad," said Kim. "Are your family still alive?"

"I think I saw my mum on a number 57 bus a couple of years back, but I couldn't exactly be sure, we haven't spoken for years and I don't even know if my Dad is still alive," said Dean wistfully.

"Do you miss them?"

"You can't really miss what you never had. My dad spent more time in the pub than at home..."

"...so do you," laughed Kim, easing the intensity of the conversation.

"Yeah, you might have a point," laughed Dean, "although if I was truly my father's son, your stock would be running a bit low!"

"What about your mum?"

"My mum had all the maternal instincts of one of those spiders who eats its family," laughed Dean dryly. "I'd like to say she did her best, but I think that might be a bit generous. When we were little, she used to lock us in our bedrooms when she went out - probably so we couldn't phone Childline!"

"Oh Dean that's awful, who's we?"

"Me and my little brother, he emigrated to Australia; we talk on the phone occasionally, but I think we both felt like we had to do our own thing, our way of leaving our past behind probably."

"Why did you leave the army?" asked Kim.

"Long and complicated story," said Dean a little cryptically.

Kim could sense his discomfort at her last question and decided to give hm a break from her inquisition! He'd divulged more in the last few minutes than he had in the last few months, so she guessed he must be feeling a little less guarded.

“I’m sorry,” she said. “I’m a nosey cow, just tell me to bog off!”

Dean smiled and assured her that it was not a problem, but his expression said otherwise.

Chapter Sixteen

They sat in the garden for so long that neither of them realised it was almost time to open the pub for the evening session. Kim hadn't changed out of her lunchtime clothes or had a shower as she often did in between shifts, and although Dean wasn't scheduled to work, he didn't leave to go home.

In contrast to lunchtime, the evening was quieter than the grave – this was no surprise and in truth, Kim was relieved to be able to take things slowly. Rosa had been due in at 6pm but Kim had phoned and told her to take the evening off, it seemed that Dean was not in a hurry to leave and would be there to help if she needed anything, which she very much doubted. By nine o'clock, the place was empty.

"Shall we have a little night cap?" asked Kim, motioning to the two comfy armchairs positioned by the fire.

"Sounds great," said Dean. "Are you sure you trust me with my alcoholic roots?"

Kim laughed. "I reckon you might have succumbed to temptation before now, can you imagine someone like Bobby working here?"

"Olivia was bad enough!" chuckled Dean.

They took their drinks over to the two chairs. The conversation flowed easily, and Kim was glad that the awkwardness of earlier had disappeared. They talked about everything from films to music and soon discovered that they had lots of common ground; bonding over a shared love of cheesy 80's pop and an aversion to Sci Fi!

"I always wanted to be one of the cool girls at school," sighed Kim. "I guess a distinct advantage of getting older is that you don't worry so much about fitting in all the time."

"I can't believe it," smiled Dean. "I bet you were always gorgeous; you just never knew it!"

Kim blushed. "You're joking, I was so skinny, I had braces on my teeth and eyebrows that my mum recommended I shave off! When I died my hair red, my dad told me I looked like one of those swan vesta matches!"

Dean laughed. "Ok, you've convinced me, you were a disaster! Mind you, I'm in no position to talk, I couldn't grow stubble until I was about twenty-five; some of my mates had a full beard at fourteen! I never got let into pubs without ID and as you can imagine, me and my brother were hardly the snappiest-dressed kids in town!"

"Poor us, eh?" giggled Kim.

"I was actually relieved when I got married. Surprised, but relieved."

"Why were you surprised?" asked Kim.

"I dunno, something to do with terrible role models for parents probably," joked Dean. "Do you know, I never once saw my wife without makeup?"

Kim sat up in her seat. It was the first time Dean had ever shared any information about his wife. She had so many questions but chose to remember that it was most likely curiosity that finished off the poor old cat!

"What never?" exclaimed Kim. "Not even at night-time?"

"Nope!" Dean shook his head. "Obviously I was away a lot, but when I was home, she always had her face on. She would have a bath before bedtime, take her make up off and reapply it to go to sleep. Then she'd get up and repeat the process. She was pretty high maintenance...I should have known then really," his face grew pensive.

Kim lightened the mood. "Good job you split up before she reached the menopause; a few night sweats and you'd have been waking up to Alice Cooper!"

Dean laughed. "There are several good reasons why we parted ways, but you do make a very good case for divorce! Anyway, enough about her, what about you, are you happy on your own?"

He turned to look at her, his eyes looking directly into hers causing her tummy to do weird little somersaults.

"I can honestly say, apart from my beautiful boy of course, that I have never been happier," replied Kim, returning his gaze.

Dean leaned in towards her. He raised his hand to her cheek, tucking her hair behind her ear. Their eyes never left each other as their lips met...

Kim felt a strange buzzing sensation in her trousers. At first, she wondered if Dean had the magic touch. She'd seen those cheesy love films where the hero was able to make the heroine reach an earth-shattering climax purely through a kiss and the power of his mind but, as reality dawned, she realised that it was simply her mobile phone vibrating in her pocket!

"Oh bugger!" exclaimed Kim, jerking away from their tender embrace as she tried, very un-seductively, to extract the insistent passion killer from her trousers. She writhed around in her seat as she tried to work the phone loose from the confines of her skinny jeans.

"Bloody pockets!"

Dean sat back in his chair looking a little deflated as Kim finally wrestled the offending phone free.

"Hello? Daniel? How lovely to hear from you!"

"You ok Mum, you sound a bit flustered?"

"No, I'm all good love," replied Kim, thinking it unwise to share with her son that she had just been snogging the staff when her phone rang! "Just my phone got stuck in my pocket, you know how it is!"

"Mum, I'm so sorry I missed Mother's Day, we had a deadline at work that I really couldn't miss. I wondered if I could come and visit next weekend instead? Nan was going to come with me too if you'd like that?"

"Oh darling, I'd love that!" Kim exclaimed, throwing an excited smile in Dean's direction.

"And Mum, there was something I wanted to ask you..."

"What is it babe? You ok?"

"Yes, I'm fine, I just wondered if it would be ok to bring a friend with me?"

"Of course you can bring a friend," replied Kim. "Any friend of yours is welcome, you know that."

"Thanks Mum, you'll like him, he's a nice bloke; I've known him quite a while now."

"Well then, I'd love to meet him. When are you coming?"

"I'm picking Nan up after work on Friday, so I guess we'll be with you around 7-ish and we'll stay until Sunday if that's okay."

"That will be wonderful darling, I've missed you!"

"I've missed you too Mum, see you Friday, love you!"

"Was that Daniel?" asked Dean rather unnecessarily but wanting to combat any weird silence that may have occurred after the call and the moments that had preceded it.

"He's coming to stay next weekend," beamed Kim. "He's bringing my mum too and I am pretty sure he's going to tell me that he's gay."

Dean raised his eyebrows in mild surprise. He wasn't shocked by Kim's news in its essence, more that he hadn't expected her to say that. "How do you feel about that?"

"Do you know what, I think I've known for ages in all honesty, and I actually couldn't care less! As long as he is happy and he's a nice person, I really don't mind what he does with his life – be happy and be nice, those are the only things I want for him."

"If I'd had children, I'd want exactly the same," said Dean wistfully.

Kim smiled, "I'm sure you'd have made a lovely dad."

Inside she pondered Dean's possible reasons for not having had children but that was a sensitive subject for some, and she certainly didn't feel like she had the right to pry.

"Anyway, I'd better be off," said Dean, rising to his feet. "It's been a crazy day and I think we could both do with going to bed."

His words hung in the air and they both shifted a little uncomfortably. Before Daniel had called, the sparks between them had begun to fly but now the mood had been broken and they were both left feeling unsure about how to behave.

“Yes, I’m knackered,” said Kim truthfully. “Thanks for your hard work today.”

“Pleasure,” replied Dean, pulling on his jacket and heading for the door.

He didn’t want to leave but he didn’t know how to stay either, so he did what he usually did in uncomfortable situations; he made a swift exit!

Chapter Seventeen

Kim put their brandy glasses into the dishwasher, turned out the lights and locked the doors; it was a little before 11 but there was very little chance of a lone punter turning up at her door now; besides, she wouldn't have let them in anyway. This was not the last chance saloon, and she was no serving wench!

She climbed the stairs wearily, having suddenly hit a wall of tiredness. As she lay in bed, she replayed the moment that she and Dean had shared just before Daniel had rung. Whilst she felt some regret that their tender moment had been cut short, she figured it was probably for the best; give them both a little time to get a handle on their feelings. If it had gone much further and they had ended up doing the wild thing, they could have found themselves in a situation that they might have regretted; and that would have been mighty tricky considering they still needed to work together!

On a practical note, Kim had also not slept with anyone other than Keith in thirty years and even before him, there'd only been two liaisons. Actually it had been more like one and a half – the first having been an awkward fumble during a night of babysitting at her Auntie Brenda's house (Brenda had actually been her mum Judy's best friend but in the early 80s it was customary to designate the title of Aunt or Uncle to any of your parents' friends) which almost got to first base, except for an unfortunate and mis-timed incident with a condom that still made Kim prickle with embarrassment.

The second of her teenage 'lovers' had been a slightly spotty lad called Mark who she thought was her soul mate but who had left her for Janine, the local trollop, rendering Kim broken hearted. After that, she had gone into a brief period of mourning during which she had spent many hours in her bedroom listening to The Cure, wearing black eyeliner and generally wallowing in her own self-pity. Then she met Keith and the rest was history. The brutal truth was that no-one had seen her wobbly bits in over three decades and they were a lot wobblier now than they had been in her youth!

She barely even thought about Daniel's 'news'. She would let him tell her when he felt ready. She certainly wouldn't push him, and she had been completely honest when she had told Dean she really wasn't bothered. As long as he found someone who would love him and treat him in the way that he deserved, she didn't care if they were man, woman or Martian!

Chapter Eighteen

Dean ran his fingers across his mouth trying to recapture the feel of Kim's lips on his. It had taken a certain amount of willpower not to sling her over his shoulder and carry her upstairs like Tarzan carrying Jane!

The intensity of his emotions had threatened to overpower his gentlemanly manners; and also, he didn't want to terrify her!

Several things had become clear to him after today. Firstly, he was pretty sure that he was in love with Kim. Secondly, he absolutely did not want to blow it, so he would take things as slowly and as chivalrously as she needed him to. And finally, he was going to tell her everything. He hoped that she would still like him after his revelation, but he also knew that he wanted something with Kim that was special and something special could only be built on honesty. He hoped that if he told her in the right way, she might be able to forgive him and love the man that he had become rather than the man that he used to be.

He would choose his moment carefully, but he was definitely going to tell her, and he'd never felt more hopeful or more terrified in his entire life!

Chapter Nineteen

The rest of the week passed fairly smoothly. Trade was steady and, thankfully, there were no major incidents; Kim was definitely enjoying the quiet life!

Things between her and Dean had not been nearly as awkward as she had feared they might be... in fact quite the opposite. They worked alongside each other in companionable silence, each of them pre-empting the other's work routines and ways of doing things. They had begun to share private jokes in the way that people who are close often do, and Kim liked how even-tempered Dean was – after Keith, who blew up more often than a balloon in a hot air factory, it was positively refreshing. Kim wondered why Dean had ever got divorced if he was this easy to live with, but then she wasn't naïve enough not to know that even the best relationships lost a bit of a shine once the love of your life started leaving poo stains in the toilet and their pants on the bathroom floor. Keith's main problem had been that he'd had all of the usual flaws, with none of the redeeming qualities that soften the edges!

Kim and Dean had not really had more than a few fleeting moments alone in a room for the entire week, but she'd noticed that when he walked past her, he would walk a lot closer than before, often brushing his hand against hers or putting his hand on her back when he needed to walk around her. Once, when she had been washing up at the sink, he had walked so close behind her, she had felt his breath on her neck, and she had involuntarily leaned back towards him. She had thought that he was about to kiss her neck and the butterflies in her tummy had been doing somersaults, but then the kitchen door had opened, and Rosa had entered with a pile of dirty plates. They had sprung apart like two scalded cats. On a couple of occasions, she had given herself a stern talking to. Her libido was out of control. Her hormones were definitely racing but they were more the kind suited to puberty than the menopause; she'd be sitting on the bloody washing machine during the spin cycle at this rate!

She had a strange feeling that Dean was desperate to get her on her own, like he had something he wanted to share with her, but she wasn't sure what that could be. She had confided in Fleur, who had rather crassly suggested the exact part of his anatomy that he wanted to 'share' with her, and Kim had shrieked in less than convincing horror at the suggestion.

"Seriously though babe, you're both grown-ups. If you like him, embrace your inner diva, and make the first move – there's no law that says he has to make a move first, it is the 21st century after all; girl power and all that," said Fleur.

"Oh my God! I couldn't," said Kim. "What if he turns me down? What if I am wrong?"

"Listen, I've seen the way he looks at you and it isn't that different to the kind of look a starving man would give a nice fillet steak," laughed Fleur. "I promise you this, he will definitely *not* turn you down!"

"I'll think about it," said Kim, "but I haven't asked a boy out in over thirty years... in fact I have NEVER asked a boy out!"

Fleur had laughed at Kim's suggestion that Dean was a 'boy.' Dean had walked past them both at that point, throwing a smile in Kim's direction which had made them collapse into giggles like a pair of teenagers – honestly, she might just as well have been back in her bedroom, applying her blue mascara, and blowing kisses to her George Michael posters!

By the time Friday came round, the chemistry between Kim and Dean was palpable and, had it not been for the fact that Daniel and her mum were coming to stay, Kim may well have heeded Fleur's advice and given Dean her very best 'come-to-bed' eyes and bollocks to whether she ended up making a fool of herself!

Thankfully, a busy pub and a pre-Easter Quiz Night special were just about saving her from humiliating herself.

A lull in drinks service around 7.30pm when round three of the quiz was well underway – an impossible round of questions on the subject of local history which only seemed familiar to 'Uncle Albert' and his mate Ernie who were both in their eighties, and the only members of the clientele likely to remember street names circa 1950 – the pub door opened to reveal Daniel, Judy, and Daniel's friend Ryan.

"Daniel!" screamed Kim, hurtling towards the door, and throwing her arms around her beloved boy.

Competition was running high, and a few disgruntled looks were thrown in Kim's direction whose outburst had meant that question number nine had been unheard by many and had needed to be repeated for fear of mutiny in the ranks – the 'Mature Minds' were particularly miffed as they were running neck and neck against the 'Loxley Lads' and were keen to secure the prize kitty, which stood at a respectable £150.

"Whoops! Sorry," said Kim sheepishly, drawing her finger to her lips and beckoning in her very welcome visitors. "Let's go into the back room," she whispered. "We can talk in there without getting lynched!"

Daniel smiled and followed his mum through to the function area at the rear of the pub, closely followed by Judy and Ryan.

"It's good to see you mum. This is Ryan."

"It's so lovely to meet you Ryan," said Kim, moving forward to kiss him on the cheek.

She suddenly wondered if it was appropriate to kiss your child's friend on a first meeting and hoped she hadn't made him feel uncomfortable. Fortunately, Ryan seemed completely non-plussed and returned Kim's greeting warmly – she liked him instantly.

“How you doing, Mum?” asked Kim, giving her mum Judy a big hug.

“I wondered when you were going to say hello,” laughed Judy. “Hello darling, it’s so good to see you.”

They found themselves a table and sat down while Kim went to get them some drinks.

“Can you manage without me for a few moments?” Kim asked Rosa.

“We are fine,” said Rosa. “Enjoy your family, I’ll bring your drinks over.”

“Thanks Rosa, you’re a star but give me a nudge if you get too busy.”

At that moment Dean came through to the bar from the kitchen. He and Kim looked at each other and smiled but he stayed in the background. Kim was aware that they both suddenly felt a little awkward. A bit of flirting and some sneaky hand touching when they were alone was one thing, but ‘meeting the family’, well that was quite another thing altogether. She was aware that Dean had already fully met Daniel and Judy and they had all got on very well together – he’d been present during the ‘Keith and Olivia getting frisky in the cellar’ incident after all, and he had backed Daniel when he'd given his father an uncharacteristic but well-deserved wallop – but things felt different now. Back then they had merely been work colleagues, maybe even friends, but now they were... to tell the truth Kim didn't know what the bloody hell they were, but they definitely weren't the same.

Rosa set the tray of drinks down on the table. "A pint of lager for Dan, a G&T for Ryan, a rum and Coke for Judy and a nice dry white for Kim."

"Perfect," said Ryan, "and proper gin glasses too – none of those tiny little social club glasses!"

"I knew I liked you," laughed Kim. "So how do you and my lovely Daniel know each other?"

Daniel and Ryan shared a look, it was only fleeting, but in that moment, Kim knew for sure that her instincts were right. She recognised that look, it was a look that signified something more than friendship.

"I'm a graphic designer," said Ryan. "Daniel has the IT contract for our firm; he does all the clever tech stuff."

"He must get it from me," laughed Kim. "I'm on social media and everything now, you know."

Daniel rolled his eyes. "Better late than never. Before she got the pub, she was still using a mobile the size of a brick and didn't know her app from her elbow!"

Kim gasped in mock offence. "Cheeky bugger!"

"He's right though," said Judy. "I think even *I* joined the 21st century before she did – I'd been FaceTiming my friends at the bridge club for years before she could even send a photo!"

"Cheers guys," laughed Kim.

They spent the next hour laughing and chatting easily before Kim suggested that Daniel help her take the bags upstairs. She wanted to get him on his own for a few minutes to see if he would tell her about Ryan. The more time they had spent together, the more she had seen how relaxed they were in each other's company and the genuine affection between them was plain to see.

"We'll be back in a bit. Mum, do you want to get the drinks in while we take the bags upstairs?"

Judy nodded and picked up the tray while Kim and Daniel went upstairs to the flat above the pub. They climbed the stairs in silence. It was Daniel who was the first to speak.

"Mum, there's something I need to tell you... no actually, there's something I *want* to tell you," said Daniel.

"Is it about Ryan?" asked Kim.

They had stopped at the top of the stairs and Daniel lowered his eyes to the ground. Kim looked at her beloved boy. To her, it was like he was five years old again, and she wanted nothing more than to scoop him up into her arms, to hold him tight, to tell him that he need never be nervous to tell her anything – she would love him with all of her heart forever.

Daniel continued to look down at the floor. Kim put her arms around him and held him. She whispered into his ear, not forcing him to look directly at her.

"Do you love him Daniel?"

Daniel took a step back and raised his eyes, "Is that okay Mum?"

"Whatever you do is okay with me," said Kim. "Be kind and be happy, that's all I've ever wanted for you; nothing more. If you love him and he loves you, then I will love him just the same."

Daniel let out a sigh of relief and Kim's heart melted at the sight of her son's worry.

"Now, because I am a massive over-thinker, I have thought long and hard about who will sleep where," smiled Kim, breaking the tension. "Does your Nan know?"

"I'm sorry Mum, I should have told you first, I just..."

"Now ssssh! It's fine. It's all fine. I get it; I'm glad she knows, and I know she'll love you whatever path your life takes. I just didn't want to give the old girl a shock by giving you and Ryan a room together if she didn't know!"

Daniel laughed, visibly relieved. "I knew you'd be fine with it; it just never seemed the right time to say it out loud if you know what I mean? I had to get it right in my own head first."

"Daniel, I love you and that's all that counts. Now let's get downstairs and have a drink, I bet poor old Ryan is panicking; I don't think my, 'come and help me with the bags' was a very subtle way to get you on your own, was it?"

"Definitely not!" laughed Daniel. "I love you too Mum."

They put the bags in the appropriate rooms, one for Judy, one for Daniel and Ryan, then went back downstairs to join the others. Daniel went and sat next to Ryan, giving him a reassuring tap on the knee.

"I think this calls for a celebration," said Judy returning to the table with a bottle of bubbles and four glasses. "Welcome to the madhouse Ryan!"

"Will your customers be ok with it?" asked Ryan. "These little villages can sometimes be a bit set in their ways."

"Fuck 'em!" exclaimed Judy. "If they don't like it, they can lump it – although you might be the only gays in the village!"

Kim and Daniel almost spat out their drinks at Judy's joke and Kim had to be banged on the back before she choked herself to death!

"Bloody hell, Mum," gasped Kim, trying to catch her breath.

Judy smiled and raised her glass in defiance – she definitely was the coolest nan on the block!

"You lot seem to be enjoying yourselves," said Dean, approaching their slightly raucous little gathering. "Are you hungry – I thought you might like a little something to soak up the bubbles?”

He placed a platter of antipasti on the table in front of them along with a basket of ciabatta slices, some marinated olives and a dish of hummus.

“You’re an angel,” smiled Kim gratefully.

“Pleasure,” said Dean, winking at Kim before walking hurriedly away.

Ordinarily he would have loved to join them. He really liked Kim’s son, and her mum Judy was just an older version of her daughter, so he definitely had a lot of time for her, but he just didn’t trust himself to be around Kim at the moment. If he had sat down beside her, the temptation to touch her hand or place his hand on her knee would have been too much to resist. He was very happy for things to progress between them – there were only so many cold showers a bloke could take without developing a case of bronchial pneumonia – but he didn’t want their ‘relationship’ to progress quite so publicly, especially if it would make Kim feel uncomfortable or put her on the spot. He also had to tell her the truth and he was resigned to the fact that the moment to come clean was not going to present itself this weekend. Once they’d gone, he’d tell her. No matter what the outcome, he couldn’t hide from his past any longer.

“Dean’s a bit off,” said Judy. “Is he ok?”

“Yeah, just busy, I think,” replied Kim.

Judy gave a knowing look in Kim's direction but said no more – it seemed that mother's intuition was running rife tonight!

Chapter Twenty

On Saturday morning, Kim received a bundle of post from her solicitor. The decree nisi had now been granted which meant that divorce proceedings were well and truly underway; in around six weeks' time she would receive the decree absolute, and she would be free of Keith forever – she guessed she should have felt a little bit sad but all she felt was relief.

The sale of their house had finally completed and all monies fairly divided, although this was not the 'fair' settlement that Keith had envisaged. Kim knew he believed completely that he had been the financial and emotional cornerstone of their marriage and, as such, should have been rewarded accordingly. His blind arrogance was actually rather funny; he'd been in and out of work (along with other women's knickers it had now transpired) more times than a fat kid living above a sweet shop, and he was about as emotionally supportive as a rubber leg!

There was a letter confirming full ownership of the pub to Kim and her name was now proudly displayed above the door, having achieved the necessary licensee status with the relevant government department some weeks back. Since Keith's explosive outburst not so long ago, she'd not heard a peep from him or his gold-digging girlfriend, but she wasn't holding her breath; Keith's ego alone would not allow him to be 'done over' by the woman to whom he had given so much love and devotion!

She fully expected some form of legal contest about the pub from Keith, egged on by the deluded Olivia no doubt, but she wasn't too worried. Her solicitor had assured her that he didn't have a leg to stand on (rubber or otherwise) when it came to claiming any kind of rights to the pub so, legally, she was home and dry. The only thing that niggled her a little bit was the chance that he would turn up again, creating a scene. She didn't think she was in physical danger, but she also knew that, whilst a little floor show of screaming matches between herself and her feckless ex might entertain the locals for a while, it would grow tired very quickly and could be bad for business if Keith and Olivia tried to make life difficult.

"You ok love?" asked Judy, interrupting Kim's thoughts.

"Yeah, fine Mum. Just sifting through the paperwork. Divorce is underway and the pub is legally mine now; I'm just worried that Keith might make a fuss."

"Whether he likes it or not, the facts are the facts; I don't think he'd turn up here, do you?"

Kim glanced in her mum's direction, her expression speaking volumes.

"He's been here already, hasn't he?" said Judy, crossly. "Did he hurt you?"

Kim sighed and inwardly chastised herself for having one of those faces that did absolutely bugger all to hide what she was thinking inside; poker-faced she was not!

"It's okay Mum. It was sorted out. He got a bit stroppy, but the police cautioned him, and Dean gave him a special 'caution' of his own!"

"Bastard!" snarled Judy. "Why didn't you tell me?"

"I didn't want to worry you. It's okay. There's a restraining order now. I doubt he'll be back but I'm sure I haven't heard the last of this. He's really pissed off that he isn't swanning around as the new landlord – you know how far up his own bum he can be!"

"I never liked him," said Judy.

"I know Mum; nor did I to be honest." Kim laughed. "Anyway, enough about him, I'm really happy now, so everything worked out fine."

"They're here!" called Rosa as she entered through the kitchen door.

Judy furrowed her brow in a confused expression.

"Oh shit! I forgot," exclaimed Kim. "We are interviewing for a new staff member. Rosa is going to sit in on the interviews – I want everyone to like them. I don't want anyone upsetting our happy little team. You can sit in too if you like?"

"Ooo yes, that'll be fun," said Judy. "Can I have a clipboard?"

Kim laughed, "Behave yourself, and no frightening the new staff!"

Rosa and Kim sat down at one of the tables in the small function room. There were two applicants to see, and they asked one of them to wait in the main bar whilst they spoke to the first one. Kim wasn't averse to taking them both on if they were suitable; the pub was reaching a point where they were in desperate need of some extra hands and Kim was just about dead on her feet most days!

Dean brought through a tray of fresh coffee and some muffins from Kate in the Women Who Wine group. They were trialling the new breakfast muffins in preparation to extend their food service. Megan had just arrived and had begun to clean the pub ready for the new day and Kim knew both she and Dean would be grilling the new staff member to see if they were up to scratch! The whole set-up had an air of the Mafia about it – Kim the 'Boss' and her mum Judy as the Matriarch, Dean and Megan as the sidekicks, and Rosa doing her very best impression of an Italian Godmother!

Daniel and Ryan had left early to sample the local sights, leaving Kim and Judy to it. All being well, they would have some time on Sunday to share a proper family meal. As much as Kim loved the pub, it could be quite restrictive, and she was looking forward to having some free time once they were properly staffed.

The first candidate sat in front of what must have looked like a fairly intimidating panel, considering this was just an interview for a bar job and not the head of MI5!

"Welcome," said Kim. "Please just try to relax and be yourself; I'm sorry there are so many of us – it wasn't meant to be this formal," she smiled as she spoke.

The candidate was a small woman with one of those faces that didn't seem to betray any kind of emotion whatsoever. She did not speak or return Kim's smile.

"So," said Kim, attempting to add some life into the conversation, "tell me about yourself. Have you worked in a pub before?"

Once again, she smiled at the woman and, once again, received no facial movement in return.

This time the woman did speak however, but in a voice without any kind of expression – a kind of monotone drone requiring so little energy that even her lips barely moved. "I worked in Loxley."

"Right," said Kim. "Did you work there for long? What were your duties?"

"Barmaid for five years," replied the woman.

"Okaaaay," said Kim, feeling like she was trying to extract blood from a stone. "Are you local?"

"Yes," replied the woman.

Kim looked at Rosa and Judy who were trying not to snigger.

Rosa stepped in to try and help Kim out. "Are you flexible about your working hours?"

"Yes," replied the woman.

"Do you like being part of a team," asked Rosa, "we have a really happy team here."

"Yes," replied the woman.

Judy wrote something down on her pad and showed it to Kim who stifled a laugh as she read the word, 'ARRGGHH!' on her mum's paper.

"Anyway, if you could describe yourself in one word, what would it be?" asked Kim drawing on all of her professional interview experience from the banking world.

Unfortunately, none of them had been prepared for the woman's answer which was delivered with a dead-pan expressionless face and from almost frozen lips...

"Bubbly."

Rosa gave a shriek and ran from the room on the pretence of needing a tissue, Judy had to work so hard to stifle a laugh that she snorted and almost choked herself and Kim stood up abruptly in an attempt to divert her brain long enough from the overwhelming desire to pee herself laughing.

“Thank you so much for coming in,” said Kim, shaking the woman’s hand. “We’ll be in touch.”

And with that, the woman left without so much as a trace of a smile ever having touched her face.

Rosa returned from the toilets, tears running down her cheeks. “I’m so sorry,” she gasped. “I just couldn’t help myself.”

Judy and Kim were now both in fits of giggles.

“Bubbly!” laughed Judy. “I’ve seen more bubbles in a pint of Bitter!”

“Now come on ladies!” said Kim trying to pull herself together. “We need to be professional here.”

“You ok girls?” asked Dean as he came over to investigate the cause of the commotion.

“Yep! Don’t ask, we’ll tell you later,” chuckled Kim, fixing the mascara that was making its way in the direction of her chin.

“Shall I show the next one through?”

The girls all took a deep breath and nodded simultaneously. Thankfully, the next prospective team member was a lot easier to talk to and clearly had not been at the back of the queue when personalities had been handed out!

Jake was a trainee accountant. He was young, smartly dressed and very easy to talk to. He’d not worked in a bar before but proclaimed himself to be a quick learner. He lived with his grandparents a few miles from the pub, had his own car, his own teeth and lips that actually moved when he spoke!

"I'm looking to make some extra money," said Jake, "but I'd also like something that is quite sociable. Accountancy is a great job, but it does mean that you spend long periods of time staring at a screen and not speaking to anyone! I can't do day shifts but I'm happy to do weekends and any evenings."

"Perfect!" said Kim, looking at Judy and Rosa for agreement.

"I think you will fit in so lovely," declared Rosa warmly.

"When can you start?" asked Kim.

"As soon as you're ready," replied Jake.

"How about this evening?" said Kim. "We could start you on a trial basis – see if we all get on – and show you the ropes. Next weekend is likely to be busy for Easter so it would be good for you to hit the ground running. Does that sound okay?"

"Sounds great," said Jake. "I see you open at 6 o'clock, shall I come about 5.30?"

"...and a bit of initiative," smiled Judy. "Thank goodness for that!"

They all shook hands and agreed that Jake would start that evening. Megan and Dean had spent quite a bit of time chatting to him whilst the girls had been interviewing the personality vacuum that had been the previous applicant, and they also thought he was great.

"The old dears will love him," laughed Megan.

"I think he'll fit in just fine," said Kim, relieved. "Now I think all we have left to do is to get someone to help Dean in the kitchen and we should be set for a little while."

"I was thinking I could contact the local college, see if they've got any trainee chefs who'd like some work experience," said Dean.

"Great idea; just don't choose anyone whose lips don't move!" said Kim.

Dean looked confused and Kim, Judy and Rosa regaled their interview with the expressionless woman with a 'bubbly' personality.

The rest of the weekend was Kim's idea of heaven. She had her family around her and there were no major incidents. There had been one slightly awkward moment when Daniel had received a phone call from his dad. Daniel had mentioned to Keith in a text message that he was coming to visit his mum and Keith had obviously been unable to resist trying to find out what was going on in his absence. Daniel had been surprised to receive the call as, not unsurprisingly, Keith was not in the habit of regularly phoning his son – it seemed that he was about as dedicated a father during separation as he had been during his marriage!

"Well, that was weird!" exclaimed Daniel, hanging up the phone. "Started telling me not to believe everything I hear?"

It was then that the whole sorry saga of Keith spitting out his dummy and manhandling Kim came out. Daniel had been fuming and had threatened to remove his dad's family jewels if he dared to touch his mum again. Kim had laughed at this and said that he should join the queue of people keen to remove Keith's most prized attributes!

"Don't upset yourself," said Kim. "There's not much he can do. I'm always surrounded by people and if he comes again, he'll be arrested. I'm sure he'll throw his toys out the pram a few more times but there's bugger all he can do about any of it. I'm not worried, honestly."

"I won't let him hurt her," said Dean.

"I'm glad you're here Dean, thanks mate."

When Dean left the room, Daniel had given his mum a cheeky wink. "Anything I need to know?"

"Don't you start!" laughed Kim. "We're just friends, that's all."

"Well, it would be totally okay if you were more than friends – he's a nice bloke," said Daniel.

"You never know," said Kim wistfully.

Now that Daniel had given her his best wishes, it was beginning to feel like a done deal with her and Dean. She didn't need Daniel's permission as such, but knowing she had his blessing meant the world to her, especially when the ink on the divorce papers wasn't even completed, let alone dry! She decided that once her family had left, she was going to give Dean the green light – just how a fifty-year-old menopausal woman was supposed to do that without looking like a deranged old trollop she had no idea, but she was prepared to give it a go!

Daniel, Ryan and Judy left on Sunday evening having enjoyed a fabulous Sunday lunch and some beautiful memories. They had laughed long and hard when Judy had shown Ryan some slightly cringey photos of Daniel as a baby – particularly the ones where he had tried to apply 'make-up' using a felt tip pen or when he had insisted that he was old enough to dress himself and had subsequently spent several months wearing a combination of dinosaur pyjamas, a variety of superhero costumes and Christmas jumpers in June!

Judy had more or less polished off a bottle of dry sherry and Kim suspected that she'd be snoring in the back of the car before they hit the motorway.

"Thanks for coming, it's been so lovely to have you all here," said Kim, hugging and kissing Daniel for the hundredth time. "I hope you'll come again, Ryan; we haven't scared you off have we?"

Ryan smiled. “It’s been lovely, and thank you for making me feel so welcome. You’re stuck with me now I hope.”

They all piled into Daniel’s smart company car, enthusiastically waving out of the windows and with Daniel peeping the horn.

Chapter Twenty-One

Today was the day. Dean had finally made his mind up.

Kim's family had left the night before and today was the day he would tell her everything. He couldn't bear the suspense any longer; lying awake every night going through a million bloody eventualities in his head – playing and replaying the conversation, rehearsing his lines, imagining her reaction.

The best scenarios were the ones where she threw her arms around him and told him that it was all fine before they fell into bed and did the sort of stuff that probably only happened in movies! The other scenarios were less comforting and usually ended with close contact of another kind - namely her fist on his jaw – but he had tried to put these outcomes to the back of his mind. Whatever the outcome he couldn't wait any longer, he needed to know where he stood, whether that meant moving forward with their relationship or standing knee deep in a bucket of crap, possibly without a job *or* a girlfriend!

One thing he was sure of was that he couldn't keep torturing himself; being in her presence and not being able to touch her was about as frustrating as declaring yourself a vegetarian just as someone offers you a bacon sandwich!

Chapter Twenty-Two

Kim woke early. Today was the day. She had decided that as soon as the morning shift was over, she would tell him. Exactly what she was going to tell him, she still hadn't quite worked out, despite rehearsing her 'speech' a hundred times in the night.

She suspected it would go something like, "...Dean, there's something I'd like to tell you..." before she turned an unfetching shade of crimson, muttered a few 'ums' and errs' and hoped to God that he wouldn't think she'd gone bat shit crazy and filled in some of the blanks!

She took extra care with her appearance, showering, washing and blow-drying her hair, applying her makeup precisely and dressing in her black jeans and the new blue silk top that she knew really suited her complexion. When she was ready, she knew she looked pretty alright for an old girl!

She came downstairs and prepared and turned on the coffee machine; she'd read in a magazine somewhere that if you wanted to sell your house you should bake bread or prepare coffee to entice the buyers in. She wasn't selling her house exactly, but she hoped the smell would be homely and welcoming all the same. She couldn't help but laugh at herself; she was sure it didn't happen like this in the movies. In movies they simply popped out a bit of cleavage and everything happened from there whilst here she was, putting on coffee and polishing shelves like she was expecting the bloody estate agent!

She opened the front door and placed the newly-painted sign advertising their opening times and popular lunch dishes next to the large tub of colourful winter pansies beside the doorway, before going back behind the bar to put on some chilled-out music and lay out the clean bar mats.

As she bent down behind the bar, she heard the front door open; it was a bit early for Rosa, and Dean always entered through the back kitchen door. She stood up wondering if perhaps the postman had come in to deliver one of her late-night eBay purchases of which she was often guilty after a couple of glasses of wine.

An attractive dark-haired woman approached the bar, pushing her expensive sunglasses onto the top of her head.

"Can I help you?" asked Kim. "We don't open until 11." She looked at the clock noticing the time to be a little before 10 o'clock.

"I'm looking for Michael Taylor," said the woman.

Kim frowned. The woman looked vaguely familiar, but she couldn't work out where she might know her from.

"Michael Taylor?" she questioned. "I'm afraid I can't help you; that name isn't familiar to me."

“I understand he works here… as a chef,” replied the woman, with an air of self-assured confidence that Kim found unnerving.

Kim shook her head. “I’m sorry, I really can’t help you.”

The woman didn’t move, holding her position at the bar with resolved determination.

At that moment the door from the kitchen to the bar swung open and Kim turned to see Dean arriving.

“Morning boss, what a beautiful morning…” His voice trailed away as he stood rooted to the spot, his eyes glued to the woman at the bar.

Kim looked from Dean’s face to the woman and back again, the recognition between them was plain to see. Dean’s face was ashen, and he looked visibly shaken. He averted his eyes from the mystery woman, looking at Kim with a mixture of horror and fear.

Kim’s frown deepened as she tried to make sense of the situation.

Dean opened his mouth as if to speak but no words came. Kim looked back at the woman who was staring directly at Dean, her eyes never leaving him.

“Hello Michael,” said the woman.

Dean shook his head, ran his hands through his hair, and left the pub.

SUMMERTIME BLUES

at the

Dog & Duck

Chapter One

Dean - Three months earlier

Dean sprinted the short distance from the Dog and Duck pub where he worked – or should he say HAD worked until about three minutes earlier – to his small riverside studio apartment. He didn't know why he was running exactly, he just had an overwhelming need to escape, to get away from the situation and also from his inner turmoil. At that precise moment, he just wished he could climb out of his own skin and disappear.

He rounded the corner at the end of his road and hurtled through the last few hundred metres to his flat. He mounted the stairs and opened his front door with trembling hands, the key dancing around the lock as his shaking fingers tried to gain entry. He almost fell in through the door as it relented on the last turn of the key. He slammed the door shut behind him and leant back, sliding down, his back pressed hard against it. He came to a seated position on the floor, drawing his knees up to his chest and curling his arms across his face.

He sat there for an indeterminable length of time – it could have been five minutes; it could have been five hours. His mind veered between total darkness - void of anything but a black emptiness that threatened to suck him in and swallow him forever - and a whirling tornado of thoughts, emotions and flashbacks that played on a chaotic loop of speeded-up motion like some kind of surreal, 1920s silent movie.

He played the morning's events over and over in his mind. The way his morning had started - vowing to tell Kim everything about his past, feeling courageous and positive that honesty would hopefully win her affections - to the utter disbelief at seeing Grace, his ex-wife, standing bold as brass at the bar, chatting to Kim, over-dressed and groomed to perfection as ever. He had noted the designer sunglasses, the tailored jacket that was definitely not from the high street, and the flawless face, meticulously made up but still devoid of any warmth or genuine expression.

He'd really felt like he and Kim had turned a corner in their relationship. Once just his new landlady, then a friend, and now hopefully something more than a friend. But the shit had just hit the proverbial fan and he knew for certain that his ex-wife's unexpected presence was definitely not a good omen; more akin to a visit from the Grim Reaper heavily disguised in a pair of Jimmy Choos and a painted-on smile.

A loud banging on the front door interrupted Dean's thoughts...

"Michael, Michael! Open up, I know you're in there!"

He ignored the banging, hoping that it would go away; like a wasp at a barbeque, providing you remained perfectly still. He then remembered that wasps generally never went away without a fight or a well-

placed swat from a rolled-up tea towel and he feared that Grace would be similarly difficult to get rid of.

"Michael! Michael!" came the voice, growing increasingly shrill, the longer it was ignored.

Dean sighed and rose to his feet. "What do you want, Grace?"

"I just want to talk," said Grace, adopting a softer tone that sent chills through Dean's body. In his experience, the nicer Grace appeared to be, the more reason you had to be afraid!

"We finished talking, three years ago, we've nothing left to say," replied Dean, still behind the closed door.

"I really think you'll be interested in what I have to say," said Grace. "Now open the door before the neighbours come out for the floor show."

'Ah, the neighbours,' thought Dean to himself. Grace had always cared deeply about how she was perceived by strangers... just a shame she didn't care so deeply about the people she was **supposed** *to care about and whom she invariably trampled on to get her own way!*

Dean opened the door, just a crack, and peered round the edge. "Seriously, Grace: what are you doing here?"

"I just want to talk to you Michael, now let me in... please? If nothing else, you'll probably want to know what your new girlfriend said when I told her your name wasn't actually Dean at all!"

And there it was, the sting in the tail, the little stab of manipulation, casually thrown into a sentence, designed to shake and unnerve her prey when they least expected it. She reminded him of one of those snakes; the kind that dance and sway their victims into submission just before they sink their fangs into the jugular!

"My name is Dean now," snapped Dean. "I thought it was time for a new start, time to throw away all of the crap from my past. Dean was always my middle name anyway – as you well know – so now I'm just Dean Michael instead of Michael Dean... not that it is ANY of your business anymore!"

"Now, now darling, don't be like that. I really do just want to talk; I just want to put things right between us; get rid of any bad feeling."

Dean almost laughed at her last comment. "Bad feeling? Bad fucking feeling? You need to leave Grace; I really have nothing to say to you."

Grace's expression darkened. She had clearly thought that Dean had spent the last three years tormented by their break-up – which in a way he had – but not because he had pined for her as she arrogantly assumed he might, but more because he deeply regretted that he had allowed her to get under his skin and throw away everything in a moment of madness.

"Michael, I really don't want to argue with you – and Lord knows I don't want to upset the cosy little set-up you have going on here," she cast her eyes disdainfully

around Dean's small apartment, "but I am here to offer you an olive branch."

"I don't want your olive branch," said Dean, as calmly as he could manage and thinking that he might quite like to take her olive branch and shove it where the sun didn't shine! "Have you split up with Tom now then?"

A look of guilty recognition appeared fleetingly on her face before she regained her composure. There it was! He knew there had to be a reason for her sudden reappearance; Grace never did anything without an ulterior motive.

"It's not about that Michael, we have unfinished business; don't you think?"

"I think our business is well and truly finished Grace, so I would really like it if you would leave, and I would also prefer it if you didn't visit here again; or the place where I work for that matter."

"I haven't told your new girlfriend about your little misdemeanour Michael, but I will if I have to..."

"Do what you fucking like," said Dean wearily. "Now please just leave me alone," and he ushered her out of the door without ceremony.

She had rung on the doorbell a further three or four times as she stood sulking on the doorstep, but Dean ignored her; something he should have done three years ago.

Chapter Two

Kim - Three months earlier

Kim was not exactly a spring chicken, and she had been what they referred to as… around the block a few times… but she seriously couldn't have been more shocked than she was in that moment. Her life was turning into one long bloody soap opera.

The woman in front of her was so polished in her appearance that Kim was pretty sure she could see her own reflection, and her air of 'everyone is beneath me' was having its desired effect. Kim felt about as intimidated as it was possible to feel and she was pretty sure she didn't look all that 'cool', standing, as she was, with her mouth opening and closing like an asthmatic goldfish.

Dean, entering through the back of the bar, had laid eyes on the polished woman for about a nano-second before he'd let out a groan like a cornered bear and disappeared out of the kitchen door like greased bloody lightning! The woman's icy stare left Dean – who for some reason was now called Michael – and directed itself firmly at Kim. Kim stood, still frozen to the spot, and for once in her life, totally speechless.

"I'm Michael's wife," said the woman with an air of arrogance that quite frankly made Kim want to smash her in the face.

From nowhere, Kim found an inner courage that she did not know she possessed, spurred on by the fact that this woman appeared to be so far up her own backside that she was getting on Kim's very last nerve. Whatever Dean – who was now Michael – had done, Kim suspected that this woman may well have driven him to it. He could explain in his own sweet time (if he ever returned), but she was buggered if she was going to allow the polished woman to treat her like something that had got stuck to the bottom of her over-priced shoes for a moment longer.

"It is my understanding that you are Dean's EX-wife," said Kim hoping to God that she hadn't been misled on that fact as well.

The look of surprise on the polished woman's face gave her the reassurance she needed – Kim's mum Judy had always told her to confront a bully head on!

"It seems to me that you might be seeking a conversation with Dean but I'd rather it wasn't in my pub if you don't mind – now if you'll excuse me, I have to get ready for opening."

And with that, Kim turned and walked into the kitchen, leaving the woman to see herself out. Considering there were obviously more than a few skeletons lurking in Dean's cupboard, she really didn't relish a confrontation with a disgruntled ex-wife without at least being armed with some of the facts; she didn't doubt for one moment that the woman would have relished making her look a fool.

Kim's exit had the desired effect, and the woman left the pub, taking care to slam the door on her way out; presumably to make sure Kim knew that she was not used to insubordination from the peasants!

What the actual fuck she was going to do now though, Kim did not know. She had a chef who was longer her chef for the immediate future at least – and who quite possibly was not even the person he had claimed to be at all – a lunchtime service to contend with, and a head that was buzzing with questions. She had spent the last thirty years with the same man and now it seemed that new liaisons were coming and going like bloody buses! When all was said and done, she actually felt quite sad – she had grown to like Dean much more than she had admitted to herself and the sinking feeling in her chest that she may have been duped was just on the wrong side of crap!

For the time being, she would just have to deal with the immediate problem of how to get through a lunchtime of orders without a chef. She opened the fridge and saw that, Dean being Dean (or whoever the fuck he was), had everything well-prepared for today; everything was ready to go, normal service would be resumed... so why was there a bloody great lump burning in the back of her throat and tears threatening to spring from her eyes?

Chapter Three

Dean and Kim - Three months earlier (less one hour)

Now that Grace had finally got the message and left, Dean paced around the flat like a caged lion. He didn't know what to do for the best, but one thing was certain, he had to come clean... ***now****. He knew Grace well enough to realise that she would be mighty peeved at being ignored and he would much rather Kim heard the truth from him. His mind wandered to Kim, back at the Dog & Duck, likely feeling that someone had just rolled a hand grenade into her life. His heart hurt when he thought of how upset she must be feeling; not to mention that he'd just left her in the bloody lurch, running out of the back door like a total coward!*

He wasn't at all sure that she'd want him to stay on as her chef, let alone her friend, but the very least she deserved was an honest explanation. He washed his face in cold water, took a deep breath, and ran back to the pub.

When he walked in through the back door, Kim was in the kitchen, trying to make sense of the day's menu. She looked up when she heard the door open.

"Hi," said Dean, sheepishly. "I am so sorry about that. I'd like to explain if you'll let me?"

Kim nodded her head, not trusting herself to speak without blubbering like an idiot.

"I'm sure you'll have put two and two together by now, but that was my ex-wife... Grace."

"I gathered that," said Kim quietly. "But why did she call you Michael?"

At that moment, Rosa had come into the kitchen having been almost bowled over by an over-dressed woman in highly impractical shoes and sunglasses with lenses so dark that they had likely impaired her vision and caused her to crash into people on her rather huffy exit from the pub!

"Who was that woman?" she exclaimed. "Almost knocked me of my bloddy feet, I don't know..." she stopped short, as she sensed the tension in the room; you couldn't have cut the atmosphere with a sodding great carving knife!

"I'm sorry, has something happened?"

"No, it's fine. Dean and I were just... anyway, it's all fine. Everything is fine, I'll just... anyway... I'll just..." and with that, Kim had left the kitchen, feeling more stupid than ever.

Rosa had looked at Dean; her face a picture of bewildered confusion.

Dean sighed and ran his fingers through his hair. "It's a long story Rosa, but I am afraid I may just have royally fucked things up... again!"

Dean's statement had done nothing to ease Rosa's confusion but, in the wise and intuitive way that she read most situations, Rosa simply kissed Dean on the cheek with maternal affection and told him that everything would work out ok. Dean had smiled at her kindness but remained unconvinced that anything was going to be even slightly okay. After that, he had simply got on with the business of getting the lunches ready – he didn't know what else to do for the best and he was fairly certain that Kim would tell him to get lost if she didn't want him there; the time for shit number two to hit the fan would come soon enough.

For the rest of the shift, Kim had kept herself busy in the bar whilst Rosa had buzzed in and out of the kitchen with the food orders and dirty plates. She didn't trust herself to speak to Dean without crying and she was more than a little worried about what he had been hiding. Did she have cause to fear him? Why had he changed his name? Had he committed a crime? The questions buzzed around in her head like a swarm of bees. Several times, customers had had to repeat their orders because she wasn't listening – her mind was so preoccupied she just couldn't focus. By the end of the shift, she was so close to madness that she didn't care if Dean was in fact Michael or Jack the Bloody Ripper; whatever he had done, not knowing the truth was torture.

The last of the customers had left just before 3pm and Rosa had hugged Kim goodbye. "Ok mia cara?" she asked.

"Long story," sighed Kim. "I'm not even sure what the story is, if I am honest."

Rosa shook her head sympathetically and hugged her again. "You know where I am mia cara. You want me to stay?"

"No, honestly Rosa, I'm sure I'll be fine."

Kim had no idea how the afternoon was going to unfold but she was pretty certain that it wouldn't be made any less awkward by Rosa staying around.

After Rosa had left, Kim continued to clean the bar to within an inch of its life. She knew they needed to talk, but it just all felt so bloody awkward and if she was honest, she wasn't sure how awful the 'truth' was going to be. It felt like such a shame that they had gone from friends who couldn't have been more relaxed in each other's company, to what felt like strangers in the blink of an eye.

It had been Dean who had poked his head around the kitchen door and broken the stalemate first. He'd paced up and down in the kitchen for at least twenty minutes before plucking up the courage to emerge; torn between an uncomfortable, yet inevitable confrontation, and just bolting back out of the door. But he had decided that he couldn't run from his past anymore. He'd hoped it would stay buried, but Grace clearly had other ideas.

"I made you a cup of tea," he said quietly.

Kim looked and smiled; a smile so weak and full of sadness that the sight of it broke Dean's heart.

"My birth name is Michael Dean," said Dean, deciding to just rip the bloody plaster off, his voice trembling. He'd been through some shit in his life, but he'd honestly never felt as nervous as he did right now. The worst of it was, that he truly had so much respect for Kim, and he'd not been at all fair; although, in his defence, he hadn't expected to fall in love with his boss. If she'd been just someone he worked for, he wouldn't have felt the guilt he felt right now and perhaps his past wouldn't have mattered so much.

"Grace and I were married for five years – most of them spent with me trying to keep her happy; Grace isn't the easiest woman to please."

"I got that impression," said Kim. "Is she the same woman you never saw without makeup?" For some reason she felt the overwhelming urge to clarify that not every conversation they'd shared had been a lie.

Dean laughed dryly, "The same one! How many wives do you think I have had?"

This last comment had been an attempt at humour, but it hung in the air like a bad smell.

"I was away a lot in the army but for the last two years of our marriage I was stationed near to our home, so I had a kind of regular nine-to-five most of the time. Things were going better than they had been for a while; we were even expecting our first baby. It was

everything I had ever dreamed of – a proper family of my own."

"Do you have a child?" Kim almost shrieked. Surely he hadn't hidden that from her as well?

Dean shook his head; the pain of the memory still cut him to the quick.

"No," he said quietly. "I'm afraid not."

Kim's defences weakened as she saw the pain in his eyes.

"...Anyway, to cut a long and painful story short, one day I came home a lot earlier than five and she had clearly not been expecting me. She was in bed with one of my closest friends..." his voice trailed away.

"Oh!" said Kim. "I'm sorry about that Dean. But why the name change; why all the secrecy?"

"I lost it Kim, I totally flipped. I chucked him down the stairs. He landed in a crumpled heap at the bottom. We had to call an ambulance and he ended up with a broken collar bone and seventeen stitches in his head; he's lucky I didn't kill him. I think I could have just left if it hadn't been for what he said..."

He paused, the guilt choking his words. He couldn't look at Kim – he hadn't spoken out loud about that afternoon's events in three years, not since he'd given his statement to the police.

"What did he say?" asked Kim.

"He said…." Dean took a deep breath as he struggled to get the words out. It wasn't that he'd forgotten exactly what Tom had said – the words would be forever etched into his memory, they'd been on replay in his head one tortured sleepless night after another – it was just that to say them out loud again after all this time meant reliving the painful truth.

Kim reached across the table and squeezed Dean's hand urging him to continue.

He took a deep intake of breath and carried on. "He said, 'I'm sorry mate but Grace needed someone to comfort her after she lost the baby.'"

"Fucking hell," said Kim softly. "No wonder you flipped. And you didn't know?"

"I knew nothing about anything it seemed," sighed Dean. "In my gut, I am not sure she was ever actually pregnant; probably a tale to manipulate whatever she wanted out of me and Tom, but in that instant, I had lost everything – my wife and the unborn child I had wanted since I was just a kid myself; I just saw red. Anyway… I got discharged from the army for aggravated assault. I lost my wife, my career and my home in one fit of temper. The pair of them agreed not to press further charges as long as I gave them the house – they've been living there ever since. I changed my name because I wanted a fresh start. I wanted to try and be a better person… a different person if that makes sense? I didn't want to be my father's son."

Kim opened her mouth as if to speak but no words came – for once in her life she had literally no idea what to say.

"I was going to tell you, but it just never seemed the right time. I wanted it to stay in the past – everything else we've shared is the truth, I promise you. I'm not the same person I was…" His voice trailed away.

Kim paused. She felt for him, she really did. She knew first-hand what it felt like to be betrayed and humiliated and she couldn't begin to imagine how Dean had felt.

"Do you want me to leave?" he asked quietly.

"No!" replied Kim. "I really don't want you to leave – besides I need you to feed the customers." Her joke echoed in the silence, doing little to relieve the tension in the room.

Dean nodded his head. "I'd like to stay… and Kim… I really am very sorry."

"Shit happens," said Kim weakly, but they both knew that things had changed between them, for the time being at least.

Chapter Four

Things had returned to something near normal, but the kind of normal where things were artificially polite and neither Kim nor Dean dared to mention 'Grace-gate' again.

Kim had felt sure that she had seen Grace in town at least once since the incident, but she had put her head down and hurried away. If it *had* been her, Kim really didn't want a confrontation – there was nothing left to say – and if it hadn't been her, she would have looked a right twat if she had hung around gawping at strangers!

She didn't know if Dean had seen Grace again and truthfully, she didn't want to know; either way it didn't change things between them. What they'd had before, had been replaced by all kinds of weird – polite exchanges, comedy side steps that ended up looking like some kind of impromptu dance to avoid brushing against each other, and elaborate avoidance tactics to make sure they were never alone in a room together. Kim still liked him very much but perhaps she liked what she'd known before; the old Dean, before he became Michael who was still actually Dean!

Kim hadn't really spoken to anyone about Dean's revelation; Megan and Rosa knew that something was up, but they had the good grace not to pry. Things with Jake, the new barman, were working out well and the pub itself was ticking along nicely. She'd had a couple of conversations with Fleur, her friend from the Women Who Wine group but she hadn't elaborated much. She actually felt like a bit of a fool; relationship dramas at her age just felt so naff.

"We all have a past," Fleur had said. "God knows you weren't exactly married to a catch yourself!"

"Well thanks for that," Kim had sighed. "You should try joining the Samaritans; I'm sure you'd be a great help for depressed callers!"

They had both laughed at this and drained their glasses, vowing to remain independent and un-reliant on men for the foreseeable future in true girl-band style. Kim didn't suppose that either of them would be burning their bras any time soon – and she could not deny that having Dean around the place for heavy lifting and reaching high-up surfaces was hugely helpful at times – but she did know that she was ok on her own despite sometimes longing for the strong arms of a certain someone. If their 'relationship' was indeed dead in the water before it had begun, at least she knew that any liaisons moving forward would be entered into on a 'want' rather than a 'desperate need' kind of basis!

Chapter Five

As the days became longer and the nights became shorter, many of the customers were beginning to enjoy the pub garden that was now bursting into life after Kim and Dean's big clean up mission in the spring. Brightly coloured geraniums adorned every possible planter, tub and hanging basket and the place was a riot of colour. Kim loved geraniums – mainly because they flowered all summer and were almost impossible to kill, even for someone with her questionable gardening expertise.

Rosa had pretty much become Dean's right-hand woman in the kitchen and the partnership was working perfectly. Both of them were great cooks and both were hard workers, so Kim never had to worry about the quality of the food or the efficiency of its service. In truth, she was torn between feeling relieved that she didn't have to endure any polite and toe-curlingly awkward shifts in the kitchen with Dean, and a little envious that Rosa got to spend so much time with him. She noticed that they now shared little private jokes together and had both become supportive of the other. Their relationship was quite maternal on Rosa's part and Kim actually suspected that it was probably the first time in his life that Dean had experienced anything that even closely resembled a mother which, at 52, was actually pretty sad. In a way she was happy for him, she just wished that life didn't have to be so bloody complicated at times! Things had jogged along so strangely for several months now that it was difficult to know how to fix – if indeed, it could ever be 'fixed' between them.

Megan was a tower of support in the bar, and she had started to work on Saturdays too. On the rare occasion when her mum couldn't look after her daughter Lottie, she would bring her in to work. Kim loved having Lottie around. She was such a sweet and sunny little girl – wise beyond her nine years – and always eager to help and do 'grown-up' jobs. The regulars adored her, and Kim was sure that Lottie also enjoyed being spoilt; someone always bought her a sneaky fizzy drink or handed her a packet of crisps when Mum wasn't looking! If things got too busy, Lottie was quite happy sitting at one of the tables with her colouring books and giving cuddles to Chester, Doris and Brian's adoring Labrador who was more than happy to be petted all day.

It had been decided that they would hold a Dog & Duck summer barbeque in the garden to raise money for a local charity for which Tony, one of the older regulars in the pub, was an ambassador. For some inexplicable reason the theme was going to be 'Hawaii,' which Kim had thought was kind of ambiguous, but she was happy to indulge Tony's ambitious plans. Tony was an avid supporter of the pub and came in most days with a group of his octogenarian mates who Kim had affectionately named her 'saga louts.' To be fair to them, whilst their collective ages totalled more than the entire population of a small village, and their aim in the men's loos was less accurate than a dart player with a lazy eye, they could certainly put the youngsters to shame when it came to drinking stamina. Kim had often wondered how their ancient bladders stood up to the extraordinary volume of bitter they managed to consume in a lunchtime session, and she was sure their pickled livers could be donated to medical science for research in the future. The great thing about such an antique gang of drinkers was that they never outstayed their welcome – they arrived before midday and left before 3pm; off and away as fast as their mobility scooters would carry them and home in time for an afternoon nap and a bit of whatever sport was on the telly.

Tony was a lovely bloke, a little bit opinionated in the way that some older folk can be when they feel they have seen it all, but he'd done an awful lot to raise money for various charitable causes over the years. He was also a little bit of a flirt and Kim was certain that he got away with far more than he might have done had he been thirty years younger!

The barbeque was to be held on the last Saturday of June. In keeping with the Hawaiian theme, customers were encouraged to attend in Hawaiian costume which Kim assumed would be some lairy shirts for the men and a token flower garland for the ladies. She certainly wasn't going to be working in a grass skirt and a bikini and she didn't relish the thought of some of her customers baring too much flesh!

Dean and Rosa had planned some tasty salads and salsa style accompaniments to go with the standard barbeque fare of burgers, sausages, and some spicy chicken wings. Tony had ordered some bunting from eBay and a local guy from the neighbouring village had been booked to entertain the guests with a medley of music and popular tunes predominantly from the 60s and 70s, singing along to a pre-prepared backing track and filling in the gaps with his guitar. The guy had promised to play between 1pm and 5pm and Kim wondered how he would manage to play for four solid hours, but Tony had assured her that he was 'fantastic' and an 'old friend;' neither of which had filled Kim with any additional confidence. As a contingency plan, if he was truly awful then Kim had planned to ply him with a few coconut rums in the hope that he'd take a break and they could put the juke box on!

Anyway, it was all for charity, so the locals were bound to be forgiving... she hoped!

The preparations were just about complete, tickets were sold out and all that remained was the delivery of meat from Jim the butcher, which was due two days before the barbeque in just over a week's time. Kim sincerely hoped there would be no last-minute catastrophes... although she hadn't had one single visit from an angry ex-spouse in months!

Chapter Six

Fran forced her mouth into a smile as Bobby modelled the truly awful Hawaiian shirt that he had just received through the post. The bright red, heavily-flowered pattern did nothing for Bobby's puce complexion and the buttons of the shirt were under considerable strain across his beer belly. More alarming perhaps, was the fact that the shirt came with a pair of matching shorts with which Bobby was also chuffed, although God only knew why – Fran thought he looked like an overgrown, giant baby.

"This will be a right laugh," declared Bobby. "Steve has got a set too."

"Hilarious," replied Fran with a tone of sarcasm that was totally lost on Bobby.

She only hoped that nobody else had fallen prey to the 'shit Hawaiian outfits offer' on eBay, otherwise the pub barbeque was going to look like a sodding idiots' convention! There was a time when she would have joined in the celebrations with more enthusiasm – no doubt going all out with her own fancy dress offering – but that was when she had been drinking. As an ex-alcoholic, going to the pub was more of an endurance test than a pleasurable outing but Bobby was oblivious to her struggle. On the rare occasion that she had suggested she stay at home whilst he went on his daily pub bender or even more bravely offered an alternative venue to the pub, Bobby had simply laughed and told her that he needed to keep an eye on her; it wasn't his fault that she couldn't 'handle her drink' after all!

Fran had laughed bitterly at the irony of Bobby suggesting that taking someone to the pub daily when they had almost died from liver failure and now the mere sip of a fruit cider might actually finish them off, was the best way to assist rehabilitation and keep them safe! She had been given tablets when she came out of hospital that she was supposed to take each day to make sure she didn't drink again – she'd been so yellow when she'd been blue-lighted to A&E that she was almost fluorescent – but lately she had allowed the tablets to lapse. Fran knew that drinking again would probably kill her, but she wasn't sure how much longer she could sit in a pub every single day, staring at other people's drinks like a fat kid in a cake shop whilst she sipped on alcohol-free wine that tasted like grape juice without the all-important 'kick.'

"So, what are you wearing?" asked Bobby.

Fran held up the sad little garland that had cost her two quid in the card shop; if she had to go and show willing then that was the best they were going to get.

Bobby rolled his eyes and left the room to further admire himself in all his splendour. Fran heard him on the phone to Steve laughing raucously as they marvelled at their own comedy genius. With Steve being a good few inches shorter than Bobby, all Fran could picture when they both arrived at the pub was a sight not dissimilar to the Crankees on LSD!

She sighed and went back to loading the washing machine, giving a one-fingered salute to the drinks cabinet as she passed.

Chapter Seven

Kim was going to be taking a little time out on the Tuesday morning that she came downstairs and opened up the doors. She had a few errands to run in town and was going to take an hour to herself to get her nails done. The pub consumed pretty much every spare minute of her time and whilst she mainly loved it, she did feel the need for a break now and again.

After the barbeque weekend, they were going to try opening the Dog & Duck all day on Thursday to Sunday, as quite often these days they were shutting the doors at 3pm with people still eager to spend money at the bar. There were a couple of groups of local builders and tradesmen who had hinted that they would like to pop in for a quick pint or two on the way home from work and Kim knew she would be daft to turn customers away.

Rosa had agreed to work whole day shifts in the week on the agreement that she didn't do any weekday evenings. Jake was keen to do as many evening shifts as there were available and Megan was happy to do a few evenings as long as she could have the time off between the end of school and bedtime for her daughter Lottie. Dean pretty much lived in the kitchen and didn't seem to mind how many hours he worked and, apart from the giant bloody elephant in the room between Kim and Dean, everything seemed to be coming together nicely.

“I’ll see you all later,” called Kim, once all of the staff had arrived.

“Now don’t hurry back, mia cara,” said Rosa. “You deserve a little break.”

Kim smiled and blew a little kiss at Rosa and Megan although rather unfortunately, Dean emerged from the kitchen at precisely the ‘kiss-blowing moment’ and Kim blushed so furiously that she felt like her face was going to explode. Dean smiled and went to say something but thought better of it and the two of them turned away from each other so quickly in a bid to gloss over their awkwardness that Kim almost bumped smack bang into the open door.

“For fuck’s sake,” she exclaimed under her breath, wondering how she could feel like such a self-conscious twat at her age. Weren’t 50-year-old women supposed to have poise and grace? She currently had about as much poise and grace as Bambi on sodding ice!

Fortunately for Kim, Dean had felt almost as uncomfortable as she had and had disappeared back into his kitchen.

“For fuck’s sake,” exclaimed Dean as he shot back through the kitchen door. What the bloody hell was wrong with him? He was so fed up with feeling this awkward around Kim that he wished he could just do something about it, but he was buggered if he knew what that was! On so many occasions he had opened his mouth to start a conversation but no matter how hard he tried he couldn't get past, "I'm really sorry I didn't tell you that I chucked my ex-wife's lover down the stairs and almost broke his neck," in his head. How else did you start an apology of that magnitude?

He'd considered just cracking into a perfectly innocent conversation to break the ice but, on the rare occasion when he'd managed to muster the balls to do it, they'd ended up talking about the meat order or the day's special, which was hardly romantic and didn't lend itself to a smooth transition into easy conversation. They had chatted together so effortlessly before 'Grace-Gate,' but now it was all completely buggered; perhaps he should just grab her and snog her face off! God knows there was enough frustrated testosterone surging through his veins, and he had certainly thought about it on more than one occasion (hence the frantic morning jogging!) but it was a risky strategy and one that was likely to get him laid or larruped… and he feared the latter was a stronger possibility!

Megan and Rosa shared a raised eyebrow and a slight grin between them. They could both sense the tension between Kim and Dean and they both wished they would kiss and make up – literally! Rosa had tried to set the scene on a few occasions, leaving the pair of them alone, whilst she and Megan hid in the garden, pretending to water the plants and peeping around corners like a couple of giggling school kids but their matchmaking efforts had so far failed. They had resolved to let things take their natural course, but this was taking a lot longer than they had both hoped.

Kim took a deep breath as she climbed into her beloved pink car which had been bought in an act of rebellion when she had finally off-loaded her feckless husband, Keith. She turned the key in the ignition, resolving to shelve her embarrassment at the morning's unfortunate encounter, and made her way into town.

She stopped at Jax the florist first, collecting a beautiful bouquet of summer flowers for the bar.

"So what's the situation with the fancy dress for Saturday?" asked Jax. "I'm not sure I'm up for showing my legs in a grass skirt at my age."

Kim laughed. "Me neither! I'm sorry about the Hawaiian theme. It was Tony's idea, bless him. I tried to talk him out of it, but you know what a stubborn old bugger he can be at times! I'm just going to wear something summery with a garland and maybe a flower in my hair."

"Phew," said Jax. "I'm alright for flowers so I think I can just about manage that! Do you need any help at all?"

"Nope, all sorted thanks hun. Meat is coming next Thursday; salads and stuff will be done on the day. A few of the lads are putting up the bunting on Friday night in exchange for a free pint... ***before*** they go up any ladders, I hasten to add... and everything else is sorted. Apparently, Mel the music man brings all his own gear and doesn't take long to set up, forecast looks pretty good for Saturday, so fingers crossed..."

"Who is Mel?" asked Jax.

"Don't ask," sighed Kim. "An old mate of Tony's who is 'bloody good' in his words. I've got the jukebox on standby just in case!"

Jax laughed. "Give 'em enough rum and he'll get away with murder!"

"That's what I'm worried about! ...Anyway, better dash. Thanks for the offer, I'll give you a shout if I get stuck. I'll see you all on Thursday," said Kim referring to the weekly Women Who Wine networking group meeting, of which Jax was a member.

"Look forward to it," replied Jax and the two women said their goodbyes.

Kim completed her last couple of errands and made her way to Helen's beauty salon overlooking the green. She loved going there, the place was a real haven of calm and tranquillity. Spotlessly clean and decorated in white and pastel pink with accents of rose gold in the mirrors and fixtures and fittings. The reception area was plush and comfortable without being cluttered, and there was always a gorgeous smell coming from the wax burner, along with the unmistakeable aroma of fresh frothy coffee that was offered to customers on arrival.

Helen was busy in one of the treatment rooms when Kim arrived a little earlier than planned and so she took a seat in one of the velvet chairs and gratefully accepted her decaff latte. She picked up one of the glossy magazines from the small side table and began leafing through its pages, beautiful girls with flawless skin and legs like a giraffe stared back at her through sultry eyes, lips pouting sulkily. Kim hoped to God they were air brushed as there was genuinely no hope for the rest of them otherwise! In Kim's experience, once you got to 50 nearly every part of your body succumbed to gravity in one way or another, unless it had dried out and shrivelled up entirely of course... But then she also didn't remember having flawless skin or giraffe legs in her twenties either!

At the sound of the back-room door opening, Kim looked up just as Helen's gaze met hers with an expression of, 'Ohhhhh... Shit!' For one second Kim was confused as to why the sight of her might render Helen so alarmed, but she soon saw the cause of that alarm. A few steps behind her was a face that Kim recognised instantly and one which looked sulkier than ever, if that were even possible...

"Olivia," said Kim calmly, acknowledging the entrance of her estranged husband's bit of 'fluff,' former bar manager of the Dog & Duck and the main catalyst for said husband's absence in Kim's life.

Olivia ignored Kim with an almost theatrical flounce. Kim suppressed the urge to laugh at this childish display, especially when she herself was the aggrieved party. Olivia had been literally caught red-handed – or red-lipped as it turned out – getting up close and personal with Keith in the cellar and now here she was acting indignant. Although part of her strop was probably due to the fact that Kim had 'stolen' the pub from Keith and Olivia and squashed their dreams of becoming Landlord and Landlady of the manor. What Kim had *actually* done was to be savvy enough to keep a pub that had been left solely to her in her uncle's will, refusing to share it with the un-entitled Keith who was firmly of the opinion that she – and the rest of the world – owed him a living!

"I bet *she* gets what *she* wants," said Olivia as she paid her bill and in a voice that was deliberately loud enough for Kim to hear. "She usually does!"

"Oh God, I am SO sorry," exclaimed Helen to Kim as Olivia left the salon. "One of the girls took the booking; I've been making excuses not to treat her for weeks."

"It's fine," replied Kim. "You don't need to feel responsible for my crap! I'm so over it all now, seriously."

"To be honest," said Helen, "it's not just the fact that she's an out-and-out trollop, but I've never particularly liked her and she wants me to do her lashes now she's got some extra cash from her sugar daddy – sorry – but I refuse to have her strutting around with a couple of dead spiders on her eyelids and telling everyone she got them done here; it could ruin my business!"

Kim laughed. "They say there's no such thing as bad publicity you know!"

"Yeah, that may work when you're one of the Kardashians, but it won't wash around here! I gave her an eyebrow wax but told her I didn't stock the lashes she wants; that's why she had a face like a smacked arse when she left."

Kim giggled. "How can you tell? When she worked at the pub, I never saw her with anything other than 'resting bitch face.' Keith's welcome to her. If they did but know it, they both did me a massive favour; I got rid of a useless husband and a useless bar manager in one fell swoop!"

Helen smiled. "Yeah, I'm sure they'd both be mighty pissed to know how much they actually helped you out! Well, as long as you're okay? I know it isn't really anything to do with me, but you've been good to our little group and the pub is just awesome now. I'm all for a bit of female solidarity!"

"Oh bless you. It's been great having you all in the pub and I'm so grateful for the way you have supported me. I don't suppose I could bung you a little tip to wax her eyebrows right off next time, could I?"

"If ever I decide to retire then I might just be persuaded – I'd love to see her face!" laughed Helen. "I don't think she'll be back anyway. I pointed her in the direction of the budget nail bar in the main town. The girls coming out of there have lashes so long they can barely open their eyes – she'll love it!"

Kim took her seat at the nail bar and relaxed back in her chair, allowing Helen to pamper her for a short while. Two hours later she emerged with glossy pink nails, a fresh brow shape and tint, some tasteful lashes and a pedicure that made her feel like she was walking on air. She had to admit she felt fabulous and so relaxed – the encounter with Olivia had done nothing to spoil her morning and was living proof that splitting up with Keith was a decision she should probably have made years ago.

When she arrived back at the pub, the place was a flurry of activity as the staff rushed around clearing up after a particularly busy lunchtime session and more drinkers waited for one last drink before they shut at three. So much for feeling relaxed, Kim rolled up her sleeves and pitched in to help.

Bobby and Steve propped up the bar, boring each other to death with their tall tales whist Fran sat in the corner like a little lost soul. The old boys were slurping the last of Shepherd Neame's finest before staggering home on creaky old legs for a well-oiled nap, and the last few clunks from the pool table signified the end of a close match where one of the players was 'definitely robbed' on the black.

In under an hour, customers were ushered out of the door, the bar was clear and polished, tables were wiped, and Megan had given the loos a quick once over before the evening session. Kim said goodbye to her staff and went upstairs to enjoy a quiet cuppa and put her feet up before she re-opened her doors.

On Tuesday afternoons, Kim usually FaceTimed her mum Judy – this being the only afternoon where she wasn't out playing bridge, shopping, flower-arranging or at any one of the many social engagements her calendar had to offer.

"Hey Mum, how's your week been?" Kim asked, as Judy's smiling face appeared on her phone screen.

"Yes, all good thanks love. What about you? Your lashes look nice."

Kim smiled, "I didn't think you'd notice but thanks. Yes, all good. We've got the summer barbeque next week, so things have been a bit hectic, but I think we are ready now. I saw Olivia in Helen's salon today."

"Little bitch," remarked Judy. "I hope you gave her a piece of your mind."

"To be honest mum, I genuinely don't care anymore. I'm actually not bothered at all."

"Yes, well that should tell you a thing or two; you're better off without that idiot in your life. Talking of men in your life have you sorted things out with Dean? He's a nice man, you know."

"I know Mum, but things are just so weird now. I'm a bit hurt that he lied to me, but then I also kind of think he was entitled to keep his past private. I'm not really cross with him, but things just feel so bloody awkward – perhaps it wasn't meant to be."

"Things have a habit of working out the right way my love, try not to worry. Now I'm going have to dash because I have a call with Anne from the local prayer chain. We phone each other once a month and talk about all the people who are poorly – it's lovely!"

"Sounds thoroughly uplifting," laughed Kim.

They said their goodbyes and Kim settled back in the chair and put her feet up. Before long, her eyes grew heavy, and she surrendered to an afternoon snooze.

When she awoke thirty minutes later, she had a crick in her neck, the telly had switched to standby, and she had thirteen unopened text messages from Keith.

They read as follows…

'You have really upset Olivia'

'I hope you are enjoying MY money!'

'I don't know how you sleep at night' (Kim chuckled at this one considering she had just woken from a very sound sleep!)

'My solicitor will be in touch'

'You can ignore me all you like – I'm not going away'

…There were several more messages of growing hysteria as Keith obviously became more infuriated by Kim's audacity regarding her failure to reply. Kim couldn't be arsed to read all of them and toyed with sending a witty and cutting message but chose instead to ignore him as she knew this would infuriate him much more than a response!

Unfortunately, she had underestimated Keith's frustration and before long, her phone was ringing.

"Keith. How can I help?" she answered.

"Don't be fucking cocky with me!" snapped Keith, before launching into a petulant outpouring.

"Let me stop you there Keith," said Kim interrupting his flow. "If you continue to rage at me like a stroppy teenager, I will hang up and switch off my phone. If you have anything to say to me, I suggest you communicate through our solicitors... otherwise I will report you for harassment...AGAIN! If your girlfriend is upset that I happened to be in the same beauty salon as her today, then I can only apologise; I will remember to ask her permission before I go next time. And with regard to YOUR pub, I think you are well aware that legally it is MY pub, but I am sorry if you do not feel comfortable with the fact that you do not have a leg to stand on. Now please leave me alone, I believe our divorce will be finalised very soon and then we can both go our separate ways properly and you can spend all YOUR money on Olivia!"

Kim could hear Keith almost hyper-ventilating with rage, and she stifled a giggle.

"What were you doing in a bloody beauty salon at your age?" snapped Keith, resorting to a low blow designed to undermine her as he had always done when cornered.

Unfortunately for Keith, Kim no longer gave a rat's arse what he thought, and his words did not make her feel like shit as they may previously have done. Instead, she simply replied, "Oh grow up Keith!" and hung up her phone.

She switched the ring tone to silent; she could check any missed calls later that may be important, but it meant that she didn't have to be irritated by Keith for a single second longer; she felt as triumphant as someone who had just swatted a particularly annoying fly!

Chapter Eight

Fleur drummed her manicured nails on the desk, "I don't know what you're looking at," she questioned with raised eyebrows to Bonnie, the older of her two Husky fur-babies who was sat on the floor beside her, head cocked to one side. "He'll be here soon and there's no going back now."

Clyde came and joined his sister, wagging his tail and nudging Fleur's hand for a tickle, "And you," she laughed. "You won't be the man of the house for much longer!"

Fleur had been dating Rob for almost five years and up until this moment they had shared their time between each other's houses; staying over at weekends and sometimes in the week. Fleur had known that something had been bugging Rob for a while now and she astute enough to have an inkling that Rob wanted to take their relationship a step further. She knew that she loved him – he was a good bloke and fun to hang around with – but she'd guarded her independence so fiercely for so long that she wasn't sure how to let go of the reins and share her life completely with another human. They went on holidays together – lots of them – they went out with friends together, they watched movies indoors together, and so, when she really analysed things she couldn't totally put her finger on what was actually going to change for them, and she knew that her fears were emotional rather than rational; she was so good at rational decision making in her business life, perhaps it was time she tried the same approach for her personal life!

Anyway, the time had come, and they'd had 'the chat.' Rob had told her honestly that he wanted more than a shared social calendar; he actually wanted marriage, the whole works, but Fleur's panic-stricken expression had persuaded him to tread a little more softly and suggest that they try living together full-time in one house. Fleur knew for sure that she definitely didn't want them to split up, so she had pulled up her big girl pants and decided to go for it – what's the worst that could happen?

Her own parents' marriage had been one of those very traditional affairs where her dad had pretty much controlled everything from where they lived to how their every penny was spent. Her mum had surrendered herself completely to marriage and had been happy for him to take the reins. They had a joint bank account that she wouldn't use unless Fleur's dad physically gave her money despite having a cash card of her own. 'I like him to offer it without me asking,' she would say. The whole lack of control over one's own life used to infuriate Fleur and she still couldn't get her head around it. Her mum had no idea about their life insurance, mortgage payments, who they banked with or when the car tax was due. She was quite happy to stay at home, ironing her tea towels and cleaning the windows. As the years went by, Fleur accepted the fact that her parents were happy with their marriage, but it wasn't a life she would ever choose for herself and almost definitely one of the driving forces behind her becoming financially independent and totally self-sufficient.

She heard the key turn in the lock and watched as Bonnie and Clyde ran to greet their new house mate... traitors; they were over the moon to see him and certainly not experiencing any cold feet!

Rob walked into the house; his face obscured by the biggest bouquet of lilies that Fleur had ever seen – he knew they were her favourite even though he always complained that they made the house smell like wee! He plonked the flowers down on the kitchen table and pulled Fleur in towards him. He smelled of the aftershave that she had bought him for his birthday and when he kissed her, she felt a tingle in several places... perhaps if her body was going to succumb to him so shamelessly then she might as well follow suit!

Bonnie and Clyde sulked as they were unceremoniously shoved into the garden whist Rob and Fleur celebrated their new beginning in the traditional way; even after five years together they were still more than compatible between the sheets and Fleur knew that the last thing she wanted was to try and find what they had with someone new. She winced at the thought of another man seeing her mis-matching underwear or God forbid hearing her fart in her sleep; one of the great things about a long-term relationship was the ability to feel relaxed in each other's company both in and out of the bedroom. She also couldn't imagine another man being able to pull off Rob's 'Elvis has left the building' joke after a passion session – he still made her laugh, and she knew deep down that was something to hang on to.

"Come on you two," laughed Rob, letting the two disgruntled dogs in from the garden. "Your mum's quite safe! Things are going to have to change around here now I'm the new top dog!"

Fleur rolled her eyes, "I've only agreed to let you move in, so I've got someone to put the bins out on a Monday morning!"

"Anything for you, babe," said Rob, patting Fleur on the bottom. "Shall we go out to celebrate?"

"I'm not sure a Tuesday night is the best for a wild night out," replied Fleur. "We could have a pint in the Dog & Duck if you like?"

"You know how to spoil me," laughed Rob.

Fleur went to have a shower while Rob dragged his suitcases in from the car. The plan was for him to rent his own house out fully furnished, so apart from his clothes and some personal items, there wasn't much to move in. He'd hired a company to pick up the larger items in the morning which they'd store in the spare room for now until they made a decision about where things would go, although Rob was under no illusions as to the amount of clout he'd have in the decision-making process when it came to the Feng Shui and organisation of his belongings! He didn't care where his stuff went, he was just glad that they'd finally made things properly official after five long years.

Once Fleur was showered and changed, they got ready to leave, but not before Rob had asked her at least ten times if she was ready yet. On the final time, Fleur had thrown a hairbrush at him and told him that asking her the same question over and over again did nothing to speed the process up! He'd done the traditionally bloke-y thing when it came to getting ready which involved changing his shirt, cleaning his teeth and glancing in the mirror for all of about five seconds before pacing up and down and waiting for Fleur to finish getting ready!

They settled the dogs down before they left and drove to the pub – they planned to get a taxi and collect the car in the morning if they stayed for more than a couple of drinks.

The pub was quite busy when they arrived – it was darts night and the visiting team had just arrived. The Bull and Arrows had travelled from The King's Head which was about twenty miles away. They had arrived in a minibus that had so many rust holes it looked like they had used it for practise! They were a rowdy bunch, their youngest player just 19 and their oldest about 90. Fleur didn't think she had seen so many tattoos in one gathering and she had certainly underestimated the loyalty of a certain local football team's supporters, the club badge being proudly displayed on an assortment of biceps – young and old, male and female!

One of the younger women on the darts team had arrived ready for the beach it seemed. She was dressed head to just below her bum cheeks in a flesh-coloured dress that left little to the imagination. The cross-over top was working at full strength to restrain her ample boobs that looked to have been the result of an expensive trip to an overseas cosmetic surgery resort. The skirt of the dress was so short that Kim had been reminded of her old grandad's words of warning about 'keeping your hand on your ha'penny,' whenever she had gone out in anything less than a full-length smock as a teenager.

As the shots flowed, the woman's 'ha'penny,' became dangerously close to a full reveal. Two of the lads on the team followed her closely for the entire evening, practically drooling like a pair of cartoon dogs in a butcher's shop. There was a tense moment when she bent over to retrieve a stray dart and several members of the pub held their breaths for entirely different reasons!

The queue for the bar was pretty substantial so Fleur and Rob had grabbed a table and decided to wait until the rush died down. Fleur felt a little nervous, she really wanted to tell Kim about Rob moving in; she felt guilty that she hadn't confided in her already, they had become really close, and they shared most things between them. Kim had met Rob once or twice but not properly. Fleur desperately wished that Kim and Dean would just stop dancing around each other and then perhaps the four of them could go out for dinner as couples… although seeing as it had taken her five years to take the plunge, she was hardly in a position to give relationship advice!

"It looks great in here," said Rob. "It used to be a bit of a dive; your friend's done well!"

"Well thank you," smiled Kim, coming over to their table.

Fleur stood up and hugged Kim. "You've done a great job babe. Can we get a drink now; we thought we'd let the rush die down before we hassled you!"

"Yes, they're all watered now, they'll be quiet for a few minutes at least," laughed Kim. "Shall I bring your drinks over?"

"No, I'll come to the bar," said Fleur, linking her arm through Kim's. She was desperate to share her news with her friend. If she left it any longer, things could become a bit awkward further down the line. "Rob's moved in…" she waited for Kim's reaction.

"Aarrgh!" screamed Kim, pulling Fleur into a hug.

"Sssshhh! Everyone's looking!"

"Sod them," said Kim. "I'm so happy for you."

"Do you think I'm doing the right thing?"

"Oh shut up," laughed Kim. "You practically live together anyway, he seems like a nice bloke, he makes you happy and he definitely doesn't seem brave enough or daft enough to try and control you!"

"He's definitely not daft enough to try that," giggled Fleur. "Yeah, you're right. He's a lovely bloke and I am really happy with him, so I figured it was about time I stopped faffing about – if I was going to self-analyse, I know this was as much about my parents' relationship as my own. I'm sorry I didn't tell you."

"Ooo get you, Sigmund Freud! Seriously it's fine babe, now what are you having... bubbles?"

"Bubbles sounds great," replied Fleur. "Any news on the Dean front; I could do with some dinner party friends?"

"I've given up there," sighed Kim. "Every time I think I'm going to say something I just clam up. It's awkward as arse between us and let's face it, we are never alone long enough to chat privately. Although the last time we actually did start chatting we ended up talking about the new menu which is hardly sexy!"

Kim put a bottle of her very best sparkling Chardonnay into an ice bucket, placing two long-stemmed flutes onto the bar beside it. Fleur reached into her purse for her card, but Kim held her hand up in refusal...

"No way, babe, my treat. You've helped me so much, it's the least I can do."

Fleur blew her a kiss and took the bottle over to Rob, whilst inwardly resolving to try and get Kim and Dean talking again – she wasn't sure how, but she was determined to try; any fool could see those two were perfect for each other.

By the end of the evening the pub looked like something from a zombie apocalypse. Kim had never seen so many thoroughly drunk people in one place, which was quite a feat considering she ran a pub! They swayed back and forth, their feet rooted to the spot and their bodies almost defying gravity by not toppling over. The unbelievable thing was that the more inebriated the visiting darts team had become, the straighter their aim had been, and they annihilated the Dog & Duck team. Kim and Rosa had both given up trying to understand their orders as they slurred and mumbled their way through the impressive list of drinks and simply resorted to bringing over a tray of refreshments that looked similar to the tray they had before! The evening had been good for the takings, but Kim wasn't sad to see them leave. Dean and Rob had manually assisted some of the leaving party, pouring them into their rusty old minibus to aid them in their passage – without the assistance, Kim feared they would have still been there in the morning taking one step forward and two steps back on repeat.

Fortunately for all concerned, the girl with the 'ha'penny' had possessed an impressive ability to hold her liquor and had somehow managed to alight the bus steps without flashing the punters which was a huge relief for most and a mild disappointment for others!

Chapter Nine

The rest of the week passed in a blur as preparations for the charity barbeque were ramped up. A couple of the regular lads had come in to help put up a large Gazebo in the garden, both for shade if it got too hot – Kim didn't want old folk fainting and dehydrating throughout the afternoon – and also in case they were unlucky enough to get rain, although the weather forecast seemed to suggest that luck was most definitely on their side.

Every available hook, shelf and wall had been adorned with tropical-themed bunting both inside and outside the pub and Kim had to admit that the place certainly looked like something special was about to happen. She'd even ordered some Hawaiian napkins for the table – she had resigned herself to the fact that tenuous or not, the tropical theme had well and truly taken a hold on the proceedings, and she figured if she couldn't beat them, then she'd have to join them! Unfortunately, when the napkins arrived, they were tiny and actually meant as paper coasters for glasses; something which Kim had always felt to be kind of pointless. She had messaged the online supplier to tell them about the mistake as she knew that she had checked the dimensions before ordering but was told that the dimensions she had been given were for the size of the box not the actual napkins! Kim had pointed out the ridiculousness of this in no uncertain terms, but the recipient of her messages had struggled to see the issue.

"When I order a dress, I ask for the size of the dress when it is made, not the size of the bloody material it was cut from!" Kim had fumed.

But no, the reply was just a standard, "We are sorry if you are unsatisfied, but we did supply the dimensions as asked, would you like to order any more?"

At this, Kim had taken a deep sigh and decided to leave matters there. It was going to cost her more than the napkins themselves to return them and they were hardly crucial to the success of the whole event - thankfully!

Early on Saturday morning, she had whizzed into the large DIY store in town for a last-minute purchase of extra barbeque briquettes; just in case the six large bags they already had weren't enough! A young lad with long blue hair dozed at the customer service desk wearing a badge that said, 'Happy to help.' He had reluctantly pointed Kim in the direction of the appropriate aisle with a bored tone that indicated he was not at all happy to help, before going back to sleep at his desk.

She had got back to the pub just as Rosa and Dean arrived. Megan was already in the bar giving the floor a last minute hoover and the tables a final wipe down – the whole place looked amazing.

"It looks great in here Megan, thank you!" said Kim. "Is little Lottie joining us later on?"

"She's at her friend's today; party and sleepover."

"Oh bless her, she'll have more fun there than surrounded by a load of old dears in grass skirts," laughed Kim.

Megan smiled but Kim couldn't help noticing that she seemed distant. "You okay darling, you seem a bit down?"

"No, I'm fine," said Megan unconvincingly. "Just a bit tired, I think," and she hurried off to put away her cleaning tools.

"She's not been herself for over a week," said Rosa, coming into the bar.

"Do you think she's okay?" asked Kim. "She's always so happy usually."

"I'm not sure," replied Rosa. "I'll try to speak to her later; things are harder for her than she lets on sometimes I think."

"You're probably the best one to speak to her," said Kim. "She loves you."

Rosa tapped the side of her nose, "I'm on the case, mia cara," she smiled.

Kim didn't know what they would do without Rosa. Sometimes she thought that Rosa was the glue that held them all together like a favourite Grandmother or an Italian Mumma. All she did know for sure was that the pub – and all of them – would be lost without her.

Dean entered the bar at that moment carrying a tray full of pastries and five creamy cappuccinos. "Come on ladies, sit yourself down, today is going to be mental so let's have a quick bite and five minutes' peace while we can!"

As if on cue, Jake appeared at the bar hatch ready to claim the fifth coffee from the tray that he knew had his name on it! "I'm starving, I've only been up about an hour, late night revision is a killer!"

Megan reappeared from having tidied things away, looking a little less subdued and definitely happy to see that breakfast had arrived. They sat together, eating and chatting about the day ahead. Lunch service had been pared back to just sandwiches and baguettes and the barbeque itself didn't start serving until 2pm. Kim couldn't imagine they'd get many walk-ins as pretty much every regular had bought a ticket for the event. The music man, who was also Tony's friend Mel, was arriving to set up at midday ready for his performance to begin at 1pm. He had sent some posters for Kim to put up in the pub two weeks before the event which showed a rather grainy photo of a bloke in a suede jacket under the headline 'Mel Plays Guitar," to which Kim had responded, "I bloody well hope so, seeing as that is what we are paying him for!"

Once they had finished breakfast, they opened the doors ready for the day to begin. As predicted, the pub was empty until just before 12, when Mel arrived. Kim had been crouched down behind the bar, re-filling the ice buckets from the ice machine when she had felt a hand on her back. She had screamed and stood upright almost poking the owner of the hand in the eye with a pair of ice tongs!

"Sorry love, I didn't mean to startle you," said the owner of the hand. "I'm Mel. I play guitar."

Kim dropped the offending ice tongs and took a step backwards. Mel might play guitar, but he didn't have much regard for personal space it seemed!

Mel was of indiscriminate age – probably somewhere between sixty and seventy-five – and was wearing what was clearly his trademark suede, single-breasted jacket and sporting a mod style haircut that made him look like somebody's grandad who was trying way too hard to be cool. A pair of dark black sunglasses perched on the top of his head, and a gold hoop earring in his left ear completed his look.

"You've probably heard of me," he said proudly.

"Yes, Tony told me all about you," replied Kim, knowing full-well that this was not what Mel had meant at all, clearly believing that he was tantamount to Paul Weller in these parts!

“They’ll all know me in here,” said Mel, trying to further convince Kim of his celebrity status.

“That’s great,” said Kim awkwardly. She didn’t have the time or the inclination to be bolstering the ego of an ageing rocker in a badly-fitting jacket and sporting a hairstyle that looked like it had been done by his mum under a pudding basin but with a couple of long bits over the ears that had been overlooked!

“I’ll show you where to set up.”

Kim led Mel out through the kitchen past Dean and Rosa who were putting the finishing touches to the salads. “This is Mel. He plays guitar,” she said with a hint of irony that was totally lost on the overconfident Mel.

Dean and Rosa both smiled but said nothing.

Kim showed Mel to the makeshift stage that had been set up for his performance – it was hardly Wembley, but it would have to do. Mel began to set up his gear which consisted of a microphone, a small speaker, and a guitar plugged into an amp, whilst regaling Kim with his entire gigging history including some rather dubious links to the Rolling Stones. Fortunately for Kim, she was called into the kitchen, and she was able to escape from Mel who would have to make do with the company of his own ego for the time being!

At a quarter to one, the guests began to arrive in earnest and before long Jake, Kim and Megan were buzzing around the bar like little bees trying to cope with the sudden influx of drink orders. Tony had been the first to arrive as mastermind of the event, wearing what would prove to be one of the standard-issue patterned shirts in garish colours – there was probably an obscure clothing supplier on eBay somewhere, who was currently rubbing his hands together with glee at offloading his entire shite shirt collection in the space of a week! Tony's wife Jean arrived wearing a hat bedecked in fruit that made her look like Carmen-bloody-Miranda which was a strange choice for a Hawaiian event and geographically about 7,000 miles east as the crow flies from the intended destination!

"If he's as good as he thinks he is, we'll have Simon-bloody-Cowell knocking on the door before teatime," laughed Kim as she took refuge from Mel's monologue to assist in the kitchen.

"Let's hope his music is less outdated than that awful haircut," replied Dean. "I could have given him a better style with one of my salad knives!"

"Oh don't," said Kim. "I've a horrible feeling that's he's going to be dreadful!"

"I'll put extra rum in the punch," said Rosa, "they'll be too sozzled to notice!"

A little after 1pm Kim's suspicions were confirmed, and Mel showed himself to be nothing like the musical impresario he imagined. It seemed he knew little more than three chords on the guitar, but he had an array of backing tracks on a tablet that he had fixed to a clip on the side of his microphone stand that were so full-bodied that he could quite literally have left the tablet playing and walked away with little impact.

He could hold a tune... just about... and basically just sung along to his prepared soundtrack whilst interjecting with the odd random chord on his guitar and curling his lip in what he obviously thought was an unbelievably sexy move. Kim thought she might just have well turned the bloody juke box on and let one of the regulars sing along in front of it! The Trading Standards would have had a field day with Mel's spurious description of himself and his musical prowess; 'Mel does a little bit of shit karaoke' might have been a slightly more accurate strap line! The bizarre thing was, the older members of the clientele seemed to be lapping it up and the old dears were gazing wistfully at the dashing Mel like a group of octogenarian groupies whilst the men nodded their heads in approval and said, "They don't make them like that anymore, Tony!"

"Thank the Lord," thought Kim. "I'm sure Ed Sheeran is quaking in his bloody boots!"

By three o'clock, the barbeque was well and truly underway, and the rum punch was working its magic. Mel was showing no signs of slowing down and Kim feared he might well fulfil his four-hour set – she only hoped he didn't do any encores!

Steve and Bobby had arrived looking like Tweedle Dum and Tweedle Dee, resplendent in their floral shirts and shorts combos. The long-suffering Fran had trudged in wearily behind them, a sad little garland around her neck, her vape clutched in her hand like a life support device. She sipped at her virgin punch quietly, looking like she was present at her own wake!

Bobby and Steve had held court, walking around together, arms around each other's shoulders, Steve almost on tip toes as he struggled to reach his arm around his friend who was at least a head and shoulders taller than him. They thought they looked hilarious, and they did, but Kim doubted that they realised the laughs they were raising were more at them than with them!

"He looks like he's going to bloody burst," laughed Doris as Kim served her a gin and tonic.

"I dread to think what his blood pressure is," sighed Kim. "His face is the same colour as that terrible shirt – he must be ten pints up already."

"Poor old Fran," said Doris. "I don't think I've ever seen her smile. I'm sure I saw her sneak a ladle of the real punch into her glass just now."

"Oh Christ," said Kim. "Isn't she on tablets? I thought she wasn't allowed to drink anymore?"

"She isn't," replied Doris. "I know you've got a pub to run, but I really don't think she should come in here; it's a disaster waiting to happen."

"I agree," said Kim. "To be honest, business or no business, I'd rather she didn't come either. The last thing I want is for people to start keeling over... or worse!"

At four o'clock there was a merciful break in Mel's karaoke routine and Tony began the raffle. Bless him, he was a lovely fella, but once he was given a microphone it was the devil's own job to get him off it! The calling of the prizes seemed to last forever and there was some confusion over the difference between the buff-coloured tickets and the white ones – the whole thing nearly descended into fisticuffs when John's wife Brenda claimed a bottle of peach schnapps on a blue ticket number 99. She had just got back to her table when she was challenged by Ron's wife Ivy who claimed that *she* had the winning ticket – it was several minutes before Ivy could be convinced that she had her own ticket upside down! Fortunately, a free glass of punch proved enough of a bribe to ease tensions and for Ivy to sit back down whilst her husband Ron told her she was a daft old bat and, 'hadn't he told her to put her other glasses on!'

The only good thing about the raffle taking so long was that Dean and Rosa had enough time to clear away most of the food trays and dirty dishes from the barbeque area and Megan and Jake had done a sterling job of scooping all the paper plates into black bin bags and getting the glasses collected and washed ready for round two – there was no way a single one of those wily old codgers was going to miss their chance of a raffle prize!

"Can Mel actually play the guitar?" asked Fleur to Kim whilst they shared a quick five minutes inside the pub away from the mayhem.

"Depends on your interpretation of 'play'," laughed Kim. "I think he only knows one chord – although that may actually be a small mercy in itself! How are things going with Rob?"

"Really good," said Fleur. "I'm not quite sure what I was worried about to be honest – we were practically living together anyway. I'm 48-years-old for Christ's sake; I've hardly rushed into things!"

"Well, you're a step ahead of me," smiled Kim. "I did rush in twenty-odd years ago and then I rushed back out again!"

"Any progress on the Dean front?" asked Fleur.

Kim began to answer but then Dean walked into the bar and her face turned the colour of Bobby's shirt and she hurried away, feeling as self-conscious as a teenager on a first date.

Dean raised his eyebrows at Fleur. “I have that effect on women,” he smiled wryly.

Inwardly Fleur screamed with frustration – these two were honestly hopeless!

Chapter Ten

Once the raffle had finally come to an end, Mel took to his stage once more and cracked into a run of reggae covers that Kim felt sure would have had Bob Marley turning in his grave! Even more alarmingly, this latest set produced some rather alarming gyrating from some of her customers as they attempted some unique 'skanking' that Kim feared may render a trip to the osteopath in the morning!

As usual, Bobby and Steve tried to out-manoeuvre each other in a series of moves that simply made them look as though they had shit themselves! When they got up onto the stage pretending to be Mel's backing singers the whole crowd erupted into fits of laughter; they really were very comical, although perhaps funnier still had been the expression on Mel's face... he had not seen the funny side one little bit and clearly took himself way too seriously. Eventually he snatched an errant tambourine from Bobby's hand and more or less shoved the pair of them off his makeshift stage, furious that they had tried to steal his thunder. This had only served to make Steve and Bobby laugh even louder and they proceeded to gyrate and limbo dance in front of Mel blowing theatrical kisses in his direction. At one point, Bobby tried to limbo under a trestle table and had collapsed on the floor in a fit of giggles, his huge belly wobbling like a under set blancmange.

Fran observed the scene with a look of resigned disgust and left her chair to go and vape in the smoking area to the side of the car park. Once Steve had finally managed to get Bobby upright, they retired to the bar to quench their thirsts. Kim served them their beers before leaving to take a tray of drinks out into the garden. Megan and Rosa were still clearing and serving tables and Dean was busy tackling the carnage in the kitchen.

Several minutes later, Kim observed Steve back in the garden but there was no sign of Fran or Bobby. She paid little attention – Fran was probably vaping her way to sanity in the car park, and it was not unlike Bobby to spend much of a drinking session in the loos, emptying his over-worked bladder as he made way to re-fill it with yet more beer. She was just returning with a tray of empty glasses to the bar when a troubled Jake emerged from the men's toilets and beckoned Kim over.

"I can't get in the toilet," said Jake. "The door is jammed, I think there is someone in there, but I can't open the door, I don't want to force it."

"I hope they're not up to trouble in there," sighed Kim.

She'd never had a problem with drugs or anything sinister at the Dog & Duck – her clientele was much more likely to be popping beta blockers than barbiturates – but she knew of a couple of pubs locally who'd had problems. "Go and get Dean, but don't raise any suspicions."

Kim went and stood at the men's toilet door, fortunately everyone was outside, and the door to the loo was slightly obscured by one of the big old beams that supported the structure of the building, so they could investigate quietly. She gave a gentle push on the door, but it was wedged tight shut.

"Everything alright?" asked Dean as he came over to where Kim was standing.

"I'm not sure. The door is wedged shut and it won't open. We've tried calling but we aren't getting an answer – there has to be someone in there though or else the door would open, surely?"

"Stand back," said Dean. "I'll see if I can open it."

He leant on the door firmly at first and then with more pressure. The door was well and truly closed. He pushed again, harder this time, and the door moved... if only by a few centimetres.

"There's definitely something in the way," said Dean, crouching down to peer through the crack that was now at the bottom of the door.

"Jesus Christ! That's feet! Someone is laying in front of the door!"

Kim and Jake exchanged a worried look and took a step backwards as Dean pushed as hard as he could on the door. The door moved further open but only slightly, the blockage in front of it giving real resistance to Dean's efforts. He carried on pushing the obstacle slowly to one side, inch by painful inch. Eventually, he was able to squeeze in through the small opening that he had managed to create with more than a considerable amount of effort.

“Bloody hell, it’s Bobby!” exclaimed Dean, crouching down to the large, immobile frame of Bobby as he lay face down on the floor, his arms stretched out at an awkward angle behind him.

“Help me turn him over,” said Dean, beckoning to Jake. “Kim, go and call an ambulance and shut the pub doors, try to keep people in the garden as much as you can.”

Kim’s heart began to race as she followed Dean’s instructions. She made the call to the ambulance service quickly and quietly before discreetly telling Rosa and Megan what was happening. Fortunately, the customers were oblivious as to the drama unfolding inside the pub and Kim instructed the girls to keep the drinks flowing while Mel strummed along to ‘Lovely Day’ by Bill Withers – how ironic thought Kim.

Inside the men’s toilets, Dean had tried to loosen Bobby’s shirt which had meant him ripping it open at the over-stretched buttons. He’d felt for a pulse, but he was struggling to find one and he was pretty sure that Bobby had suffered some form of heart attack. It didn’t take a genius to work out that a man, many stones overweight, who smoked like a chimney and drank like a fish, and whose face was an alarming shade of purple, was sailing pretty close to the wind in the health stakes.

“I’m going to give him mouth to mouth,” said Dean to Jake, calling his army first aid training into action. “I’ll keep going for as long as I can, but you may need to take over if my arms give out.”

He put one hand under the back of Bobby’s head, pulling his chin up and back with the other, to open his airways. He began pressing firmly in the middle of Bobby’s chest, hands clasped together, arms outstretched…”One, two, three, four, five, six, seven, eight, nine, ten…” he counted, before squeezing his thumb and forefinger over Bobby’s nose and expelling one long puff of air into his mouth. Again and again, he repeated the process, yet still Bobby lay motionless.

“Fucking hell, do you think he’s dead?” exclaimed Jake.

Dean didn’t answer, he just kept pressing and counting but deep down he suspected that Bobby had been dead the moment he had hit the floor.

Kim circled the garden, silently counting heads, in a kind of secret roll call. There were certain members of the crowd who must not be allowed anywhere near the inside of the pub – Steve, for example would be the absolute worst person to witness what was going on. He had a loose tongue at the best of times and the last thing Dean needed right now was help from someone who would try and give him the benefit of his questionable wisdom, nor did they need the whole sorry saga to be announced at full volume to the rest of the pub.

“Fran!” said Kim suddenly. “Megan, go and find Fran, I think she’s in the smoking area. We need to tell her before she finds out by accident!”

Megan hurried off to find Fran, and Kim went round to the front car park to wait for the ambulance. It was only another two minutes – although it felt much longer – before the welcome sight of the blue lights appeared in the distance and only seconds later before it turned onto the forecourt.

“He’s in here,” said Kim, meeting the two paramedics as they jumped from the vehicle.

She ushered them in through the front door and through the pub to the toilets where Dean was still tirelessly working on Bobby. Jake was standing by the door, his facial expression a mixture of shock and pure horror at the events unfolding in front of him. The paramedics rushed in and took over from Dean who was breathing heavily, beads of sweat trickling down the side of his face.

“Well done mate, we’ll take over from here,” said one of the medics. “Have you found a pulse, is he breathing?”

“I’ve been doing CPR for around 15 minutes,” said Dean. “No movement and no visible signs of life. We found him collapsed on the floor – not sure how long he'd been there."

At that moment, Fran appeared in the doorway, her face ashen. "It's okay, love," said Kim, putting her arm around Fran's shoulders and knowing for certain that nothing was even slightly ok.

The paramedics had worked and worked on Bobby for what had seemed like hours but was in fact little more than half an hour. All the while, Bobby lay motionless, the merest glimmers of life having left his body long-since, it seemed.

"I'm sorry," said the paramedic. "I'm afraid he has passed."

Fran let out a strangled cry and almost fell into Kim. A small crowd had assembled in the pub, roused by the sight of the ambulance in the carpark.

"Let's go back outside, folks," said Fleur, observing the scene before her and instantly realising that something dreadful had taken place. "Nothing to see here, let's leave these people in peace." She threw a sympathetic glance in Kim's direction and motioned that she would take care of things outside. Kim smiled weakly and nodded her gratitude.

The ambulance men heaved Bobby's huge frame onto a stretcher and covered him over with a blanket. They wheeled him out to the waiting vehicle as Fran looked on speechless.

“I’ll go with her,” said Dean. “You going to be okay Kim?”

“Yes, yes of course. You look after Fran, we’ll be fine here… and Dean… thank you.”

Dean smiled and guided the bewildered Fran in the direction of the ambulance leaving Jake, Kim and Megan standing silently and none-the-less bewildered as they watched the sombre group leave the pub.

“What do we do now?” asked Jake.

“There’s not much we can do,” sighed Kim. “I’ll just give this floor a quick wipe over,” she winced as she noticed the small patch of blood on the floor from where Bobby had fallen. “Then we will have to go back outside and brazen things out. I’m not making any big announcements, I’m sure the gossip chain will be well under way by now anyway and I don’t want to share any news publicly until Fran has given her blessing. If anyone asks directly then we can say that he has collapsed and been taken to hospital – we don’t need to go into gory details.”

Megan stood guard on the toilet door whilst Kim cleaned the floor and then the three of them made their way to the garden in silence. The unstoppable Mel was still strumming the same three chords on his guitar and singing along to a Motown medley whilst the more pissed members of the gathering danced in front of him, none of them the wiser as to the tragic events that had just occurred inside the pub.

Fleur came over to Kim and handed her a well-deserved brandy; she also offered one to Jake which he took gratefully with shaking hands, although Megan declined hers. They continued to clear tables, serve drinks and clear plates almost on autopilot. Rosa was an absolute powerhouse in the kitchen making sure that nothing would be left for Dean to clear when he returned.

Kim was so grateful to her little team and especially to Fleur who was living proof of the phrase that had something to do with 'friends in need.' There were a few awkward questions to answer, and Kim knew that amongst the more astute members of the clientele, lots of hushed conversations were taking place; the noisy arrival of an ambulance and the gaping hole left by Bobby's absence were strong indicators that something was seriously amiss if nothing else.

Steve cut a pathetic figure in the brightly coloured shirt that now seemed at odds with the dark change of tone of the afternoon, sipping quietly on a rum and coke, his usual bravado now conspicuously absent. Kim felt quite sorry for Steve, him and Bobby had sometimes been an annoying double act, but she knew they had real affection for each other, and they had both certainly brought character to the pub no matter how irritating that had been at times!

The afternoon seemed to drag on forever and Kim wished she had been able to close the doors and chuck everyone out; she had not been particularly close to Bobby, but the death of another human being was no small thing by anyone's standards.

The British Summer proved to be the saviour in the end, with rain clouds beginning to gather around six o'clock and encouraging the guests to search for shelter before the heavens opened. Inevitably this disruption in the flow of proceedings meant that several customers fell by the wayside and either began to weave their way home or wait for ordered taxis. Kim would be eternally grateful to Fleur who had managed the exit of Mel, which in itself had meant at least a twenty minute rundown of how the crowd had 'lapped him up' and how there weren't many musicians who could play like him; a point which Kim could definitely not disagree with on many levels!

Poor Steve was literally poured into a taxi, barely able to stand after trying to literally drown his sorrows in rum and coke, and the lovely Brian and Doris had promised to look in on him in the morning as he only lived a few doors away from their house. Tony and Jean left the party buoyant at having raised well over a thousand pounds for their charity and not fully aware of the enormity of what had taken place, for which Kim was grateful. Poor Tony had put his heart and soul into his Hawaiian barbeque, and she would have hated his efforts to have been completely overshadowed or disregarded.

By seven o'clock the pub was empty, and Kim took the decision to close the doors permanently for the day. Any walk-ins would have to find another watering hole.

"Why don't you all get yourself off home. Thank you so much for everything, but you could all do with a rest – it's been quite a day," said Kim.

"Would like us to stay with you?" asked Rob.

Kim smiled, thinking now more than ever that Fleur had definitely found a good one in him – she would have been mad to let him walk away.

"We don't mind," added Fleur.

"No honestly, I'm fine," said Kim. "I'm just going to try Dean's mobile and see how things are at the hospital then I think I'll have a hot bath and an early night. I am physically and emotionally exhausted!"

"If you're sure, mia cara?" said Rosa, kindly.

"Seriously, I'm fine, now go on shoo, the lot of you," smiled Kim as she ushered them to the door.

Fleur and Rob gave Jake a lift home and Rosa travelled in Megan's car; Kim hoped they would use their respective journeys to decompress from the tragedy. She looked around at the pub, now gleaming and spotlessly tidy, not a trace of the carnage that had occurred earlier. The team had done an amazing job and she was so thankful that she wasn't looking at a bar full of dirty glasses right now; she didn't think she could have found the energy.

She poured herself a large brandy and sat in the chair by the fire, pulling her mobile from her handbag to call Dean. Just at that moment, the handle on the front door rattled and she called out...

"Hello, who is it? We are closed – sorry!"

"Only me," came Dean's familiar voice.

Kim pulled the door open and threw her arms around Dean without a thought. He returned her embrace, pulling her in tight towards him, his strong hands stroking her back as he held her close. She looked up at him, tears pricking the back of her eyes as she studied his face; her relief at seeing him almost overwhelmed her.

Dean's expression grew serious, and his eyes burned into hers with an intensity that did funny things to her insides. The next thing she knew, his lips were on hers and she returned his kiss with a passion that she was not sure she had ever felt; unless she counted the first time she had clapped eyes on David Essex in a red neckerchief and a leather waistcoat!

Chapter Eleven

"Whoops!" said Kim, snuggling into Dean's chest as they lay in her bed together a mere thirty minutes after Dean had walked in through the front door!

"Is that a good whoops or a bad whoops?" asked Dean.

"A good whoops, I hope," replied Kim, "although I wish I'd worn better knickers and shaved my legs. I don't even want to think about the state of my bedroom!"

"I really wasn't all that interested in your knickers," Dean laughed, "and don't worry, I didn't shave my legs either!"

Kim gave him an affectionate punch on the arm. "You know what I mean. You've barely been up to the flat before now and the first time you do, you're in my bed. It's a long time since anyone saw me naked... unless you count my gynaecology nurse!"

Dean rolled over onto his side and propped himself up on one arm. "I've wanted to do this from about the second time I met you and I wouldn't change a thing – apart from the dramatic events of today of course."

"Oh God, I'm so selfish, I almost forgot about Bobby. How is Fran?"

"She's okay, I dropped her off at home, but I said I'd go round there in the morning – she didn't say much, but then she doesn't ever talk much at all anyway. She just looked numb to be honest. I'm not sure if she loved him or loathed him half the time, it's difficult to tell really."

"I hope she doesn't drink tonight," said Kim. "We could be having two funerals instead of one if she does."

"Yeah I did worry about that," said Dean, "but she assured me she'd be able to resist. I didn't know what else I could do."

"You were so calm," said Kim. "Thank you so much for taking charge."

"The army has its advantages," smiled Dean. "I'm so sorry I hurt you Kim, I didn't know how to break the ice and make things okay again between us."

"Well I think the ice is well and truly broken now," laughed Kim. "What did they say at the hospital?"

"Massive cardiac arrest," said Dean. "As I suspected he would probably have died instantly which is a blessing in a small way; at least he wouldn't have known much about it."

"Small mercies," sighed Kim. "Not exactly the way I wanted the day to end. Will you stay over tonight?"

"It's taken months for me to find a way to be with you, I'm not going away that easily," replied Dean. "You're stuck with me for tonight at least. I guess tomorrow we will have to find a way to deal with the fallout but for now I suggest we have a little night cap and get some sleep – we can even compare hairy legs again if you like!"

What followed was the longest, shortest night of Kim's life. They stayed awake talking for hours, snuggled into each other; they even made love for a second time which was even more delicious than the first time, now that urgency had been taken out of the equation. Kim couldn't remember ever having done the wild thing twice in one night...*ever.* And when she considered that she was on the wrong side of 50, menopausal, and not in the same shape that she had been as a young woman – downstairs *and* upstairs so to speak – she felt bloody fantastic and surprisingly 'chafe' free! If someone had suggested that she'd be engaging in sex marathons at her time of life (well maybe it was more of a jog than a marathon, but it was still a big deal in her book), she'd have been wincing and reaching for the Canesten at the very thought. The hesitance she had initially felt at baring her wobbly bits had vanished into thin air and Dean had quite literally made her feel like the most beautiful woman in the world which was pretty bloody amazing when the mere sight of her reflection made her recoil most days. She felt fantastic. She also felt a little bit guilty for feeling fantastic when poor Bobby was lying in a hospital morgue, but she just couldn't help herself. All the tension between her and Dean from the last few months had disappeared and she felt safe and invincible at the same time. Dean had handled the whole terrible ordeal with Bobby with such control and compassion that she felt nothing but respect for him, along with a renewed admiration that had finally overcome the awkwardness between them.

She had hoped to wake before Dean in the morning so that she could go to the bathroom and quickly brush her teeth and remove the remains of last night's mascara, and maybe pinch her cheeks and apply a little lip gloss like they did in the movies, before jumping back into bed and lying in a restful sleep pose looking like a goddess. Unfortunately, Dean's army training meant that he was always awake long before most other mortals and Kim feared that he had already caught sight of her bed hair, smudged makeup and dribbly cheeks!

What if he had left? What if he had woken, taken one look at her and instantly regretted their mid-life shag-fest?

"Breakfast?" said Dean as he poked his head around the bedroom door.

Kim inwardly chastised herself for being such an insecure twat and resolved to embrace her inner goddess once more. Anyway, fuck it! Even if he had regretted their night of passion – and it certainly didn't look like he had - she'd had a great time, whatever happened going forward!

"What time is it? Is it late?" asked Kim, pulling herself up in the bed and pulling the sheets up to hide what was left of her modesty.

"It's just before nine, but I thought we ought to get up and about before Jake arrives, he's usually here before eleven on a Sunday. We probably need to have a bit of a talk about Bobby too – did you want to make any kind of announcement? I also promised to check on Fran; I feel like I ought to make sure she's okay at least."

"Yes, you're right. There's lots to think about today."

"I also didn't want you to feel uncomfortable if people started arriving and I was up here with you," said Dean, sitting on the bed beside Kim and placing a mug of tea and a slice of toast on the little chest beside her.

"You don't regret it do you?" asked Kim.

"Not at all," said Dean, kissing Kim on the top of her head. "I couldn't regret it less if I tried. I just want you to be ok with whatever this is. I will follow your lead, you set the pace and I will follow. I want you to feel comfortable that's all. I'll tell anyone who wants to listen – but only if you want me to."

"I appreciate that," said Kim truthfully. "I don't mind people knowing but maybe we just take things slowly and see how we go, does that sound okay?"

"Sounds perfect, now let's get dressed and I'll go check on Fran before the pub opens."

"It feels a bit wrong to just carry on as normal," said Kim. "I mean, just getting on with cooking Sunday dinner when a man has died!"

"Life goes on unfortunately," said Dean. "But if you wanted to shut the pub, that's entirely your call."

"No, I think we will open as normal," said Kim. "I imagine there'll be a few people wanting to know what happened and some of them might need to talk about it – this might be the place where they come to off-load, if you know what I mean."

"I know exactly," said Dean. "I think Jake and Megan were more shaken up than they let on – it was quite traumatic, especially for someone without any experience of that kind of thing."

"Well then, we shall be their safe place," said Kim, jumping out of bed and kissing Dean on the lips.

Chapter Twelve

Fran looked up as the knock on the door interrupted her thoughts. The room was still dark, the thick velvet curtains that had seen better days still able to block out most of the light despite their shabby appearance.

She hadn't gone to bed last night, just dozed on the sofa gazing blankly at the whisky in the drinks cabinet, its amber liquid like a magnet pulling her in as she fought to resist. If she was honest with herself, she didn't think she wanted a drink because of the grief she felt, nor for the undeniable shock of yesterday's events (although the way Bobby had lived his life, it wasn't the biggest surprise that he had gone the way he did), she wasn't really even sure that she wanted a drink for the taste of the drink itself. No, if she was brutally honest, she wanted a drink just because she could. Now Bobby was gone there was nothing stopping her, no one to tell her she couldn't, she was free to do whatever she liked.

The knock on the door became louder and more insistent. So many times, Fran had thought that Bobby was the root of her problems. The reason she felt trapped. The reason she was sad. The reason she felt out of control of her life. But now he was gone and in principle she was freer than she had been in a long time, but yet she felt more trapped, and sad, and out of control than ever. Bobby had driven her mad at times and mostly she had resented him, but now the deafening silence that was left by his absence was all-consuming and for perhaps the first time in her whole entire life it had suddenly dawned on her that she was the root of her sadness. She was out of control of her own life and the realisation made her sadder than ever. She wasn't pleased that she was free of Bobby like she had often dreamed she might be and whilst he hadn't always been good for her the thought that she now might actually have to take some control of her own was utterly terrifying.

"Fran, Fran! Are you in there?"

Fran heard Dean's voice calling through the letterbox. It was time to face the music. Time to play the grieving widow, time to be what other people would expect her to be because it finally dawned on Fran that she didn't have one single fucking clue who she really was at all!

Chapter Thirteen

Dean walked back to the pub from Fran's house. The poor thing had looked like a rabbit in the headlights. Dean suspected that Bobby hadn't always been the easiest person to live with but then he also suspected that Fran had probably relied on his 'strength' more than she realised. He worried that if she didn't swim after Bobby's death she could very easily sink and disappear without trace, possibly into the nearest whisky bottle.

He felt a little guilty at the conflicting emotions running through his head. On the one hand, yesterday had been a shit storm of a day that had left a lot of sadness and trauma in its wake, yet on the other hand it had been one of the best days of his entire life. The night with Kim had been more than he could ever have hoped for. He was determined not to bugger things up this time. He vowed to take things at her pace and to prove to her once and for all that he had been worth the wait. He felt like a lovesick teenager – without the acne and the squeaky voice mercifully – and it felt bloody great!

"All ok?" asked Kim as Dean walked in through the kitchen door about an hour after leaving for Fran's house.

"Yeah, she looks a bit lost, poor love – we'll have to keep an eye on her. I've offered to help her with funeral arrangements."

"Aw, my hero!" smiled Kim, kissing him on the lips.

Dean took his chance and pulled her in towards him thanking his lucky stars that he was now 'allowed' to do this. Just at that moment Rosa walked into the kitchen and the two of them sprang apart like scalded cats.

Rosa just laughed and said, "It's about bloody time," and left the kitchen whistling, 'Here comes the bride.'

"Well that's that buggered then," laughed Dean. "The cat might have jumped from the proverbial bag!"

"Oh, fuck it!" laughed Kim. "Do you know what? Life's too bloody short and we aren't getting any younger. We'll just be how we want to be and see what happens – what's the worst that could happen anyway... unless you run off with the new cellar maid too!"

"I don't think I'm Rosa's type," said Dean trying to play it cool but grinning like a Cheshire cat.

"Right, let's get on then, we've got a tough day ahead of us I fear and just because you've bonked the landlady it doesn't mean you can start slacking!"

As predicted, the events of the day before were the talk of the pub. Bobby had been a larger-than-life character in the Dog & Duck and many of the locals had known him since he was a teenager; slightly thinner than in recent years and just as gobby, but still with a voracious appetite for lager, apparently. Bobby had lived his life to excess, and it seemed that his less-than-healthy choices had finally caught up with him.

Kim had taken the precaution of phoning the hospital, mainly to check that she hadn't dreamed Bobby's demise; she had an irrational fear of breaking the sad news to everyone only to find that Bobby had made a miraculous recovery and was sitting up in a hospital bed somewhere taking the piss out of the other patients and driving the nurses mad! Of course, deep down she knew this was ridiculous but maybe it was just her brain's way of accepting what had happened. She realised she had never actually seen a dead body before, her dad had died when she was too young to have gone to see his body, and she didn't think that the death of Rory the hamster was quite in the same league!

Once she had been reassured – if that was even the appropriate term – that Bobby was indeed no more, she steeled herself for the inevitable questions that were sure to follow throughout the day's service.

Dean had confirmed that, although subdued (not that it was easy to tell the difference between one day and the next with Fran), Fran was indeed alive and had not succumbed to the demon drink. The rest of the session had passed without too much difficulty with many of the regulars expressing their condolences upon hearing the news of Bobby's passing. Brian and Doris, although not always Bobby's biggest fans, took on the role of sharing the news discreetly and respectfully to those whom Kim was unable to speak to, and Fleur and

Rob popped in just to check that Kim was bearing up okay. It did not escape Fleur's notice that things had changed between Kim and Dean, and she had given a conspiratorial thumbs up to Kim when Dean wasn't looking. Kim hadn't been able to hide her smile even though she pretended that it was 'no big deal'; they could have a conversation about the gory details later on.

Rosa had fussed around in the caring way that she always did, and Jake seemed calmer after a good night's sleep. Megan wasn't working and so Kim had made sure she called to check that she hadn't been too affected. She thought that Megan sounded quiet on the phone and not quite like her usual self, but then she guessed that she was probably tired and perhaps still a little shaken. All things considered, things were as good as could be expected and life had indeed carried on, just as Dean had said it would, and in the relentless way that it often did, regardless of occurrences that were life-changing for some. Steve was distinctly conspicuous by his absence and Kim suspected that he might remain absent for a little while yet. The truth was, Steve only knew how to hold court in a room, he had no default method, and holding court right now probably seemed brash even to Steve's thick skin.

All in all, Sunday was an emotional roller coaster. Obviously, all talk was of Bobby and there was a much more subdued atmosphere in the pub than usual. Later that evening when Fleur had phoned to check that the day hadn't been too traumatic, Kim had given her the full rundown of her and Dean's first night together – minus the dodgy knickers and the hairy legs! Fleur had screamed so loudly down the phone that Kim thought she might lose an ear drum but deep down she felt blessed to have a friend who was so happy for her, and not just because it meant that Fleur had gained a new pair of dinner and drinks buddies!

The police had called for Kim to make a statement as a formality, and she had phoned the hospital again to double check what needed to be done next, if only to assist Fran if she needed it. Kim agreed with Dean that Fran was fragile at best, and she didn't think she had family, let alone any friends, to help with the inevitable upcoming arrangements.

Chapter Fourteen

The weeks after Bobby's death had passed in a blur. The pub had ticked on by, and things between Kim and Dean were surprisingly comfortable. They worked together without friction and their free time was spent in similar harmony. Since their first night together, Dean had barely gone home at all, and they had been easily accepted as a couple by their friends and customers. Kim hadn't realised that a grown-up relationship could be so thoroughly undramatic, and she sometimes wondered if she was missing something or if she should be waiting for the shit to hit the fan but, for the time being at least, things couldn't have been better between them.

She hadn't heard from Keith since her unfortunate encounter with Olivia in Helen's salon and she hoped this was proof that he had finally got the message and given up; although knowing Keith, she felt sure there might be at least one more little tantrum on the horizon. She hadn't even heard from him when their Decree Absolute had landed on the doorstep. Dean had asked if she felt okay when she had opened the envelope, but she had been totally honest when she had told him that she felt nothing but a sense of closure and excitement for her future.

Bobby's funeral arrangements had finally been made for the last Wednesday in July. In some cultures, the dead were buried within 24 hours of death, and it had always baffled Kim how that kind of efficiency was even feasible. The British culture seemed to drag things out for as long as possible whilst grieving relatives sat around waiting and waiting, with the funeral looming over them like the Grim-bloody-Reaper.

The plan was for Dean and Kim to travel in the funeral car with Fran – mainly because she had no one else to go with – and then after a short ceremony at the local crematorium, there was to be a wake at the Dog & Duck, Bobby's favourite place and one he definitely spent more time in than anywhere else.

The ride to the crematorium was made in total silence. Fran made no sound at all – neither through tears nor words.

There had been a tense moment when Dean, Steve and a couple of the other lads from the pub had attempted to lift Bobby's coffin; for one dreadful moment Kim had envisioned a macabre scene in which they had dropped their weighty load resulting in Bobby rolling out down the hill, resplendent in his red Hawaiian shirt and shorts clutching a pint of lager and a king-sized cigarette. Bobby had been a giant of a man in every way and the strain on the men's faces as they attempted to lift the heavy coffin had been proof of that.

Steve had given quite a touching eulogy for his 'best mate Bobby', although Kim had suspected that Bobby had actually not only been his best mate but more likely his *only* mate. Once outside the crem, Steve had proudly laid a small arrangement of flowers that had been crafted into the shape of a pint of lager and, whilst this had been meant as a touching tribute by Steve, Kim had thought it a little insensitive seeing as it was probably the drink that had been the cause of his demise; a bit like placing a wreath of flowers in the shape of a bus for someone who had been run over by one!

Back at the pub, the customers had used the excuse of Bobby's death to drink their collective body weights in alcohol and Kim couldn't deny that their outpouring of grief had certainly been good for business. By the end of the early evening, the jukebox had been pumped enough with money to provide a soundtrack to Bobby's entire life playing every track he had ever loved, from Motown to Reggae. There was even a rendition of Jonny Cash's Ring of Fire in remembrance of the infamous curry incident when Dean had put extra chillies in Bobby and Steve's curries and they had both refused to admit defeat or acknowledge that the heat was ruining them – even Steve had laughed at that one, once he realised they had been tricked.

Fran had stuck to her non-alcoholic drinks but had said little throughout the proceedings at all until the last few minutes of the evening when she had given an impromptu rendition of an old Irish folk song that had rendered the pub crowd speechless and reduced them to tears.

At the end of the evening, as Kim had ushered the last of the flock from their venue of remembrance, she had gone into the ladies' toilets to turn off the lights and close the windows. At first, she hadn't noticed anything untoward until she noticed a pair of feet under one of the doors. She was beginning to wonder if the pub toilets were cursed; it seemed to be one thing after another!

"Hello, anyone in there?" said Kim, knowing full well that someone definitely was in there, but reverting to a rhetorical question as is often the case when people don't quite know what to say.

"Just coming," replied a quiet voice.

"Megan, is that you? Are you okay?" asked Kim.

Megan emerged from the toilet looking anything but okay. Kim could see that she had been crying, despite her attempts to dry her face and conceal her tears.

"I'm fine..."

"You're not bloody fine," said Kim. "Is it the funeral?"

"No, it's not the funeral, I'm fine honestly."

Kim put her arm around Megan's shoulders. "Come on now Meg, you can tell me, we look after each other here."

With that Megan descended into floods of tears and buried her head on Kim's chest. "Come on now, it can't be that bad surely...?"

"It's much worse," sobbed Megan. "Kim, I'm pregnant!"

"Not blind date BMW guy?" asked Kim, certain that Megan hadn't disclosed that their relationship had progressed past the one awful blind date stage!

"It's much worse than that," said Megan softly. "It's Lottie's dad!"

Kim furrowed her brow in confusion...

"He was always a selfish git," explained Megan. "Always dropping in and out of our lives in between whatever new shiny object had caught his attention, but I always wanted more you know? I wanted Lottie to know her real father. Well, he came back a couple of months ago, said he'd missed me. Turns out he just needed a bed for the weekend before his latest adventure. I swore that was the last time and I really meant it, I'd finally got him out of my system and now look! My mum will go fucking spare – I just can't tell her. She thinks he is a useless bastard...!"

"Calm down," said Kim gently. "Does he know?"

"He's gone on some Asian tour," sobbed Megan. "Gone to 'find himself', whatever the bloody hell that means!"

"So, he's not likely to show up and give you or Lottie any trouble?"

"He couldn't care less about either of us... his own daughter, for God's sake!"

"You know what," said Kim. "Bollocks to him then, it's his loss. If he can't see how lucky he could have been then let him go and bloody well find himself; preferably up a long creek without a paddle!"

Megan smiled weakly.

"Do you want to keep the baby?" asked Kim quietly. "It's your choice you know, and I will support you whatever you choose."

"I just couldn't," sobbed Megan. "I don't want to bring another baby without a father into this world but... I just couldn't..."

"Then you listen to me, my girl. You will be father *and* mother to that little baby, and you will do a better job than he ever could, just as you have done with Lottie. If he's going to be a crap father, then your children are much better with no father! Children need love and stability, and you can give them both by the bucket load."

"But what about my mum?"

"You are going to have to tell your mum, but she will love you just the same. I can't guarantee she won't give you a lecture and I am sure she won't be overjoyed, but once she calms down she will love you all just as she always has. I am happy to come with you, but I think you would be better to go on your own; I'd hate your mum to feel hurt that you told me first. You have me and Dean and Rosa to look after you and we will always be here for you – like a gang of mad old aunties!"

Megan laughed. "Thanks Kim, I've been going out of my mind worrying. I didn't want to believe it at first."

"We all knew you weren't yourself. Now why don't you go home and get some rest. You can tell your mum in the morning when you pick Lottie up."

"What about my job?"

"Your job here will always be your job my darling, and when you get too fat to waddle around, we will step in and help you – we are family now whether you like it or not!"

"Thanks Kim," said Megan.

"My pleasure," smiled Kim. "That's what mad old aunties are for! Now I want you to ring me tomorrow when you've told your mum and let me know how you are. If you need me to pick up Lottie, then you only have to ask. How was she about her dad coming back?"

"To be honest, I don't think she likes him very much, he doesn't really pay her much attention and I think she was quite pleased when he left. She doesn't even know him really."

"That girl will go far," smiled Kim. "Are you going to be okay on your own... did you want to stay here tonight?"

Megan faltered in her reply and Kim stepped in. "Right, that's it, you're staying here. Dean can make you breakfast in the morning. Big conversations should never be done on an empty stomach!"

"Who am I making breakfast for?" asked Dean as he encountered the two girls on their way out of the ladies' loos.

"Just enough for a little one," replied Kim, motioning towards a very subdued Megan.

Dean didn't ask for any further information, sensing that now was not the time. "Breakfast is my favourite meal of the day," he smiled. "The more, the merrier!"

That night after an exhausted Megan had gone to sleep in Kim's spare room, she had filled Dean in on what had been happening. Dean had been sympathetic but also a little bit excited at the impending patter of tiny feet and Kim thought it had made her love him just a little bit more.

Chapter Fifteen

Megan had left the pub after several cups of tea – she certainly hadn't been eager to leave. She hadn't said more than a few words all morning and the poor girl had looked like the weight of the world was upon her shoulders. Dean had done his best to make upbeat conversation but even he had given up trying to get her to smile. Kim's heart went out to her but somehow she knew that things would be alright in the end. However tough things were at the moment, Kim could never bring herself to see a new baby as anything but a blessing.

Daniel had rung just before the pub opened at eleven.

"Hi Mum, how's it going?"

"All good thanks darling, everything okay with you?"

"Yep, all good, how was the funeral – not that funerals are known for being a bundle of fun?"

"Yeah, it was okay. As you say, they're never too much fun but we gave him a good send-off, I hope. What's happening in your world... any gossip?"

"Well, it's funny you should ask that, Mum," said Daniel, "but I do have a little bit of news!"

"Yes...?"

"Ryan has asked me to move in with him and I've said yes! We're going to rent my flat out and see how things go to start with."

"Oh Daniel, I'm so happy for you," shrieked Kim honestly. "I think he's lovely."

"Thanks Mum, I haven't told Dad yet – I'm not sure he's fully on board with the whole Mr and Mr thing just yet."

"He'll get over it," laughed Kim. "He may be an absolute pillock at times, but he does love you in his own special way. He won't disown you, but I wouldn't hold your breath for a moving-in card!"

Daniel chuckled. "I wouldn't have expected one if I was moving in with a girl either. I don't think he even knows when my birthday is, beyond knowing it is sometime between Autumn and Christmas! I know he's my dad, but he's never really had much room in his life for anyone other than himself."

"Well, I will send you two cards if that helps," smiled Kim.

"Thanks Mum. We thought we'd pop up in a couple of weeks if that's ok? It might mean bringing Ryan's dog though; would you mind?"

"Ooo no! I love dogs; it'll be nice to have one about the place for a couple of days. Will you bring your nan up with you too?"

“I daren’t come without her; she’d bloody kill me,” laughed Daniel.

“Anyway, I’d better dash darling, I think I can hear the beer delivery. I’ll see you in a couple of weeks – love you lots!”

Kim hung up the phone, her heart full as it always was after speaking to her boy.

Sure enough, the beer delivery had indeed arrived and there was the usual clanging and banging as new barrels were rolled down into the cellar and old ones removed. She had seen quite an increase in the number of barrels they now ordered as trade grew.

Kim had engaged in conversation with Nigel, the regular delivery guy who usually served the Dog & Duck. Nigel was a man with a not dissimilar physique to the barrels that he delivered – he was almost as wide as he was tall, not fat exactly, just solidly built! Nigel had a habit of repeating back every element of a conversation to the recipient and this morning had been no different.

“Have you got the extra bitter I ordered?” asked Kim.

“The extra bitter?”

“Yes, the bitter please Nigel. Can you put them at the back of the cellar?”

“The back of the cellar?”

"Yes please," Kim had sighed. "Have you sent the invoice?"

"The invoice?"

"Yes, if you could email the invoice that would be great. How's your family?" said Kim, attempting to free herself from the constraints of a looped conversation.

"The family?" repeated Nigel without a hint of irony.

"Yes Nigel, your family, are they okay?

"Are they okay?"

At this point, Kim had taken a breath and busied herself with counting the barrels. She hoped to God he never got bloody dementia; his poor wife must have the patience of a saint!

Once Nigel had left, Kim returned to the kitchen to check the day's bookings. "Bloody hell, that Nigel is a lovely fella, but the constant repeating drives me batty."

"The constant repeating?" asked Dean innocently, ducking as Kim chucked a well-aimed bread roll in his direction.

"We're a bread roll down for lunch now!" he laughed.

Chapter Sixteen

Megan turned the key in the lock of her Mum's front door; her heart was hammering in her chest and her palms were sweating – she hadn't felt this nervous since she'd got caught bunking off school with her best friend Julia and they'd been rumbled by her mum's next door neighbour Elsie (a nosy old bint with a love of juicy gossip), drinking cheap cider from the corner shop up at the local park. Still buzzing from the cut price alcohol, Megan had raced all the way home in an attempt to beat her mum there and try to sober up and play the innocent. Unfortunately, she had forgotten that the day in question had been one of her mum's early shifts and so she had torn up the path almost bumping into a triumphant Elsie who had obviously got quite a sprint on for an old girl and who had quite clearly imparted her deliciously inflammatory news with eager efficiency. Even more unfortunate was that the now futile run that Megan had taken to beat her adversary had caused the cider to swish around in an alarming fashion inside her empty stomach (she had been going through the awkward teenage aversion to food that came from imagined body imperfections), causing her to eject the contents of her stomach with some considerable force all over the unsuspecting Elsie's 'housework slippers'. Elsie had stood with a face like thunder although for once, mercifully speechless. Over the years, Megan and her mum, Carla, had re-lived the story that they now referred to as 'the cider incident,' with humour.

Carla had confessed that she had secretly been quite pleased to see the loose-tongued Elsie brought to an abrupt silence for once in her life, particularly as she, 'Never had a good bloody word to say about anyone – what goes around comes around…'

'…or up…' Megan had laughed.

But this was different. This was not just a bit of drunken hi-jinks that could be remedied with a strong black coffee and a few hours' kip. This was life changing. Megan had so much respect for her mum. Her own dad had buggered off when she was small and Carla had worked her backside off to raise Megan by herself, often working two jobs to make ends meet.

When Lottie had come along, Carla had embraced the job of 'Nanny' whole heartedly, pouring as much love onto her granddaughter as she had her own. She had been less than impressed with Megan's choice of Baby Daddy – she had always found Brad to be selfish and feckless and she had always known that one day he would break her daughter's heart, something which she took no pleasure in being proved right on – but she suffered him as best she could for the sake of her girls. In fact, Carla was quite happy when he eventually left; in her eyes no father was definitely better than a crap one! So, Megan was now under no illusion as to how Carla would feel about Brad… again! But the thing she feared the most was that her mum might lose respect for her. She knew she had been an idiot and she knew she had let herself and Lottie down by falling for his well-worn lines but the thought of being a disappointment to her mum really cut deep.

Megan pushed the front door open, fighting the urge to run back down the path – thankfully she'd had something more substantial than two litres of Strongbow this time and therefore the risk of projectile vomiting was at least one less hurdle that needed to be dealt with.

"Is that you, love?" called Carla from the kitchen. "Lottie's just gone round to see Millie – they've got a new puppy of all things, so I guess that's her gone until lunchtime!"

Millie was the little girl who lived with her family two doors up from the little house where Megan had spent her childhood and the pair of them were practically joined at the hip. It had been a great source of comfort to Megan that Lottie had a little friend to play with when she spent time at her Nan's, especially being an only child… until now, of course. The enormity of what she was about to share hit her again with no less ferocity than when she had peed onto the little white stick and willed there to be only one pink line, repeating it over and over in her head like a mantra. Unfortunately, Mother Nature had other plans and the second pink line had sprung into vision practically before the wee was dry on the stick, resplendent in all its bright fuchsia pinkness, shining in the little window as if to underline the news that she had been dreading

– 'Baby number two is on the way, you are UP THE DUFF!'

"You ok? Megan? Megan? ...Megan you're scaring me, what on Earth has happened?" Carla's voice rose a full octave at the sight of her daughter's pale complexion.

"Oh Mum, I'm so sorry. I'm such a fucking idiot!" and with that, Megan collapsed into Carla's arms as if her heart would break.

Once Megan's crying had subsided to empty sobs, staccato breaths shuddering through her body, her mascara now a black smudged memory smeared across her cheeks, her nose dripping in the most unattractive fashion; Carla was the first to speak,

"You're pregnant aren't you?"

Once again Megan began to wail.

"Right, you listen to me my girl, you will never again allow that bastard to make you feel this way again do you hear me?"

"I haven't told you who the father is yet," sniffed Megan.

"I know you well enough to know exactly who the father is. You haven't been on a proper date for over a year and I'm pretty sure BMW guy was not your type! You're only ever at work or looking after Lottie and you were never the type for one-night stands, so I can only assume that it was him. Besides, Lottie told me she had seen her dad, but she didn't want to tell you that she didn't like him very much in case she upset you!"

"Poor Lottie," said Megan quietly. "What have I done?"

"Lottie will be fine," said Carla kindly. "She has a wonderful mother and although her father is an idiot, she isn't like to be troubled by him – I assume he isn't sticking around?"

"He doesn't even know," said Megan. "He left to go travelling and to 'find himself', whatever the bloody hell that means. I didn't find out until he was long gone."

"Well hopefully he will find himself up a bloody gum tree!" laughed Carla, angrily. "We will be just fine. Lottie will have a new little brother or sister to love, and I will have another grandchild. We will love this baby just as much as we love Lottie – just promise me you're done with him now, don't fall for anymore of his old crap!"

"Oh Mum, I was worried you'd hate me!"

"My darling girl, I could never hate you. I might think you're an idiot now and again, but I will always love you to the moon and back. I am so proud of you. You are an amazing mother and the best daughter, so come on dry your eyes... you are an ugly crier!"

Megan laughed. "Thanks for that Mum! Will you help me tell Lottie?"

"Of course, but you won't need my help. Children will only ever respond to news in the way it is presented – if you treat it like a wonderful surprise then Lottie will feel exactly the same. Does Kim know?"

Not for the first time, Megan was grateful for her mum's wisdom and composure in the face of a crisis. She also marvelled at her uncanny intuition.

"I can't lie to you Mum. I told Kim last night. I'm sorry I didn't come to you first, but Kim found me crying and she was so kind to me – her *and* Dean; I stayed there last night."

"Listen, I'm just pleased they looked after you, she's a lovely woman that Kim, and I get it... sometimes you just need to work things out in your own head first. I'm a bit too close, I understand that."

"I love you Mum, you're amazing," said Megan, throwing her arms around her mum and holding her tight.

"I love you too baby girl, now let's go and rescue this poor puppy from Lottie before she hugs it to death!"

Chapter Seventeen

Daniel and Ryan arrived on Saturday morning with a very excited Judy in tow. Kim had filled her in on the developments between her and Dean and Judy was like a clucky mother hen – thank God she was past the whole baby-bearing stage or she feared Judy would have started knitting already! Perhaps, when Megan was ready to share her news with the rest of the pub, then Judy would be able to divert her broody affections. Kim had a feeling this new baby was going to have a bigger extended family than your average Mormon!

"No dog?" Kim remarked, remembering that Daniel said they were going to bring Ryan's dog with them.

"I'm afraid she has strayed from the path of righteousness," laughed Ryan. "My one dog is going to be a few dogs before too long! She's resting at home with Nanny!"

Kim rolled her eyes but said nothing; there was clearly something in the air!

It had taken less time than Kim had predicted for Megan to share her news and she loved how supportive her family were – she included Dean, Rosa and Jake in this collective and once again thanked her lucky stars for all of them.

The day had passed in a flurry of activity. The pub was so clean it practically shined – the result of Megan's overactive hormones and an unstoppable desire to 'nest' at every available opportunity. The poor girl had looked so upset when Kim had found her sobbing in the toilets, and she was relieved that her mum Carla had supported her daughter without the need to blame or pile judgement onto a situation that had already caused Megan enough guilt and self-recrimination. Megan appeared as if a weight had been lifted and whilst Kim didn't for one minute expect that the next few months would be plain sailing, she knew it would all be okay in the end; in her view, a new baby bought only love if you embraced it.

There had been a brief lull in trade between three and six o'clock when a new wave of customers had arrived in search of an evening meal in the sunny pub garden. Megan had left for the day and Rosa had stayed on to help Dean; despite her earlier vows of 'no weekday weekends'. Bobby's death was now fading to a memory and Kim felt a pang of guilt for how quickly life had appeared to move on; but then that was how life had to be, she supposed, none of us are expendable.

Dean and Rosa were working and laughing together in the kitchen, their partnership now so well-formed that even the arrival of hungry hens on their way for a raucous night out in the town did nothing to fluster them. The bride arrived in the usual garb of white dress and veil made from someone's leftover net curtain, a pink sash diagonally over one shoulder proclaiming her as the 'Bride To Be'. A group of excited fake-tanned, mini-skirted friends followed in her wake, a rainbow of brightly coloured T-shirts declaring their roles as 'Team Bride'. Bringing up the rear were two older ladies, reluctantly wearing their lurid group T-shirts over more sensible shift dresses patterned with indiscriminate floral designs. Their T-shirts announced them as 'Bride's Mother' and 'Groom's Mother' respectively and whilst the bride's mother was happy to play along and carry one of the many inflatable penises within the group, the groom's mother looked as if she might have been sucking on a lemon and couldn't wait to leave! Kim doubted that either of the mothers would still be part of the entourage much past nine o'clock.

Sensing the need for stomachs to be lined, Dean made sure to supply plenty of bread with the girls' meals and Rosa had delicately suggested that perhaps a good portion of her famous lasagne might be just the thing to provide a pasta barrier against the ensuing Prosecco and Sambuca-shot onslaught!

The girls were loud and excitable, and Kim wasn't overly disappointed when their minibus arrived to take them into town. She didn't want to be a party pooper but there was only so much cackling laughter and 'dare the hen' games that her customers would take. Fortunately, by the time the bride-to-be had reached number five on the list of dares she had been given –

which was to kiss the top of a bald man's head – the bus had arrived, and the pub garden was restored to a calmer atmosphere, rescuing the poor old Colonel (Kim's octogenarian, ex-military regular) from the tipsy bride's advances; the unexpected stimulation might well have finished him off!

Kim's mum Judy was in her element, collecting glasses and cleaning tables, Jake was a dab hand behind the bar meaning that Kim was able to snatch a few moments here and there to chat to Daniel and Ryan who were working their way through a bottle of house red and an extra-large portion of cheesy chips as the last of the sun began to sink below the line of trees that lined the secluded garden.

"The garden looks lovely, Mum," said Daniel.

"It's great, isn't it? I love it out here, I'm so glad it's being used properly now, I don't think they did anything apart from store a few old barrels and a sand bucket full of fag ends before we came here!"

At that moment there was a screech of tyres coming from the road at the front of the pub. The screech seemed to go on for ages before there was an almighty crash, an alarming crunch of crumpling metal and the continuous sounding of a car horn that sounded as if it was under constant pressure or had somehow been stuck into the on position.

"What the bloody hell...?" yelled Kim, hurtling round to the front of the pub car park with Daniel and Ryan in hot pursuit directly behind her.

Upon hearing the commotion, Dean and Rosa had left the kitchen and raced around the side of the pub to join the growing crowd. Even the 'laid-back-to-the-point-of-horizontal' Jake had left his place behind the bar and emerged from the front door to observe the chaotic scene in the car park.

The sight that confronted Kim was like something from a soap opera. The sound of Neil Diamond's 'Cracklin' Rosie' blasted out from the car stereo, barely audible above the incessant blasting of the horn that echoed out from the crumpled remains of a small sports car, its front wing now permanently altered from where it had collided with the big green wheelie bin to the left of the side gate that led around to the garden. Mercifully the wheelie bin had served as a convenient barrier to the car's forward trajectory which, had it continued, would have taken it through the side gate and quite possibly into the small wooden shelter that served as the pub smoking area and contained a very bemused and surprised collection of hardcore smokers. Kim shuddered at the very thought of 'what if'.

Dean appeared at Kim's side just as the occupant of the mid-life crisis vehicle extricated themselves from the now distinctly reduced seating area, that was once the driver's side of the car.

"Dad, what the bloody hell are you doing?" bellowed Daniel.

"I came to shee yoo shun," slurred a less than sober Keith. "And what the fuck is he doing in my pub?" he yelled, pointing a finger at Dean before toppling backwards and landing in an undignified heap on top of the last old sand bucket full of fag ends that Kim had yet to dispose of.

"For fuck's sake Keith, you could have killed someone!" Kim could barely contain her anger or her contempt for her pathetic former husband. "I'm going inside to call him a taxi. You'll have to wait with him Daniel. I'm sorry to put this on you but if I stay here a minute longer, I'm likely to hit him over the head with that fucking bucket!"

Kim strode back into the pub whilst Rosa shooed the few nosy spectators back into the garden. "Nothing to see here, back you go. Bloddy idiot!"

Mercifully the taxi arrived within a few minutes and reluctantly accepted its inebriated passenger. Dean, Daniel and Ryan had more-or-less manhandled Keith into the taxi and bribed the driver with an extra twenty quid to make sure he got Keith out of harm's way. Then they had rolled the mangled mess that was once Keith's pride and joy into a corner of the carpark, disconnected the horn and left it parked where it could await towing from the local breakdown garage. By rights, they probably should have phoned the police to report Keith for drinking and driving but Kim had taken the path of least resistance, just thankful that the only thing Keith had hurt was his pride and his precious car.

Kim had fumed her way through the rest of the shift, she really thought Keith was regressing – he had never been a paragon of virtue but these days he was behaving like a hormonal teenager!

"I'm so sorry about your dad," she said to Daniel later that evening. "Did you tell him you were coming here… not that you shouldn't of course!"

"It's fine Mum, honestly. It's not your fault. I told him we were visiting because I thought it might be nice to catch up with him for a coffee or something. I was planning on arranging to meet him somewhere. I didn't expect him to plough his way into the carpark – he could have really hurt someone!"

"I know, darling. I don't know what's going on in his head at the moment, he's being a bloody nuisance. But this isn't your fight."

"Seriously Mum, don't worry, it's fine. If I am honest, I was probably only seeing it out of a sense of duty, you're the most important person in my life."

Kim smiled and hugged her precious boy. The last thing she wanted was a doorstop showdown between her old and new significant others – it was all a bit 'fish-wife chav' for her liking – but she also knew that the conflict was all of Keith's own making; karma was presenting herself as quite the bitch it seemed!

Once the pub had emptied for the evening, Kim, Dean, Judy and the boys had slumped onto the comfy bar sofas and poured themselves a well-earned nightcap. Kim loved the pub when it was empty, it felt so peaceful after the hustle and bustle of a busy shift. They began to laugh and reminisce in the way that families often do and both Dean and Ryan fitted into the conversation like feet into a pair of well-loved slippers; it was as if they had always been there.

Kim began to feel the tension leaving her body and her pent-up frustrations from earlier eased with each sip of brandy and each jovial exchange. Just as she had mentally drawn a line under the afternoon's events, they were interrupted again by a frantic banging on the front door...

"For fuck's sake," said Kim for what felt like the hundredth time of the day, her calm demeanour leaving her in much less time than it had taken to arrive. "I swear to God, if he's back I'll bloody kill him myself!"

Dean opened the door to find a tear-stained Olivia on the doorstep.

"Is he here? He said he was coming back to her!" she screamed, pointing an accusatory finger at Kim.

Kim just about managed to maintain her cool, although the same hadn't quite been true for her mum Judy who had launched a few expletives in Olivia's direction that Kim wasn't even aware she knew… she wasn't even sure she had heard some of them herself!

She had calmly and politely told Olivia that she wouldn't take Keith back if he came bringing Gold, Frankincense and bloody Myrrh, and that if she didn't leave her pub immediately then she couldn't hold Judy responsible for what she was about to throw at her! It certainly explained a lot about the afternoon's fiasco – for Keith and Olivia it seemed that the honeymoon period was most definitely over.

"You haven't heard the last of this," screamed Olivia as she was ejected none-too-ceremoniously out into the warm summer evening.

"That is exactly what I am afraid of," sighed Kim!

AUTUMN CHILLS

at the

Dog & Duck

Chapter One

Megan rolled awkwardly out of bed and shuffled over to her bedroom windows, opening them as wide as the hinges would allow. Even though the summer was drawing to a close, the nights were still uncomfortably warm, especially when her belly was swelling at such an alarming rate. Her swollen ankles ached, even having been raised for the duration of her fitful night's sleep, and a bead of sweat was making its way rather unattractively down between her shoulder blades.

Megan's 9-year-old daughter Lottie had woken her in the night for the third time in a row which had been unheard of before the visit from her wayward father several months before – the same visit that had resulted in the unplanned baby growing inside her. Even though Lottie knew little about her father – he had certainly never been anything close to what a 'Dad' might be – his visit had really unsettled her. Not least because it had reminded her that she didn't have a father like most of her school friends, but also that there was to be a new addition to her little family which up until now had consisted of herself, her mummy and her nanny. Megan knew that Lottie was anxious about sharing her and her mum with their new family member and that perhaps she might be pushed out when the new baby arrived; not something that was easy for a nine-year-old to process or put into words. Both Megan and her mum had tried to talk about the new baby in only positive terms and in a way that gave Lottie opportunities to look forward to being an amazing big sister, but they were both fully aware that no amount of affirmation could put a positive spin on the fact that Lottie's biological father was a monumental twat, and a ridiculously selfish twat at that!

Megan was actually pleased that he hadn't left a forwarding address when he'd left to 'find himself', after their brief reunion, at least she didn't have to wrangle with the decision of whether to tell him about his impending paternity. This way, she could keep him out of the picture without a shred of guilt. Unfortunately, try as she might, she just could not get excited about the arrival of her second child, all she felt was fear and indifference, there was nothing even close to love, and for that she felt terribly guilty.

The shards of the late summer sun beamed in through the gap in the half-drawn blinds. Megan looked across at the clock: 5.58am. She sighed and decided against going back to bed; it would only mean tossing and turning for an hour before falling into a deep sleep, ten minutes before the alarm went off and feeling like crap for the rest of the morning. She pulled her cotton, summer dressing gown around her bloated middle, tears pricking the back of her eyelids as she caught sight of herself in the long wardrobe mirror. She wished she felt glowing, she wished she felt excited, she wished she felt something other than despair. This was not the life path she had planned for herself and Lottie and, not for the first time, she chided herself for having been gullible enough to fall for Lottie's dad's smooth-tongued bullshit… again!

She made her way down the steep stairs in her tiny, rented house to the downstairs bathroom that had probably looked modern about 30 years ago but now looked grubby no matter how much she scrubbed it. Her landlord did the bare minimum and there was no way her barmaid's wages allowed for home improvements. She loved her job at the Dog and Duck, and she couldn't have wished for a better friend and boss than Kim, but each month was still a juggling act when it came to paying the bills. She flicked the switch on the kettle and went into the bathroom. One of the many joyous things about pregnancy was the need to wee with unnatural frequency. The only problem was that her belly was now so large, as was the baby it seemed, that when she sat down to wee nothing would come out no matter how much she felt as if she would burst. The midwife had told her that 'baby' was probably pressing on her bladder and stopping the flow and so she should press on her belly just below her bump on the right-hand side. This had now become a force of habit and as Megan pressed her distended bladder, she was reminded of one of those big cartons of wine where you pushed the button to release the flow; how alluring she must look!

She peed for what felt like an eternity before washing her hands and returning to the kitchen to make herself a cup of tea and to get Lottie's packed lunch and breakfast ready. She had stopped in the shop on the way home to pick up a punnet of strawberries – Lottie's favourite – and had bought some of the lemon and raisin pancakes that Lottie loved so much; anything to put a smile back on her beloved daughter's face. It was only a few weeks until her tenth birthday and Megan so wanted to make it special – after all, double digits was quite a milestone in a little person's life – but what with her minimal budget and a new baby on the way, Megan feared that all she could give Lottie was more stuff to worry about.

She resolved to chat to her mum later on that day, she was always great for advice, and she loved Lottie just as ferociously as Megan did. If it came to it, perhaps Kim would give her a couple of extra shifts at the pub – although in her current state and the rate at which she was expanding, they'd be rolling her in and out of the pub with the beer barrels!

Chapter Two

Dean turned the key in the lock to his small studio flat just a short distance from the Dog and Duck where he had been enjoying the benefits of working for a landlady with whom he was completely besotted. Since their 'on-off-will they-won't they' relationship had finally become most definitely 'on,' he hadn't been back to his apartment for more than a whistle-stop visit to pick up clean clothes and check the mountain of free post that had dropped onto his front door mat. Unfortunately, tonight, he was going to have to sleep over as he had a landlord check in the morning along with some other exciting household stuff, including his obligatory 6 monthly boiler check to make sure he didn't snuff it in the night from carbon monoxide poisoning!

He was actually dreading sleeping alone for the first time in weeks and he already felt like a lovesick teenager. As far as he was concerned, Kim was the ying to his yang and he was quietly confident that she felt the same. They laughed together, worked together, talked for hours and were still managing some pretty awesome sex, despite their combined ages totalling over a century! Their relationship had got off to a pretty troubled start and Dean was forever grateful that Kim had managed to forgive him his chequered past and the fact that he had thrown his cheating wife's lover down the stairs and almost landed himself in prison for manslaughter. Fortunately, his former best mate had survived and graciously decided not to press charges provided Dean gave him his house and his wife; as far as Dean had been concerned, that had been a very dark cloud with a seriously silver lining! Unfortunately, his ex-wife Grace had re-appeared on the scene now that his ex-best friend had also discovered that she was a giant pain in the arse and threatened to blow his life apart. Some awkward confessions and the sad but timely death of Bobby, the resident pub alcoholic, had meant that Dean had been able to prove to Kim that he was good in a crisis and actually not the raving lunatic she had feared he might be. Now, that was all behind them and their relationship had gone from strength to strength. Grace had slunk back into her ivory tower, licking her wounds when Dean had told her in no uncertain terms that he was not interested in one single hair on her meticulously coiffed head, and Kim and he had begun to share the kind of companionship that he had previously thought was nothing but a pipe dream. As in every element of life they still had one large and disgruntled blot on the landscape in the form of her obnoxious ex-husband Keith, but Dean had vowed to remain cool, despite what Keith and his gold-digging ex-Dog and Duck barmaid girlfriend Olivia, threw their way; he wasn't going to risk losing everything for a second time by losing his rag.

The last contact they'd had with Keith had been when he'd crashed his mid-life crisis sports car into the pub wheelie bins after a few shandies and a row with Olivia. Olivia had later come storming into the pub, like an over made-up fishwife threatening all kinds of retribution and Dean feared that, as promised, they hadn't quite heard the last of them just yet. It was funny what an unsatisfactory divorce settlement did to people; unfortunately for Keith the pub had been left solely to Kim in her late Uncle's will and after their divorce, she had duly claimed it as such. Keith had clearly thought he was worth much more, despite having shirked rather than worked, during their 30-year marriage, and he was aimlessly flapping about trying to think of ways to claim what he mistakenly thought was rightfully his. They hadn't heard from either of them in several weeks. Dean didn't want a single penny of Kim's money, he felt ridiculously lucky enough just sharing their time together and running what was fast becoming a food destination on the list of local pubs and eateries, and he was keen to enjoy their quiet life, but he also couldn't shake the niggling feeling that when Keith and Olivia were quiet, it was more worrying than soothing.

Dean wandered around his flat, which in truth didn't exactly take long. The living accommodation in which he had once taken so much pride now looked sparse and unwelcoming. His military training meant that he had always been a stickler for a clean and tidy living space but now he really didn't have the enthusiasm to do anything past knocking down a couple of enormous cobwebs and flicking a duster over the bare surfaces. If he was honest with himself, this place didn't feel like home anymore. Home was the Dog and Duck; in fact, home was anywhere that Kim was, and he wanted nothing more than to live with her until he was old and grey... although a glance in the mirror showed him that the 'grey' was already well and truly established, disguised by the fact that he kept his hair cropped short to his head. He hadn't dared ask Kim if he could move in officially, he didn't want to push her so early in their relationship, but he hoped that she'd get so used to seeing his toothbrush in the bathroom that he'd become a permanent fixture without forcing the issue!

Chapter Three

Kim sat in the pub garden as she enjoyed a quiet cup of tea in the late afternoon sunshine. They'd had a long summer and had been blessed with many days of blue skies and sunshine. Today was the first day that she had actually been alone in the pub for quite a few weeks; discounting the customers of course! Dean hadn't really left since the day that Bobby had died, and they had finally 'sealed the deal' on their relationship. Bobby's death had been tragic – although not overly unexpected for a man who had been the size of two men and drank the same quantity of beer as two men might – but it had also meant that she and Dean had at last overcome the awkwardness that had previously existed between them.

She couldn't remember a time when she had felt so happy and contented in another human's company, especially a male human! They got along great, he was capable and reliable, he just got on with things, and he didn't mind pulling his weight; he didn't even leave his pants on the bathroom floor! She might have thought that the way things were could be classed as a cause for concern – the old adage about if things seemed too good to be true had often popped into her head – but Dean's skeleton had leapt from his closet in quite a dramatic way long before they had officially become a couple so she felt that, unless he was a secret spy or an international jewel thief, their cards were pretty much wide open on the proverbial table. Her own relationship had ended in hideous, and very public technicolour, when Keith had copped off with Olivia in the cellar, so they were both an open book to each other whether that had been their initial intention or not! In truth, Kim loved the raw honesty between them and the fact that they had very few secrets left to share; she hoped it would never be necessary to divulge the fact that she occasionally took a sneaky pee in the shower or that she still harboured a guilty crush on Richard Gere and often dreamed of a 'Pretty Woman' or 'Officer and a Gentleman' kind of rescue that involved her being gracefully scooped up into a pair of strong arms without flashing her knickers!

She had even toyed with the idea of asking Dean to move in permanently – she thought he was keen, especially when she considered the fact that he hadn't been in any rush to leave – but she didn't want to blow things by appearing too needy. The truth was that at fifty-something, she wasn't quite sure how the whole dating thing worked anymore, when was too soon? Was it cool to play it cool, or was it now the role of the independent, modern woman to take the lead and be bold enough to ask for what she wanted? She was buggered if she knew. All she did know was that Dean had only been gone a couple of hours and she missed him already; she was dreading sleeping alone tonight.

She slurped the last of her tea and made her way back into the pub. Monday afternoons were typically quiet and the evenings weren't much busier, but she still had to make sure that the pub was open and ready for business. Rosa was pottering around in the kitchen just tidying up and humming softly to herself. Even though the pub was now open all day, there were no customers in the bar and Rosa just liked to keep busy. Megan had looked tired when she had come in earlier that day and Kim had packed her off early; she worried that she was finding it difficult to cope with the prospect of having two little mouths to feed and care for. Megan's mum was a tower of strength and supported Megan and Lottie whole heartedly, but still, it was a lot to deal with.

"You okay, mia cara?" asked Rosa.

"Yes, all good, thanks. Just feels strange without Dean here don't you think?"

Rosa smiled and gave Kim a wink before humming 'Here comes the bride'.

"Oh sshhh you!" laughed Kim. "I just meant he's normally around that's all!"

Rosa smiled again and blew kisses at Kim. Kim threw a tea towel in her direction in mock indignation, but she knew that Rosa only ever had her best interests at heart. She was also a wily old bird and usually knew much more than she let on about most things! Kim adored Rosa, and she had been like a mother to her, especially with her own mum being at least a couple of hours' drive away – she was forever grateful that she had her in her life.

“Shall we have a little something before the people come?” asked Rosa, dishing two generous portions of her famous homemade lasagne onto a plate before Kim had the chance to answer.

Kim nodded her reply and collected two sets of cutlery to take through to their favourite table in the bar where they often ate and put the world to rights. She knew she wouldn’t eat later on, especially as Dean wasn’t here clucking around her and generally looking after her in the way that he did, so she was grateful to share Rosa’s ‘piece de resistance’!

They ate and chatted about the upcoming week – darts on Tuesday, a pool match on Wednesday, the Women Who Wine ladies’ business meeting on Thursday lunchtime and a quiz night on Friday; it was going to be a busy one!

Monday passed uneventfully although, as suspected, Kim did not sleep soundly. After a night of fitful sleep and some weird and disturbing dreams during which she flitted from sitting in a packed bar in her underpants to eating a lasagne full of maggots, she gave up and went downstairs to make a cup of tea and check that the front door was locked for at least the hundredth time. Despite her protestations and assurances to the rest of her team, Keith’s dramatic collision in the car park followed by some pretty wild threats from a hysterical and vengeful Olivia had rattled Kim and deep in her gut she was expecting more unwanted confrontation. The fact that the pair of them had been so quiet these last couple of months did nothing to ease her concerns.

She looked at the pub clock and saw to her dismay that it was still only 3.25 in the morning – even she couldn't justify getting up and starting her day that early... besides, she'd be knackered by lunchtime if she did. She jiggled the front door lock one last time and climbed wearily back upstairs to the flat that she now called home. She crawled into bed, placing her phone on the nightstand beside her and plugging her earphones into a guided meditation on YouTube.

"...concentrate on your breathing... breathe in for four... hold for four... and sloooowllly release... one, two, three, four... walk down the steps, one, two, three, four... deeper... deeper... deeper... five, six... seven..."

Kim didn't remember reaching the bottom of the steps.

"Buzzzzzzzzz, buzzzzzzzzzzzz, buzzzzzzzzzz..."

Kim woke up with a jolt, her phone jumping around on the side as it vibrated to alert her to an incoming call. She rolled over, tangling herself up in the lead of her headphones as she made a futile reach for her phone. Her headphones twisted their way further around her neck as the phone slid onto the floor, almost garrotting her in the process.

"For fuck's sake," she swore as she ripped the murderous headphones from her ears. She reached down to retrieve the phone from where it had somehow managed to wedge itself between the bedside cabinet and the leg of her bed in a position that she couldn't have achieved if she'd been a bloody, fully trained marksman. Just as she finally curled her fingers around the offending phone it stopped vibrating and with a dramatic 'ping' the battery died, and it went completely silent.

"For FUCK'S sake!" she said again, louder this time; she was beginning to sound like she had developed a bad case of Tourette's!

She hurled herself from the bed, snatching the phone from its place of refuge and ripped the sodding headphones from their plug, before throwing them unceremoniously across the room. She located the charger on her dressing table in the corner of the room and plugged the phone back in. No sooner had it received 1% of battery and she had managed to turn it back on, was it buzzing furiously again…

"Hello!" she answered, none too calmly.

"Oh God babe, are you ok?" Dean's frantic voice echoed down the line. "I've been calling you for ages, I was just about to run over there!"

"No, I'm okay," said Kim, instantly softening at the sound of his voice. "I just got attacked by a pair of headphones, half-strangled my bloody self, then my phone died, and I had to put it on charge… other than that I'm great!"

"I'm not sure you're safe to be left alone," laughed Dean. "Was everything okay last night? I've got the boiler man coming at ten, so all being good I should be with you by eleven thirty at the latest."

"Yeah, it was all okay. I checked the front door was locked at least a hundred times; it was weird here without you." Kim inwardly cringed at how corny she must have sounded.

"I missed you darling, the place feels like a tomb without you here."

"Hark at us, like a pair of lovesick idiots! Well, get your arse back here and I'll warm you back up," giggled Kim.

"Oooh, I like the sound of that, anyway gotta go I think that's the front door."

"Hang on, what's the time?" asked Kim, looking at the clock as she asked the question. "Oh my Christ it's five to ten! No wonder you thought I was in trouble – I must have slept like the bloody dead. Rosa will be here any minute and I'm not even dressed!"

"Mmmm, even better," said Dean, his attention now distracted from the persistent doorbell.

"Cool down, Romeo! Go and answer that door and I'll see you later!"

Kim hung up the phone, grinning like a Cheshire cat; she hoped he always made her feel this way. She crossed the landing in the direction of the bathroom as she heard Rosa's voice ringing up the stairs.

“Good morning mia cara, coffee?”

“Coffee would be awesome, I’m running late, just going to jump in the shower.”

“No rush mia cara, when you’re ready.”

Kim took her time under the shower, falling into a deep sleep in the early hours of the morning had seriously messed with her body clock and she felt as sluggish as hell. She knew they were well prepared for whatever the day threw their way, she was blessed with the best people in her little team. Megan had given the pub an extra good clean yesterday as she had an appointment with the midwife that morning; Kim hoped that she would find a way to embrace this new baby, it was horrible watching Megan so clearly torn emotionally. She resolved to chat with Rosa and Dean when he got back, to see if they could find a way to help lift her spirits.

Kim finished her shower and applied some gradual tan moisturiser – it made her feel better, and the bottle promised to ‘tone and firm’, which was a welcome but somewhat bold claim she feared. She gave her hair a quick once over with the hairdryer and dressed in an emerald green maxi dress that was cool yet flattering; obviously this was just the first thing that she had laid her hands on in the wardrobe not something that had been carefully chosen for Dean’s return after an entire night away!

Kim heard the bolt sliding back on the heavy old front door and completed her morning routine with more haste – no matter how organised they were, it wasn't fair to leave Rosa in charge of the bar and the kitchen. She added a quick slick of raspberry kiss lip-gloss and slid her feet into her favourite silver flip flops – not too bad if she did say so herself! She made her way downstairs, opening the door to the bar...

"Jesus fucking Christ Almighty!" she exclaimed catching sight of Bobby, sitting at the bar, larger than life, resplendent in the garish red Hawaiian shirt that he had worn on the day of his earthly departure.

"It's okay," said a voice from behind Bobby's giant form. "It's just a cardboard cut-out... it's great though, isn't it? It's like he's still here in the room!"

Kim clutched her hand to her chest, her heart beating wildly. "Jesus Christ, Steve, you gave me a bloody heart attack," she exclaimed before cringing at the insensitivity of her chosen euphemism considering that Bobby's demise and been the result of exactly that!

Steve, aka Brag Pit, aka local pub know-it-all and Bobby's best mate, stepped out from behind the life-sized cardboard cut-out of his dear departed friend. "I had it made specially, it would have been the old boy's birthday today, I thought it would be nice to have a drink with him."

Kim had just been about to reply that, 'No, it wasn't great, and that she'd be buggered if she was going to be staring at Bobby's puce-coloured cheeks and jumping out of her skin every five minutes,' but then she had seen the elation on Steve's face at having brought his mate in for one last pint and she didn't quite have the heart to tell him that Bobby would have to leave the building one last time!

"Gave me the fright of my bloddy life," exclaimed Rosa as she appeared from the kitchen.

Kim rolled her eyes and shuddered. Quite frankly the apparition of Bobby was creepy-as-fucking-hell, but she supposed she'd have to suffer it for today at least.

"Bloody hell!" gasped Dean as he too came through from the kitchen. "I thought I'd seen a ghost!"

"It's great, isn't it?" grinned an oblivious Steve. "We're having a drink for his birthday."

Dean smiled at Kim. She stood on tip toes to kiss him on the cheek, "Don't you dare say a word," she whispered into his ear.

Chapter Four

Bobby's impromptu birthday celebration had been a raucous affair, almost as if Bobby was conducting it from beyond the grave. His long-suffering girlfriend – an ex-alcoholic who had sat in the pub, day in day out, sipping on a sin-free drink whilst Bobby chucked enough pints of lager down his neck to sink a battleship – had come to the pub to join in the birthday celebrations. It was difficult to tell if she was having a nice time; Fran never looked anything other than melancholic and she rarely spoke, but she stayed nevertheless. Kim and several of the locals watched her carefully, it was not beyond her to try and sneak a drink of something stronger than she ordered, but one more drink could potentially kill her, and Kim did not relish the idea of another death in her pub – she was running a public house not a bloody mortuary!

Lunchtime ran into evening and Steve had drunk both his share and Bobby's. By nine o'clock he could barely stand, and Kim took the decision to call him a taxi, reluctantly agreeing to 'look after' Bobby until Steve came to collect him in the morning. When the darts team had arrived at seven, they had embraced the ghost of Bobby and he had been bought more drinks than when he was alive!

"Bloody hell," Brian – other half of Doris, and one of Kim's favourite regulars – exclaimed when he and his wife came in for dinner. “He ain’t got no better looking with age has he?”

Kim giggled, “Sssh! Don’t upset him, I don’t want him coming back to haunt us!”

Doris rolled her eyes. “At least he talks a bit more sense than he used to!”

Once Steve had been poured into his taxi, Kim and her team had continued to race around serving the thirsty customers and accommodating the visiting pool team. Fleur had popped in to say hi and had similarly been surprised to see Bobby at the bar in glorious technicolour.

“I didn’t know it was Halloween just yet,” she whispered to Kim. “Are you warding off evil spirits?”

“Oh don’t!” sighed Kim to Fleur with whom she had now become firm friends since her arrival at the pub over half a year ago. Fleur had been a catalyst in the growing popularity of the pub, encouraging her Women Who Wine ladies’ group to hold their regular meetings there and she and Kim were now inseparable.

“You heard any more from Fred and Rose?” asked Fleur, using the rather non-PC nicknames she had adopted for Keith and Olivia.

“Not a peep. Makes me bloody nervous if I am honest. He’s much less dangerous when he’s making a noise.”

"Isn't that what they say in an emergency?" laughed Fleur. "Deal with the quiet ones first cos if they're making a noise you know they're alive and less dangerous!"

"Exactly! I can't believe lady muck is gonna give up that easily. Last I heard, she was seen in the travel agents in town booking an all-inclusive to the Costa del Sol. The rate she's working her way through Keith's money, it'll be gone by Christmas, and I wouldn't be surprised if she's deluded enough to believe that she'll get 'her' pub back!"

"Well at least you've got your own personal bodyguard now," smiled Fleur glancing in Dean's direction.

Kim blushed. "Bless him, he stayed away last night, and I can't believe how much I missed him. When I was married to Keith, I couldn't wait for him to go out... trouble was, he always came home!"

"Talking of going out, has Dean spoken to you about the weekend after next yet?"

Kim frowned in confusion just as Rosa came over. "It's all sorted mia cara, I'm holding the castle!"

"I think you mean holding the fort, Rosa," said Dean as he plonked an antipasti platter for two on the bar. "Table six... and it was meant to be a surprise!"

"Ay, ay, ay," sighed Rosa in a theatrical tone, sounding for all the world like an Italian Don!

"Will someone please tell me what the bloody hell is going on? It sounds like you have all been scheming behind my back?" said Kim.

"Sorry babe, my bad. I thought he was going to tell you today," said Fleur.

"I was," laughed Dean, "but once we'd got the pub to ourselves... if you know what I mean?"

Kim blushed and slapped Dean playfully on the arm.

"It's okay, we know you're doing it... even at your age," laughed Fleur. "Now I've ruined the moment I'll leave Dean to explain, but you're going to love it!"

Dean kissed Kim on the cheek and explained that he and Fleur had been in cahoots to arrange a little weekend trip away for just the four of them – Kim, Dean, Fleur and Fleur's long-term boyfriend Rob. They had arranged for Rosa to look after the place while they were away, and Megan's mum Sandra was going to come in and support her daughter and Rosa if she needed help. Jake the barman had also agreed to work the whole weekend.

"It's only one night; we go Saturday morning and come back Sunday evening. It's a spa hotel with a golf course, so me and Rob will have a game while you girls relax and then we're booked for a nice meal on Saturday evening. You don't hate surprises, do you?" asked Dean a little anxiously.

"Oh babe, I love it! I can't remember the last time anyone planned a surprise for me, thank you! Although do you think that Rosa will be okay here on her own?"

"She's going to stay over if that's alright with you? I thought you'd prefer someone on the premises?"

"I think that's a great idea and I'd rather she stayed here than have to go home in the dark. Will she be okay on her own here do you think? I worry a bit about her. I wonder if Megan and her mum would like to stay here with little Lottie as well? Might be a brief change of scenery for them – I know Megan hasn't been coping too well and poor Lottie is a bit unsettled."

"I almost wondered that myself," said Dean. "If you don't mind a houseful I reckon that will be perfect, if they're up for it."

Kim threw her arms around him and ignored the cries of... 'get a room!' from a couple of the customers. It had been a long time since anyone had done anything so thoughtful for her – excluding Daniel and her mum – but she couldn't remember Keith ever having surprised with anything more than a parking fine or a broken promise!

Kim had spent the rest of the evening on a high. Rosa had thought it a great idea to have Megan and her little family come and stay, and a quick phone call to Megan had confirmed that the feeling was mutual.

Throughout the evening, excited discussions with Fleur in between service had revealed their intended destination via a few photos on Fleur's phone and it looked amazing; a beautiful country hotel set in beautiful grounds, overlooking the golf course where the boys were set to enjoy eighteen holes while the girls lazed by the indoor pool and got pampered by the resident beauty therapists.

They were set to leave in a week's time, early on Saturday morning returning on Sunday around teatime and Kim felt like an excited child looking forward to Christmas. Later on that night, when Kim and Dean lay in bed together cuddled up, chatting about their trip, Kim couldn't remember ever feeling so content. To add a very juicy cherry to top of her cake, she had received a phone call from her son Daniel to say that he and his other half Ryan were coming for a quick visit on their way to their holiday destination on Monday – the day after Kim and Dean got back. Daniel had also offered to bring Kim's mum Judy with him so that she could stay whilst they were away, and he would pick her up on their way home. Life didn't get much better than this – a thriving pub she now loved, great staff and friends, a boyfriend she adored and a visit from her precious family; yep, she really was a lucky girl!

Chapter Five

Kim jumped at the sight of Bobby who seemed to have taken up residence at the bar. She was never going to get used to his life-sized effigy, a permanent grin on his face, his Hawaiian shirt now even less appropriate as the summer came to a close and the autumn nights began to draw in.

"He's going to have to go," she said to Rosa, who had also jumped when she had 'bumped' into Bobby earlier that morning.

"He freaks me out," said Rosa, "it's a bit weird don't you think?"

"It's positively creepy," sighed Kim. "I'll have to have a word with Steve. I know he misses his mate, poor thing, but this is a pub not a bloody cemetery! I'll broach the subject when I get back from my weekend away, I don't want to upset him but if he wants to keep him, he'll have to take him home!"

"Poor old Bobby," chuckled Dean. "You know how much he loved the pub!"

"Oh sshh you! Why don't you take him back to your place?"

"Sod that!" said Dean. "My landlord will think I've got a lodger!"

"Lottie nearly had a heart attack," said Megan waddling through from the toilets where she had been finishing her morning's cleaning routine. "I brought her in with me when I dropped the new loo rolls in yesterday... scared the bloody life out of her!"

"I know, he's going to have to go, I'll have to find a delicate way to broach the subject with Steve, I can't really say it's cause he's scaring the customers! How you doing today babe, you sleeping any better?" asked Kim.

"Some nights are better than others, my mum bought me one of those long sausage cushions that you can wrap around your lumpy bits; it's helped a bit, but I still need to pee at least four times a night!"

"Aw bless you, it might be better when the nights get cooler, you've got a way to go yet! Have you thought any more about Lottie's birthday?"

"It sounds awful but I'm dreading it. She's so unsettled at the moment, and I feel permanently like I'm letting her down. I want to make it really special for her, but I don't have the money for anything lavish and if I am honest, I don't really know what to do for the best."

"She just needs love," smiled Rosa. "She'll be okay, expensive gifts aren't the answer to much, at the end of the day."

"She's right," said Kim, kindly. "Lottie has more than enough love from you and your mum and that's worth more than any present you could buy her. We can make sure she has a special day; we can have a party here for her. We can decorate the back room, put some balloons up."

"I'll make her favourite chocolate cake," said Dean, "you know how much she loves chocolate."

Megan's eyes began to fill with tears, her bottom lip trembling.

"It's going to be fine love, honestly. You're a great mum and Lottie will be the best big sister. Trust me, once the baby comes things will fall into place," said Kim, putting her arm around Megan as she saw her start to crumble.

"It's such a mess, and I just don't know if I can..." Megan's voice trailed off as she struggled to find the words, the tears now spilling onto her cheeks.

"You can and you will," said Kim, quietly. "And what's more you'll be amazing once the worry goes away. You're just anxious about the future right now because this wasn't something you planned. Plus, whether you admit it or not, you're feeling let down by Lottie's dad and angry that you let your guard down. But honestly, this baby will bring you love... I promise."

"Bloddy bastard," exclaimed Rosa. "At least he's done the decent thing and buggered off; you'd be much worse off if he'd stuck around to poke his oars in. We're your family now."

Megan smiled through her tears at Rosa's misquote of an English saying, something she was now famous for. "I don't know what I'd do without all of you. I'm so lucky to have you."

"Nonsense," said Kim, "we are lucky to have you, and little Lottie. And now you're going to give us another little person to love. You're part of this crazy family now whether you like it or not!"

At that moment, Dean reappeared from the kitchen, having slipped quietly away whilst Kim and Rosa had been comforting Megan. "Hot chocolate anyone? I'm not much use when it comes to pregnancy and hormones, but I reckon that chocolate is usually a safe bet in most situations!"

"Oh yes," sniffed Megan, blowing her nose on the serviette that Rosa had just thrust into her hand. "Seeing as alcohol is now out of the question, I think chocolate sounds perfect!"

As they sipped the velvety hot chocolate topped with cream and a dusting of chocolate powder, they chatted about Lottie's impending birthday in a few weeks and Kim was pleased to see that Megan began to lose some of the worry from her face. Deep down, Kim knew that things would all be fine in the end, no matter how anxious Megan felt currently – babies always brought love in her eyes. Whatever happened, Lottie would have the very best birthday a little girl could hope for; she may not have been entirely sure what that would look like, but she knew that they would pull it off together.

Chapter Six

Dean sighed as he swept up the broken glass from the kitchen floor. “You need to keep that back door closed when we’re out, babe,” he said as Kim walked in behind him, carrying the last of the shopping bags from the car.

“What do you mean?”

“You must have left it open when we went shopping. Next door’s cat has let himself in again and knocked the glasses off the drainer,” replied Dean, scraping the last of the debris into the bin. “Mind where you’re walking and don’t come down here without something on your feet until I’ve hoovered.”

“I’m certain I closed it up before we left,” said Kim.

“Well unless the cat has got a key, I reckon you forgot,” laughed Dean. “Never mind, it was only a couple of glasses, it’s all done now.”

“That’s bloody weird. I could have sworn I shut it – I’m going mad in my old age.”

“Well mad or not, you’ll do for me,” said Dean, planting a kiss on Kim’s cheek. “You shouldn’t leave the place open though, babe, when there’s only one person in.”

“I know, that’s still bloody weird though,” said Kim.

They finished unpacking the shopping just as Jake popped his head around the door. “Everything okay?" he asked.

“Yeah, I think next door’s cat has been having a party in the kitchen,” sighed Kim. “There was glass everywhere when we came in.”

“Oh bloody hell, sorry about that. I’ve been down in the cellar. We haven’t had a soul in all afternoon, so I nipped down and sorted a couple of the pipes out. I didn’t hear a thing!” exclaimed Jake.

“Not to worry,” said Kim. “I must have forgotten to close the door when we went out, no harm done. No problems this afternoon otherwise?”

“Nope, all good,” said Jake. “Just me and Bobby – as quiet as the grave you might say.”

Kim laughed. “Well at least he’ll scare off any demons! Promise me you’ll keep that door locked up when we’re away though, won’t you? Dean’s right, it’d be easy enough for someone to sneak in the back if you’re all busy in the bar. I’m more worried about your safety than anything else, especially if the girls are here on their own.”

“No worries boss, I’ll look after them don’t worry!”

At that moment Kim’s phone began ringing and she made her excuses to go and chat to her mum on face time whilst Dean and Jake chewed the fat about cellar maintenance.

Judy was her usual bubbly self and Kim could hardly keep up with her social life – bridge, bowls, flower arranging, afternoon tea – the woman never stopped! They chatted for around half an hour before saying their goodbyes and each expressing their excitement about Judy's impending visit the week after next.

The rest of the week passed without too much drama, apart from an unpleasant incident with the wheelie bins that had somehow been upended overnight spewing several days' worth of food scraps all over the car park and providing an unexpected feast for the local fox and his nocturnal friends. It had taken over an hour for Kim to sweep and wash the rotting food away and Dean had spent just as long trying without success to fix the lids on the bins that had been catastrophically damaged in the fall. They now had the problem of bins without secure lids until the council could replace them. Fortunately, Dean had managed to cobble together a less-than-pretty makeshift bin store, which would keep them out of harm's way until the job could be done properly.

Megan had popped in with Lottie after school on the Thursday afternoon before Kim and Dean's night away and Lottie had seemed much chattier than of late.

"I can't wait to come and stay here Auntie Kim," she said, excitedly. "Mummy said we can stay up until midnight and I can serve the drinks."

"That's not exactly what I said," smiled Megan. "I said we could maybe have a movie night and you can help Rosa to pick up the glasses."

"If you're a really good girl, Mummy might forget the time," whispered Kim conspiratorially. "Anyway, it's not long until your birthday, are you excited? Do you know what you want yet?"

"Am I allowed three friends to my birthday tea here? Mummy said I can only have two, but Jade Smithers got really upset when I said I was only inviting Emily and Jessica O."

Kim laughed at Lottie's use of her friends' surnames to tell them apart from others with the same name in her class. "Three is fine darling, we don't want to upset Jade Smithers! So do you know what you want?"

Lottie lowered her eyes to the ground. "She wants a puppy," exclaimed Megan, but I've explained that it's not really possible in our little house, especially as my landlord wouldn't allow it."

"Puppies are a lot of work," said Kim, kindly. "Maybe one day you'll have one; at least your new baby brother or sister won't need walking!"

Lottie smiled. "If I can't have a puppy, I'll just have a party then."

Kim chuckled, "And it's going to be the best party you could wish for! If you put your head in the kitchen, I think Uncle Dean might do you a hot chocolate."

Lottie skipped off to the kitchen, momentarily distracted from her ambitious birthday wish list.

"Thank you," said Megan. "She's wanted a puppy for ages, but it just isn't practical and I'm not sure I could cope with a new baby and a new dog!"

"Yes, I think that's probably a bit much at the moment," said Kim. "Dean will cheer her up, she's got him wrapped around her little finger!"

"Ooh, I forgot to ask you," said Megan. "Did you notice the security lights were out in the car park?"

"No, when did you notice that?"

"Yesterday when I left, they usually ping on when I leave but they didn't. I'm not sure but one of them looked like it was bent the wrong way."

"Bloody brilliant," exclaimed Kim. "It's one thing after another at the moment. You heard about the sodding wheelie bins, didn't you? There was rotten cabbage and maggots all over the carpark – one of the old food bags had somehow got wedged in the drain and blocked it too. We didn't notice it until yesterday when there was stale water flooding out around the drain and now the lights... I think he's come back to bloody haunt us," she said grimly, nodding in cardboard Bobby's direction.

"Oh don't," Megan winced. "He creeps me out staring at everyone!"

"I know," said Kim. "Don't worry, he's going, straight after the weekend whether Steve likes it or not. Every time I come down the stairs I nearly bloody wet myself. My mum'll have a blue fit if he's still sitting there when she comes to stay!"

Megan laughed, "Do you think Fran will want him?"

"I'm not sure she wanted him when he was alive," chuckled Kim. "Can you imagine having him sitting in your living room watching your every move?"

"No I bloody can't! Lottie, come on, we've got to go, Nanny's coming round at six."

Lottie came bounding out of the kitchen, a chocolate smile plastered on her face.

"No guesses what you've been up to," giggled Kim. "See you both later. I'll get Dean to look at the lights but make sure you keep the place locked up whilst we are away."

"We'll be fine," said Megan. "There's going to be five of us here to look after the place – six if you include the grim reaper over there! Seriously, it's one night, we'll be fine, and you need to go away and relax!"

"If you insist," smiled Kim. "I'm happier that you've got Jake on hand if you need him; he's a good lad."

"Exactly! You have nothing to worry about. It's about time you had a break, you look after everyone else enough, now stop worrying!"

Kim hugged Megan and kissed Lottie on the top of her blonde head, squirreling a sneaky chocolate bar into her coat pocket.

"I saw that," laughed Megan.

Kim and Lottie shared a look of feigned innocence.

Once Kim had waved goodbye to Megan and Lottie, she went to find Dean who was scratching his head and looking up at the security lights, having overheard Kim and Megan's earlier conversation.

"Christ knows what happened to this light, it's bent right down on the bracket and the bulb is blown."

"Do you think it could have been a bird or something? It can't have been the wind, can it?"

"You'd need a hurricane to cause this sort of damage, but I guess it could have been a bird or…"

"…or what?" asked Kim.

"I don't know, I wonder if it could have been tampered with but I'm not sure how or why anyone would bother," said Dean. "They weren't the best quality, perhaps you should consider some better-quality lighting and put it higher up?"

"Let's have a look when we get back," said Kim. "It probably wouldn't be a bad idea now the nights are getting darker; I might even see if we can get some CCTV put in, there was a couple of burglaries in the village last week."

"Yes, probably not a bad idea – a camera or a dog are usually the best deterrents! I'll see what I can do but I don't hold out much hope; we'll definitely do something more permanent when we get back next week."

"Thanks babe, I don't know what I'd do without your help."

Dean smiled and blew her a kiss before going back to wrangling with the offending light and a long-handled screwdriver. Kim hoped they weren't next in line to be the victim of any thefts although she figured that they were probably safer than most houses as the pub was rarely without anyone at home. Nevertheless, she resolved to get things tightened up before the month was out – better safe than sorry.

On Thursday evening, Kim took the opportunity to go upstairs and do a little packing for the weekend whilst her capable little team took control downstairs. They had the monthly quiz the evening after on the Friday and it had become quite popular both with locals and visiting quiz enthusiasts – it was usually a busy evening and she didn't imagine she'd get much time to take a breath, let alone pack her bag. Kim had always envied those women who were able to go away with a small overnight bag containing an impossibly stylish 'capsule' wardrobe that covered every eventuality from daytime through to evening with just one carefully chosen top, a jacket and two pairs of shoes. Her own packing style resembled that of a Tasmanian Devil with a severe case of multiple personality disorder! She'd always start so calmly with one outfit to travel in and one for the evening before suffering a crisis of confidence and throwing in shirts, dresses, trousers, jumpers and everything but the kitchen sink just at the last minute, only to arrive at her venue and realise that she had simply packed a load of random contradictory stuff that was wholly incompatible and about as far away from a 'cohesive' look as it was possible to get! This time she resolved to make a decision and stick to it, packing one dress for the evening with a nice jacket and laying out some pale pink jeans, a T-shirt with a heart design, a fitted denim jacket and her new white trainers with the silver detail. All in all, she was pretty pleased with her efforts although she did throw in some smart trousers and a glitzy top... just in case! Fortunately, she also remembered to pack a swimming costume for the spa – she had brought this last year and hoped it still fitted and was also still able to deliver the body shaping and tummy flattening that it had promised on the label. She also chucked some pretty pyjamas that were ridiculously impractical for the cold winter nights but that were a little sexier than the fleece onesie with the tail and bunny ears that her mum had bought her for Christmas!

Chapter Seven

The quiz night contestants started arriving promptly as usual and the pub was full by seven o'clock even though it didn't start until half past. A hum of excited chatter filled the bar as tables were pushed and shunted around to accommodate the different team configurations. Brian and Doris were part of a team of six called the 'Silver Foxes', whilst eight of the Women Who Wine group had formed their own team aptly named 'Wonder Women'. A very serious and highly competitive team, 'Les Quizzables', from The White Hart in one of the nearby villages had arrived in formal dress looking like they were about to make their appearance on University Challenge and who would likely spend the night nursing half a lager each, after begrudgingly paying the five quid a head necessary for the prize kitty. They were sore losers and had often been known to question scoring outcomes before leaving with their tails between their legs if they felt they had been wrongly judged. If they won however, they would strut around the pub performing some kind of lap of honour, although still not buying any more drinks.

The quiz continued to be hosted by Jim the butcher's daughter-in-law, Laura, and the rest of the pub seemed able to overlook the possible potential for bias that might be afforded to 'Jim's Meaty Minds', in exchange for a tray of homemade pork pies and some of his world-beating Lincolnshire Sausage Rolls.

Bobby maintained his usual seat at the bar and Kim feared that even the locals were becoming attached to his ghostly presence, if only for the comedy value provided by a giant cut-out of a bloke in Hawaiian wear propping up the bar of an English country village pub in late September! Even Fran had taken to sitting beside him when she came to the pub, and he had been a part of many a drunken selfie; he was going to have to go before he became a bloody tourist attraction! Kim still wasn't convinced that he wasn't haunting the place and, if she hadn't known she was being ridiculous, she wasn't entirely certain that he hadn't hidden the spare key to the back door that she couldn't locate for the life of her. However, she wasn't about to voice that little concern out loud – only last week there'd been an article in the local gazette about a woman who had been almost force-fed HRT when her long-suffering family had frog-marched her to the doctor after the menopause had sent her a bit doolally. Kim could just imagine Dean's face if she told him that she thought Bobby's ghost was hiding her stuff! There was nothing for it but to steel herself for an awkward conversation with Steve in the hopes of persuading him to help Bobby's spirit exit the building one last time – either that or they'd be having an alternative Guy going on the fire on Bonfire Night!

At precisely 7.30 p.m., the eager quizzers began to grow restless, and Kim diplomatically drew Laura's attention to the large clock on the wall before they had a full-scale mutiny on their hands.

"Settle down ladies and gents, get yourselves comfy and let us begin," said Laura over the mic. "No conferring please, and if you shout out the answer and another team steals then that's your own silly fault."

Laura was referring to an incident the previous month in which a new member of Les Quizzables had inadvertently called out one of the answers in their eager drive for victory. Unfortunately, this extra point had been just what the Silver Foxes had needed for the win and there had been much disgruntlement from the hapless contestant's teammates. They had tried, unsuccessfully, to call foul play, but Laura ran a tight ship and was having none of it. The Silver Foxes had perhaps revelled a little too enthusiastically in their triumphant win – almost to the point of gloating – but had the Quizzables been a little less pompous then perhaps a little more diplomacy may have been employed! In the end, it was Kim's opinion that you reaped what you sowed, and that pride almost always came before a fall.

By 8.30 p.m., the quiz was well and truly underway, and at times you could have heard a pin drop. Even the juke box had been turned off between rounds and the only time there was a burst of noise and activity was when there was a break in questions and there was the inevitable dash for the loo and the bar. This meant that during the questions, Kim and Rosa were twiddling their thumbs and during the breaks they were running around like two blue-arsed flies! Dean kept the food to bar-snacks-only on quiz nights, or things that could be eaten with fingers or just a fork; proceedings were far too intense to allow for a full-blown meal!

By 9.30 p.m., Laura was just finishing the final round of questions on pop lyrics and there were hushed discussions on which singer's 'guilty feet had no rhythm'. As the quiz drew to a close, there was one last rush for the bar whilst Laura did the final tally on the scores. They had taken to having impartial markers due to the 'creative' nature of some teams' tactical scoring especially when the sweet smell of success was within sniffing distance! By 10 p.m. the Wonder Women had been declared the worthy winners, having smashed the round on capital cities, much to the disappointment of the silver Foxes who had been convinced that Rio de Janeiro was still the capital of Brazil and needed confirmation from Google to convince them otherwise. The prize kitty had been a respectable £210 but the glory of the win was priceless!

Rosa had planned to stay the night at the end of the shift as Kim and Dean were going to be leaving first thing in the morning. Dean and Rob had a tee time of 8am at the hotel which was a good hour's drive away and they also needed to pick up Fleur and Rob on the way. As much as the quiz had been a roaring success in terms of the night's takings along with the pub's continuing good reputation, Kim was not sorry to see the last of the customers depart. She was shattered and also really looking forward to her night away.

"Well done ladies," said Dean as he brought through two very welcome coffees at the end of the evening. "Another quiz night smashed!"

"I'm pooped!" said Rosa.

"Are you sure you're going to be okay this weekend?" asked Kim.

"Now sshh mia cara! It is just ONE night. I have Jake and Megan and Megan's mum, so I will be just fine."

"And don't forget Lottie," laughed Dean. "I'm sure she thinks she's actually going to be running the place!"

"Bless her," said Kim. "Well, I have every faith in all of you and I can't deny I'm not looking forward to it. Just make sure you lock everything up when you close – there's been a bit of trouble in Loxley you know."

"I will make sure," said Rosa. "Now I am off to my bed, or I will be good for nothing in the morning!"

Dean bolted the front door and double checked the back before turning off the lights and following the girls upstairs. Kim was never more pleased that she had done her packing in advance – God knows what she would have managed to cram into a bag if she was under pressure!

Chapter Eight

Kim was awake twenty minutes before the alarm went off – she hadn't felt this excited in a long time. She disabled the alert on her phone and padded into the kitchen to make a cup of tea. It wasn't long before she felt Dean's arms snake around her middle as she stirred the milk into the cups.

"Good morning gorgeous. I hope you are aware what you have signed up for?"

"What do you mean?" giggled Kim enjoying the feel of Dean's lips on her neck.

"Just, you know what happens in hotels right?"

"Sleeping? Eating?" replied Kim.

"Yes, sleeping and eating but also I just wanted to warn you that 'hotel sex' is an actual thing!"

"Sssh!" laughed Kim. "Rosa is here!"

"Just saying..." said Dean, patting her gently on the bottom before retreating to the bathroom.

Kim sighed. She really was very happy and so grateful for her good fortune.

Kim and Dean managed to get ready quietly enough that Rosa could still be heard snoring softly in the spare room. They bundled their overnight bags into the boot of the car and drove the short distance to

Fleur and Rob's house where the two of them were waiting on the front path like a couple of excited kids.

Kim and Fleur sat in the back of the car nattering about everything from what they had packed to wear, to titbits of local gossip about who might be seeing who, whilst Dean and Rob sat up front discussing perfect golf shots and whether it was best to use a 9 or a 5 iron.

They stopped for a quick coffee and a wee at the motorway services where they were charged the equivalent of two Full House specials at the Dog & Duck for three under-sized skinny lattes and a Frappuccino. The traffic was a little sticky around the ring road but other than that they had a good run and were soon on the B-road that would take them to their weekend retreat. The entrance to the hotel looked promising with a long, wide, gravel drive that swept up to an imposing building standing in manicured grounds with several large, white marble statues of Greek Goddesses with missing arms and a muscular Adonis with a very small appendage!

"Well this looks alright," said Fleur, as Dean chose a parking space.

"Not sure what that's all about though," said Rob, pointing to a line of mobility scooters parked neatly in a bay to the left of the reception entrance.

"We have got the right place, haven't we?" asked Kim.

"I hope so," replied Dean. "It's definitely same as the online photos... unless there's an old folks' home nearby which looks the same!"

Fleur and Kim giggled.

They retrieved their bags from the car, along with Dean and Rob's golf clubs, and made their way through the glass doors to the reception desk which was located in what would probably have been the Entrance Hall to the old manor house as it once was. Grand oak panelling covered the walls, original stone tiles covered the uneven floor. There was a spectacular vase of flowers on the desk; a mix of scented white lilies, blue hydrangea blooms and dark green eucalyptus stems. Kim couldn't help but notice that both couples joining them in the queue for the reception desk were a fair bit older than them – maybe even collectively! – but she didn't pay too much attention.

The receptionist recorded their names in the hotel register and allocated them their rooms which were next to each other on the second floor. They were directed to the lifts and instructed to turn left on arrival at floor two before taking the short walk along the corridor to rooms 214 and 216.

"Can anyone smell cabbage?" asked Dean as they entered the lift.

"It smells like school dinners," agreed Rob.

Fleur and Kim rolled their eyes at each other, but Kim did have to secretly agree that there was a quite significant aroma of cabbage and the kind of musty smell that one might ordinarily associate with a charity shop. The lift stopped at their floor, and they all got out. The corridor stretched almost as far as the eye could see and it quickly became apparent that they were in fact in a relatively modern extension that had been added to the rear of the original building.

The decor here was much less grand than the foyer had been and was more reminiscent of a budget airport stopover than a country estate. It did not escape their attention either, that on the way to their rooms they passed at least six mobility scooters parked outside the room doors patiently awaiting their mobility challenged passengers. They exchanged a wry glance but none of them said anything.

Once they arrived at their rooms, they agreed to drop their bags and then Dean and Rob would head off for the golf course whilst Kim and Fleur made their way to the hotel bar for a light breakfast before heading off to the spa.

"I'm sorry babe, it looked a lot nicer on the internet," said Dean apologetically as they entered their room.

The room itself was clean and tidy but it definitely was not a patch on the reception area – they'd clearly spent the design budget on a good first impression!

"It's okay babe, seriously. It's just nice to be away and I'm sure we'll have a lovely time – it's just nice being here with you and I'm really grateful for the thought."

"I just wanted it to be perfect... like you. You know I ...." Dean's voice trailed off as they heard Rob's quiet tap on the door.

Dean looked at Kim with an intensity that was powerful, and she felt her cheeks redden beneath his gaze. If she hadn't known better, she was almost convinced that he'd been about the drop the L-bomb, but surely it was too soon for that wasn't it?

"Don't forget what I said about the deal with hotel rooms," said Dean lightening the mood.

Kim laughed. "Go on, you. You need to concentrate on your game!" and she kissed him a little too long for the time they had.

Rob knocked again, "Come on you two, I hope you're not up to anything in there – hotel sex always comes after dinner!"

"See? What did I tell you?" laughed Dean.

Dean opened the door and joined Rob, giving a small wave to Kim as he left. She was frankly a little embarrassed about the way her lady parts were reacting currently and was glad that she was going for a cool dip in the hotel pool! She and Fleur made their way down to the hotel bar to receive the coffee and croissants that they had ordered on their arrival. There were very few guests around at such an early hour and the peace was lovely. The musty smell from earlier persisted throughout their passage and there were more mobility aids visible outside several of the rooms.

An elderly couple sat in the corner of the bar slurping noisily from two cups, the matching saucers shaking below in trembling fingers. Halfway through their breakfast, two more couples passed through the bar area on their way to the dining room and Kim duly noticed that each member of the party could have given her at least twenty years.

"I'm feeling surprisingly sprightly all of a sudden," whispered Fleur.

"I'm glad you said that I was beginning to think I was being ageist! Is it me or is there the definite air of 'old folk's home' about the place?"

"Yeah, it does feel a bit like an Octogenarian Butlins," giggled Fleur, "and I can definitely still smell cabbage!"

They finished their coffee and croissants before leaving for their first spa treatment of the morning which was a relaxing back and shoulder massage. They had two more treatments booked throughout the morning before they were due to meet the boys on the terrace for an antipasti platter and a glass of bubbles. They had then planned to spend the afternoon walking in the nearby nature reserve where there were ponies and deer roaming free, before heading back to the hotel for a siesta and a shower ahead of their evening meal.

As they left the bar, an influx of guests passed them on their way to breakfast and Kim and Fleur both stifled a giggle as they were almost mowed down by the convoy of electric scooters that queued in the hallway like the line at the local Post Office on pension day!

"This *is* a hotel and not a retirement home, isn't it?" whispered Fleur. "I keep expecting Victor Meldrew to jump out from behind the curtains."

"I don't believe it!" shrieked Kim, hardly able to contain her laughter.

The girls' mirth was met by some icy stares from the inmates and Kim imagined that it had been a long time since anyone had come here for an actual good time! Things didn't get any better when they entered the spa. Kim didn't wish to be judgemental but there were a couple of old ladies floating around on inflated pods in the heated pool who looked eerily still when they entered the room and Kim found herself subconsciously scanning the walls for signs of a defibrillator or at least a panic button! It was a relief when one of the ancient bathers let out a less than silent fart, creating her very own impromptu jacuzzi in the water!

"I think I might hold off on the swim," said Fleur with a grimace. "It's like an episode of fucking Cocoon in here, talk about God's waiting room!"

"Oh don't!" chuckled Kim. "I hope the masseuse is a bit sprightlier or we could be in trouble!"

Fortunately, the masseurs were young enough to be the great-grandchildren of most of the residents and, if they ignored the scent of lavender and lily of the valley that seemed to ooze from every pore of the treatment rooms, the beauty treatments were actually very enjoyable.

Dean and Rob had been the only two men on the golf course actually able to complete the course without a buggy and an oxygen mask and they had also wondered if the hotel write-up had been as truthful as it might have been; although in fairness, it had simply stated 'a peaceful, adults-only retreat suitable for couples and those looking for a relaxing stay,' which wasn't entirely inaccurate... there just hadn't been any clarification of the age of the adults, this being more 80 to 90 than 18 to 30!

Fortunately, they did not allow lack of common ground with the fellow residents to mar their time away and they were able to enjoy their beautiful walk in the countryside just the same. The evening meal had caused a few more raised eyebrows when they discovered that there was indeed cabbage for dinner although the rest of the food had been pleasant enough. The restaurant tables had been closer together than they might have liked and brought a whole new meaning to the phrase 'intimate dining,' and they were all in total agreement when Dean suggested they take their after-dinner drinks onto the terrace to avoid the evening's entertainment which consisted of a tribute to Dame Vera Lynn and hits from the fifties!

"I'm so sorry babe," said Dean when they were lying in each other's arms later that night. "I hope it wasn't too disappointing. I really wanted it to be special."

"Well, it's certainly been unexpected," laughed Kim. "Honestly it wasn't your fault, I've had a lovely time and when we are old and grey, we'll have the perfect place to come and stay!"

"I can't wait!" said Dean. "Now what about those other hotel rules we talked about?"

Kim giggled as Dean made his advances, she was beginning to have quite a fondness for hotels already!

Chapter Nine

Kim had very much enjoyed 'hotel sex'... both times... and she awoke feeling blissful. It had been agreed that they would all go into town for breakfast – as much as they were trying not to judge, they all rather fancied the idea of some younger company and a less sombre atmosphere; anywhere that didn't smell of cabbage!

They showered and dressed and for once, Kim was pleased with the wardrobe choices she had made when packing. Usually, she always regretted whatever she had chosen to wear, feeling inadequate to others around her – she would go 'smart casual' and everyone else would be 'yuppy chic,' she would go 'boho hippie' and her company would be 'jeans not dresses,' she always felt like she got it wrong but this weekend she had felt great. Perhaps it had something to do with the way Dean made her feel, or that she was totally comfortable in Fleur and Rob's company but whatever it was, she was determined to enjoy it.

They drove to the neighbouring village as it was too far to walk and quite frankly the narrow roads without footpaths were more than a little dangerous for a casual stroll. They found a lovely French café in one of the side streets with a sweet little patio for diners that was packed with tubs of olive trees and bright-coloured geraniums that were just about hanging on to their summer flowers. They took a table for four in the corner of the courtyard where the autumn sun was still strong, and it felt warm and summery. Kim ordered a croque monsieur and a gorgeous little tarte aux fraises for dessert; she excused herself to go and use the toilet while they waited for their food to arrive. She applied an extra slick of gloss in the bathroom mirror before returning to their table.

She was met with silence as she returned and one look at their faces told her that something wasn't right; Dean looked positively ashen.

"What's the matter, what's happened?" she asked, her voice rising in panic as she mentally considered every possible disaster.

At times like these, her thoughts always went first to Daniel and then to her mum. Daniel often joked that whenever he didn't immediately answer her phone call, she would instantly assume that he had befallen some freak accident and got sucked into a swamp or disappeared down a sink hole!

"Tell me!"

"There's been an incident at the Dog and Duck," said Dean quietly.

"Oh my God, are the girls okay?"

"The girls are fine," said Dean. "No one is hurt but there has been a small flood."

Kim exhaled deeply. At that precise moment all she felt was relief. As much as she loved the pub, as long as the people she loved were okay then she would confront whatever else came her way. Even so, she couldn't deny that she felt concern.

"Is it bad?"

"It doesn't sound good," said Dean grimly. "That was Rosa on the phone, she's in bits. Apparently, she's been trying to call all morning."

Kim took her phone out of her bag and tapped the screen display – nine missed calls!

"Oh bloody hell! I didn't think to check my phone. I didn't have much of a signal and I just forgot all about it, I feel terrible now. Are you sure they're okay?"

"They're fine babe honestly, just a bit stressed I think – but I reckon we should head back. I'm sorry about your weekend."

"No, of course we have to go back," said Kim. "Don't be daft, I'm fine, just worried about them... and I'm sorry to cut the weekend short. I could get the train if you guys wanted to stay?"

"Don't be silly," said Rob and Fleur in unison. "We'll come with you; you might need some help."

Kim smiled in gratitude and the four of them made their excuses to the restaurant owner who kindly wrapped their food for them to eat on the journey.

The car ride back to the pub veered between silence and intense discussions, each of them predicting what could have happened. Kim had made a quick call to

Rosa to say that they would be with them in an hour or so and that she should just stay calm until they got there. Rosa had sounded really upset on the phone apologising profusely, but Kim had assured her vehemently that she knew without doubt it would not have been anything other than an accident; Rosa didn't have a bad or incompetent bone in her body.

Kim almost leapt from the car as they pulled into the car park with Dean, Fleur and Rob close behind her. The front door to the pub was wide open and the smell of damp hit Kim's nostrils before she had even crossed the threshold. The pub floor was awash with water although not ankle deep as Kim's overactive imagination had first feared.

Rosa, Megan and Sandra were frantically trying to swoosh the puddles of water out through the open door and little Lottie was doing her best to help. The chairs had been put up onto the tables to try and clear the area as much as possible, while the cardboard cut-out of Bobby had sunk to the floor in a twisted position as if he had just kind of melted onto the ground. His red face and inane grin now distorted by the wet and swollen card peered up at them from his resting place between the bar and the juke box and he looked more macabre than ever. The vibrancy of his cherry-red Hawaiian shirt looked at odds with the grey puddles of water that surrounded it; rather fittingly, his glass of beer was still clutched between his cardboard fingers.

Upon seeing Kim, Rosa rushed forward, throwing her arms around her.

“Mia cara, I am so sorry. This is all my fault. I am so sorry mia cara. I turned it off, I was sure I turned it off!”

Kim held onto Rosa tightly offering words of comfort. “Rosa calm down, please don’t blame yourself.”

Once Rosa’s sobs had subsided, Megan’s mum Sandra had been able to explain that they had been woken in the early morning by the sound of running water. The taps in the bar sink had been running for quite some time it seemed, although Rosa was certain she hadn’t left them on before she went to bed.

“I checked everything mia cara,” she wept.

“Rosa please calm down,” said Sandra, soothingly. “Honestly Kim, I don’t know what happened, but I cannot honestly believe that Rosa would have left the taps on. She checked everything a hundred times before we went to bed. One of us would have noticed. If we hadn’t had such a busy night, we might have heard it sooner but we were all exhausted when we went to bed and we must have slept pretty soundly.”

“Honestly, it’s fine,” said Kim. “Seriously it’s not actually as bad as I was expecting to be honest. It’s just a bit of water. Fortunately, we don’t have carpets in the pub anymore and it really won’t take long to clean things up. We’ll close for today and get it mopped up – please don’t worry yourselves, I’m just sorry you’ve had such a stressful time.”

"Kim's right," said Dean. "It looks much worse than it really is. Me and Rob will have this cleared in no time, won't we?"

"Absolutely," said Rob, rolling up his sleeves in readiness.

"Right, I'm going to put the kettle on," said Fleur, "and we are going to go and sit in the back garden whilst the boys clear the worst of the water. Then, once we have a cuppa and a chat, we can come and tidy things up. We'll be done by lunchtime in time for a well-earned brandy!"

"Perfect," said Kim. "Lottie, I think this calls for chocolate biscuits all round... and look on the bright side... at least we haven't got to exorcise Bobby anymore!"

The tension in the room began to subside and Lottie followed Kim into the kitchen on the hunt for biscuits.

One hour later, the water had been cleared and they all pitched in to give the bar a last wipe down and open all the doors and windows to air the last of the damp – it really had looked much worse than it was thankfully, although Kim and Dean both knew they would be talking later about what could have caused it. One thing was for sure, Kim didn't for one second believe that Rosa would have gone to bed and left the taps running.

By lunchtime, they had collected fish and chips from the local chippie and were enjoying a well-deserved stiff drink in the garden – with the exception of Lottie and Megan of course – crisis averted and normality once more restored. No matter how much stress had been caused, Kim was just forever grateful that the people she loved so much were all safe; when all was said and done, nothing else really mattered.

They could probably have kept the pub open, but Kim thought that everyone could do with a break and so she put a sign out the front saying that the pub was closed due to a plumbing issue which wasn't a million miles from the truth. Fortunately, there were no bookings for Sunday lunch as the first part of September was often quiet once the kids went back to school and, due to the early morning panic, Rosa hadn't started any food preparation so there was little or no wastage.

After lunch, Kim hugged Rosa and told her for the hundredth time not to beat herself up about something that was clearly just an accident. She didn't voice her concerns that both she and Dean were worried that there could have been some form of foul play, although neither of them was entirely sure how, nor by whom. A phone call to Jake had confirmed that all the doors were locked when he left because he had rattled the handles from the outside just to make sure, knowing that the girls were staying over by themselves. If anyone had tried to break in, then there would have been some signs of forced entry and Kim was pretty certain that the noise would have woken at least one of them.

"Maybe she did just leave the tap on," said Dean. "Even a trickle of water can become a lot of water over a period of time."

"Yes, that had occurred to me," sighed Kim. "As much as I am suspicious, I really can't see how someone could break in without waking anybody and why would they bother?"

"Well, we both know there are two people with quite a grudge but like you, I can't see them breaking in without making a row and they definitely wouldn't have been allowed into the pub whilst it was open. Perhaps this was just an accident but whatever it was, we need to get some better security sorted out, just in case."

"I agree," said Kim. "Let's head into town tomorrow and get some new lights and we can get a simple CCTV set up from the electrical store on the industrial park – anything will be better than nothing and it might just provide a deterrent moving forward."

Early the next morning, Kim and Dean got up to check that all was well, but the pub had actually dried out quite nicely and, fortunately, it was still warm enough for the potential for damp to have been averted quickly. Kim's mum Judy, and Daniel and Ryan, were arriving a little after lunch time, so it was decided that Kim would hold the fort once they arrived whilst Daniel went with Dean to the industrial park. Daniel was pretty clued up when it came to anything remotely technical, and so he was likely to offer a better second opinion than Kim who had only just discovered FaceTime!

Kim threw her arms around her mum when she arrived, it was so nice to see her, and it was in times of difficulty that she realised how much she missed having her around. Her whole life, she had either lived with her or within a few minutes' drive and consequently the Dog and Duck felt like a long way away.

"Hey Mum," said Daniel, pulling his mum in for a hug after his nan. "It's good to see you."

"It is SO good to see you too my darling. Where's your car, I didn't hear you pull up?"

"No, we decided to get the train after all, we got a cab from the station; my car is in for a service and Ryan's company car is being upgraded, we'll just book a taxi to the airport on Wednesday morning – the train ride was quite nice actually."

"Don't be daft, I'll give you a lift," said Dean, coming in from the garden where he had been weighing up the best position for the new cameras.

"We're going early – you okay with that?"

"Listen, I was in the army for years, I struggle to sleep in past 5 a.m., so early is no problem for me!"

"Great, thanks Dean," said Daniel.

Once they'd had coffee and caught up on all the gossip, including the recent events at the Dog and Duck, it was almost two in the afternoon and lunchtime service was coming to an end. Daniel and Dean set off for the industrial estate in Dean's car whilst Kim, Judy and Ryan finished helping Rosa to clear the last of the washing up, wiping down tables and washing the glasses.

Rosa left at three o'clock, hugging each of them in turn before she left.

"Bless her, she was so upset, but I'm thinking perhaps it was just an accident," said Kim to her mum.

"These things happen," said Judy. "We all make mistakes, especially as we get older."

"Exactly," replied Kim. "No harm done and at least we got rid of Bobby without too much drama – I was dreading telling Steve it was time for Elvis to leave the building... again! You okay, Ryan?" she asked, noticing that Ryan hadn't spoken since Dean and Daniel had left.

"I'm just going to say it," blurted Ryan.

Kim and Judy looked at him quizzically...

"I know it's not been long, and I know it's perhaps not what you expected, and I know that maybe you might think it's a rush, but..."

"Aaarrrggghhh!" screamed Judy. "You're going to propose to Daniel, aren't you?"

Ryan shifted in his seat his eyes fixed on Kim, waiting for her response.

When Kim spoke, her eyes were filled with tears, "Oh Ryan, I couldn't be happier. Daniel loves you; I know he does and I am just so glad that he has found someone to love him back!"

The relief on Ryan's face was palpable. "Oh Kim, thank you, I was so worried you might not approve!"

"Silly boy!" laughed Judy. "We would LOVE you to marry our Daniel!"

Kim raced behind the bar and re-appeared with a chilled bottle of bubbles, "This calls for a celebration!"

"I was going to ask him when we're on holiday so can we keep it a secret for now?" asked Ryan.

"Mum's the word," giggled Judy and Kim in unison.

They were both grinning like a pair of Cheshire cats and neither of them could contain their excitement.

"The only thing I ask is that you text me the moment you have asked him!"

"I hope he says yes now," laughed Ryan.

"He will definitely say yes," said Judy. "He is mad about you. Oh Kim how lovely is this?"

"It's the best news ever," smiled Kim.

By the time Dean and Daniel returned from the superstore the tell-tale signs of the afternoon celebration had been cleared away and Kim and Judy had adopted their very best poker faces. The system that Dean had bought proved fairly simple to install and Daniel was a great help when it came to linking the technology to an app on Kim's phone. They had installed two cameras, one above the back kitchen door where it was quite isolated and another on the corner of the pub with a good view of the carpark and side entrance. They had managed to conceal the cameras quite cleverly on the edge of the window boxes that Kim had taken great pains to install and fill with colourful blooms as part of her mission to make the Dog and Duck more inviting, as opposed to the ramshackle building that had greeted her on her first sighting of the place.

Once the work was finished, they were ready to receive their evening guests and Kim felt much more secure knowing that they had taken steps to make the place a bit safer, even though she was now convinced that they had been the victims of an unfortunate accident and nothing more.

Steve had been crestfallen to learn that his best mate and drinking buddy had unfortunately met an untimely end for the second time and Kim was reminded of the title of a Bond movie – You Only Die Twice! Kim was just glad that she had a legitimate reason for Bobby's departure that didn't involve her saying that the sight of him just creeped her out.

Judy was in her element, helping Jake and Rosa behind the bar and she was an absolute godsend on Tuesday night when the visiting pool team did their very best to drink the place dry along with a large party of ten who had booked a table in celebration of a birthday. Dean and Rosa had done a sterling job with the food and the diners were over the moon, especially when Dean brought out a cake complete with sparkler-style candles.

Chapter Ten

Daniel helped Dean to load the large suitcase that he and Ryan had packed for their holiday into the back of the car at 6 a.m. on Wednesday morning. Kim hugged Ryan at the door, giving him a conspiratorial wink and planting a kiss on his cheek.

"Good luck and don't forget!" she grinned.

"Promise," replied Ryan.

"Break it up you two," laughed Daniel, "I'm getting worried that you are the new favourite!"

"You'll always be Mummy's little soldier," exclaimed Kim, hugging her son tight to her.

"Have fun," waved Judy who had appeared at the door behind Kim.

"Bloody hell, I bet the Queen doesn't get a send-off like this," laughed Daniel, "we're only going to Europe!"

Dean bundled the two boys into the car whilst Kim and Judy waved frantically from the doorway.

"Oh my God Mum, I can't wait!"

"I know, isn't it wonderful," sighed Judy.

Kim was actually relieved that the boys had left, it had been murder keeping their secret, she only hoped Ryan would pop the question sooner rather than later.

The week flew by, they had been busier than predicted and it was great having Judy there to help out. Jake came in most evenings and Megan's mum Sandra had taken to supporting her daughter as she grew bigger and more weary. The worry of Lottie's impending birthday was also weighing heavy on her mind.

"I just wish she could see what a fantastic mother she is," sighed Sandra as she and Kim took the rubbish out to the bins one morning.

"I know, bless her, Lottie will be fine, I actually think she feels some of Megan's anxiety," replied Kim.

"I've tried to tell her that," said Sandra, "but it ends up sounding like more criticism if you know what I mean?"

"Yeah, I get that. All we can do is to support her and trust that things will work out okay. We will make Lottie's birthday the very best it can be."

"Thank you, Kim. I can't tell you how much it means to know how well you look after her."

"We love her," said Kim, "plain and simple. Don't feel like you have to come in and help, you know her job is safe here, don't you? We will happily take up the strain whilst she is struggling."

Sandra hugged Kim. "I know that but if I can help then I am more than happy, this is a very special place, and you should be very proud of yourself."

"I actually am quite proud of myself," smiled Kim, "but I couldn't have done it without Rosa and Megan and Dean of course. I'm very lucky. If you're not busy you're welcome to take on Megan's shifts when she gets nearer her time?"

"That would be amazing," replied Sandra. "I love it here and it would be a great way to support Megan – I know she worries that she might lose her place here."

"She'll always have a place here for as long as she wants it," said Kim.

On Saturday morning, Kim got the call she had been waiting for. Daniel phoned to break the news that Ryan had indeed proposed in a beautiful restaurant with a sea view and unsurprisingly Daniel had said yes. Dean had laughed when he had heard Kim and Judy screaming loud enough to bring old Bobby back from the dead. It had taken quite a while for them to come down from their high and Daniel had held the phone away from his ear until they calmed down in order to avoid permanent damage!

After several rounds of congratulation in which the phone was passed back and forth between Kim and Ryan, Judy and Ryan, Kim and Daniel, Dean and Daniel, and Judy and Daniel, Daniel had finally persuaded Kim to hang up and assured her that they would celebrate properly when he returned on Wednesday afternoon.

"Well, I think Mum's happy," laughed Daniel when they had finally hung up.

"Yeah, I reckon she's okay with it," smiled Ryan.

After a busy Saturday, it was well past midnight by the time Dean and Kim went up to bed. They checked that the CCTV was operational and that all the doors were firmly locked, as they had done religiously each night, before they climbed the stairs. The CCTV cameras appeared to be working and, although they didn't make for overly interesting viewing, the images were clear enough. There had been one rather messy visit from the local fox who had taken a liking to Rosa's leftover lasagne, the parcel delivery man had been caught red-handed slinging Kim's delivery of coffee pods behind the wheelie bin without leaving a delivery card and despite the fact that they had most definitely been in, and Jim the butcher had had his five minutes of fame with a rather impressive rendition of one of his favourite tunes while he had delivered the meat on Friday morning! Kim was grateful that the replay of the CCTV footage was so thoroughly uneventful and also reassured to know that it was working well should they ever need it in the future...which she hoped they most definitely would not.

Kim had never been happier to see her bed. Her feet ached and the adrenalin rush that she had experienced after Daniel's call had left her well and truly pooped!

She climbed into bed and felt the warmth of Dean's body as he wrapped himself around her.

"Good news about Daniel, eh babe?" asked Dean kissing her neck.

"Oh Dean, I'm so happy for him – it's bloody brilliant. I'd like to hold a little party here for them or maybe they could get married from here!"

"Hang on a bit, they've only just got engaged – give them a chance!"

Kim giggled, "I know, I'm so excited for them though."

"We need a party for a certain little lady first," said Dean. "I think Lottie needs to be spoilt and Megan needs to know that things will be okay in the end."

"You're right, we'll make it really special for her. I...." Kim's voice trailed off. She had just been about to drop the L-word, but suddenly she felt self-conscious.

"We could say it together at the same time, if it made you feel better?"

Kim turned around to look at him. "How do you know what I was thinking?" she asked, a little glint of mischief in her eye.

Dean smiled. "Just a hunch, but if you were about to say something that means you like having me here and you are a big gooey mess when I'm around, then I feel the same!"

"It's not too soon, is it?"

"Too soon for what? We aren't getting any younger!"

"Speak for yourself," laughed Kim, "but if you think it's okay then I'm pretty sure I love you."

"I'm pretty *certain* I love you," replied Dean, "but then I think I was pretty certain on about week two of meeting you. I was just playing it cool!"

They kissed, slow and tender, and Kim wished she hadn't been so tired – there were things she would have liked to have done with him right then that required more energy than she had currently! One thing she did know was that she was very happy.

Chapter Eleven

The noise that woke them was one which had resonated through the whole pub; a loud, metallic-sounding crash that seemed to come from the very depths of the building followed by something which could have been a crackle, or maybe a whooshing sound.

Dean sat bolt upright in bed and grappled for his trousers that lay discarded on the floor beside him. He switched on the bedside lamp motioning for Kim to stay where she was and placing a finger to his lips.

“Be careful,” she whispered, pulling her dressing gown around her, and picking her mobile phone up from the bedside table.

At that moment there was a loud bang which sounded like the kitchen door being slammed and Dean ran to the bedroom windows that were at the front of the pub and overlooked the carpark.

“I’m calling the police,” he bellowed out the window, as two shadowy figures ran around the side of the building and jumped into a vehicle, before a screech of tyres signified their speedy departure.

“Fucking bastards,” he exclaimed.

Ignoring his earlier instruction, Kim followed him as he flew down the stairs at speed, jumping several steps at a time. They exited the door at the bottom of the stairs which led directly into the bar. The whooshing sound that they had heard earlier was now clearly audible and appeared to be coming from the cellar. The door from the bar to the kitchen was wide open and they could see that the back kitchen door was also open. Dean wrenched open the cellar door and the whooshing sound now become an almost deafening gushing. The cellar light was on, and it was only seconds before Kim and Dean were able to see the source of the noise. A torrent of beer spewed from every barrel, the pressure causing the liquid to shoot out like lava from an erupting volcano. The foamy liquid was flowing over every surface, weaving its way under the boxes of wine and bar snacks that were stored in the cellar, some of which had already started to collapse as they gave way to the saturation. It did not take long, mere minutes, for each barrel to discharge its contents and any attempts to stop the flow would have proved futile, such was its ferocity.

Kim and Dean stood ankle deep in the sticky brown liquid, its malty aroma mingled with the stench of wet brown cardboard and brine, a solitary packet of pork scratchings bobbing at their feet. Some of the large wine boxes had been slashed open and rhythmic droplets splashed into the brown river below like tear drops.

It felt like ages before either of them spoke; both of them silenced by the shock of the scene in front of them.

"This wasn't an accident, was it?" asked Kim, stating what they both knew to be the bleeding, bloody obvious.

"We need to phone the police," said Dean grimly. "This was sabotage Kim, and I think we both know who was responsible."

"But why?" said Kim, her voice breaking. "Why would they do something so horrible?"

"Because they are selfish bastards, that's why. Are you insured?"

Kim nodded. Her feet were freezing in the cold beer, but she did not think that was the only thing that was causing her body to shake so uncontrollably.

Dean pulled her into his arms, his hand cradling the back of her head as she finally let the tears fall. They must have looked a sorry sight, standing in silence, except for the sound of Kim's sobs and the eerie splash, splash, of the last of the pub's stock as it found its path down walls and shelves into the malty river below.

"Right, that's it. We aren't wasting another moment crying over that selfish fucker," said Dean. "You phone the police, and I will run the video – see if we can get any footage. Once the police have been, we need to get as much of this liquid out of here as we can – try and limit the damage."

At that moment, Judy had appeared at the top of the steps. "Jesus Christ Almighty!" she exclaimed. "What on earth happened?"

Kim had almost forgotten that her mum had been staying with them in the confusion, and the sight of her caused Kim to burst into tears once more.

"Now you stop your tears, my girl. Dean is right. We are not crying over that bastard anymore. Come upstairs and I'll help you call the police."

Several hours later, the three of them sat in the bar as the first of the morning's light began to stream in through the windows. It was funny how at odds the bright sunshine was with the mood and the scenes of destruction in the cellar, but then nature was like that; it stopped for nothing and no one.

The police had been quite prompt in their response to Kim's phone call and had taken witness statements from each of them. The CCTV video footage had shown two grainy figures entering through the back door and the same figures exiting quickly around the side of the pub before taking off at speed in a car. Unfortunately, although it was fairly obvious that the two people on the video were a man and a woman – one being much taller and heavier set than the other – it seemed that the intruders had taken the precaution of wearing dark clothes with hoods pulled up over their heads, obscuring their faces. The car had not been one that either Kim nor Dean recognised but they had managed to get a partial glimpse of the number plate which began with M and ended with the letters SAP, something which had raised an ironic smirk from Judy.

What had become clear from the video was that the intruders had got in using a key and had therefore most likely evaded being caught sooner this way, having made very little noise gaining entry.

“I knew I couldn’t find that bloody key,” Kim had remarked, remembering that she had searched high and low for her missing spare back door key just days before their weekend away. “But how did they get it?”

The police had explained that there were many surprisingly easy ways in which a perpetrator could gain entry if they had enough bare-faced cheek, and Kim had to agree that Keith and Olivia had plenty of that between them!

The main thing troubling all of them now was that firstly, Keith and Olivia had a key to the Dog and Duck and had clearly shown that they had no fear about using it, and secondly that the CCTV video had not been clear enough for the police to make an arrest. They would try to trace the vehicle plate number and see who the car might be registered to, but even that might not give much more than circumstantial evidence and blame would be difficult to prove in court.

The police had advised that they change the locks on the Dog and Duck and consider installing an alarm system for further protection. They would pursue their enquiries but warned Kim not to be too hopeful. They had given her a crime number so that she could present it to the insurance company but for the moment there was little they could do but wait.

"I don't know how much more of this crap I can take," sighed Kim, rubbing her eyes as exhaustion washed over her. "And it doesn't seem like he's going to get any comeback – slippery little bastard!"

"This is what I suggest," said Dean. "Obviously we need to change the locks and, for the time being, I am going to sleep down in the bar."

"Oh Dean don't do anything daft, will you?"

"Don't worry babe, I promise. The first sign of any noise or trouble, I'll be on the phone to the police. We need to catch them at it. All we need is a good quality photo of them in action and we can present it to the coppers."

"Do you think they will be back?" asked Judy.

"I'm afraid I can almost guarantee it," said Dean sadly. "They want to get Kim out, or at least ruin her; I don't think they will be happy until she goes. We need to play it clever and beat them at their own game. I'm going to have a drive round today and see if I can spot that car, it can't be that far away."

"Why don't I just bloody ring him and tell him I know?" said Kim.

"Don't let him know you're rattled. For a start it'll give him a massive kick and it might make him a bit cleverer

– which won't exactly be hard! This way, they might get sloppy, and we'll have a better chance of catching him."

"I feel a bit guilty now; I was starting to think that Bobby was haunting us! I'm not sure if I'm relieved or not!"

They ate breakfast in silence, each of them deep in thought and each of them furious in their own way. Judy because she was worried about Kim, Kim because she was worried about her staff and Dean because he felt he should have been able to protect Kim better; one thing was for sure, he wasn't going to let Keith cause any more damage than he already had done.

The rest of the weekend passed in a blur as they tried desperately to sort out the carnage caused by Keith and Olivia – they may not have had proof, but Kim was in no doubt that it had been him. At least she hoped it was, otherwise, she had made more enemies than she realised!

Unfortunately, they'd had to close the pub for a second weekend and through to Tuesday afternoon, and the effect on takings could not be maintained long term. Fortunately, the insurance assessors had been very helpful and had been satisfied with the copious amounts of photos that Dean had taken along with the police report and crime number as proof of no blame on Kim's part.

The pub regulars had been incredible, each of them helping in whatever way they could. Everyone from

Steve to Jim the butcher had rolled up their sleeves to help clean and clear the cellar. Brian and Doris had rallied around bringing trays of sandwiches for the working parties and the ladies from the Women Who Wine group had each offered support in terms of help to clean and donations of fresh flowers, and scented candles to brighten the place up once the clear-up mission was complete. Even a couple of Kim's affectionately nicknamed 'saga louts' had offered to help although, at times, this had proved more stressful than helpful; there were only so many items a pair of shaky old hands could carry at any one time!

All the staff had worked tirelessly to rescue as much stock as they could and to get the pub ready for re-opening. Fleur and Rob had been a tower of strength with Rob offering muscle power to the operations and Fleur acting as a great shoulder for Kim to cry on – which she had done many times – and also as supportive listening ear when Kim had needed to rant about Keith....which she had also done many times! One thing they both agreed on, was that by the time they had brought Keith to justice – which they were determined to do – he would be wishing he had never been born!

Chapter Twelve

Kim had not rung Daniel to share her tales of woe whilst he'd been away, she saw no reason to interrupt his holiday or cause him unnecessary worry – no amount of worrying would change the facts – so she had resolved to tell him when he got back. In fact, Dean was going to explain the situation when he picked Daniel and Ryan up from the airport on Wednesday afternoon. Kim had agreed that he would probably be less emotional than she might be and could engage as more of an impartial witness so to speak. Granted, Dean had felt more than a little angry by Keith's actions, but he didn't have the emotional ties that Kim or Daniel had once had.

"What annoys me the most," said Daniel after Dean had broken the news to him, "is that Dad must have known how scary that could have been for Mum and now how unsafe she feels in her own home."

"I think that's the probably the bit he's enjoying the most I'm afraid," said Ryan gently. "I know he's your dad but he's obviously out to cause as much trouble as possible. He wants half of the Dog & Duck and if he can't have it fair and square, then he's going to do his best to make it impossible for your mum to stay."

"The worst of it is," said Dean. "We can't prove it was them because the CCTV is too grainy, and they were smart enough to keep their faces covered; I reckon they are going to get away with it. We still haven't found the car yet either."

"It will bite them on the arse eventually," said Daniel. "The one thing I do know about my dad is that he hates to be ignored and he literally will not be able to resist shooting his mouth off at some point; the truth will come out eventually."

"I hope you're right," sighed Dean. "Your mum is pulling her hair out and your nan has been worried about how safe she is. I feel awful that I couldn't do more to protect her... and the staff come to that."

"It's not your fault. Daniel's right, this won't last for ever, something will happen before long, even if we have to give things a little nudge," said Ryan.

"We'll get them eventually," said Dean. "Now let's not dwell on it anymore. Your mum is so excited about your good news, and I don't want this to spoil things anymore than it already has. We've got a great team of staff and the regulars have been amazing. Let's count our blessings and hope they run out of steam before too long!"

They had barely turned into the car park before Kim had run out to greet them flinging her arms around Daniel.

"I'm so happy for you darling. It's such amazing news, I was busting to let the cat out of the bag!"

"Yes, Ryan told me you and Nan were in cahoots," laughed Daniel. "It was a total surprise, but a lovely surprise – I know it's quite soon but life's too short!"

"Absolutely," said Kim. "If you're happy then why wait?"

"I'm so sorry about Dad; I can't believe even he could be such an arse!"

"It's over now, son. I'm not getting too upset any more – that would just give them what they want... let's hope karma is a real bitch!"

Dean and Ryan planned to stay until the weekend and leave on the Sunday afternoon as they were not back to work until Monday. Kim didn't say anything out loud, but she felt hugely comforted by the fact that the place was full; Keith and Olivia's 'visit' still played on her mind. Replacing the lost stock and clearing the place up had cost a pretty penny but luckily it didn't look as if the insurance pay-out was going to take too long, thank God she'd had the foresight to get a comprehensive policy; ironically this was something that Keith would never have done, he didn't believe in paying 'unnecessary' premiums!

Dean continued to sleep downstairs on a blow-up bed, even with a pub full of people and new locks on the doors, he still felt frustrated that he hadn't heard their intruders before they'd got down into the cellar. They had an appointment with an alarms company for the following week and he didn't feel he could rest easy until that was underway. It was now clear to Kim that she hadn't lost her keys and that Rosa hadn't accidentally left the tap on, which was both reassuring – it was good to know that she was not mad and the pub wasn't possessed by Bobby's ghost – and unnerving, to think that Keith had once been close enough to steal her keys (she still didn't know how he had managed that) and had also been in the pub whilst Rosa, Megan, Sandra and Lottie had been home alone.

On Thursday, Daniel and Judy had driven into town to run a few errands and to get a printed copy of the photo of Daniel and Ryan's engagement that they'd taken on holiday – Daniel had thought it would be nice to get a framed copy for his mum and nan. They visited a few of the little shops in Loxley before driving to the superstore on the outskirts of the town. The carpark was heaving, and Daniel had struggled to find a parking space. As they made their way to the supermarket, Judy chatted away happily about her friend's daughter's godson who had just secured a promotion, even though he was diabetic!

"…he always was a clever lad…" Judy stopped dead in her tracks.

"You okay, Nan?" asked Daniel, coming to a halt several paces in front of Judy and turning to look at her as she become uncharacteristically silent.

Judy suddenly sunk down on her haunches behind a large white van and began gesturing wildly to a place just behind Daniel. "That's it," she whispered, "that's it! Get down!"

"What on earth are you talking about? What's '*it*'? What are you doing?"

Judy reached out an arm almost toppling from her crouched position and grabbed a very confused Daniel by the trouser leg. "Come here!"

She continued to drag him by the trouser leg and and squeezed him in next to her, pulling him down to her level and shuffling them both to an even less visible position behind the white van.

"Nan, what *are* you talking about?"

"That's the car!" proclaimed Judy triumphantly. "I'd recognise that number plate anywhere... SAP!"

Daniel frowned before realisation dawned. "Do you mean Dad's car, the one on the CCTV?"

"That's it," said Judy. "Quite fitting don't you think?"

Daniel stifled a giggle. "Well, I am certainly impressed Mrs Marple, but would shall we do about it?"

"They're coming back," squeaked Judy, her excitement now almost palpable. "We need to follow them!"

Under any other circumstances, Daniel might have thought his nan had completely lost her marbles, but desperate times called for desperate measures, and he made a dash for their car, keeping low to the ground like some sort of comic strip detective. He slid below the front windows and crawled into the driving seat – he wasn't sure how he was supposed to see where they were going, let alone drive the car whilst sunk so low down, but he didn't see that they had many other options. If they made their presence known then he wouldn't have put it past his dad to deny all knowledge of the offending vehicle – they *had* to link Keith and Olivia to the car and they *had* to find out where it was parked. It definitely wasn't Keith's mid-life crisis car so perhaps it belonged to Olivia – one thing was certain, they weren't going to find out without a bit of subterfuge.

As soon as Daniel was in the car, Judy shot round the back of the van, along the row of parked cars and into the passenger seat – she was surprisingly agile for her age. She reached into the back seat and thrust Dean's yellow beanie hat into Daniel's hand.

"Put this on so you aren't recognised!"

Daniel almost laughed out loud but did as he was told. "You sure you don't want me to wear glasses and a fake moustache?"

"I'll crouch down and you follow them... and don't bloody lose them!"

"Yes, boss," replied Daniel with a mock salute.

Judy ignored his sarcasm and sank so low in her seat that she was in danger of disappearing into the footwell. "Here they come, let's go!"

Daniel had never tailed another car in his life – unless he counted the time, he'd had to follow a funeral procession when his best mate's mum had died but that was hardly the same thing and also much slower! All in all, he managed to keep a couple of cars behind Keith and Olivia, staying just far enough back to see them but not close enough to get spotted, although he wasn't sure what would happen if he *was* spotted; presumably his dad was blissfully unaware that Daniel was 'on to him', and there were still no laws against occupying the same road as your dad even if he was a massive knobhead!

Keith's car had left Loxley on the ring road and driven along the dual carriageway to one of the neighbouring rural villages. Daniel held back as the battered Vauxhall turned into one of the side roads leading to a less than salubrious housing estate nestled amongst farmers' fields. Daniel and Judy waited in silence as they watched the Vauxhall turn into Randall crescent. Figuring that the road would be true to its namesake, Daniel decided to leave the car where it was and follow on foot, gambling on the fact that a semi-circular close was more of a destination than a through road.

He and Judy got out of the car and walked into the crescent. If they had been at all worried about being spotted, they needn't have bothered. A semi-circle of houses bordered a large communal green that was overgrown with trees and a variety of bushes. A group of teenagers sat smoking in the middle, whilst several younger children sped around the central space on bikes and scooters of varying sizes and states of disrepair. Every now and then, one of the youngsters would shoot off the green, across the road, and up and down the kerbs, before racing back to the middle. There was not a cycle helmet in sight and never once was there any hint of awareness that the road was still a public highway. Daniel was relieved that he hadn't bought the car down here, he didn't relish playing dodgems with a group of hyperactive toddlers.

However many bikes and scooters there were in motion, there seemed to be many more abandoned in the front gardens of almost every house. The semi-detached dwellings had large front gardens and in most cases a driveway, although many of these were home to cars that did not seem likely to be moving at any time, most of them missing several crucial parts from windscreens to wheels and many more jacked precariously on piles of bricks. There was not one house in the crescent that didn't look in a state of disrepair – broken front doors, cracked windows and the shabbiest collection of material posing as curtains from towels to bedsheets, hung in the windows as if thrown there.

"You can tell a lot about a person from the state of their curtains," said Judy.

Daniel smiled, "I knew you'd say that!"

Daniel and Judy tiptoed along the edge of the path keeping close to the line of overgrown hedges that bordered each of the front gardens. Keith's car had been more abandoned than parked, outside a house with a faded red front door. An old leather sofa sat in the front garden upon which sat an ample bosomed woman smoking a roll up. Keith and Olivia could just be seen in the distance appearing to be in heated discussion with the stationary woman. Olivia began gesticulating, pointing her finger aggressively at her passive counterpart. Keith stood for just a few minutes before retreating into the house with Olivia in hot pursuit, her no doubt insightful tirade now directed at Keith's disappearing form.

"Well, he's fallen on his feet there," smirked Judy.

Daniel didn't reply but sighed in despair. No wonder his hapless father wanted everything that Kim had, but then if he'd been less of twat, he might have still had it. Whatever way you looked at it, his mum was well rid. Perhaps he should have had a bit more respect for his dad but then in Daniel's book, respect was something you earned, and Keith had never earned anything much his whole life. It was a sad fact but just because you were related to someone, it didn't make them a good person.

"What shall we do?" asked Judy.

"You stay here. I'm going to sneak round the other side and try to get a picture of the car parked outside the house. At least we know where they are staying and hopefully, if we can link the car to them, that will give us a bit more ammo with the police. I'll take a photo of the whole number plate too; then I reckon we get the hell out of here!"

Judy went back to wait in the car while Daniel snuck round to take some photos. Fortunately, the ample bosomed woman had been consumed with the task of rolling herself a new fag and had not even noticed that she was the star of someone else's camera roll – her apathy was breath-taking!

Daniel jumped into the driver's seat next to Judy and wasted no time in getting them back onto the ring road in the direction of home. Pulling into the car park of the Dog and Duck, its spectacular window boxes still bearing the last of the summer blooms and not a broken scooter or jacked up car in sight, Daniel felt great relief that he was definitely a 'mummy's boy!'

Chapter Thirteen

There had been much discussion about what they might do about the newly-acquired intelligence after Judy and Daniel's super sleuthing. In the end it was decided that they would pass the details of where the elusive getaway car had been located along with the full number plate to the police, but that they would also do a little 'further enquiry' of their own. Daniel had suggested that he would give his dad a call just 'out of the blue'. He would mention that he was staying with his mum but would not discuss any of the recent events that had occurred. Daniel was certain that Keith's curiosity would get the better of him and he was likely to ask questions that could potentially incriminate him; they would work out their next steps after the phone call.

"You know what you could do?" said Ryan. "Why don't you tell your dad that Dean is running us back home on Saturday. You could also mention that your nan and your mum are coming along for the ride. It's not a complete lie, we *are* going on Sunday, but I reckon he'll pay another visit if he thinks Kim and Dean aren't going to be here."

"That's not a bad idea," said Dean. "We could move my car and hide in the garden or something?"

"I don't know Dean; it could all get a bit nasty. I don't want you getting into trouble," said Kim.

"I think it's a bloody brilliant idea," said Judy. "If he comes round, I'll confront him. He won't lay a finger on me, and Daniel and Dean can just take some photos as evidence."

"I'm not sure, Mum."

"Nonsense!" said Judy. "If we don't catch them in the act they'll keep coming back and make your life a misery – enough's enough!"

"She's right babe, we can't spend our lives looking over our shoulder," said Dean.

"Okay, but no heroics – knowing our luck we'll get arrested instead of him! Besides we'll have the alarm fitted in a week or two."

"About that," said Ryan. "I don't know if it's something you've thought about, but there's not a much better alarm system than a dog and if you remember, my dog went and got herself knocked up! All the puppies sold but we've got one boy left - my mum's been dog sitting whilst we've been away. I don't know how you feel about having a dog but it's just a thought?"

"Have you got a photo?" asked Kim.

Ryan scrolled through his phone to find a picture of 'Dog', as he was currently known.

"Mum is of indeterminate origin, but we think she's part Rottweiler, part Labrador and part something that was probably large and scruffy. We have no idea who dad was – little trollop – but if he's anything like his mum, Dog is likely to be large, scruffy, clumsy and overly affectionate!"

Two chocolate brown eyes peered out from a black whiskered face, a brown splodge over each eye and a little patch of white under his nose that looked a bit like a love heart.

"Oh my goodness, he's gorgeous," cooed Kim.

"What's Mum like with kids?" asked Dean.

"Are you thinking what I'm thinking?" asked Kim.

"I just think a pub without a dog is like a bowl without a fish," laughed Dean, "and there is a certain little girl who was desperate for a puppy for her birthday?"

"We'll take him," said Kim, throwing caution to the wind. "I'll check with Megan of course but he can be our gift to Lottie. He can live at the pub, but Lottie can name him and see him whenever she likes. We'll have him whatever, but it feels like a gift from the Gods!"

Megan had cried when Kim told her their news. "Oh Kim, she'll be so happy, thank you!"

"It's no problem. Selfishly I want the dog for the pub anyway, but if we can make Lottie smile then it's a win, win, in my book!"

Lottie's party was planned for the following weekend so it was decided that Daniel and Ryan would make another trip up and bring Dog with them. He would have Saturday to settle in before being the guest of honour at Lottie's party on the Sunday. After all the crap that had been going on of late, it felt wonderful to have something good to look forward to. Daniel and Ryan had to go back for work on Monday, but Judy decided to stay on for another week and travel back with them after Dog's arrival.

"Right, I hate to be a party pooper," said Daniel, "but I need to ring Dad now. I'll go and take it in the back room, I'll start laughing if you're all gawping at me. I'll record it just in case."

Kim poured them all a stiff drink while Daniel went to phone Keith. Rosa, Megan and Sandra joined their huddle whilst they all sat in expectant silence.

"Hello?" Keith's voice answered and Daniel noted that he did not recognise his own son's number.

"Hi Dad, how's things?"

"Daniel, is that you?"

"Unless you have another son in your life?" Daniel's joke fell flat, and Keith did not respond. "Anyway, just thought I'd see how you were? I'm visiting Mum on the way back from holiday. Me and Ryan got engaged."

"Are you at the pub now?" Keith asked, ignoring Daniel's news and maintaining his customary self-absorption.

"I'm in the garden," Daniel lied, "just having a quiet pint. What you been up to?"

"I heard there's been some trouble at the pub?"

"We didn't get back from holiday until yesterday," said Daniel, deliberately evading the question.

"She can't afford to keep losing all that stock, is that dickhead still there?"

"If you referring to Dean, Dad, then yes he does still work here. How's Olivia?" Daniel asked noting Keith's reference to the lost stock; he was dropping himself in it just as predicted.

Keith ignored Daniel's enquiry about Olivia and tried another tack; he was clearly becoming frustrated at the lack of gossip on offer. What he really wanted was for his son and ex-wife to be crying down the phone, begging him to leave them alone. Thinking that his efforts had caused little disruption was irritating to say the least.

"When you going back, son?"

"Dean is driving us back on Saturday. Mum and Nan are coming too. Will I see you before then?"

"Who's looking after the pub if you're all out?" asked Keith.

"Mum's going to close at three. One of her regular customers is having a big birthday bash and most people are going, so she said she'll close early. They're coming home after they've dropped us off, I think. So will I see you before I go?" Daniel repeated his earlier question.

"Not sure mate, I'll let you know," and with that Keith hung up the phone.

Daniel returned to the bar as six eager faces turned towards him.

"Well, he asked about the lost stock, didn't give a shit about my engagement and couldn't get off the phone fast enough when I told him we were all driving down to my place together. I reckon he'll be round here on Saturday!"

"Oh Daniel, I'm sorry babe. I wish he could show you more love," said Kim, sadly.

"Seriously Mum, I expected nothing less. To be honest I'm actually not that bothered anymore."

Chapter Fourteen

Plans were made for Saturday. It felt unnerving to think that Keith and Olivia might actually be watching the place, but the possibility was almost a certainty. It was decided that Kim and the family would 'leave' in Dean's car just in case and that they would park it on Frank and Barbara's drive just down the lane. Frank had been a pub regular for years, he was a lovely old chap and he and his wife Barbara were happy to help – they could also be trusted not to spill any secrets! Once the car was hidden away, they would return to the pub through the garden gate which was pedestrian only. Dean and Daniel were going to sit it out in the shed, Judy and Kim were going to wait safely upstairs and Ryan and Jake were going to wait in the back bar hidden from view; that way they had all exits and entrances covered. Kim didn't want any of the girls involved and so none of the barmaids were coming back after the morning session. They had all resigned themselves to a long day. The fact that Daniel had mentioned Kim and Dean's return the same evening meant that hopefully Keith and Olivia would seize their opportunity sooner rather than later. There was no guarantee when, or indeed if, they would come but it was their only shot at catching them in action.

Kim hardly slept a wink on Friday night. Her dreams were weird and fitful and by four in the morning she had given up on sleep and gone downstairs to make herself a coffee. She was surprised to see Judy down before her; it seemed that she too had been unable to sleep and was sitting drinking coffee with Dean in the bar next to his inflatable bed that had barely been slept in. Kim hoped desperately that today would provide some form of closure; she didn't wish Keith any harm, but she just wished he'd piss off and leave her alone!

The grand departure happened at around 3.30 p.m. Some of the regulars were in on the secret mission and by 11.30 the pub was uncharacteristically full for such an early hour with Kim's faithful, and curious, customers positioned around the room, pretending that they always started drinking before midday, reading newspapers and twitching every time the door opened. If it hadn't been so bloody stressful Kim would have laughed – it looked like a scene from an Agatha Christie drama, each of the characters playing their part before the criminal was revealed! Kim wasn't quite sure what they expected to see, especially as their mission wasn't due to start until the afternoon, and whilst she was grateful for their show of solidarity, she guessed it was primarily born out of curiosity!

By 3.25, Kim was waiting by the car with her coat on, her heart beating in her chest. They made the short journey to Frank and Barbara's drive, parking their car under a tree in a hidden corner of the large private driveway. They crept back along the lane, filing in through the back gate and taking up their positions. Dean and Daniel found the two small camping chairs in the dark little shed that was home to several large spiders, Kim and Judy waited upstairs in the bedroom, peeping out of the front window through a crack in the half-closed blinds and Jake and Ryan took their positions in the back room.

The kitchen door had been locked but the new internal security bolt had not been pulled across – the plan was to make entry not too easy but also not impossible; besides, if entry was easier, there would hopefully be less damage.

Five o'clock came and went and the light was fading fast. Kim had almost begun to despair, questioning her own sanity at agreeing to such a ridiculous plan – just what the fuck she expected them to do if the shit really hit the fan she didn't quite know!

"There's someone in the drive," whispered Judy.

Kim shifted her position at the edge of the window squinting through the slats of the blinds.

"Sneaky bastards," she exclaimed. "They've come on foot!"

She reached for her phone and sent a quick message in the 'Operation Keith' family WhatsApp group – Daniel had wanted to call the group 'Operation Knobhead', but Kim had declined saying it wouldn't look very professional if they should have to share any evidence with the police!

She quickly typed a message… 'there's people in the caravan…' predictive text having intervened in her panic to get the message sent.

"We're on," whispered Dean to Daniel, "I think your mum's a bit stressed."

"Unless they're setting up camp," laughed Daniel.

"I wouldn't put anything past them," said Dean. "Right, we just hold fire until we get a message from Ryan. We want to catch them in full flow."

Keith and Olivia tiptoed across the car park and through the side gate that led into the garden and the back kitchen door. They had once again donned their black hoodies that they had bought especially for their clandestine missions, taking care to pull the hoods up as far over their heads as possible. Keith noticed that the lights in the pub were all out and laughed at how easy this whole thing had been. They could literally have strolled right in through the front door, but it didn't hurt to be careful, there were some proper nosey bastards around here!

They approached the back door and Keith pulled the key out from his trouser pocket. He wriggled the key around in the lock, but it would only go in less than half way; turning it was impossible.

"Smart little bitch has changed the lock," he whispered to Olivia. "Never mind we'll get in easy enough."

Inside the pub, Ryan and Jake heard the smash of glass as Keith struck one of the small panes with a rock that had been left by the door – this was just too simple, like taking candy from a baby! He reached his arm in through the jagged hole and turned the key in the lock.

"For fuck's sake Olivia," he exclaimed, as Olivia, just a little too full of Dutch courage toppled forward, causing him to scrape his arm on the broken glass.

Blood began to drip down his arm covering the door handle as he twisted it to gain entry.

"Will you fucking calm down?" he grumbled.

Olivia giggled and muttered incoherently. Finally, the door gave way and they both stumbled into the kitchen.

Dean and Daniel tiptoed from their spidery hideout and crept up through the garden keeping close to the darker edges. As they got to the back door, they could hear cupboards being ransacked as Olivia searched for bottles of cleaning products. Meanwhile Keith was getting busy in the freezers, locating the electrical switch to turn them off and opening the doors – their plan was to turn off the power, before covering the meat and produce in bleach rendering it inedible, before making their way into the bar and the cellar to wreak yet more havoc. By the time they had finished with this place it would be uninhabitable – the great thing was, they had plenty of time and nobody around to disturb them!

Almost simultaneously Dean and Daniel, and Ryan and Jake appeared at both the front and rear exits to the kitchen.

“I wondered when I’d see you again Dad,” said Daniel calmly.

“I thought you said they were out?” demanded Olivia.

At that moment Kim and Judy appeared from upstairs, “I never liked you, not in thirty-odd years did I ever like you,” exclaimed Judy.

“Well the feeling was mutual you old cow!” snarled Keith.

“I think you need to leave,” said Kim. “This is pathetic even by your standards.”

“Don’t patronise me you fucking bitch, this is MY pub!”

“I’m just calling the police,” said Ryan, his phone to his ear. “This has gone on long enough.”

“This is none of your business you faggot,” yelled Keith.

“I think you need to leave,” said Dean, “before I forget I’m a reasonable person!”

“You can’t prove anything,” yelled Keith, grabbing Olivia by the arm and dragging her out behind him.

“Do we just let him go?” asked Kim as she watched them leave.

“Let them go,” said Dean. “The police will be here soon, and we can let them deal with him.”

"But he could be right," said Kim. "We don't really have any proof, if he's not here when the police arrive..."

"True, but I do have a photo of him with his head in the freezer," laughed Jake who had been quiet up until that point. "He's also left half his DNA on the door handle, and I had my phone on record the whole time – I reckon we've got enough!"

"Oh my God, I could kiss you," shrieked Kim. "Let 'em think they've got away with it – it'll be so much more fun when they get an unexpected visit from the police!"

Fortunately, the food produce was quickly put back in the freezer with no harm done, and the only thing that needed fixing was the pane of glass in the back door. It was several hours by the time the police had been and taken more statements, the blood on the door handle had been swabbed and photos and recordings had been shared. The police had more than enough for an arrest and Kim was happy to leave the rest of it in their capable hands, she wasn't cut out for long term surveillance!

It was almost ten o'clock by the time they sat down, and Kim got pretty pissed within a very short space of time. The combination of a very long day, a substantial amount of adrenalin surging through her veins and two very large glasses of wine consumed at speed on an empty stomach, meant that she was in bed and snoring before her head had hit the pillow.

Dean had half-carried and half-dragged her up the stairs as she proclaimed her undying love for him, Daniel, her mum, and anyone else who may have known her!

"She's had a stressful day, bless her," laughed Daniel. "Mind you, I'm glad it's all over, it can't have been easy."

"I hope they throw the bloody book at them," said Judy.

It wasn't long before they all climbed the stairs wearily. Dean was pleased to sleep next to Kim for the first time in several nights – despite her drunken snoring. Secretly, he had been terrified that he would lose his rag and mess things up and he was forever grateful that he'd had Daniel and the rest of the boys to keep him on track. Only he knew how close he had come to paying Keith a visit, and that would only ever have ended badly.

Chapter Fifteen

The rest of the week was thoroughly uneventful by comparison. Dean drove the boys back down South on the Sunday and Kim spent her time preparing for the following weekend – a party for Lottie, a new puppy and more time with her precious boy.

Kim and Judy had brought so much stuff for Dog that the back room was beginning to look like a pet shop! A cosy little basket with fluffy grey lining, some cuddly toys, food bowls, a lead and collar, soft blankets for the sofa – which he of course was not allowed to sit on! – worming tablets, flea drops and chews for cleaning his teeth. Kim hadn't been this prepared when she was expecting Daniel.

Megan was so excited for Lottie, and it was great to see the gloom and anxiety of previous months slowly lifting. She still didn't feel joy at her impending arrival, but she was maybe coming to terms with it. The fact that her Lottie was going to have the kind of party that only dreams were made of, brought her much comfort.

On Saturday morning Kim opened the door to Daniel and Ryan. Cradled in their arms was a ball of black fluff, wrapped in a soft cream blanket decorated with little bone motifs.

"Meet Dog," said Ryan, handing the warm little bundle over to Kim.

It was love at first sight.

That night, Dog slept in his basket beside Kim's bed, her hand resting on his warm little body to comfort him. Twice in the night she and Dean had taken it in turns to pad downstairs, bleary eyed, to wait patiently while Dog went 'wee wees' in the garden. Unfortunately, one of the wee wees turned out to be a false alarm and a tiny little mishap meant new, clean blankets at the entrance to his bed. By the morning, Dog had somehow ended up snuggled in between Kim and Dean, his soft little head on the pillow, snoring gently.

Chapter Sixteen

On Sunday morning, the finishing touches were made to Lottie's party room. A balloon arch in unicorn colours had been placed around the door and fairy lights twinkled in every corner. A beautiful handmade birthday cake took pride of place, courtesy of Kate the baker, from the Women Who Wine group and Dean had been true to his word making enough variations of chocolate goodies to satisfy even the sweetest tooth! A pile of beautifully-wrapped presents awaited the birthday girl; almost everyone in the pub had bought a gift for Lottie and the little girl had unwittingly gone from having very little to unwrap, to a veritable hoard.

Megan had been so emotional the evening before, she'd blamed it on pregnancy hormones, but actually she was just bowled over by the kindness she'd been shown.

When Lottie arrived, she too had burst into tears. "This is the best party ever, Auntie Kim," she said.

Lottie and her three little friends enjoyed a special manicure and pamper session from Helen, Kim's beauty therapist friend, and there were lots of 'oohs' and 'aahs' as Lottie opened the enormous pile of presents.

Kim had asked Megan to bring Dog down to Lottie, she wanted him to be a gift from all of them.

"So Lottie, you've got one more present," said Kim, as Megan crept upstairs to collect Dog. "But I warn you this is not an ordinary present. This is a very special present that will take up a lot of your time – are you ready?"

Lottie nodded, her eyes wide with excitement. She sat on the floor, her arms outstretched as instructed.

"We can't take him home darling, he has to live here, but he's yours to name and care for, Auntie Kim and Uncle Dean will just look after him while you're at school," said Megan, entering from upstairs and placing a blanket containing a curled up and very sleepy Dog into Lottie's arms.

"Is he really mine?" asked Lottie, tears streaming down her face. "This is the best birthday ever!"

After that, there was not a peep from the girls as they cooed and fussed over Dog who was lapping up the attention like a pro.

"Thank you," said Sandra, hugging Kim tight, "you've made my daughter and my granddaughter very happy and I can never thank you enough for that."

"It's not the worst thing I've had to do," laughed Kim, "but you're welcome!"

"So, what will you call him?" asked Ryan. "He can't be called Dog forever."

"I think I shall call him Teddy, because he looks like a teddy bear," said Lottie.

"Perfect," said Kim.

"Phew!" said Dean. "I was worried you'd name him something embarrassing!"

Later in bed that night when the last of the cake crumbs had been hoovered up and the party streamers had been collected from some pretty weird locations, little Teddy slept soundly in his basket at the side of the bed, worn out from what had been a pretty exhausting day for a puppy.

Judy, Daniel and Ryan had left to drive home around teatime and Kim had been sad to see them go. It had taken a whole lot of persuasion to get Lottie to leave and Kim had a feeling she'd be a regular visitor moving forward!

"What do you reckon will happen to Keith and Olivia?"

"I'm not sure," said Dean, "but even if they only get a caution, it'll mean they're unlikely to come back. We'll have an alarm next week and now of course we have Teddy to keep us safe!"

Kim laughed, as Teddy gave a long snore as he began twitching and dreaming in his basket.

"Yeah, I must admit I do feel much safer with him around! Thanks for everything though, I know it's been a bit shit lately but thank you, I couldn't have got through it without you."

"Well, if that's the case," said Dean, "and I really am indispensable, I was wondering if it wouldn't be a bit too soon for us to make it official? Perhaps my toothbrush could live alongside your toothbrush, if you understand what I mean…?”

CHRISTMAS GIFTS

at the

Dog & Duck

Chapter One

"It still tastes of fucking onions," exclaimed Kim as she took a bite of the choc ice she had taken from the freezer for a quick sugar boost.

"I think we'll have to bite the bullet and clear that freezer out completely," replied Dean. "Clear it, defrost it, and scrub it. The smell has penetrated everything. We'll get away with a little hint of onion on our savoury stuff, but I don't think onion ice cream will ever catch on!"

One of the repercussions of Kim's ex-husband's attempts to sabotage the pub a few weeks back had been the raw onions that he and his girlfriend Olivia had managed to hide in the freezer during their clandestine 'visits'. Kim and Dean had thought that they'd managed to abort the feckless pair's mission without further casualty, but it seemed that a couple of their 'gifts' had slipped through the net. It was worrying to realise that they had been in the pub undetected more times than Kim had first thought, but then it had also transpired that the missing back door key had been taken rather than lost.

The stakeout that Kim and her Dog and Duck family had staged had not been without drama but it had meant that Keith and Olivia had been caught in the act with enough concrete evidence for the police to arrest and charge them with criminal damage and several other offences relating to harassment. Since his arrest,

Keith had completely gone to ground but Olivia had been seen parading around the local area wearing a rather fetching ankle bracelet – curtesy of HMP – like some bloody badge of honour!

Fortunately, the conditions of their conviction meant that 'Bonnie and Clyde', as Dean now referred to them, weren't allowed within spitting distance of the pub and Kim was cautiously confident that the drama was now at an end. Any more visits, and the pair of them would end up sharing a bunk and wearing his and hers grey tracksuits and sliders with socks! ...Although Kim did think it rather fitting that the placement of the onions meant that they had left a nasty smell under everyone's noses!

Kim chucked her half-eaten choc ice into the bin; she didn't think even she would ever be desperate enough for sugar to give onion ice cream a go. She began to pull the food items from the freezer, stacking them in one of the many cool bags that she seemed to have accumulated each time she went shopping – it was about time they came in useful. The whole point of reusable bags was that you took them with you to re-use, but every time Kim went to the supermarket, she left the bags behind and bought more to add to her collection; menopausal brain fog was real!

Teddy sat at Kim's feet watching as joints of meat and packs of sausages were pulled from the freezer, his expression ever hopeful.

“This isn’t for you Teddy baby,” laughed Kim, as Teddy gave her his very best puppy dog eyes.

“He’s starving, bless him,” said Dean.

“Yeah, he does look malnourished!”

Teddy was just about 5 months old and growing at an alarming rate. He’d been in their lives for just a few weeks, having been presented to Megan’s daughter Lottie as a birthday present. The deal was, that he would live at the pub and Lottie could visit whenever she liked, desperate as she had been for a dog of her own.

Lottie and her mum Megan lived in a rented house which meant that they could not have pets – it was also pretty small, and Teddy was beginning to take up quite a lot of room! He was also ridiculously clumsy. He appeared to have little control over his long gangly legs, and he was forever knocking things over with his long tail, or pouncing ready to play and destroying most of whatever was in his way as he did so!

With a new baby brother or sister on the way, Teddy had been the perfect way to make Lottie feel special and was helping her to deal with some of the fears she had about the new unexpected addition to her and Megan’s little family of two. Megan had very much struggled to come to terms with her impending arrival, having been ‘loved and left’ by Lottie’s wayward and now very absent father. Seeing her daughter so happy again had certainly helped her to allay some of her own worries and fears for the future.

Lottie adored Teddy and the feeling was entirely mutual, although Teddy seemed to adore everyone, and Kim doubted that he'd ever be much use as a guard dog, as had been part of the plan... unless he could lick the intruders to death! Lottie came by most days after school to see Teddy and he would hurtle through the pub from wherever he was sleeping or chewing on a discarded sock or a stolen tea towel and practically throw his huge gangly frame at her. They would then hurtle round the garden together before collapsing in front of the telly, both stretched out on the sofa, Lottie almost buried under a mass of black and chocolate brown fur. Kim and Dean still had few concrete ideas as to Teddy's true parentage, but he was big and hairy with a soft squishy face and floppy ears that looked as if they belonged to two different dogs! He was never going to win any awards at Crufts, but he had wormed his way into their hearts more than Kim had imagined possible. The regulars loved Teddy, the staff loved Teddy, even the postman loved Teddy; he was a clumsy, messy, loveable oaf!

Once the freezer had been cleared of its onion-y aroma, Kim put the kettle on for a quick cuppa before the lunchtime rush. She could hear Rosa singing in the bar area as she polished the counter to a healthy shine. Dean had prepped the sandwich fillings, and the homemade pie for today's special was in the oven – chicken ham and leek... no onion!

"Let's have a quick cup of tea before the crowds start pouring in," said Kim placing two mugs on the large stainless-steel table that stood in the centre of the kitchen, the place where Dean would plate up once the orders came through.

"I don't think we'll be super busy today; Mondays are always a bit of a lull after the weekend," he said, taking the mug of tea and settling on one of the kitchen stools.

Kim took a deep breath. She had been wanting to speak to him for several days now, but she never seemed to find the right time. She didn't know why she was so bloody nervous, their relationship was refreshingly uncomplicated, and she had never felt so at ease in another person's company – let alone a bloke – as she did Dean's. She was pretty sure she knew what his answer to her question would be but there was still that nagging feeling that perhaps she had misread the situation; old mind monkeys that refused to keep quiet. She had thought several times about a grand gesture, or at least a candlelit meal but that just served to make her feel even more nervous. She decided to just go ahead and blurt it straight out...

"Dean, I wanted to ask you something. I want you to be totally honest with me and I'm sorry if this makes you feel pressured, it's really not meant like that... look just be honest, okay...?"

"Blimey, this sounds serious, spit it out girl!"

Kim reached into the cupboard next to the fridge and pulled out a small, blue gift box, tied with a white ribbon. The box had been in there for over a week when she had formulated plan number 45 of 'how to ask him', but still she had bottled it several times over.

Dean furrowed his brow in confusion.

"Look I'm just going to give you this and let you decide. You don't have to say anything." Kim's words came out in a rush.

She knew she was talking way too fast, but she was so nervous, and she wasn't totally sure why. She handed the box to Dean who was more confused than ever. He pulled the ribbon undone and opened the small box. Inside there was a shiny silver key. The key opened the new lock that had been fitted on the back door to the kitchen; the door that they used as their main entrance to the pub and their flat.

"I just thought you'd like to make it official... move in properly... but only if you want to... it's fine if it's too soon..." her voice trailed away, and she felt like she might pass out or wet herself!

The relief she felt when Dean grabbed her into his arms was palpable.

"Is that a yes?" she asked. "I was so worried you might think it was too soon, it's really fine if you'd rather wait, I just thought you're here most of the time anyway and there doesn't seem much point in you paying rent on a flat you never sleep in, but please say if you'd like to wait..."

At that point Dean kissed her so passionately that she felt she might wet herself for an entirely different reason altogether and Teddy started barking and pawing excitedly at his mum and dad who seemed to be involved in some kind of wrestling game... and he loved to wrestle!

“Best bloody contraceptive in the world,” laughed Dean pushing Teddy away playfully. “Babe, I’ve been wanting to make things official for months, but I didn’t want to make you feel pressured. I’ll phone the landlord and give notice today... I’m so glad you asked me. I love you so much!”

Kim gave a huge sigh of relief. “Thank fuck for that!” she exclaimed. “Honestly, I wasn’t this nervous when I took my driving test! Is it okay to tell my mum and Daniel now? I know they’ll be happy for me. Not that much is changing really, you’ll just have lots of spare cash to spoil me with!”

“And there was me thinking that you only wanted me for my body!”

Kim laughed, “I’ll have your body too if you’re lucky.”

They began snogging like a couple of hormonal teenagers just as Rosa walked into the kitchen.

“Get a bloody room you two love bugs!”

“I think she means lovebirds,” laughed Kim. “Dean’s moving in Rosa!”

"That's great mia cara, but I thought he lived here already!" chuckled Rosa. "Now are you two going to get any work done?"

Kim and Dean reluctantly let go of each other, having been 'reprimanded' by Mama Rosa! Kim felt so relieved that he had felt exactly the same as her, although considering he hadn't actually left the pub for more than a night or two since they had got together, she had to agree with Rosa that not much was going to change. Things just felt 'official' now and she couldn't quite put her finger on why that made her feel so different. All she knew was that the 'different' was definitely a great kind of different.

Chapter Two

The rest of the shift passed uneventfully although they had been much busier than anticipated considering Monday was supposed to be their quieter day. Once the plates had been cleared and washed, Kim went upstairs to share her news with her family and of course her best friend Fleur. Dean had to go into town to run a few errands and Rosa was in the bar until six, when Jake would arrive to help out with the evening shift.

As she had hoped, Kim's mum Judy was overjoyed with her news and said that as far as she was concerned it had taken too bloody long! Kim listened patiently whilst Judy filled her in on the medical ailments of the entire sewing circle members, bridge club, and prayer chain combined, and she was delighted to learn that Gloria's suspected tumour had in fact been a rather nasty boil that had been dispersed by the application of a warmed-up milk bottle opening!

Fleur had screamed her delight down the phone and had been pleased to learn that she was not alone, having taken the plunge with her boyfriend herself a few months back and agreeing to live together; although it had taken her a few years as opposed to a few months!

Kim had hung up on Fleur and gone through to the kitchen in the flat to make a quick coffee before phoning her son Daniel. She had left him until last as she knew that his workday usually finished around four and it was now just a few minutes past; give him time to get in the car and start his drive home, as that was when they usually did most of their catching up.

She had just put the milk back in the fridge when her phone rang, and she noticed it was an incoming video call from Daniel. Her heart leapt as she made her usual jump to catastrophic conclusions whenever Daniel called unexpectedly or out of the ordinary. Daniel often joked that his mum was prone to over dramatising where he was concerned; if he didn't answer one of her calls immediately, Kim would instantly assume that he had befallen some outrageous freak accident involving quicksand, avalanches and sink holes on the drive home from work!

He didn't normally video call her after work as he would be driving, and so her mind went into overdrive even more than usual. "You okay babe?" she asked as she clicked the green answer button on the call.

"Calm down mum, everything's fine," laughed Daniel. "I literally just said to Ryan that you'd make some random assumption about my welfare!"

"Oh, shush you, it's what mums do. Is that Ryan behind you?"

"Hi Kim, you get two for the price of one today!" said Ryan as he appeared directly behind Daniel.

“Where are you? You aren’t at work, by the looks of things?”

“We had a day off,” replied Daniel. “Mum, we’ve got some news...”

“And....?” questioned Kim, her heart racing in nervous anticipation.

“Don’t worry, it’s good news. Well at least I hope you think it’s good news. Ryan asked me to marry him yesterday... and I said yes!”

Kim grinned like the proverbial Cheshire cat, tears rolling down her cheeks.

“Are you happy?” laughed Daniel. “I take it those are happy tears!”

“I can’t tell you how happy I am,” blubbed Kim. “It’s wonderful darling, congratulations!”

“That’s a relief,” said Ryan. “I worried I should perhaps have asked you first...”

“Don’t be daft, I’m over the moon. It’s so funny cos I was just about to call you and tell you some news of my own.”

“Oh God, I’m not getting a new brother or sister, am I?” laughed Daniel.

“Jesus Christ no!” exclaimed Kim. “I’ve asked Dean to move in with me... officially. Is that okay?”

"It's bloody brilliant mum, I think Dean's great, and you deserve a bit of happiness at last. Just one more thing..."

Kim took a deep breath, "I'm not sure I can take much more excitement."

"We'd like a Christmas wedding, and we'd like it at the pub. How do you feel about that?"

"I feel like I'm going to burst," shrieked Kim. "I think it is absolutely perfect."

"There's no rush, but we also thought sod it, why wait? Neither of us will be wearing a dress and there won't be all the drama associated with your average wedding. We just want a quiet ceremony, some good champagne and the people we love to share it with us – life's too short for waiting!"

"I couldn't agree more," replied Kim. "You tell me what you want, and we'll do it, does Nan know?"

"I'm going to phone her now," said Daniel.

"...and what about your dad?" asked Kim tentatively.

"I'm not sure," sighed Daniel. "I'd rather he didn't come if I am honest, and I'm sure you won't want him there."

"Let's wait and see," said Kim. "These things have a habit of working out by themselves, I'm not worrying about him now, I've got a hat to buy!"

Kim came off the phone feeling on cloud nine. She went down into the bar and threw her arms around Rosa, sharing her lovely news in between tears of happiness.

"A wedding mia cara, that is so fantastic!" squealed Rosa hugging her back. "And it will be so lovely to have it here, we can make the place look beautiful. Does Dean know?"

"They've only just told me. I'll tell him when he's back from town, but I know he'll be over the moon. I'd love you two to get together on the food – do something amazing!"

"Consider it done! Now in Italy, we always toast good news, so what shall it be?"

"You read my mind," laughed Kim, reaching into the fridge for two small bottles of vintage Cava that had become quite popular with their younger customers who were enjoying a dry-er version of the traditional Prosecco. The mark-up on the bottles was outrageous in Kim's view but it seemed they were happy to pay it - especially for special occasions - and this was certainly a special occasion in Kim's eyes.

By the time Dean came back from town, Kim and Rosa had polished off three of the small bottles each which equated to almost two standard bottles between them and they were feeling very little pain.

After Kim and Rosa had slurred their way through their news Dean had headed into the kitchen to fix them both something to eat and a large cafetière of coffee! Rosa had gratefully accepted a lift from one of the regulars at the end of her shift and Kim had been ushered upstairs by Dean to enjoy a hot bath and an early night whilst Dean and Jake had held the fort. The day's excitement had proved a bit much and she had been fast asleep by 7.30, curled up in front of the telly with Teddy keeping her feet warm. At closing time, Dean had come upstairs and bundled her into bed, still snoring her head off!

Chapter Three

"Sorry about that," laughed Kim, in bed the next morning. "I think I had a bit too much excitement for one day."

"I think the three bottles of Cava might have had more of an impact than the excitement... but I'll let you off. Although... you do owe me!"

Kim shrieked as Dean pulled her unceremoniously on top of him, making her squirm and giggle as he kissed her neck. Teddy, who had been dead to the world in his basket just seconds earlier, awoke with a start and hurled himself onto the bed, eager to join in the game. Kim squealed as he thrust his big wet nose in between hers and Dean's faces, covering both of them in soggy wet doggy kisses, his tail wagging furiously as he took part in what he obviously thought was a family game of rough and tumble!

"Sod off!" cried Dean. "I'm trying to seduce your mother here!" which only served to rile Teddy up even more and he jumped and leapt back and forth across the bed, tangling himself up in the duvet, leaving both Kim and Dean without covers and dripping in doggy slobber!

"I give up," laughed Dean. "Bloody dog! Come on, let's get you some breakfast then perhaps me and your mum can have a cup of tea in peace."

"I don't think that Teddy has much idea about peace!" said Kim. "I'll take the tea though. Did you phone your landlord?"

"Yep, phoned him yesterday afternoon. He's a nice enough guy and I don't think he'll have much trouble getting new tenants, the flat's in a good area. I told him I'll move my stuff out this week, but I'll hand the keys back officially at the end of November; I'm paid till then anyway. I should get my deposit back, there's no damage and as you know, I am the model house guest!"

"Yes, you do have certain talents that make you quite nice to have around," said Kim, "you are very good at DIY and cooking, for example!"

"Nothing else?" asked Dean.

"Well, if you feed the dog and bring me tea, I could be persuaded to show you," replied Kim with a wink.

Dean practically hurled himself downstairs, feeding the dog in record time and leaving a bemused Teddy in the kitchen with the back door open in case he needed a wee. They had made sure that the garden was secure since getting Teddy, so he was safe enough on his own for a short while.

The next half an hour of the morning passed in rather a pleasant way and Kim finally rose from her bed feeling like some sort of wanton sex goddess – she didn't remember a time when she'd enjoyed sex so much. Keith had been the kind of man who only did 'it' on

Sunday mornings. Sunday mornings at eight o'clock to be precise. The total lack of spontaneity had made their sex life something of a chore and Kim had begun to view it like a trip to the dentist – a necessary evil, that involved some light drilling but that was usually over quite quickly! As the years had gone by and Keith had become even less agreeable and more of a drinker, the only fortunate side effect to this permanent state of oafishness had been the declining regularity of their Sunday morning trysts and Kim had been more than happy to say nothing and avoid it altogether. She'd even sabotaged the Teasmade - which had been a wedding gift from Keith's mother – leaving the kettle part to boil dry and damage the element. This gave her a reason to spring out of bed on a Sunday morning and make the tea herself; losing a weekend lie-in was a sacrifice she had been willing to make! Yet now, here she was, dragging her lover back into bed for mid-week nookie; she was out of control!

Chapter Four

Megan dragged the hoover around behind her as she waddled her way through her cleaning routine. She didn't remember being this large or this uncomfortable when she was pregnant with Lottie, although she had been more positive about the whole baby/pregnancy thing back then. She still had over two months to go, and little junior wasn't due until the New Year, but at this rate she felt like she was going to burst.

She knew that she wasn't really coping but she didn't want to let Kim and Dean down. The midwife had told her that her blood pressure was higher than she would have liked, and Megan knew that she was going to have to take her advice and rest up whether she liked it or not. She already felt guilty enough about not loving her bump in the way that she had with Lottie, but she didn't think she could bear the guilt if she caused the baby some harm in any way.

She had chatted with her mum Sandra just the night before whose advice had been to come clean and speak to Kim. Kim and Sandra got on great and they'd already agreed that Sandra would take over from Megan whilst she was out of action. Sandra had been covering Megan's shifts in the bar pretty much consistently these past couple of weeks, but Megan had tried to continue her cleaning duties at least in part.

She sat down in the chair as she felt a sharp twinge move across her stomach, twisting her insides into knots and causing her to inhale sharply. It was no good, she was going to have to stop before the choice was taken from her hands.

"You know it's time, don't you?" said Kim kindly as she came down into the bar and sat down beside Megan as she struggled to catch her breath.

Megan began to cry, "I just wanted to feel normal for a little while longer."

"Now you listen to me," said Kim. "Hanging on for grim life is not going to help you or the baby... or Lottie for that matter. We have already agreed that your mum will stand in for you, which she is more than happy to do. This isn't a failure you know... this is the sensible thing to do."

"You're right," sighed Megan. "I'm being a stubborn idiot, aren't I?"

"A little bit," smiled Kim. "We will still see you every day. Lottie won't let you off the hook that easily – she won't be away from Teddy for too long."

"She loves that dog. Shall I ring my mum today?"

"I would," said Kim. "She will be upset if you don't look after yourself, she loves you both so much."

"I know, I'm so lucky to have her. I don't know what I'd do without her..." Megan's voice trailed away as she choked back the tears.

"It's going to be fine," said Kim. "This baby will come, and you will fall in love."

"But what if I don't?"

"You will, I know you, and I know you will. It's only the fear holding you back. Now come and have a coffee and we will phone your mum together."

"Thanks Kim, I'm so sorry."

"Shush!" said Kim. "And if you say sorry one more time, I won't give you any of Rosa's homemade chocolate cake!"

An hour later, Sandra had arrived after a tearful phone call from her daughter and a new working rota had been decided. Sandra was to take over Megan's role completely so that her daughter could take some much-needed rest and in return, Megan had offered to babysit Teddy if Kim and Dean needed to go out at any time; news which was bound to be gleefully received by Lottie who was devoted to Teddy.

Kim had felt so much love as she watched Dean fuss over Megan, doing what he always did in times of crisis, which was to feed the needy!

On Saturday morning they had received a tearful phone call from Rosa whose sister had been taken poorly over in Naples and she had requested some time away to go and visit her with her own children and grandchildren. There was no doubting that things would be a little hectic whilst she was away, but Kim had of course told her absolutely that she must go and see her. Thank goodness Sandra was on board full time now! Dean had given Jake a call and he had agreed to take as many shifts as they needed since his accountancy training broke early for the Christmas period which was a real stroke of luck; under the circumstances, things seemed destined to work out better than first feared.

Rosa was booked onto an early flight on Monday morning and was likely to be away for at least a couple of weeks. The pub diary was already filling up with bookings for Christmas parties even though they were only just into November. Almost every Friday and Saturday night they had at least two large parties joining them for work dos with many more booked for Sunday lunchtimes. The only time they didn't do food was on a Sunday evening which gave them a very small window in which to recover from the onslaught!

Alongside the food reservations were the Christmas Karaoke, Christmas Quiz Night and the all-important Christmas Meat Raffle which was to be hosted in the last week of November with profits going to a local children's hospital to help fund a party for its patients, especially those who were unable to be at home for Christmas. Kim had been really touched at how many tickets had been sold, with many of her regulars making generous donations to the very worthy cause. She was regularly reminded of what a great bunch her customers were; a far cry from the miserable old farts convention and troublesome drunks who had come as part of the fixtures and fittings when she had taken the pub on almost a year ago. How things had changed – it felt like yesterday and a lifetime ago all at once.

Any patrons who had caused more than their fair share of grief had been asked to find an alternative venue and the troublesome drunks had mostly gone when Olivia had left – knowing that their chances of getting drinks on the house were now about as rare as rocking horse shit!

One of Kim's favourite regulars was an old boy called Ernie who was as wide as he was tall (which was only about five foot four!) and had a thick white beard. He often sat on the bench outside the pub puffing on a hand carved old pipe, dressed in a cable-knit sweater and flat cap, come rain or shine, and looking more like Captain Birdseye than the man himself!

He drank Bitter from his own personal glass that was kept behind the bar and was engraved with his initials. Apparently, he had been coming into the pub for years and whilst everybody knew of old Ernie, no-one actually knew where he lived or where he came from. He said very little, but he smiled often and loved nothing better than pottering around the pub and clearing glasses from tables, which was very helpful when they were busy.

Someone had suggested that they should host a Santa's Grotto – Kim couldn't remember which bright spark had made this suggestion, but all she knew now was that it was on the notice board, which in pub terms meant that it was practically carved in stone! The next hurdle had then been to find someone willing to play 'Santa' for the afternoon, and whilst Steve's offer had been well intentioned, Kim didn't relish the thought of the pub know-it-all holding court for an entire afternoon and becoming even more self-important than he already was. Besides which, Steve was built like a 'streak of piss' according to Doris's husband Brian and had tattooed knuckles and an eyebrow piercing – hardly the Father Christmas vibe that the children would be expecting. Added to that, the fact that Steve's big mouth would be flapping about like a bird in a wind tunnel, pathologically unable as he was to be discreet about anything, he was unlikely to conjure up the air of mystery and magic that Kim hoped to provide for any visiting children.

As Kim was tactfully trying to decline Steve's kind offer, Ernie had offered his services in exchange for a pint of Mild and a steak and kidney pudding. Kim had somewhat over-zealously accepted once she had got over the initial shock of hearing Ernie say more than four words consecutively out loud. Steve had tried unsuccessfully to hide his disappointment, not for one moment understanding why Ernie was a more suitable candidate for the role despite the round physique and sodding enormous white beard! He had sulked at the bar for an hour or two before realising nobody was all that interested. The truth was that they had all been quite pleased for a little break from his usual puffing and blowing.

And so it was sorted, that Ernie, with little need for disguise other than a red suit and a pair of wellies, would sit in an armchair in the back room each Saturday afternoon from three till five for four weeks from the middle of November until the middle of December. He was to be well fed and watered after each session and presents were being donated by local businesses in exchange for some mutual promotion in the pub's ever-expanding social media development thanks mainly to Kim's best friend and marketing guru Fleur.

It felt strange putting up Christmas decorations in November. Kim had always steadfastly refused to put up any decorations before the 1st of December in her previous life, but she was fast learning that pub life was very different to any form of normality she had previously known. They had decided to go all-out with the decorations, particularly as the back room was to be Santa's home for the next few weeks and Kim had soon realised that the meagre box of decs containing some threadbare tinsel and a rather wonky angel that she had brought from home when she moved in, were really not going to cut it!

She had decided to go shopping with Megan and Lottie for more decorations after school on Wednesday. She had thought that it might cheer Megan up a bit, and she was certain that Lottie would be in her element choosing trinkets for the makeshift grotto. There were no pub events on a Wednesday and Dean and Jake were quite capable of holding the fort with help from

Sandra who was an absolute natural behind the bar. Some of the girls from the Women Who Wine group were popping in for drinks later in the evening and had offered their services to help decorate and Jax, the local florist, was bringing a handmade wreath for the door and had arranged delivery of a real tree from her supplier.

Kim was looking forward to Christmas more than she had done in a long time. Since Daniel had left home, Christmas with Keith had been a depressing affair with him spending most of it watching crap Christmas telly and eating his own body weight in mince pies and nuts, flicking little bits of shell all over the bloody place as he wrestled with the nut crackers. When he wasn't at home, he'd been in the pub and Kim had lived for the few days when she would see her mum and Daniel over the festive period. This year was set to be very different. The days and nights were to be filled with company and laughter, over-the-top decorations and Kirsty MacColl's Fairytale Of New York on repeat on the jukebox. Her mum and Daniel were coming to stay and now they had a Christmas wedding planned on top – life really was bloody marvellous!

Kim and Megan drove to Lottie's school and picked up a very excited little girl who chattered at a hundred miles an hour all the way into town. The journey took a little longer than anticipated on account of the fact that they got stuck behind a suped-up VW Golf driven by a youth who looked no more than about 12 years old! The car had been fitted with two enormous exhaust pipes – presumably to make it go faster or at least make the noise of a really fast car – and had one of those skirt kits around the bottom that meant it only cleared the ground by a whisker. The car was so low to the ground that the driver was forced to drive at a snail's pace over the many speed bumps located en-route and practically came to a grinding halt negotiating the ramp into the carpark. Kim thought it was more than a little ironic that a car that had been modified to go as fast possible – complete with 'Fast and Furious' decals – was now so hindered by its modifications that it would have been quicker to get out and push the bloody thing!

The girls spent a blissful couple of hours visiting every bargain pound store and pop-up Christmas shop in the vicinity, collecting a haul of festive sparkle that Rudolph himself would have envied – fairy lights, baubles, tinsel, garlands for the fireplace, a pair of gold woven reindeer, a three-foot-high snow man that danced when you clapped your hands, and tea light holders in every Christmassy shape imaginable.

Kim's little pink car was packed to the gunnels as they made their way home, stopping briefly to pick up a takeaway burger for Lottie on the way. The nights were drawing in and it was quite dark by the time they arrived, even though it was still not yet six o'clock.

They dragged the bags in from the car, enlisting willing helpers to help them with their bounty. The pub soon became a flurry of activity. The tree had been delivered and Dean was busy removing the top in the garden with a saw as it was too tall to fit into the room! Customers and staff began unpacking the decorations like a bunch of excited kids. Fleur and Rob had arrived, and the men were soon put on 'high up' duties and anything requiring a hammer or a screwdriver.

The time flew by and before they knew it, it was nine o'clock.

"I'd better take her home," said Megan, as a tired Lottie let out an involuntary yawn.

"I'm not tired Mum!"

"Maybe not," said Sandra. "But Mum's right, you've got school in the morning. You okay getting home darling?"

"I've got to shoot off," said Jax, "I'll drop you back if you like."

"Thanks Jax, you're a star," replied Kim. "And thanks for everything; the wreath looks amazing!"

By 10pm the pub was fully decorated, every surface, corner and ledge housing some form of Christmas cheer. It looked incredible: warm, inviting, and ready for an unforgettable Christmas.

Chapter Five

Rosa chewed her nails as they waited in the boarding room of the airport. She watched with affection as her youngest granddaughter slept in her dad's arms - Rosa's youngest son. It had been a long time since they'd had a family holiday and Rosa just wished it was in better circumstances.

It had been several years since Rosa had been back to her family home, the place where she had grown up. Long, hot days filled with Mediterranean sunshine, where she and her friends would walk the narrow, stone streets, buying Gelato from old Signor Agosti and giggling at the attentions of the local boys, strolling between tall apartment buildings designed to keep the walkways cool in the searing heat.

It was in these streets that she had met her darling Paulie – the boy with the jet-black curls who had won her heart, the boy who had taken her for rides on his moped, sneaking off to share secret kisses behind the old church. Their wedding had been a rather sudden affair, when Rosa had found out that she was carrying their first child not long after her seventeenth birthday. Their Catholic parents would never have been able to withstand the shame of a grandchild born out of wedlock, but Rosa regretted nothing...well almost nothing. Her and Paulie had gone on to share many wonderful years of marriage, leaving to start their new life in England. Paulie had been an amazing husband

and father, working hard to provide a good life for his family – how she missed him. To her, he would always be the boy with the jet-black curls.

“Come on Mum,” said Rosa’s daughter Isabella. “That’s our number.”

Rosa smiled and stood as they were called to board their flight. It was true, she had so many fond memories, but she also had some dark ones too. Memories that she had chosen to keep buried. The same memories that had kept her away from Italy for so long. Even Paulie hadn’t known the full truth; she just prayed that she would be able to let old scars stay healed.

Chapter Six

On Sunday morning, Kim came downstairs to find Sandra chasing Teddy round the pub, a Christmas bauble clenched between his teeth.

“This dog is such a bugger!” she laughed. “He knows he shouldn’t have it; he just wants a game. He won’t even chew it; he just wants me to chase him!”

“I hate to point this out to you, but you are sort of giving him what he wants,” said Kim.

“Yeah, you might have a point there! He’s got us all wrapped round his little paws!”

Teddy was persuaded to relinquish the bauble in exchange for a chicken chewie, although the tell-tale signs of his morning thievery shone on his whiskers and muzzle in the form of some silver glitter residue. Sandra and Kim shared a frothy cappuccino before the day’s trading once the pub was clean and tidy. Kim felt prouder than she had ever done for how the Dog & Duck looked now, resplendent in its Christmas finery; it bore almost no resemblance to the damp, dark and neglected place that she had walked into in January. She remembered the despair she had felt then compared to the pride she felt currently – she couldn’t have wished for a better outcome.

There was lots to be done today. Daniel was making the necessary phone calls to try and secure a registrar for his and Ryan's upcoming nuptials and then they had a family Zoom call planned to agree arrangements and finer details. Kim wondered if her mum Judy would be able to handle a group video meeting but, as Fleur had rather bluntly pointed out, Judy was more technically capable than Kim was, despite having come on in leaps and bounds since taking over the pub in January and joining the 21st Century!

The video call was to be set up in the function room at five o'clock once Sunday dinners were over. Jake had agreed to manage the bar, and the rest of them would be there if a catastrophe occurred. Jake's new girlfriend had offered to come and lend a hand just in case and, whilst Kim was sceptical about having his new love interest behind the bar, especially one he'd only been seeing for a few weeks and whom she'd never met, Dean had persuaded her to give it a try.

"If she's no good, we'll be around and if she is, we might need her over Christmas. We are probably going to need extra help for Daniel's wedding – you don't want to be working the whole way through it."

"Fair point," replied Kim. "I wonder what she's like?"

"Well, Jake's a nice bloke, and he's no fool, so fingers crossed..."

Sunday dinners were a roaring success as usual with Dean's now famous Yorkshire puddings gathering quite a reputation as they exploded in the oven, rising to impressive dimensions. Once plates had been cleared and the pub returned to something like normality, Kim set up the laptop in the back room. Fleur and Rob had arrived and of course Sandra, Megan and Lottie were an enthusiastic part of the planning mission. Jax had come along to offer her floristry expertise and Kate the baker – another member of the Women Who Wine group – had popped by to discuss making a cake for the wedding which was to be her own generous gift to Daniel and Ryan. The only person missing was Rosa and Kim was sad that she couldn't be a part of the plans, but she had promised to relay every detail to her when she phoned later in the week. In truth, Kim was a little worried about Rosa who had seemed distant before she left; she would speak to her properly during their phone call.

Once they were all settled, a huge dish of leftover roasties and a bowl of thick rich dipping gravy on the table in front of them, Fleur set up the laptop ready to start the call. There was a chilled bottle of Chardonnay in the ice bucket on the table and a couple of glasses of lemonade for Lottie and Megan who were of course not drinking. Lottie had also been provided with an impressive tray of snacks courtesy of Uncle Dean who spoiled her terribly!

"It's okay, she's got a few strawberries as well," Dean said, meeting the raised eyebrows of both Kim and Megan as he placed the goodies in front of Lottie. "Just make sure you eat the healthy stuff too, or we'll both be in trouble," he winked at Lottie.

Teddy sat beside Lottie, his eyes ever hopeful as he carefully watched every bite she took!

"Right, here we go," said Fleur. "We're live!"

They huddled around the laptop as the faces of Judy and Daniel and Ryan came onto the screen.

"Hey Mum, hey my darlings, it's so good to see you," said Kim. "I'm so excited about all of this, I can't tell you. How did you get on with the registrar?"

"Yes, all good," Daniel replied. "We were going to aim for a few days before Christmas but the only date they had was 'Christmas Eve Eve'; apparently, they had a cancellation because the groom ran off with the bride's sister! That's the 23rd, it's not too close, is it?"

"It's perfect darling, it's all so romantic. Is he coming to us, or will you go to a venue?"

"No, he comes to the pub, I thought we could set the ceremony up in the room you're in now. We've got Ryan's parents, Nan and about four friends coming, but that's it. Anyone who wants to come from the pub is more than welcome, but I'll leave that up to you to organise. I'm going to get our guests to book into hotels nearby, but they can make their own arrangements. All we need to do is talk about food and timings. We had a couple of ideas about some decorations, but we are pretty easygoing to be honest."

By the time the call had finished they had decided that Dean would prepare a buffet-style wedding breakfast that people could eat at their leisure; the boys wanted a relaxed atmosphere. The ceremony was set for 1pm and was due to last about forty minutes. Ryan was sending some digital photos to Fleur who had offered to create a slide show of memories and photos to show on the big screen usually reserved for football matches and other sporting events. Daniel's only real request for decorations had been the addition of two giant light-up initials for D and R which would look great as a backdrop for photos and as many candles as the pub could safely light. The Christmas decorations in the pub were so exquisite that the place already looked fit for a Christmas wedding and Kim had offered to get some chair covers for the ceremony in Daniel's planned colour scheme of dark green and red to go with the Christmas theme. Both he and Daniel had ordered suits in the darkest green with a wine-red tie and Jax had pledged a flower centre piece of red roses and dark green foliage to compliment. She was also going to make some unique holly and ivy styled buttonholes for guests. There was to be a large sprig of mistletoe hanging in the entrance to the room and one above where the ceremony would take place for the grooms' first kiss. Kate's idea for the cake had involved a lot of chocolate and an assortment of red berries and edible green leaves to really complete the scheme. Lottie was over the moon to be chosen as the chief – and only – bridesmaid.

"Oh my word, it's going to be beautiful," shrieked Judy through the microphone.

"Oh Mum, isn't it going to be just amazing," said Kim, a lump forming in the back of her throat.

She was overwhelmed with everyone's kindness and generosity, and she really didn't know how she was going to hold it all together until the 23rd!

Later in bed, that night, as she cuddled into Dean, she said, "I'm so lucky Dean. I just feel so blessed."

"We all are babe, we all are."

Chapter Seven

The following week passed in a blur and before they knew it, they were almost at the end of November. The nights were well and truly drawing in and there seemed to be less and less daylight filling the days. The only thing Kim liked about this time of year was the cosy candlelight and the opportunity to light the fire in the old brick inglenook fireplace. There was nothing so welcoming as a roaring fire on a dark and gloomy winter's day. The weather had been unusually mild for the time of year, but she had lit the fire nevertheless!

On the last day of November, Dean was due to go back to his old flat and hand over the keys as his tenancy officially came to an end. Fortunately, his landlord had managed to find a new occupant which had made Dean feel less guilty about potentially leaving him in the lurch just before Christmas. He had cleared pretty much all of his stuff out of the flat, leaving only a few big items of furniture behind, some of which had been there when he moved in and some which he no longer needed and had agreed to leave for the new occupier. He'd been quite down on his luck when he had moved in and so he was happy to do his bit and help out the new people, figuring that what went around, came around. Anything they didn't need or want could be donated to charity and Kim had made it very clear that she was not about to house any of his stuff 'just in case'. If he needed it, fine, but if not they were starting their uncluttered life together as they meant to go on.

Keith had been a bloody nightmare for hoarding old bits of tat or collecting unwanted 'antiques' that were basically other people's old bits of tat but that he swore would be 'worth a fortune' in the future... Lovejoy he was not! Fortunately for Kim, Dean's army training meant that he disliked clutter as much as she did and was fully on board with a bit of order; he was unbelievably tidy for a bloke!

They had arranged for Kim to drop Dean off at the flat on the afternoon of 30th November, whilst he waited for the new tenant. She had to nip to Jim the Butcher's shop to pick up the last of the produce for the Christmas Meat Raffle and then she would collect him on the way back home. Dean didn't have a car of his own, but there seemed little point in getting a second car that would sit on the drive most of the time. He was happy to cycle if he needed to go anywhere local and he was secure enough in his own skin not to feel emasculated driving or riding in the pink car that Kim had bought in a 'sod off' gesture of defiance to Keith after his departure!

"You sure you'll be okay?" Kim asked Sandra as they prepared to leave.

"No problem, Megan is popping in with Lottie after school, so I've got a spare pair of eyes if I need a wee! Jake's coming in at six anyway."

"We'll be back way before then," said Kim. "It's just gone three now, so I reckon we'll be home by five latest. Hopefully the new tenant won't be late – Dean said they're due at four – so I'll dash over to Jim's while he waits and pick him up on the way back here."

"No rush, drive safely. I'll see you when you're back."

Kim and Dean left through the back kitchen door, with Kim locking it behind her. She knew it was daft, but she still felt uncomfortable leaving it open when her staff were in the pub alone. She was totally over Keith and Olivia's little sabotage campaign, but she couldn't deny that it had left its mark. You could easily see people coming in the front door if you were behind the bar, but Keith had proven just how easy it was for someone to sneak in through the back if you were busy.

"She'll be fine, Megan will be here soon, and she's got Teddy with her," said Dean.

"That's what I'm worried about," laughed Kim.

They drove into the neighbouring village before turning off towards the dockside development where Dean's soon-to-be previous home was situated. Kim marvelled at how quickly they had become an item and how safe she felt in their relationship; something she would not have dreamed possible just a few months ago. She often had to pinch herself to believe that in under a year she had ended a thirty-year marriage and moved her new lover in... permanently; not to mention taking on and transforming a pub she hadn't wanted! Her old self might have spoken words of caution, warned against moving too fast, but her new self said, 'Bollocks,' to waiting around! She was happy. She was in love. And what's more she didn't feel the slightest bit anxious about the future; she just had this feeling that it would all be okay.

"Right, see you in a bit," said Dean, kissing her on the cheek as he opened the car door. "Hopefully they won't be late, and I'll meet you back here in half hour or so."

"No regrets?" asked Kim.

"Only that I wish I'd met you sooner."

"Soppy git! See you soon."

Dean waved and blew a kiss as Kim pulled away from the front of the apartment building. He hoped this new person wouldn't take too long. He couldn't wait to be free of the last symbol of his old life and start his new one with Kim... officially.

He climbed the stairs one last time to his flat. Although the circumstances of his occupancy had been less than joyous, he had enjoyed living here. Having his own space and time to decompress after the traumatic way that his marriage had ended had been good for him, even though it might not have felt that way at the time. He'd never forgotten that one tiny twist of events on that fateful day could have meant a life sentence in entirely different living accommodation altogether! The flat itself, had been clean and tastefully decorated and living close to the riverside had been good for his soul. But now it was time to move on and he had never been more ready.

He turned his key in the lock, slightly surprised that the door hadn't stuck on the usual pile of useless junk mail that had greeted him on all of his previous visits. He began to wrestle with the small silver ring that attached the two keys to his keyring, struggling to release them in readiness for the new owner.

He swore softly to himself as he pinched his forefinger in the tight metal overlap, a small blood blister popping up angrily as he pulled it free, the keys refusing to budge. As he continued to fiddle with the unrelenting ring, he became aware of another presence, he was not alone.

"Hello Michael, I hope you don't mind. I had an extra key cut so I could move some bits in. The landlord said you'd be totally fine with it."

Dean looked up. Even before his eyes met hers, he knew instantly who the other presence was. He'd recognise that patronising, silky tone anywhere and the scent... he couldn't believe he hadn't recognised that perfume the moment he'd opened the door. The strong, almost overpowering smell of soap and flowers, the scent that she'd always worn because in her words, 'it made you smell wealthy.'

"Well, I am totally not 'fine with it'," snarled Dean. "What the fuck are you doing here?"

"I'm the new tenant, darling. I just fell in love with the place when we met last time, and I thought it would be nice for us to be near each other again."

"Are you fucking mental? We didn't *meet* last time, you followed me back here after you barged UNINVITED into my life. And I quite literally cannot think of anything worse than being within a ten-mile radius of anywhere you are!"

"Oh Michael, don't be like that. I appreciate we might have got off on the wrong foot..."

"The wrong foot? The wrong FUCKING FOOT? And DON'T call me Michael!"

"Don't be silly darling what else should I call you?"

"You're right, you're absolutely right..."

The almost triumphant, yet subtle raise of Grace's left eyebrow did not go unnoticed by Dean as she thought that she'd won... as she fully expected to.

"You're right, Grace. It doesn't matter what you call me. Because whatever you call me, I will never be listening, not now and not in the future. I've moved on with my life. I'm happier than I have ever been..."

"...with a barmaid?" sneered Grace.

Dean ignored her insult. She was here for a reaction, and he was going to rise above it; no matter how much she pushed his buttons!

"Kim is a landlady and a bloody brilliant one at that – not that it is any of your business. The fact is that I am leaving this flat and whether you decide to live here or not is totally irrelevant to me. You don't affect me any more Grace. I just don't consider you at all anymore."

The slight twitch in Grace's jaw belied the anger that Dean's comment had riled but she said nothing. Dean finally freed the wretched keys from their host and, pushing past her, slammed them unceremoniously onto a small side table in the open living area. As he prepared to leave, Grace stood between him and the open front door behind her.

"I always used to affect you Michael. I'm pretty sure you could still be persuaded..."

Dean's expression changed to one of horror, his eyes wide like saucers.

Unfortunately for Grace, she misread this horrified expression for one of lust as she stood before him, her long coat now in a crumpled heap where it had fallen onto the floor, as she dropped it from her shoulders.

"Oh my God," exclaimed Dean.

"I knew I could still have you if I really wanted to," purred Grace, standing before Dean, resplendent in a black Basque, stockings and long black boots.

"Oh fuck off Grace!"

Grace looked confused as she followed Dean's gaze. She turned around to find Kim standing in the doorway behind her.

"Oh dear, I hope I haven't put the cat amongst the pigeons." Her sinister smile belied the untruth of her statement.

"You forgot your paperwork," said Kim, ignoring the barely dressed Grace standing between her and Dean. "Did you know she was going to be here?"

"I swear darling I had absolutely no idea. Apparently, she is renting the flat now. I'm so sorry I genuinely didn't know..."

"I believe you. Have you got everything? ...Are you completely finished here?" asked Kim throwing a deliberate and pointed glance in Grace's direction.

"I love you," said Dean.

"I love you too. Shall we go?"

"Excuse me, but I believe we have unfinished business here, Michael," said Grace indignantly.

"His name is Dean, and as far as we are *both* concerned, this business is well and truly finished. Now grow up and put some bloody clothes on – you'll catch your death! You ready, babe?"

"I've never been more ready," replied Dean, stepping around Grace to join Kim in the doorway.

"I'll be living just around the corner," yelled Grace, her poised demeanour slipping somewhat.

"Live where you fucking like," laughed Dean. "Makes no difference to me!"

Chapter Eight

"You sure you're okay?" asked Dean for the hundredth time on their way back to the Dog and Duck.

"Seriously babe, I'm fine. But if you ask me again, I'll make you walk back!"

"I honestly didn't know she was going to be there. I think she's lost the bloody plot."

"I completely believe you – I think she's just not used to getting her own way, that's all. Now let's forget about her and get this meat back into the fridge; I think we've had enough problems for one day. I couldn't face cancelling the Meat Raffle too!"

"Well, I know where there's a bit of old mutton going begging if we get stuck…!"

"You are going straight to hell," laughed Kim.

"I sodding well hope so, I won't know a bloody soul in the other place!"

Once they had unloaded the Christmas meat haul into the fridges, there was just time for a quick cuppa before the Saturday night service began in earnest. Kim and Dean had both decided not to share the afternoon's events with anyone, they didn't want their lives to become a soap opera. Although Kim would probably definitely tell Fleur at some point!

Saturday was busy. Most people had been paid at the end of the month and the Christmas spirit was starting to infiltrate even the most reluctant of revellers. The jukebox had already started to ring out the sounds of 'I wish it could be Christmas every day,' and whilst Kim was thoroughly enjoying the buzz and building excitement, she was certain that come the end of December she'd be glad of a Christmas break!

The following day, on the Sunday, the pub was packed to the rafters. The Meat Raffle was to be drawn at 4pm and there wasn't a spare seat in the house. They had raised an unprecedented amount for the local children's hospital and Kim loved the fact that most ticket holders were just happy to have taken part, even if they didn't win the free-range turkey or the honey roasted ham. Personally, Kim wasn't even that keen on Turkey, considering it to taste like a rather dry and over-priced chicken... but to each their own!

There had been a few tense moments when the difference between buff- and white-coloured tickets had caused some minor disagreement, but all in all the raffle went without a hitch. Brian and Doris had magnanimously put one of their tickets back after winning three prizes on the bounce and for fear of being accused of foul play, but generally the banter was good natured and well-meant.

The Grace incident had been well and truly put to bed and neither Dean nor Kim had mentioned it again. Kim was never more certain of anything than she was of Dean's loyalty – besides, she didn't think he'd be stupid enough to put his ex-wife back in his old flat if he was planning a secret affair! The fact that neither of them felt the need to discuss it showed how little it had impacted them, something which would have really pissed Grace off. Kim didn't know her well, but she had seen enough to know that the best way to hurt Grace was to be indifferent to her!

Rosa was due back on Wednesday and Kim had really missed her. She'd tried to talk to her on the phone, but the line hadn't been altogether clear, and it had been difficult to have a deep and meaningful conversation. Kim hoped she was okay. She understood that her sister had been poorly, but she just had a niggling feeling that there was more to Rosa's melancholy than her sister's illness alone. The one thing that she had managed to glean from their phone call was that the patient was now on the road to recovery and the prognosis looked good, which was a blessing at least. Kim planned to go and see Rosa at her house before she came back to work, the pub wasn't always the best place to find peace and quiet for a private chat!

Chapter Nine

Rosa had breathed a sigh of relief when the plane landed – she was a nervous flyer and was always tempted to get out and kiss the tarmac as they disembarked! All in all, the trip had gone better than she had first feared and in many ways she had finally managed to lay some old ghosts to rest.

Later that day, she had been surprised by an unexpected knock at the door of the neat and tidy little cottage that she had shared with her husband Paulie for the last few years of their marriage before he had passed. Living there was bitter sweet – there were so many treasured memories in that house, from the big old armchair next to the fireplace that had always been Paulie's chair to the olive tree in the garden that had been planted specially to remind them of home, but there were also the memories that reminded her of the time when she had lost him. She'd lost a piece of herself that day, one which she knew she would never get back but she tried to be thankful for the good times.

"Kim!" she exclaimed as she opened the Mediterranean Blue front door.

"Hello stranger, I'm not disturbing you am I?"

"Of course not, mia cara, I'm just surprised to see you here – is everything okay?"

"Everything is fine," said Kim, stepping forward to hug Rosa. "I was just a bit worried about you that's all. I felt like something was wrong when you left... a bit more than your sister being ill? Tell me to sod off if I am poking my nose in!"

Rosa smiled and beckoned Kim in, leading her through to the little kitchen at the back of the house. She motioned for her to sit at the kitchen table, with a view of the garden through the French doors. Kim felt like she could have been in a little Italian village somewhere far away, as she looked out at the whitewashed stone steps, terracotta plant pots – now awaiting planting once winter was over – and the olive tree that stood proud and tall beside an ornate metal bench.

"Even in the winter, your garden looks lovely Rosa."

Rosa smiled. "Paulie always loved the garden here."

"So, how is your sister?"

"She's much better, mia cara."

"...and everything else? Are you okay or am I barking up the wrong olive tree?!"

Rosa laughed. "Paulie would have loved you so much. You are woofing at exactly the right tree!"

"You don't have to tell me anything, I just want you to know that I am here if you need me. I can't tell you how much you mean to me and how much you have helped me, this past year. I seriously couldn't have done it without you."

Rosa wiped a tear from her eye with the white lace hankie that she always kept in her pocket.

"A very long time ago, when we were young, my sister Francesca and me, we were very close. The same hair, the same clothes, the same taste in boys..."

Kim sat quietly as she listened.

"When I met Paulie, he was so beautiful. Jet black curls, dark skin. He drove a moped – they were very cool back in those days – and he had a six packet..."

Kim laughed. "I think you mean a six-pack Rosa!"

"I never really knew what that was – your funny English nicknames – but he had good muscles!"

"Anyway, me and Paulie we fell in love like a flash! From the day I met him, I just knew. We became inseparable, we were never apart. But Francesca, she was jealous. I guess I can understand it, looking back. First it was always me and her and then Paulie came, and we drifted apart. Unfortunately, she just took things a bit too far..."

"You don't have to tell me if you don't want to," said Kim, reaching across the table to lay her hand on Rosa's.

"It's so long ago but it took me so long to forgive her. If we hadn't left they would have taken her away from me. I would never have known her…" Rosa began to dab at her eyes with the same lace hankie.

Kim continued to hold her hand but said nothing.

"I fell pregnant with my Angel when I was barely seventeen. We called her Angel because that's what she was to us – an angel sent from God. My sister was cross with me for deserting her for Paulie but I think she was more cross because Paulie chose me and not her – all the girls loved him!"

"In those days, to get pregnant before marriage was a sin. My parents would never have lived with the shame. Girls who messed up got sent away to have their babies and the babies were adopted… I couldn't lose her Kim, I just couldn't!"

"You were born to be a mother," said Kim softly, "you have the biggest heart."

"…Francesca threatened to tell my parents, she overheard me and Paulie talking. We had to run away, whatever happened we just couldn't lose our baby. It wasn't their fault it was just how things were… old-fashioned Catholic ways. We came to England, we got married and our little Angel was born. My father died before he ever got to meet her and my mother always blamed me for breaking my father's heart. We made our peace but a lot of years were wasted."

"Oh Rosa, I'm so sorry. Is that why you were worried about seeing your sister?"

"She broke my heart but as the years went by, I missed her. Just so much time had gone on, so much water in the river."

Kim smiled at Rosa's misuse of the old saying.

"I should have forgiven her, but it just got harder to talk about it the more time went... like we had missed our chance. And when Paulie died it was even harder."

"So how were things when you went back?" asked Kim.

"Actually, better than I feared. Francesca was so sorry. We were all young and hot-headed... Italian blood! We hugged, we cried. I'm so glad I went, I would never have forgiven myself if she had died before we had the chance to let go of old wounds." The hankie that Rosa was using was being put to the test as the tears flowed freely now.

"You mustn't blame yourself, Rosa. We all do things we regret in the heat of the moment, and she did really hurt you. But things are good now and maybe things were meant to be this way, maybe before would have been too soon?"

"You're right, mia cara. Things are good now but I don't think Paulie would ever have let go – stubborn Italian blood! Maybe we could only make our peace when it was just us two left. Now shall we have coffee?"

Kim nodded gratefully as Rosa left the table to tend to the coffee maker now bubbling away on the kitchen side. After a generous cup of good, strong espresso and a slice of homemade orange cake, the world seemed a brighter place. The two women continued to chat and put the world to rights before the winter dusk began to draw in and Kim was reminded that she had a pub to run!

They hugged warmly before saying their goodbyes and Kim once again thanked her lucky stars that the Dog and Duck had brought Rosa into her life.

Chapter Ten

"Everything alright, I thought you'd left home?" smiled Dean as Kim walked in through the kitchen door.

"Everything is absolutely amazing, my love," said Kim, kissing Dean on the cheek.

She thought she may tell him a little about her conversation with Rosa at some point but for now, it was a discussion which would remain between the two of them only.

December seemed to have caused time to speed up and the days were whizzing by in a blur – there seemed to be something going on every day. The Father Christmas visits were going down a storm and Ernie had been a real trouper. He seemed to have been born for the role and Kim wondered what he had looked like as a little boy; she couldn't have imagined him ever looking any different, but then not many babies were born with a bushy white beard and face that looked like a crumpled brown paper bag!

Some days the queue for Santa's grotto was so long that Dean had taken to handing out chocolate bars to their little visitors whilst they waited.

Teddy was in his element, seeing every small child as a potential playmate and the Rudolph antlers and 'Santa's Little Helper' neckerchief that Fleur had bought him were a real hit with everyone who encountered him, rendering lots of 'ooos' and 'aahhs'! There had been one tricky moment when he'd stolen a small stuffed bear from the hands of one of Santa's visitors, clearly mistaking it for one of the many toys that Lottie brought him to play with. The aggrieved youngster had wailed at an ear-deafening pitch which had sent Teddy into a frenzy as he mistook the noise for his cue to play. After a fruitless chase around the pub, the bear now minus an arm clenched between Teddy's teeth, they had given up the chase and the small wailing child had been placated with a new present from Father Christmas and a slice of Rosa'a homemade chocolate cake. Fortunately, the child's grandparents were regulars in the pub and were able to see the funny side of the incident whilst enjoying the free mulled wine that Kim had served them as a peace offering.

An unrepentant and oblivious Teddy had grown bored and retreated to his basket once people had given up the chase, where he had promptly fallen asleep and begun snoring loudly, the small one-armed bear beside him.

Daniel and Ryan's wedding was to be held on the 23rd of the December, the day before Christmas Eve and Kim was like a kid, literally waiting for Christmas. The plan was that they would arrive on the morning of the 22nd in time for the Christmas Karaoke that same night. Ryan was planning to go home with Fleur and Rob and stay the night with them so that Groom and Groom could keep the tradition of not seeing each other before the big day. A whole posse of regulars had been enlisted to add the final decorations to the back room where the wedding would take place once it had been 'de-grotto-ed' and Father Christmas had finally left the building.

Dean was going to be flat out that day preparing the buffet for the wedding breakfast and he and Rosa had devised a table of goodies fit for royalty. Megan was so big and uncomfortable now that she was to be on light duties only, folding napkins and fixing mistletoe and holly to the candle holders that were to adorn every table top and window sill; all of which could be done in a seated position! Fortunately, Jake's new girlfriend had taken to the bar like a duck to water and had been a godsend over the past couple of weeks when things had gone crazy. She was a lovely girl and was very popular with the customers, which Kim hoped was down to her personality as much as her ample cleavage and the tiny skirts she wore! Jake seemed besotted and gazed at her with a similar expression to the one Teddy wore when watching Dean carve the Sunday roast beef! All in all, things were on track, if a little hectic.

Chapter Eleven

"Arrrgggghhhh!" screamed Kim as she hurtled out of the front door, the moment she heard Daniel and Ryan's car pull into the carpark.

She practically threw herself into Daniel's arms before he was fully out of the passenger seat.

"Hi Mum! Bit excited?"

"Oh my God darling, I've literally been like a coiled spring!"

"She's driven me bloody mad," laughed Dean as he appeared to help unload the car.

"Hello darling," said Judy, pulling her daughter in for a hug once she had set Daniel free. "It's all just so wonderful, isn't it?"

"Oh Mum, I literally can't wait!"

Ryan's parents, John and Dot, were the last to exit the car, unfolding themselves from the back seat into which they had been crammed with Judy for over two hours!

"It's so lovely to meet you both," said Kim, kissing them both on the cheek. "We've heard so much about you and we are definitely a fan of your lovely son – welcome to the Dog and Duck!"

Once the car had been unloaded, they headed into the bar for a cup of tea and a sandwich. They all talked at once at a hundred miles and hour and it was a wonder that any of them knew what had been said by anyone! Kim and Dean loved John and Dot who fitted into the group like long lost family. Eventually the conversation descended to a little above fever pitch and preparations for the Christmas Karaoke began in earnest.

Zane had set up his karaoke equipment the day before as this was also going to be the sound system for the wedding celebrations. Zane had become quite popular around the local area and his set-up was much more professional than it had been a few months previously when he had first started his DJ career. He still sported the same floppy fringe that covered most of his face and he was still entirely dressed in black but he had certainly learnt a lot about how to set up a gig rack. Kim didn't ever think their conversation would progress much past 'hello,' and 'I'll have a VRB please,' but he was good enough at his job not to make Kim feel nervous.

The first of the 'decoration task force' had begun arriving just after lunch and by two o'clock the back room was heaving with dedicated helpers. The chairs were lined up and covered in their fancy new covers, the top table that was serving as a kind of altar for the registrar had been decorated with the deep burgundy cloth that matched the colour scheme and Jax had delivered the spectacular flower arrangement that was to take pride of place. Kate had delivered the cake, the arrival of which had been greeted by a round of applause, so spectacular was it in all its chocolate-y glory. Fortunately, the pub was already beautifully decorated and only the tea lights needed to be added; although Kim had made the executive decision of hiding the tea lights away until after the karaoke, all she needed was a tipsy reveller to take it upon themselves to try and the light the bloody things and they could be celebrating bonfire night all over again!

By six o'clock the place looked incredible and Kim couldn't have felt prouder or more grateful to the gang of helpers that had now become friends as well as customers. There was just time enough for a quick shower and outfit change before the Christmas karaoke began. Sandra, Jake and Jake's girlfriend Sophee with a double 'e' were going to man the bar, whilst Kim and Dean were on clean up duty and keeping the bar as chaos-free as possible before the next day's wedding – the last thing Kim fancied was a massive clear-up mission on the morning of her only son's nuptials!

Everyone was in high spirits as they arrived for the evening's entertainment. Bobby's widow Fran had accompanied Steve for the evening, and although they made an odd-looking couple, Kim was grateful that despite Steve's big mouth and delusional sense of self-worth he was at least looking out for his dear-departed friend's vulnerable former partner. Fran had made the same bland and ill-fitting outfit choices that she always did, except for the addition of a pair of dangly snowman earrings and some Christmas bee-boppers, which looked rather at odds with her less than cheery disposition as they bobbed jauntily above her head. Kim had often wondered if Fran's less-than-jovial disposition had been the symptom of her long-suffering relationship with the over-exuberant Bobby but nothing much had changed since his demise and she had begun to suspect that Fran, like Eeyore, was just one of those people who was destined to be gloomy.

The evening got off to a raucous start from the get-go, with none of the usual 'warming-up' period needed to get people in the party mood – the Christmas spirit was well and truly flowing it seemed. Daniel and Ryan's friends had checked in at the nearby guest house where they were to stay whilst they attended the wedding and they had arrived at the pub full of excited congratulatory chatter. Kim liked them all instantly, but then she hadn't doubted for a moment that she wouldn't – Daniel and Ryan were great people and great people usually attracted great friends!

First up was Steve (unsurprisingly), whose rendition of Tom Jones's 'Delilah' raised an enthusiastic bout of audience participation in the chorus, particularly for the 'Ha, ha, ha, ha' parts! Kim thought she may actually wet herself when Dean and Judy performed 'Fairytale of New York'; she never knew that her Mum knew so many of the words and listening to her sing, '...you scumbag, you maggot, you cheap lousy faggot,' had caused some side-splitting laughter from Daniel and Ryan.

Fran's rendition of 'Danny Boy' brought a hushed reverence to the evening and by the time she had finished there wasn't a dry eye in the house; Kim still marvelled at how such a meek and mild character as Fran could produce a performance that any self-respecting musical Diva would have been proud of.

Megan sat propped up in the armchair by the fire and Kim couldn't help noticing how tired she looked – only a few more weeks and baby would be making his or her appearance; personally, Kim couldn't wait, it had been a long time since there had been the patter of any tiny feet in her life, and she missed the days when Daniel had been a youngster.

More hilarity had ensued when Daniel and Ryan had given a purposefully camp and cliched rendition of 'YMCA' with John and Dot thoroughly appreciating the humour, and all in all the evening was a great start to the wedding celebrations.

"What a great night, babe," shouted Fleur above the singing. "I bet you can't wait for tomorrow!"

"Oh Fleur, I'm so proud of him."

"What's the situation with his dad?"

"I told him I was happy to go along with whatever made him happy. The only line I drew was that Olivia would not be welcome to attend; not that he'd have wanted her here to be honest! I left it up to him but I'm quite glad he's decided not to invite him. I haven't pried, but I'm not sure he's even told him about the wedding at all – he's still pissed off with Keith's shitty reaction the last time he saw him. It's a bit tragic when you think about it, but you just know he'd have been a giant pain in the arse; Keith never could keep his mouth shut!"

"Well, you know what they say, you can't choose your family!"

"...And that would be comforting if I hadn't actually chosen Keith," laughed Kim. "But then, if I hadn't married him, I wouldn't have had my lovely Daniel so it was a sacrifice worth making in the end!"

"You definitely took one for the team there," laughed Fleur. "Anyway, we'll probably head off in a bit. Rob's looking a bit squiffy already and I don't want him with a raging hangover tomorrow if we are in charge of one of the grooms – besides, the weather is bloody awful out there!"

"Yes, I did notice the rain coming in. They forecast storms but fingers crossed it doesn't get too bad. Drive carefully and thank you for everything."

"Any time, babe."

They had practically poured Rob into Fleur's car and by the time they had said their goodbyes and come back into the pub, they were soaked through to the skin. The unusually warm weather had been replaced by a rather aggressive storm that had apparently made its way across the channel. Kim hoped that it would start to wane by the morning; it seemed that all the big calamities that had befallen the Dog and Duck in the past year had been of the wet kind, what with over-flowing sinks and flooded cellars – although both of those had been the result of Keith and Olivia's shenanigans and, despite his God complex, Kim didn't think that Keith was quite able to control the weather just yet!

As the evening came to a close, the storm refused to quieten – rain fell from the sky in sheets and the windows rattled as they were battered by the raging winds.

"I hope this storm eases," said Judy with a worried expression. She'd never been a lover of storms and this one seemed particularly aggressive.

"We'll be fine Nan," said Daniel. "I'm sure it will blow over... Ha ha!"

Kim slapped him affectionately at his cheesy humour. "Well, if that rain doesn't ease soon, your guests will be arriving by boat in the morning!"

By midnight, the pub had been cleared and tidied and the guests had left to go home. Casual invitations had been made so that whoever wanted to attend would be made welcome outside of the immediate wedding party. Jake had left with Sophee, but Rosa had opted to stay for the night (she and Judy were going to bunk in together) so she could be there bright and breezy in the morning to help with preparations. Ryan's parents had managed to find a 7-seater taxi to their hotel which they had shared with the boys' friends. Megan, Sandra and Lottie were staying over in one of the spare rooms. Lottie was looking forward to being chief bridesmaid and had gone to bed exhausted but ridiculously excited at around nine o'clock.

"I think I'll head up if you don't mind," said a tired Megan. "I feel shattered."

"Sleep well darling, try and have a lie-in tomorrow, there's plenty of us here to sort Lottie out, the rest will do you good."

"She looks a bit washed out," said a worried Sandra to Kim, as she watched her daughter leave for bed.

"Yes, she does look tired," agreed Kim. "But then, don't you remember yourself, that last few weeks of pregnancy seems to take forever. I really struggled in the last month – swollen ankles, a leaky bladder, a belly that felt like a boulder..."

"Sounds great," said Daniel, sharing a grimace with Dean.

"There'd be no bloody babies in the world if it was left to you fellas!" laughed Judy.

Kim and Dean checked that the doors were locked securely and that no windows had been left open, the way the rain was hammering on them, there'd be puddles in the morning if they weren't tightly shut!

They all climbed the stairs one by one, each of them worn out from the evening's partying and the adrenalin rush caused by the anticipation of the next day. Kim doubted she'd sleep at all, but she knew she'd be knackered if she didn't at least try.

Chapter Twelve

Kim sat bolt upright in bed as a loud crash reverberated through the pub. She reached across to nudge Dean, but his side of the bed was already empty. Teddy was pacing the bedroom, clearly agitated. The rain that had begun to pour last night had intensified and there was an atmosphere of impending disaster that made Kim very uneasy indeed.

She threw her fleecy winter dressing gown around her shoulders and climbed out of bed. She glanced at the clock which showed the time to be just a little after 6am. The room was in total darkness. Teddy remained glued to her side she descended the stairs into the bar area using the torch on her phone just as Dean appeared from the back kitchen, a worried expression on his face.

"I don't want you to worry babe, but one of the sheds has collapsed in the garden. Now of course this doesn't really affect anything that's happening today, but I am a bit worried about how bad this storm is."

Kim ran her fingers through her hair, a flurry of emotion coursing through her.

"It's really dark in here," she said, just noticing the lack of lighting behind the bar.

"I think the power is off too," said Dean.

"Oh Dean, no! What are we going to do?"

"Try not to worry, it might only be temporary. I'll see if I can get the news on my phone and check out what the forecast is doing and I'll make a call to the energy company... see if we can get an update."

At that moment, Daniel, Judy and Sandra appeared thought the bar door.

"You okay darling?" asked Judy, looking at Kim first and then Daniel.

"Listen, let's not panic just yet," said Daniel, noticing his mum's worried expression. "As Dean says, it might only be temporary and we've still got a few hours..." he was trying to remain calm and upbeat but Kim noticed the slight wobble in his voice that betrayed his anxiety.

They all went into the kitchen where Dean had lit the gas hob and was boiling a pan of water so they could all have a cup of tea – a very British response to war, famine and impending disaster!

It had to be said that the weather forecast was not optimistic, and the storm was showing no imminent signs of easing for the next three days! Each of the kitchen inhabitants did their very best to put their own positive spin on the current turn of events but there was no hiding the tension in the room. There were three questions on everyone's lips, but no-one was brave enough to say them out loud... what if the power didn't come back on? What if the groom and the guests couldn't get there and most importantly how were they going to stage a wedding without a fecking registrar?

By eight o'clock, they had decided that they were going to have to come up with some sort of contingency plans...just in case. Kim volunteered to try and phone the registrar to assess his intentions and Daniel was going to call Ryan to see how the land lay in that department, both with his parents and their friends.

By nine o'clock the mood in the kitchen had moved from nervous to downright bloody sombre and more in keeping with a wake than a wedding. It had transpired that the registrar lived in a road that had been flooded, and his only mode of transport was a small Fiat 500 which was only likely to be able to make the journey to the pub with a couple of oars and a sail!

"What the bloody hell are we going to do?" wailed Kim.

"Right, let's think about this logically," said Dean. "The only way anyone is going to arrive at this wedding is if they have a big-ass four-wheel drive, so who do we know with one of those?"

"Jim!" said Kim and Dean in unison.

As a butcher and coming from die-hard farming stock, Jim never drove anything that wasn't equipped to tackle a muddy field and a bit of inclement weather!

"I'll give him a call," said Kim.

Fifteen minutes later, Kim emerged with something resembling a faint smile on her face. They still had no power and there was still the little matter of a car park that looked like the River Nile, but at least Jim had readily agreed to ferry any stranded wedding guests to the venue. What's more, Jim had also promised to give Brian and Doris a call as he knew that their son also drove a vehicle that might be able to cope with the treacherous roads.

"We can't turn the lights on," said Kim.

"Listen, we have a registrar and wedding guests arriving – fingers crossed," said Judy, "which is more than we had an hour ago."

"True," said Dean. "I'll light the fire so it's nice and cosy and God knows we've got enough candles and tea lights to conduct our very own séance!"

"It will look beautiful in here," said Sandra, "and all that matters is that our two grooms are happy – it'll be something to tell the grandkids!"

As the day progressed, Kim resolved to remain as cheerful and positive as possible although it was difficult when the rain and wind refused to quieten for even a few minutes. They had been without power for most of the morning and Dean had worked to prepare as many of the hot buffet items as he could in frying pans or pots on the gas stove although most of it was already done. Fortunately the cold meats had been roasted in advance and the significant drop in temperature meant that, if necessary, any perishable items could be kept outside if the fridges got too warm. On pain of death, no one was allowed to open the cellar door to keep it as cool as possible for as long as possible.

At least the bar was warm, as poor Dean had battled the elements to bring in enough logs to keep the fire stocked throughout the day. By midday, they had done as much as they possibly could. The bridal party had gone 'old-school' and done their hair with rollers, having had no access to hairdryers and curling wands. The candles had been lit and the buffet table laid. As many phone calls as they could make rallying for help had been made and Dean had done his very best to secure any garden furniture or loose fixtures that could cause a hazard – there wasn't much to be done about the water in the car park nor the shed that was now in pieces all around the garden. The pub looked beautiful, its warm cheery glow almost defiant against the dark, raging elements outside. All they could do now was wait and wait...

By 12.30. Kim began to pace. The pub was eerily empty and as they sat there in their finery Kim was reminded of something her nan used to say about 'being all dressed up with nowhere to go...' Lottie had been a little trooper and despite her obvious worry, she had continued to smile and be as helpful as she could. She looked as pretty as a picture in the burgundy red satin dress with the green sash that they had chosen specially in the big department store in town. Daniel sat on a stool at the bar, unusually quiet and chewing his fingernails – Kim's heart ached as she watched her handsome boy trying to hide his concern.

At 12.45, there was a ‘pop’ as Dean released the cork on a bottle of bubbly.

“Right, come on you lot! Have faith. This wedding is going ahead – it might be a little behind schedule, but we are going to celebrate this wonderful day and thank God we all have each other.”

“Hear, hear,” exclaimed Judy. “Let’s raise a toast to our precious Daniel and our beautiful Lottie and say a little prayer!”

They each took a glass, wishing as hard as it was possible to wish.

Just at that moment the door flung open, a gust of wind and a whoosh of rain blowing a small party of die-hard attendees into the pub.

“Fuck me, it’s blowing a hoolie out there!” exclaimed Brian as he and Doris almost tumbled into the pub, resplendent in wedding suits and wellies.

They were soon followed by Daniel and Ryan’s friends and John and Dot who had arrived in relays, having been rescued by Jim the butcher and their son Adrian who had collected the waifs and strays from around the villages in their hardy vehicles. There was an uproarious and collective cheer when the registrar arrived looking more than a little dishevelled having waded through the car park in the long white tunic style robes that he wore for ceremonies and looking rather like a soggy ghost!

Ryan finally arrived with Fleur and Rob just before two o'clock and the relief on Daniel's face was palpable.

The ceremony finally went ahead at two o'clock, just one hour behind schedule, which was an absolute miracle in the circumstances! Lottie was the perfect bridesmaid and Teddy carried the rings in a little pouch attached to his collar which had to be wrestled from his teeth as he tried to play tug of war with his precious cargo!

There was literally not a dry eye in the house as Daniel and Ryan said their vows and gave and exchanged rings and Kim felt like she might actually burst with pride. All of her friends and family had rallied round to make this day special despite the weather and she could never repay them for their dedication to the cause. The wedding guest list may have been much smaller than expected, but in no way did it detract from beauty of the event. In fact, Kim was secretly quite pleased that only the most special people had made it through – Brain and Doris, Daniel and Ryan's friends, Ryan's parents from the guest house, Fleur and Rob, and of course, the absolute heroes of the hour, Jim and Adrian and their wives. Even Rosa had been collected along the way – she had been threatening to, 'bloody well swim there,' if she had to – she wasn't missing the wedding for anything!

At eight o'clock that evening, the power was restored to yet more cheers as they celebrated into the night. Little thought had been given to how any of the party were going to get back home and as the storm continued, there was further drama added to the already dire conditions when the temperature dropped to below zero for the first time that year. What had been wet rain was now icy rain, and driving and travelling conditions were now going way beyond treacherous.

"I don't think we can risk people going home in this tonight," said Dean. "It's bloody treacherous out there."

"I know, I was thinking the same thing, what shall we do?" replied Kim.

"I think we need a bit of the old 'Dunkirk spirit'," laughed Dean. "You got any spare bedding?"

And so it was that the night ended with guests wrapped in a mis-matched assortment of spare blankets and bedding, stretched out on every available sofa and bench seat the pub had to offer. The Dog and Duck looked like a cross between a halfway house and a wartime bunker – but Kim had never been happier and she was just thankful that everyone had stayed safe. Although, the sight of a sozzled registrar, still wearing the robes that he had arrived in, stretched out in front of the fire, snoring and looking for all the world like the Ghost of Christmas Past, was an image that would stay with her for a very long time!

Chapter Thirteen

Kim awoke early again the next morning, disappointed to hear the rain still hammering on the roof top, although it was definitely lighter than before. There was now a coating of ice on the windows too which meant that much of the rain had probably frozen and road conditions were likely to be worse instead of better.

At least Daniel and Ryan were officially married, although they'd had to forego their romantic night in a plush hotel in exchange for a night in their mum's spare bedroom. Hopefully they had many more years ahead of them in which to make amends and it *had* been their idea to stage a wedding in December after all!

Kim snuggled into Dean's arms as he wrapped his warm body around her back.

"No funny business this morning," he murmured. "We've got a house full of strangers and most of your family – not the ideal conditions for romance!"

"Yes, I think we'll have to postpone our Christmas nookie," Kim giggled. "Shall we go downstairs and assess the damage? I'm pretty sure there'll be a few people wanting a cup of tea and a bacon sandwich before they brave the journey home – if they can get home that is!"

"I'll see if Jim and Adrian can help me clear a path in the carpark. I think we are going to have to put a bit of grit down if nothing else. This pub's going to be busier than Bethlehem this Christmas if we aren't careful!"

They both dressed in warm tracksuits before going downstairs, today wasn't the day for dressing up. Kim feared there was going to be a lot of elbow grease needed in one way or another.

When she reached the bar and surveyed the scene, the place was more of a disaster zone than she had envisaged. They hadn't cleared up with the usual vigour that they normally used, and it didn't help that there were so many bodies in various stages of sleep scattered around the place. Dean went through to the kitchen to make a start on the mass-catering breakfast that was likely to be needed, while Kim chucked another couple of logs onto the glowing embers of the fire, roaring it back into action.

By nine o'clock everyone was awake, fed, and dressed, although they all looked a bit ridiculous in last night's wedding attire! The blankets had been folded and ferried back upstairs and Jim, Dean and Adrian had gone out into the car park to assess the damage. The torrential rain had now given way to some pretty harsh sleet that was driving its way onto the ground in angled lines of ice-cold water. The sky was grey and heavy and the sun was nowhere to be seen.

The car park was a treacherous mess of large puddles of water, some of which had accumulated an ice coating that lay camouflaged and dangerous amidst its watery companions. They were going to have a devil of a job to get people home safely and Kim hoped that the two utility vehicles parked on the highest bits of ground to avoid the flooding would be up to the job. Dean, Jim and Adrian had done what they could to grit the drive and had cleared any ice or puddles where possible, but in truth it had been a fruitless task.

"I'll take the registrar and the girls home," said Adrian referring to his and Jim's wives, "and I'll phone back to report on the roads. If we are going to get stuck there's no point losing both vehicles at the same time."

"Agreed," said Jim. "As soon as you give me the nod, I'll get Daniel and Ryan's friends and parents back to their hotel so at least they can get a change of clothes. Then I'll come back for Brian and Doris – you okay with going last, you two?"

"Fine by us," said Doris. "We'll stay and help Kim get cleaned up."

"I'll come with you," said Dean to Adrian, "just in case you need a bit of muscle."

"Be careful," said Kim.

"Can we help at all?" asked Ryan. "I feel bad leaving you all to it."

"It's fine," said Dean. "Just look after everyone here, hopefully we won't be too long."

It was at least an hour before Kim received a call from Adrian, to say that they had arrived safely. The roads had been treacherous and some of them impassable, but they had managed to find a way through, after some careful driving and a few detours.

"I'll leave now then," said Jim. "You going to be okay?"

"We'll be fine," said Kim. "Just please be bloody careful!"

They hugged goodbye to Daniel and Ryan's friends. Ryan's parents hugged their son warmly and Kim could see that they were as proud of him as she was of Daniel.

"I'm sorry it was a bit dramatic!" said Daniel, "but thank you so much for coming."

"We'd have been disappointed if there hadn't been any drama from the only two gays in the village," laughed Daniel's friend Alicia.

"We couldn't be happier for the pair of you," said Dot, "it'll certainly be a wedding to remember in lots of ways!"

Once they'd left, the remaining party sat round the fire chatting about the events of the past twenty four hours. The pub was still pretty full. Rosa of course hadn't gone home; Judy and the two grooms were clearly not going anywhere and Brian and Doris were the last of the guests to be getting ferried back when Adrian returned. Sandra and little Lottie were sitting colouring at one of the pub tables whilst Megan was still in bed. Fleur and Rob hadn't dared to risk the drive home either.

"Is Megan okay?" Kim mouthed to Sandra, not wanting to alarm Lottie.

Sandra left Lottie to her felt tips and came to sit beside Kim. "I think she's just tired, but she's not herself."

"Maybe she's coming down with something?" asked Kim.

"Maybe," agreed Sandra. "I'll let her sleep a bit longer then I'll take her up a cup of tea. Thanks for giving her the best of the sleeping options last night."

"Don't be daft. I wouldn't have had it any other way."

They continued to chat and drink coffee by the fire. The pub was now clean and shiny, having been restored to its former glory by a band of willing and very capable helpers. In some weird way, Kim was selfishly quite pleased to have a bit of quality time with the people she loved most, without the distraction of opening up to customers; there's no way they'd be opening their doors in this weather – even the hardiest of drinkers would be thinking twice about venturing out today!

Just as Kim was wondering what was taking Adrian so long, they received a call to say that they'd been held up by a fallen tree in the road. Emergency services were on their way, but it was likely to be some time before they'd get through. Kim had quickly phoned Jim to alert him to the road block and he'd gratefully told her that he'd come back round the other side of the village which, although a much longer route, would hopefully be clear.

Around midday, Sandra popped upstairs to check on Megan but she returned with a grave expression.

"Everything alright?" asked Kim.

"I'm not sure. She feels very hot and she's very uncomfortable, I don't know whether we should call a doctor – will they even come out in this weather?"

Kim beckoned Rosa and Doris over to the door, taking care not to alert Lottie's attention. Both women had children of their own and she thought that perhaps they could offer some words of wisdom under the circumstances. Judy caught her daughter's eye and moved over to keep Lottie occupied, seeming to intuitively understand Kim's thoughts from the expression on her face.

The four women climbed the stairs and entered the room as quietly as they could. Megan was propped up on three big pillows, but her face was the colour of ash. She looked to be running a temperature and little beads of sweat had begun to gather across her cheeks and forehead.

"She's burning up," said Doris. "I don't like the look of her one bit."

"What do you think we should do?" asked Sandra, her face etched with worry.

Megan let a cry of pain, drawing her knees up to her chest and twisting her head to one side.

"She needs an ambulance," said Kim, pulling her phone from her pocket and dialling three nines before waiting for an answer. "Rosa, you go and get a bowl of water and we'll see if we can cool her down. Doris, go downstairs and keep everyone calm; whatever you do, don't let Lottie up here. Keep an eye out for the ambulance..."

"Hello, emergency services, which service do you require...?"

The voice on the other end of the phone interrupted Kim's instructions and she began to relay details of Megan's situation.

"Ambulance please, and quickly. We have a young pregnant mum here and I think she's in early labour..."

Kim and Sandra exchanged a look that spoke volumes.

Downstairs, Judy, Daniel and Ryan did their best to keep Lottie entertained whilst fending off any questions about her mum. Brian waited anxiously by the door, keeping a lookout while Doris tried both Adrian and Jim's mobiles. Thirty minutes passed and there was still no sign of the ambulance. The storm had taken its fair share of casualties and the hospital services were more stretched than ever. Jim was stuck in a long line of traffic, all the cars that were avoiding the fallen tree having taken the alternative route, and there was no reply from Adrian, his phone going straight to voice mail.

The tension in the room was palpable but it was nothing compared to what was happening upstairs. There was now little doubt that Megan was in labour, the waves of pain evident on her face. She'd only had two of what Kim thought to be contractions, but the second had left its mark more visibly than the first. Megan was burning up and drifting in and out of lucidity.

"I wish that bloody ambulance would come," said Sandra, through choked back tears. "I don't know how to help her..." Her voice trailed away as the very same terrifying thoughts entered her head that were currently spinning around in Kim's mind.

What if the baby didn't make it? What if Megan didn't make it?

The bedroom door flew open, and Dean burst into the room. "They've cleared the tree, but Jim's stuck in traffic. How long for the ambulance?"

"I don't know," replied Kim. "It's been nearly an hour now."

"Shall we take her? The road is quite clear at the bottom and we can pick up the dual carriageway from there?"

They both looked at Sandra, searching for her response.

"We can't leave her," she replied weakly. "Are you sure we'll get through?"

"I'm sure," said Dean. "We literally just came that way. We could be at the hospital in under fifteen, but it's totally your call..."

Sandra nodded almost imperceptibly, and Dean disappeared back downstairs without a word. He returned with Adrian, Daniel, Ryan and Rob and between them, they carried Megan as carefully as they could down the narrow staircase. Lottie cried out as she saw her mum carried into the back of the Land Rover and Judy put her arms around her to comfort the little girl's sobs.

"Shush now darling, Mummy will be just fine. She's working hard to bring you a new little brother or sister."

Judy wrapped her coat around Lottie and carried her out to the car so that she could give her mummy a goodbye kiss before she was whisked off to the hospital; Adrian and Dean up front, Sandra cradling her daughter in her arms in the back seat.

"Now what?" asked a visibly shaken Ryan.

"Now we wait... and pray," said Kim.

Chapter Fourteen

Kim didn't think there had ever been a situation in her life when time had moved so slowly. The ticking of the old pub clock seemed louder than before as it marked the passing of the hours, almost mocking them in their anxious vigil.

Words were only exchanged through necessity and to keep Lottie as calm as possible. It was remarkable how many ways the little group found to keep themselves busy – anything to distract them from the thoughts racing through their heads.

Rosa made endless cups of tea – many of which grew cold and were poured down the sink whilst Daniel, Ryan, Rob and Brian went out into the garden to begin to clear the debris from the obliterated shed; a job which was totally unnecessary in the circumstances, but which provided a masochistic test of endurance that went some way to helping them avoid the horror of their current situation. Talking about childbirth was never going to be a comfortable topic for men – gay or straight – it seemed!

Doris made a call to the hospital to cancel the ambulance and inform them that Megan was on her way and Teddy sat glued to Lottie's side with the kind of sixth sense that only animals seem to possess when it came to knowing that something wasn't quite right.

An hour after Dean had left, Jim finally returned, his face showing the concern he instantly felt on being given the news. As the father to a daughter of a similar age to Megan, he could only imagine what they were all feeling at that moment in time.

Chapter Fifteen

Dean gripped the handle above the passenger door as Adrian navigated the icy roads as quickly and as safely as he could. Every few minutes, he looked around to check that Megan was still conscious, her cries piercing though his heart. He had grown to love Megan and Lottie as if they were his own and the responsibility he felt to get her to the hospital safely was immeasurable.

Fortunately, Adrian was a skilled and capable driver, having lots of experience across country. They reached the hospital in double quick time and Dean leapt from the car before it had properly come to a halt.

He tore through the automatic doors, running up to the reception desk, his message coming out in a garbled mess…

"She's in labour… it's too early… she's not well… you have to come quickly… please!"

The hospital reception sprang into action. Nurses and hospital staff seem to emerge from every direction before a stretcher was wheeled out at speed to the waiting vehicle. Megan was loaded onto the stretcher and the last thing Dean had seen was Megan being whisked away, with Sandra clinging onto her daughter's hand as she ran alongside the moving stretcher.

"Well, that was fucking intense," exclaimed a visibly shaken Adrian. "What the hell do we do now?"

"We wait mate, we just sit and wait," sighed Dean.

Chapter Sixteen

Several long hours later when Dean didn't think he could stomach one more cup of hospital coffee, an exhausted and emotional-looking Sandra emerged from a lift on the left-hand side of the corridor. Both Adrian and Dean jumped up simultaneously, spilling the dregs of their now-cold refreshments.

"It's a boy," sobbed Sandra, "it's a baby boy!"

"...and Megan?"

"She's fine... She's tired and sore. It was touch and go for a little while but mother and baby are doing okay thanks to you two. Honestly, I cannot thank you enough, you'll never know what you've done for my family." At this last outburst, the tears flowed freely down Sandra's face. "Would you like to see them, just for a minute?"

"Of course," said Dean.

They entered the small private delivery room to find Megan propped up on the pillows. She was pale, but much calmer than she had been a few hours before. She was cradling a small bundle wrapped in a hospital-issue blanket, there having been no time for such luxuries as an overnight bag and new baby clothes.

"I'm going to call him Harry because that's Lottie's favourite name for a boy. Harry Dean... if that's okay with you?" Megan raised her eyes towards Dean, whose eyes filled with tears.

"That's bloody marvellous," he beamed.

Chapter Seventeen

The phone call came at one in the morning. Kim leapt on the phone as if it were an unexploded bomb...

"Yes?" she gasped, feeling several pairs of expectant eyes fixed on her as she took the call.

"It's a boy," said Dean.

"Oh thank God! Is Megan okay?"

"She's fine. A bit worn out but doing well. It's a boy, Kim, and he was born at one minute past midnight!"

"A Christmas baby! Our own little Christmas miracle!"

"She wants to call him Harry Dean, I just can't tell you what that feels like."

"Oh my darling, that's just wonderful. Will you be home soon?"

"Me and Adrian are going to leave now, poor bloke is knackered! We won't be long."

"Well just make sure you get here in one piece – I love you Dean, and thank you!"

Kim hung up the phone.

"Well come on then," exclaimed Judy. "Don't keep us in suspense any longer, are they both okay?"

"They're fine and it's a boy, 'Harry Dean'... probably the best Christmas gift ever!"

Chapter Eighteen

After the phone call, it hadn't been long before Dean and Adrian returned. Adrian had picked up Doris and Brian and they'd left to go home after the most eventful Christmas they were ever likely to see! Jim had finally left, having hung on for hours in case they had needed him again. Kim couldn't express how grateful she was for their love and support.

All that was left behind was a small shell-shocked little gathering, each of them struggling to take in the magnitude of the weekend's events; a wedding, a storm and a birth were quite a lot of action for two days! They'd cracked open a bottle of their very best brandy to toast the new baby and to celebrate Megan's recovery – it had been a rocky road up to this point.

By the time the news had been shared, discussed and dissected it was almost three in the morning.

"I think we ought to go to bed," said Kim at last. "We have a little girl upstairs who needs a visit from Father Christmas more than she ever has done, we have to make Christmas special for her, no matter how shattered we all are."

In the morning, a sleepy Lottie came downstairs to find her stocking full of goodies from Father Christmas, just as it would have been if her mummy had been at home. There were a few tears, but she was soon consoled with the news that she was now a big sister to little Harry Dean and that Uncle Dean and Auntie Kim were going to drive her to the hospital later that day so she could give her new brother and her mummy a cuddle.

They sat around a Christmas table laden with leftovers and goodies that Dean and Rosa had managed to cobble together – having had no time to prepare a traditional roast dinner which was hardly surprising given the circumstances! Kim didn't think she'd ever enjoyed a Christmas dinner quite so much.

Later on that afternoon, Kim and Dean had set off for the hospital; Lottie almost bursting with excitement in the back seat.

Chapter Nineteen

Megan gazed down at her precious bundle. How could she have thought that she wouldn't love this baby? It took almost losing him to realise how much love she had for him before she'd even met him, and she felt so guilty that she'd almost wished him away.

She looked up as the door burst open.

"Mummy!" Lottie cried.

"Hello darling, did Father Christmas come? I'm so sorry I wasn't there but little Harry was desperate to arrive in time for Christmas!"

Sandra took baby Harry carefully from Megan's arms and instructed Lottie to sit on the armchair in the corner of the room. Very carefully, she placed him in his big sister's arms. Lottie's face lit up as she gently kissed the top of his head.

"Are you crying?" Kim teased Dean as he sniffed rather unflatteringly into his sleeve.

"Me, never! Tough as old nails, me!"

They didn't stay long. Both Megan and Harry needed their rest if they were to be allowed home from hospital before too long. Despite being four weeks early, Harry was a strong and healthy baby and the nurses were confident that he would be able to go home within the week if all went well.

A tired and emotional Sandra reluctantly left her daughter and new grandson at the hospital under doctor's orders – Megan wasn't the only one who needed a rest.

"I'll see you in the morning, Mum. Now stop worrying and go and get some sleep. Lottie could do with a little bit of time with you too. Me and Harry will be fine here; we'll be asleep before you're out of the car park!"

"She's right, Sandra," said Kim kindly. "You look exhausted and I'm sure Lottie would like to show you what Father Christmas brought for her."

They said their goodbyes and travelled back to the Dog and Duck, Lottie snuggled into her nan on the journey home.

The rest of Christmas day passed peacefully by comparison and when teatime came, everyone was dropping off to sleep in front of the TV. Rosa had finally left to spend what was left of Christmas with her own family and Fleur and Rob had gone home to collect their fur babies from their over-worked dog sitter!

By nine o'clock, the Dog and Duck was silent, its occupants all sleeping soundly.

Chapter Twenty

Megan and baby Harry had come home from hospital on the last day of December. Both were doing well and showing little signs of their traumatic birthing journey. Daniel and Ryan had finally left for their mini-moon in the plush hotel that had originally been booked for their wedding night. The hotel had agreed to move their stay considering the unprecedented events that had taken place and whilst Kim had been sad to see them go, she was happy that they would finally get some 'normal' time together without any freak accidents of nature or the unexpected arrival of Christmas babies!

Megan, Lottie and Harry had gone to stay with Sandra so that she could look after them all whilst Megan recuperated. Judy had stayed at the pub to see the new year in with her daughter, and things had returned to something close to normal – although Kim wasn't entirely sure what normal looked like anymore!

There was a small event planned for New Year's Eve and whilst Kim would normally be up for a celebration she was a little done with celebrating and, if truth be told, she was starting to get more than a little sick of Christmas tunes on the jukebox – Noddy Holder could bog right off with his 'Christmas every day' wish!

Nevertheless, she put on her glad rags and prepared herself for the evening's event. They had only planned to put on a Christmas playlist and turn the TV on at midnight so that the punters could watch Big Ben chime in the New year; with any luck they'd be able to get rid of them before the party poppers hit the deck! Kim felt a bit uncharitable for not wanting to fully enter into the spirit of things but truth be told she was shattered – physically and emotionally!

"You need a break, love," said Judy. "Why don't you and Dean have a few days away? I'm sure me and Rosa could hold the fort for a couple of nights."

"I might just take you up on that, Mum. It's been an emotional rollercoaster of a Christmas, that's for sure!"

If Kim had hoped for a quiet evening, she was certainly going to be disappointed. The pub had never been busier. Christmas had been quiet, what with all the apocalyptic weather, and it seemed that the punters were making up for lost drinking time! Despite her earlier reluctance, she couldn't help but feel lucky that she was here, in this place, with all these people – some funny, some vaguely annoying, some loveable, some downright bonkers, but they were her bonkers tribe and she loved them!

At ten to midnight there was a wave of hush as the jukebox was turned down unexpectedly.

"Who cut the bloody music?" yelled one of the party goers.

"Settle down," said Dean, taking the microphone from its stand beside the juke box. "I've cut the music because I have a little announcement to make."

"What's he on about?" said Kim, frowning in confusion at Judy.

"I think we should raise our glasses and toast our amazing landlady Kim. She came to this pub one year ago and, to be honest, she almost did a runner when she caught sight of you ugly lot..."

A wave of laughter and a cheer rippled around the room.

"...but lucky for you, she's got a strong stomach and she stayed. And I think you'll agree that the Dog and Duck has never felt so bloody amazing..."

More cheers erupted.

"...so I would like you to raise your glasses in toast to Kim, the best pub landlady around and the future Mrs Dean Bennet... if she'll have me!"

An expectant hush descended on the room, it was so quiet, you could have heard the proverbial pin drop. Kim raised her hands to her gaping mouth.

"Well come on then, give him your answer," shouted Steve from the back of the room. "If you blow him out then you can marry me."

"Christ alive, you better bloody marry him if that's your alternative!" bellowed Brian.

Kim nodded. "Yes! Yes, I would love to be Mrs Bennett."

“Thank Christ for that,” exclaimed Dean, breathing a sigh of relief, “I was worried you were going to be running off with Steve for a minute… no offence, mate!”

Kim ran forward and jumped into Dean’s arms, kissing him passionately to cries of, “Get a bloody room!” just as the chimes from Big Ben rang out to mark the beginning of the New Year.

Chapter Twenty one

Kim climbed into the car beside her new husband-to-be. She took one long look at the Dog and Duck before Dean started the engine ready for their two night break away, gifted to them by Fleur and Rob as an engagement present. Apparently they had been in on the surprise along with Judy, Rosa and half the bloody village – Kim had definitely been the last to know!

As she looked at the pub that she now called home, the place where people had left and entered this world, where relationships had broken down and new ones had formed, it was hard to reconcile herself with the despair that she had felt when she had first arrived twelve months earlier.

Her life had taken a path which had been full of twists and turns, some of which had been painful and others that had brought joy, but she knew that wouldn't have changed a single a part of that journey. The Dog and Duck had brought Dean into her life and friendships that would last a lifetime. She had spent one whole year as the landlady of the Dog and Duck, and she hoped that there were many more to come...

About the Author

Karen Stanley is a former teacher and Assistant Headteacher with a long-standing passion for books and all things bookish. She is a many times published author; writing Chick Lit and children's books. Karen now coaches new writers from initial idea through to publication with her publishing house Mabel & Stanley Publishing, alongside her own writing endeavours.

Karen is a proud wife, mummy, and nanny and likes nothing better than spending time with her family or walking the dog on her local beach where she takes her 'brain breaks' and finds inspiration. She loves satire, and the humour in real life situations and characters, and enjoys writing books that are light-hearted and reflect the quirks of everyday life.

karenstanley-author.co.uk

Printed in Great Britain
by Amazon

12176979R00317